QUEER POWER
Escaping the Fright

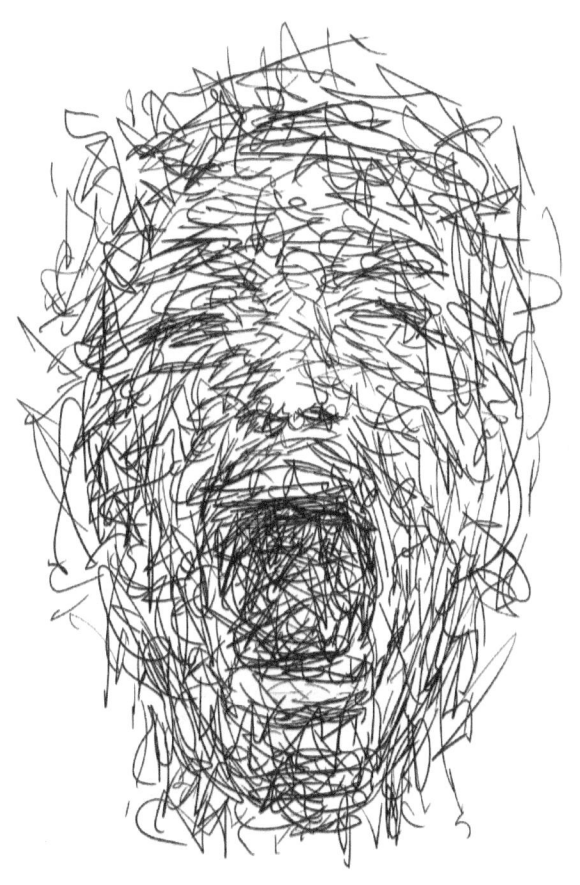

John G. Hartness • Nicole Givens-Kurtz
Rachel Brune • JD Blackrose
Michael G. Williams • Jason Roach

THRILLER • MYSTERY

GOLD DUST

PUBLISHING

★ ★ ★

FANTASY • HORROR

e-book ISBN-13: 979-8-9929748-5-0

Paperback ISBN-13: 979-8-9929748-6-7

Hardback ISBN 13: 979-8-9929748-7-4

Cover design by: Susan Roddey

Edited by: Lynn Picknett

Layout by: Jason Roach

Printed in the United States of America

Special Thanks

Gold Dust Publishing would like to thank all of the authors, editors, and cover artists who have contributed their blood, sweat, and tears to making this book happen.

Contents

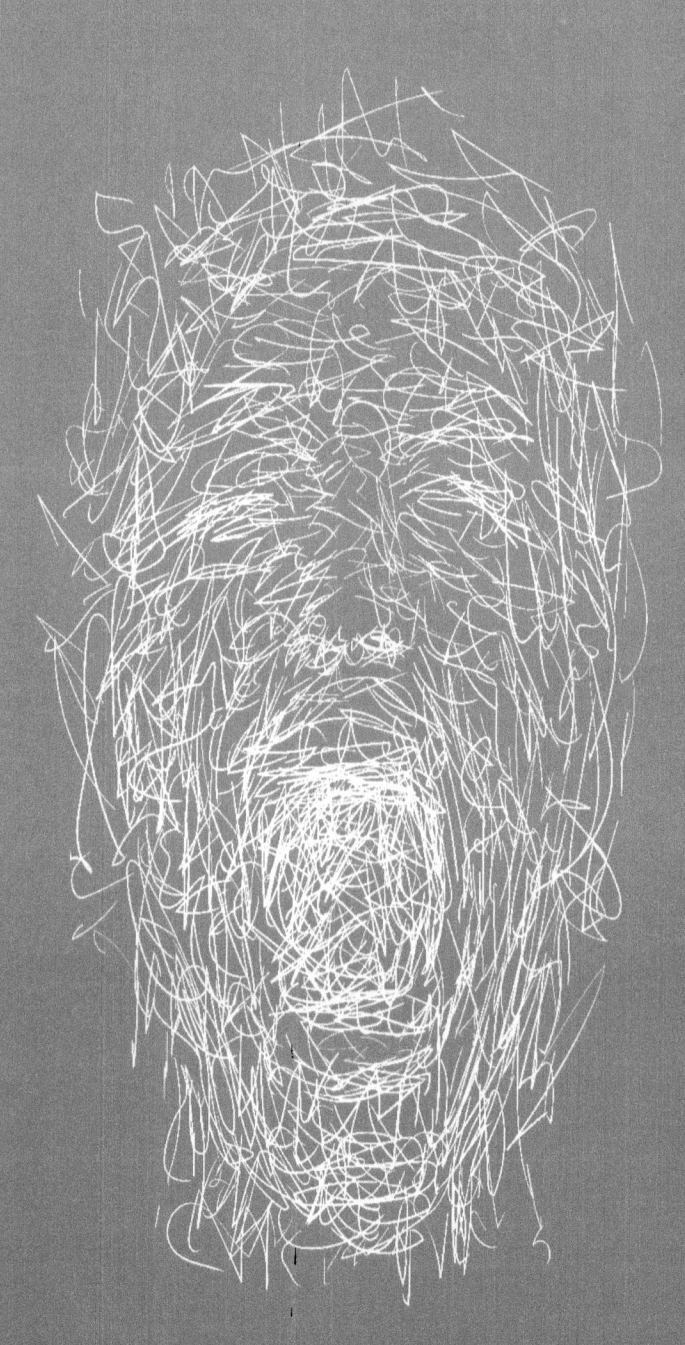

Sprout

By Nicole Givens-Kurtz

1

"The dead get to walk away, but we remain." Dr. Nadya Singleton stood beside the 3-D visual projection of the planet, Noorbi's, southern hemisphere. Inside the crowded, stuffy briefing room several other scientists took notes, whispered amongst themselves, and studied the projected blue sphere. The M-class planet with its puffy white clouds and crisp cerelan sky hovered above the center of the conference table.

She zoomed in on the highlighted area, illuminated in yellow and jutting up from the rest of the orb. With hands splayed, she stretched the visual to showcase her point, the glowing location. It brightened the dim space. The shuffling of feet and bodies spoke to the anxiousness and uncertainty looming in the tense air. For Nadya, their concerns didn't matter. A crisis bubbled in the hot cauldron of those villages and to prevent it from spreading, her team—the members in this room—had to swallow the acid mix of fear and draw courage.

Afterall, they were Intergalactic scientists.

Brave words from a coward, her inner critic said.

She pushed down the urge to shout at her internal consciousness to *Hush!* It had been five years since the shuttle crash and IO Officer Brown's death. She still bore scars both outside and inside from the incident, but now wasn't the time to reopen them.

A planetary crisis didn't care about her post-traumatic stress disorder or her bubbling terror at having to get back into a shuttle, let alone lead a mission.

"Doctor?" Her partner, Dr. Leslie Gupta, cleared her throat. It was a hint to tell Nadya to get on with it.

Right.

"This mission is classified SL01 Omega. Directly from the Noorbi council, in concert with IO command. This evening, at eighteen hundred hours, our global monitors received an alert from Uzuri, a southern village. The leader reported the population had perished, seemingly overnight. She awoke to find most of her residents either dead or dying. No fever. No vomiting. No signs of anything disease or environmental in origin." Nadya rotated her right hand clockwise. The 3-D image turned to reveal a transcription of the alert. It had originally been submitted in Noorbian. She swept right and the scientists' devices lit up. "You can read the entire alert for yourself, at your leisure."

"Dr. Singleton, do we know if environmental has been completely ruled out?" Doctor Reginald Perez, botanist, raised his hand. His black-square glasses caught his device's glare and cast his eyes in shadows. "We want to be sure of what we're walking into there."

"The reason we do this work, Dr. Perez, is because we don't," Nadya said. "We've sent drones to scan the atmosphere around the village for airborne viruses or bacteria. Dr. Gupta's team completed this work earlier today. Dr. Gupta."

Dr. Leslie Gupta nodded at her and stood.

"Yes, of course. We ran the scans using the drones from the closest village, Ukweli, about 482 kilometers away. Not exactly close, but we discovered it to be clear of any known viruses or bacteria. This appears to be isolated, but we don't know how long it's been infected or much more than what our drones reported."

"*Known*," Reginald added. "Known viruses or bacteria."

"Correct. We can form any hypotheses from here, but we need to go there to confirm. This is a fact-finding mission as much as it might be preventative. If a threat is determined, we'll be tasked with ascertaining its impact and reporting to the council." Nadya pointed to the 3-D visual. "There's no way to know if there is an unknown agent involved in the villagers' demise without going to the hotspot. We need more data."

2

She called up the drone's images. Bodies lay scattered across the lush grounds like forgotten, discarded dolls. People appeared to have dropped where they stood. The drone's flyover provided aerial pictures, but they needed specifics, to tag and test, to get samples and witness, firsthand, the situation.

"No one sought safety or appear to be in distress other than they're dead." Reginald pushed up his glasses and leaned in to peer closer. "Are those maggots?"

"This is a grisly jigsaw puzzle." Francis Adu, forensic pathologist, checked her tablet and glanced at the drone images. "In this heat the bodies will start to decompose. We're losing evidence by waiting. It's already 2100."

"Right. That's why we're leaving as soon as we can," Nadya said. "We suspect the village leader may be alive somewhere, but we have move quickly to confirm."

"I have a question." Marcelo raised his hand.

Nadya swallowed the groan pressing at her throat. *Why would the council send a novice regent on such a potentially dangerous venture?* The only clear answer was for him to spy on her, her team, and the project. The council and their perverse loyalties to their interests had planted him in with them. Then another thought occurred. *They must not trust my ability to lead.*

"Ah. Everyone. Team. This is the new regent to Noorbi, Marcelo Duili. He'll be accompanying us on the mission. Go ahead with your question." Nadya gripped her tablet so hard her hands throbbed.

He nodded in greeting.

"Dr. Singleton, are there any reports from the village from a day or two before?" Marcelo gave a small smile as if the question contained some humor. "Being there may be some witnesses who reported something strange or felt suddenly ill."

"Sir, there haven't been any reports prior to the leader's contact today. The Noorbians are like ghosts. They don't have a digital footprint." Nadya turned her attention back to the images rotating before her. "For now, we keep the grisly details under wraps."

"Understood," Leslie said.

"Great. We'll divide into four teams. I'll lead Alpha Team, Dr. Gupta, Beta, Cole can you handle Delta Team and Calhoun, Gamma?"

Cole raised his hand in confirmation. Calhoun said, "Yes, ma'am."

Despite the generic titles, each team had unique responsibilities. Gamma Team was comprised of ten soldiers responsible for infrastructure. Beta Team included six scientists, counting Leslie—biologists, entomologists, and a microbiologist. Cole lead the combination team of scientists and soldiers, Delta Team. Dr. Francis and most of the pathologist crew rounded out that group. Nadya's team didn't have any soldiers and mostly provided organization and oversight. It was her, Dr. Perez, and both pilots, Williams and Reyes, who had certification in various scientific work.

"We leave in three hours. If there are no further questions, you are dismissed. Rendezvous at 22:00."

The overhead lights warmed, revealing the flat gray walls and black table and chairs. The scientists shuffled out through the automatic doors, heading toward their departments and homes to say their goodbyes and prepare to explore the great unknown.

Always the mission.

Most of her team were scientists, then soldiers. Cole was a soldier, through and through, so was Gamma Team. Nadya waited until they all left before shutting down the visuals.

Except for one.

Marcelo stood by the door. His piercing hazel eyes peered across the room to her. "You ready for this? There's much your team doesn't know about the incident."

Tell me something I don't know. He's already questioning me.

She cleared her throat.

"Yes, but that's the nature of our work—discovery." Nadya glared, unsmiling. "We'll meet in Hanger Three, Regent Duili."

"Please, call me Marcelo. We're going into this together. There's no need for the formality."

This time he did smile.

"I'm an IO scientist. There's always a need for formality, *sir.*"

Nadya adjusted her satchel across her shoulder and walked out into the sprawling Intergalactic Organization's Noorbi complex. It ate up roughly 80 square kilometers of land provided by the Noorbi Council. It included IO housing and research facilities for IO scientists to study the planet, its fauna, and its flora.

No way would she let him lure her into the supposed one IO motif. Marcelo's reputation as a braggart and a troublemaker proceeded him. It was most likely why he'd been sent to the outer rim planet in the first place. Slow paced. Friendly inhabitants. Less chance of him causing trouble.

The rumors hadn't been wrong about his striking good looks. The regent wore dark robes crafted from the aria trees' leaves. Lightweight and breathable the garments absorbed sweat and wicked away moisture. All the Noorbians wore them. Marcelo's shoulder length hair, reddish and straight with a touch of a wave, brushed his collar. He had perfect bow lips, nice cheekbones, and great teeth. He did not disappoint the eyes. She had a wonderful partner, but Leslie knew she appreciated beautiful things.

Once she exited the biomedical suite of conference rooms and labs, she headed down a long corridor toward the housing unit. It rested on the northern side of the complex and burrowed underground. Many of the cabins were below Noorbi's surface. Hollowed out from stone and rock, these housing units remained cool in the otherwise sweltering planet heat.

As she walked, the panthers—the Noorbi called them chumbas—roamed the facility intermingled with the soldiers and the scientists. With those who gave permission, these four-legged animals connected, via psychic link, to their partners. Several IO scientists joined with them, and the biology section actively studied those relationships. With those who gave permission—but Nadya knew Obe would tolerate no such interaction.

Your stress level is elevated, Obe spoke into her mind. A soft, growling followed the panther's words. *You are worried.*

You know we've been partnered far too long for me to hide my feelings from you. Nadya smiled at the warmth flooding through her. *See you when I get home.* The telepathic link's range was limited.

After Officer Brown's death, Obe helped heal her mind. The black chumba would comfort her when her episodes erupted or when her nightmares threatened to tear her psyche apart.

The lift dinged. She entered with others and pressed the button for her floor. The glass cylinder dropped, speeding downward so fast, so effortlessly, the illuminated floor numbers flickered in rapid session. The container grew emptier as people got off at their respective floors until only three remained.

At Floor 19, Nadya exited and headed down the narrow hallway lined with embedded LED lights. The earthen walls spoke to the planet's hardened interior. The integration of soil and steel, tree roots, and digital wiring all blended into what Nadya called home. She'd been on outposts and ships since she joined the Intergalactic Organization after medical school at twenty-eight. None of those places felt like she belonged. Nowhere was home until Noorbi, until Obe and Leslie. The constant shifting of locations and missions forced her to form micro relationships. Forever changing and brief, her connections to fellow scientists, soldiers, and friends evaporated once she left port for the next journey.

Noorbi provided stability.

It was this planet where she met Leslie toiling away in the labs and she felt the sort of instant connection Nadya never believed existed. All the mushy, love-at-first-sight garbage didn't happen in real life. People had more depth than their appearance and behaviors went far beyond the surface's outer packaging.

She had to eat all those beliefs when she spied Leslie that day while touring the complex. The director stopped in the biolab, and there, she met Leslie, the lead scientist. Nadya's knees actually weakened, like some worn cliché. She pushed through it and with a confidence she didn't feel, she introduced herself. Leslie said later, she could tell Nadya wasn't as confident as she presented.

As she was the director of the science complex, Nadya had pushed her feelings away, as she'd done often since joining the IO.

Nadya's medical school dean declared she'd sold herself short by consulting with the IO. Her mom and her gran said the same thing. They didn't understand her attraction to travel, to adventure or desire to help others. The IO improved her quality of life. She wanted to see the galaxy, to get off planet, and explore.

And she did.

But it had cost her.

When you're IO, trauma follows you.

They don't put that in the brochures or recruitment vids. All those smiling faces lured scores of new recruit each earth year.

"Finally." She pressed her hand against the reader to the right of her door. The green light scanned her palm, running the laser beam over it and illuminated to a brilliant blue when verified. "Home."

The door whooshed back. No sooner had she crossed the threshold than Obe leapt onto her, sending her crashing against the now closed door. Big paws pressed into her shoulders. Obe panted, pink tongue out ready to deliver happy licks.

"Obe!" She hugged the massive panther, running her hands over his soft blue-black fur. His tail wagged in joy, the lighter tabby-like stripes a blur. "I've missed you too, but I have to pack. And I have to go."

I know. Obe relented and released her. He padded behind her as she went to her bed. The small, one-room cabin contained a bed, a bathroom, storage beneath the bed, and a sectioned off corner with a pantry for non-perishable items. She ate in the cafeteria with the other IO personnel and scientists, but she had a tiny microwave and fridge.

She took down her rucksack from an overhead shelf. "This alert is concerning. Nothing. No hints of what happened to the villagers. They could've been killed by a maniac but all at the same time. Unlikely. They could have ingested some rancid plant, but you'd think they'd avoid those. We just don't know."

There have been, as you say, conversations among us. There is a strangeness in Uzuri. Obe settled on his thick cushioned pillow at the base of Nadya's bed. He laid his head on his two front paws.

"A strangeness?" Nadya grabbed some clothes from her under-bed drawer and put them into the larger bag. She picked up socks and her undergarments. "What's strange?"

We are unsure. No one has been to the southern region in many generations. Obe rolled to his side. *It is not safe for our kind there.*

"Not safe? Why?" Nadya paused and looked at him. Something in his tone caught her attention. The thread of fear, perhaps? No, the chumbas feared nothing. So, why didn't they go to the southern region?

Give us a scratch. Obe reached out to her, paw extended in her direction.

Nadya walked over to him, crouched down beside his pillow, and scratched him behind the right ear. Obe shimmed onto his back, giving her access to his belly. She put her hand there and patted his smooth dark stomach, watching Obe begin to glow in pleasure. Unlike Earth's cats, these big panthers didn't purr, but glowed when happy. Obe closed his eyes as she continued her scratching and stroking his soft fur, now along his side. His purple light took over the standard-issue white illumination, turning her quarters into a cocoon of royalty.

"Now, tell me. Why aren't there chumbas in the southern region?" Nadya stopped petting and stood up to resume packing. If she wanted to get a decent meal before leaving, she needed to hurry. Once on the mission, who knew when she'd be able to eat anything but bar rations.

Obe opened his yellow eyes and yawned as if it all bored him. *Men would disappear from Ukuri. It did not mean they* left.

"What does that mean?" Nadya shook her head. The chumbas' logic and beliefs didn't align with humans' and sometimes, because of the language differences, confusion happened.

Obe didn't reply.

"You can't utter cryptic things and not elaborate." Nadya sat on the bed. Obe inched forward until he reached her and placed his head in her lap.

It will be a difficult journey. You do not like flying or field activities.

Nadya nodded. "No, I don't, but I also don't have a choice. I-I will be up for it."

You are, but beware your hubris.

"I don't know how long I'll be gone. This mission has many unknown variables. You may not want to stay here while I'm away."

I can stay along with Raki and Min, or I could come along…

Nadya sighed with longing. "Obe. You said chumbas don't go there. Not to mention, this is a sanctioned IO investigation…"

In concert with the Noorbi council, Obe countered.

"Yes, but…"

You humans, your emotions make you dangerous.

Nadya couldn't argue with him on that point.

Obe licked his front left paw.

They say death lingers in Uzuri.

2

Metal clanging echoed throughout Hanger Three and into the hallways, snaking through the IO complex. Rapid footsteps announced the rest of the crew's arrival. Nadya turned to find six members of the science team walking with purpose, carrying their gear. She fought back the acidic rise in her throat. Her quivering belly wanted nothing to do with flying or being away from the massive buildings.

Maybe eating a late dinner wasn't a good idea.

"Oy, doctor, we're ready. Right?" Reginald waved at her, shouting over the din.

She gave him a thumbs up, not really trusting herself to speak.

The heavier equipment had already been loaded onto four crafts. The engines' loud rumblings shook the hanger's thin separation walls with their forceful idling, impatient to take off, eager to work. She couldn't be further from that. Of course, she wanted to get to the bottom of the mystery. Two things could be true at once.

Nadya wore her IO uniform, a one-piece, body-skimming garment in the Intergalactic Organization's blue and white colors, paired with her black military boots. Despite its snug fit, the uniform wicked away moisture. With her close-clipped hair, her mini-afro kept her cool on the hot planet. The weight of the mission pressed down on her, and they hadn't even left yet.

"Ready to discover the secrets of Uzuri?" Reginald said once he reached her. "Beta Team will save us all. Right Ed?"

A skinny, dark-skinned man stopped, startled to hear his name. When he spied Reginald, he frowned and shuffled on to their shuttle.

"Edgar knows his stuff," Nadya said. "This might be a mass poisoning."

"Why aren't I on Beta Team? I'm usually on the same team as Ed. You know two are better than one."

"I need you with me. Plus there's a lot to organize. You're great with details," Nadya said. She didn't want to tell him he was her emotional support human.

"I'm too brilliant to clerk for you," Reginald said.

Nadya laughed. "Don't worry. You'll get plenty of field time."

A flurry of activity buzzed around them. Soldier and scientists readying to launch. Chatter and a few giggles rose above the buzz. No one appeared nervous or anxious. This was old hat. Routine.

Trust your training.

A digital beeping announced the arrival of another person. She turned to the monitor. The visual revealed the regent himself. In moments, he appeared in the flesh, stepping into the hanger sans his robes, and dressed in an IO soldier uniform. It included a gun belt and a zippered jacket, an arched collar, and matching blue boots. His long hair had been pulled back in a ponytail and the style showed of his cheekbones. His salt-and-pepper goatee made him looked seasoned, mature, and more in charge.

"Dr. Singleton, Dr. Perez," Marcelo greeted them as he kept moving toward the shuttle with his gearbag in one hand and his weapons bag in the other.

Weapons?

Nadya's clammy skin and dry mouth kept her from replying right away. She finally managed a "sir" to his back.

Reginald laughed.

Nadya rolled her eyes at him. "Hush you."

Marcelo's new look disarmed her. His presence had a direct impact on her. *Damn him.*

"Come on. Let's load up and get this mission launched," Nadya said to Reginald. She adjusted her rucksack and started for the first shuttle on the left. "I want this to go smooth and fast. The more samples we can gather, the faster we can get back here and determine what happened out there."

And the sooner I can get back to my safe, familiar surroundings.

Reginald nodded. "Yeah. I know."

She climbed onto the spacecraft with her hands damp and her stomach balled into a knot. The other team members swarmed in right behind them. Nadya didn't like the regent being on this mission, but she comforted herself by noting it would be over soon.

A simple mission—get info and return back to base.

Pilots William and Reyes were already seated at the two navigation consoles. Pilot Williams signed and spoke aloud to Pilot Reyes, who was deaf. Three more bucket seats rounded out the small shuttle's seating area. Nadya took her seat beside Reginald and inserted her communications ear piece.

Beside her, Reginald recounted horror stories about other missions, like the one about the infestation of hostiles that had shown up for their first mission, the one where they ran out of food, and the one time they discovered water on a barren planet but it evaporated once it was removed from the ground.

"Reggie, you're not helping me relax."

His eyebrows rose. "You do look a little green around the gills. Don't vomit in here though, the smell will last the entire trip."

"I'd clean it." Nadya pouted at his lack of faith in her abilities.

He chuckled. "Your facial expression…I'm kidding!"

"I'm not going to be sick, anyway." Nadya folded her arms, but her words were stronger than her stomach.

She did have many more important things to focus on.

How did those people die?

"So, tell me about this, Dr. Perez," she took her seat behind the cockpit's pilot. "You're a legitimate scientist…"

"Yes…"

"…what's going on out there?"

"I don't know," Reginald said, with a shrug. "I have a feeling…I know, not scientific, but I feel we should leave well enough alone. If it isn't biological, as far as we can determine, it may be a new strain of something for which we aren't prepared a spillover event."

Nadya paused while securing her seatbelt. "Well, there's no one alive who can tell us. We have dealt with these types of scenarios before on many planets…"

"…and always with a deadly learning curve," Reginald added.

"We need to know." Nadya gestured to the viewer. "To get ahead of it."

"Do we *need* to know?" Reginald pressed his lips tight as if restraining the rest of what he wanted to say from escaping. His nostrils flared, and he released a heavy sigh.

"Of course, we do! Whatever is out there most likely won't stop. It's a threat to us, the chumbas, and the Noorbians. If history has taught us anything, it's that once anything gets a taste for killing, it'll keep going. That's from bacteria to serial killers."

"That sounds ominous." Marcelo took the seat behind her and Nadya shot him an annoyed look over her shoulder.

"I assigned you a seat in your own craft, sir, with Gamma Team," she said, disdain lowering her tone.

"I'm overriding you, Dr. Singleton. I want to see if I can access the computer's files on previous missions." Marcelo strapped himself into the seat behind her. "Maybe I can determine an anomaly we missed on previous visits to the village."

"Yes," Reginald said. *He could do that from any of the shuttles. He's here to spy on me.* "That would be helpful."

"No. There haven't been any visits." Nadya wondered if Marcelo read the briefing she'd prepared.

Marcelo shot her a smug smile. "Not in sixty-three years."

Nadya just looked at him, before pivoting around to her console. She shook her head. "You can try, but no one's *been* to the southern village."

"Not even on classified fact-finding cloaked missions?" Marcelo said, without looking up at her. "You probably don't have clearance to view those."

"I assure you, *Regent*, I do!" Nadya shoved on her headset and waited for the pilots to finish checking their craft for liftoff. Soon they'd be underway. Once she started working, she could push the pompous regent out of her hair.

We've already checked those black boxes after every flight. No one's been to that village, hence why we had to get the drones to fly over!

Her annoyance flooded her system with adrenaline, racing fast and hot. She couldn't focus on anything, except punching his grinning face. Add her already heightened insecurity about being confined in a shuttle, and Nadya wanted to dissolve into a puddle. She also wanted to punch the smugness from his face.

You are made of stern spirit, human. Obe's thoughts blossomed in her mind. *You are leader. Are you not?*

Could she hear him this far from her quarters? *Did I imagine it? It sounds like something Obe would say.*

It didn't matter.

She straightened in her seat. *Yes. I am.*

Nadya looked around the tight U-shaped seating and its five IO scientists and regent. She wasn't only a scientist, she was also a soldier. "I am."

Reginald stirred, already half asleep. "You say something?"

"No," Nadya answered. *Not to you, Reggie, but to myself.*

At that, the spacecraft fired up.

"Time to go," Reginald said becoming fully awake thanks to the engines.

"Finally." Relief washed over her. *The sooner we start, the sooner we'll return.*

Ahead, the hanger's door yawned open to reveal the inky night sky bespeckled by stars. The ship lifted from the platform as another one took its place. The ship shuddered from the force as they shot out into space. A few of the other team members watched from the windows, and she guessed they were probably seeing the landscape for the first time. Most of them arrived to Noorbi in stasis. When they woke, they were already in the IO hangers.

Nadya braced herself by embedding her finger and palm prints into the chair's two armrests. The other scientists in other vessels launched one by one, bursting into the evening's twilight, a series of ships sailing on the blackened sea.

When they reached a cruising altitude, Marcelo asked, "How long is the flight?"

Nadya rolled her eyes. "You have a copy of the briefing, including the mission overview, sir. Everything you need to know is there."

13

"I'm making conversation, Doctor," Marcelo said with a grin. "That's all."

I don't care.

"There's some audio ASMRs you can listen to, sir." Reginald saved her from delivering a snarky response. "Those work wonders for calming jitters."

Marcelo said, "I don't have the jitters…"

Reginald glanced over his shoulder at the regent. "Of course not, sir."

Nadya muted her microphone to hide her laughter.

Marcelo looked like he'd eaten a lemon. Now, maybe he'd sit quietly for the remainder of the flight.

Maybe.

The flight to the southern region kept them cloaked in dark; only the console and controls remained illuminated. Beside her, Reginald's head bobbed in a series of snores. His folded arms would jerk each time his head leaned too far forward. Nadya felt sorry for his subconscious and security belt. They worked hard to stop him from face-planting into his console.

She looked back at her tablet. Incoming information scrolled across the screen, rehashing what they already knew. She didn't know who or what lay ahead. The not knowing was the worst. Suddenly, she thought of Obe's warning.

Why?

Nadya closed her eyes to calm their burning. Too much screen time left them parched. What if it was an environmental incident? They could be the wall between a possible epidemic. Containment mattered now. Her mind shifted to the question niggling at her. *Was it airborne? Was it edible? Was it humanoid?*

"How long till arrival?" Marcelo's alto voice sliced through the computerized workings' low hum.

"Another hour or so, sir," Pilot Williams answered. A burst of static blotted out her other words.

"Why doesn't the IO have a presence in this section of Noorbi?" Marcelo said. "There aren't any delegates from these regions' councils."

Nadya threw her head back against the bucket seat. *Was he really going to talk the entire trip?*

14

Reginald spooked her. "The southern parts are the hottest and hardest places to live for humans. The Noorbians have adapted to the climate, and even many of them fled north. The harsh environment makes communities a challenge. Many villages are sparsely populated and far apart."

"Meaning?" Marcelo pressed.

"I thought you were asleep," Nadya said to Reginald.

"Dozing," he said, then to the regent: "The lack of organization made it hard to get any participants for council. Each village has its own leadership and, due to the space between them, they are used to their independence."

"All of which was included in the briefing," Nadya said.

Marcelo became quiet after that.

Nadya didn't pay too much attention to the goings and comings of council members. Her work, Leslie, and Obe kept her busy. It hadn't occurred to her to question why no one from those regions had seats.

She closed her eyes again.

What awaited them?

Death.

She shuddered as a coldness filtered through her.

That wouldn't be the worst of it.

It's amazing what a human body could live through.

Obe's words floated forward in her mind.

Men would disappear from Ukuri. It did not mean they left.

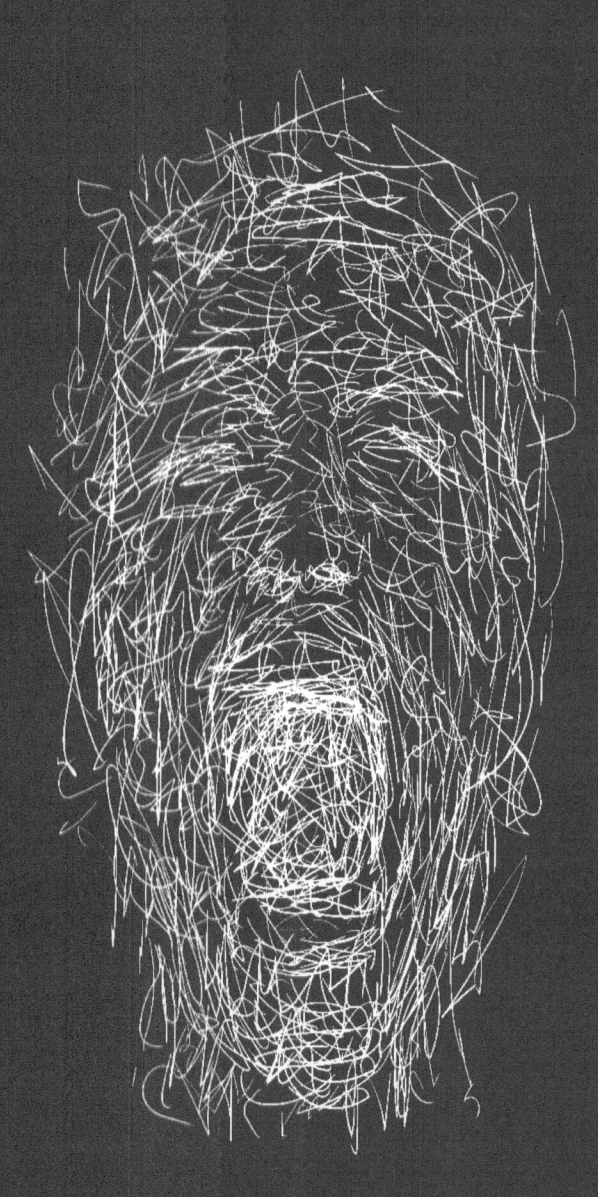

3

Hours later, Pilot Williams's soft voice brushed Nadya's ears. "We're here."

Nadya leaned forward to see the canopy of trees coming closer as their shuttle swept over them. The ship's mounted light illuminated the ground below as they searched beneath the ship's mounted light, they searched for a clearing in which to land. From this vantage point, everything resembled a dark sea, undulating waves of trees swaying as if with currents gently licking the air. The earlier drones' images provided clear footage of the village, but being this close to it brought home the area's lush environment. It was a jungle.

"Going to land in that clearing over there," Pilot Williams said, notifying the other shuttles to follow her. "There may be space for all of us. I can't get a clear read. Something interfering with the visual..."

"I can manually navigate if you need an extra set of hands," Marcelo said from the rear.

Pilot Williams sighed, her voice tight. "It isn't navigations that's giving me fits. It's the viewer. It keeps flickering. Something must be stuck on it."

Nadya shook her head. They were too high still for it to be something stuck to it. Birds didn't fly into the shuttle because of an invisible barrier around the craft. It should have protected the viewer too.

So why didn't it?

One of the things about exploration was you needed good tools, effective tools, to get work done.

"Did we hit something on the flight down here?" Reginald asked, wiping sleep from his eyes. "I didn't feel anything if we did."

"No, I don't think so," Nadya said, looking through the wide front window. For now, she ignored her tablet which had a direct feed from the shuttle's viewer. Squiggly lines rolled across the screen, disrupting attempts to see clearly, so she used her eyes and watched. The niggling of suspicion crawled over her. The tech had to work, or they would be in trouble. Most of them had been trained on how to survive and maneuver when technology wasn't an option, but it made things more difficult. And their mission already had a number of challenges.

"The barrier's still in place?" Nadya kept her voice light.

Williams said, "Yes, ma'am."

When her knuckles ached, Nadya realized she'd been squeezing the armrests for dear life. With a cough, she rubbed her hands on her thighs and said, "Let's, uh, wait until we get down there to see what's going on."

"Once we land, I and two of the flight crew will look over the shuttle and run diagnostics," Marcelo said, spooking Nadya again.

She'd almost forgotten he was on board.

"I used to be a pilot and ship navigator," he added. "I know my way around IO shuttles."

Pilot Williams inclined her head. "Yes, sir."

Reginald turned to Nadya. "This is an omen. We're not wanted here."

"Don't start your mother's chants and beliefs now. We need factual information, not feelings and intuition and spirt talk." Nadya unbuckled her seatbelt. "Focus on the task we have a hand. Discovering the threat. Saving lives."

Reginald sucked his teeth and gave her a half-hearted shrug of agreement.

She sounded way braver than she felt, but she'd been in the IO a long time. Faking confidence came along with rank and promotion. *Courage is being scared and doing it anyway.* That's what she learned from her grandmother. She'd have to apply it now, as she'd done on other matters throughout her thirty-five years.

"Dr. Singleton." Leslie's smooth voice broke through the tension. "We've landed roughly a quarter of a mile from your current location. We're disembarking. We'll head your way and rendezvous there."

"Affirmative, Dr. Gupta." Nadya's heartbeat faster at the idea of seeing Leslie. They did work well together, but the formal addressing of each other kept Nadya from saying something unprofessional like, take off all your clothes or let me kiss your lovely mouth.

"Okay, Dr. Gupta's team is headed this way. Let's suit up before going out. We don't know what's out there." Nadya turned to Reginald. "Masks too."

"You don't have to tell me twice." He adjusted his seatbelt.

"Got it." Marcelo gave her a thumbs up.

Williams discovered a spot to land a short walking distance from the village, but it had only room for their shuttle. The vessel gave a shudder once it touched down, rocking as its landing gear whined in protest.

"That does *not* sound good." Marcelo stood up.

Nadya ignored him. She unbuckled her belt and went to the rear of the craft. With sweaty hands, she took one of the protective suits out of its packaging.

"We can wait to we get to the hotspot to put these on," Marcelo said.

"No. The shuttle scans for known pathogens, but since we don't know what's taken place, there may be unknown viruses our scanners can't detect. We don't want to take additional unnecessary risk. You're free to stay here and monitor."

"You won't get rid of me that easily, Doctor," Marcelo said to Nadya.

Damn. Nadya thought.

Pilot Williams said, but she used her hands to sign her words. "If your offer to help with the shuttle still stands, Reyes and I can use it."

Pilot Reyes turned in his seat to wave. His inner ear pieces wrapped around his earlobe to accommodate his cochlear implant.

Now that they'd arrived, she quelled her impulses to snatch open the door and race out into the air.

Can't be anymore reckless than Mr. Regent can.

Marcelo said, "Will do."

With that settled, Nadya took a deep breath, let it out slowly, and focused on ensuring her gear lacked holes, tears, or gaps. Marcelo took the hint and didn't bother her with more questions or idle chit chat. Maybe the seriousness of their plight had finally weighed in on the new regent.

In the artificial light, Nadya made out the trees' sway in the distance. Amongst the canopies, thatched roofs poked through like little brown hats. There wasn't any illumination within the village. No one was left to light the lanterns or turn on the torches.

"Night vision on folks. It's pitch black out there." Nadya lowered the goggles and switch them on. She spoke into her embedded microphone. It connected her to her teams. "When you're ready, step out. Pilots, please stay back and monitor. We may need a quick pick up and getaway, depending on what we find."

"Roger," Leslie replied. "We're making our way to you."

"Delta Team has landed and headed to the rendezvous site," Cole said.

"Gamma Team's on the way," Calhoun reported.

Great, the other three teams of scientists had landed safely and had everyone accounted for. That gave Nadya some relief. The first big step went well. Leading a mission felt a lot like jumping into an ocean. It's big, intimidating and unpredictable, but once you take the initial plunge and come up for air, the swim seems doable.

The shuttle door hissed as it lowered, ending in a loud *thunk*. Heat rushed in, pushing back against the cooler interior.

"You never get used to the heat on this planet," Reginald said from behind her.

"No, you really don't." Nadya released a deep, steadying breath.

"There's going to be a lot of sweating," Reginald said. "Stay hydrated."

"Good point." Nadya walked down the landing. "I'm glad our unis wick away moisture because goodness we're going to have a lot of it."

"Ew!" came Leslie's voice through the earbud connection. "Such stimulating discussion."

"Aren't you scientists? Human sweat can't be more gross than the digging through elephant feces on Quatar looking for the sacred bowl it ate," Nadya said.

"Why would you make the sacred bowl edible in the first place?" Reginald said.

Leslie laughed and a few others chuckled too, their mirth rippling through their shared communications devices. Connected.

It felt good to break the tension. They could be silly and loose. Too soon they'd have to be serious and professional.

Here everything goes.

4

The teams assembled at Nadya's shuttle. She watched them, all covered from head to toe in their protective gear, their faces behind clear shields with filtered ovals for breathing. The equipment remained outside the clothing, and with gloved hands, several fidgeted.

Ready to get started, no doubt.

"All right. Let's go. Be aware and mindful of where you step and what you observe. Signal if you come across anything strange or potentially violent," she said. The hazard suit's mask distorted her voice. It not only stripped away bacteria and airborne microscopic viruses from the air, but it removed the humanity too.

"You have your designated orders on what to do once we reach the village. The travel there is through this jungle according to navigation."

Leslie walked over to her, at the head of the group. "We understand. Let's go do this." She squeezed Nadya's arm.

How did she know I needed that bit of comfort? My voice sounded confident. Strong. Right?

Fear kept its finger on her spine, sending chills down it, making her shudder. Nadya tried to suppress them, but maybe Leslie, being the perceptive scientist, noticed.

"Right. Let's move on out." Nadya raised her arm and waved them forward.

They started across the clearing and into the mouth of the massive jungle. Thick greens, lush blues, and crisp yellow vegetation sprouted from trees; flowers and fungi decorated the ground and towered over them.

The odor hit them once they hit the jungle's edge. Grumbles and comments erupted at once.

"Why does it smell like corn chips?" Calhoun asked.

"Corn chips and decomp," Cole said. "Weird."

Edgar said, "What are corn chips? Are they like Zabra fruit?"

Laughter answered him.

Then Leslie's calm and patient voice said, "Yes, Dr. Adu."

Many IO scientists came from all over the galaxy. It didn't surprise Nadya he didn't know about corn chips.

"The village is through here," Reginald pointed in the tiny trail twisting through the undergrowth. "It's like a blackened, open mouth."

"Stop it!" Leslie said, her voice stern. "We must be on point and focused."

"I am being focused." Reginald adjusted his mouthpiece. His eyebrows crouched in an annoyed V.

All alarm bells rang inside Nadya, too. The hairs on the back of her neck tingled in warning. The familiar but bitter taste of fear coated her tongue. She gripped her torchlight. The light's beam trembled and she made herself steady her hand.

"C'mon. The night's not getting any younger," Cole said. With his broad shoulders and rugged posture he parted the group and entered the jungle, taking point.

"You heard him," Nadya said, and fell into step behind him.

Bright, yellow ferns brushed against her legs, and the scratchy sound of bear grass filled the air. Ahead, Cole led with his torch, securing a way forward. The footpath, created by villagers traveling back and forth, didn't have pavement. So, the plants wandered from the edges and into the trail. The overhead moon didn't cool them off or make the way brighter. The canopy blotted out much of its illumination.

"It's so quiet," Leslie said in a hush. "Where are the animals? The insects? The nocturnal creatures?"

"Good question. Maybe they're hiding from us, or the light frightens them," Cole said.

"They're watching," Reginald added. "They're always evaluating new prey or predators, gauging how dangerous we are."

"Reggie!" Nadya couldn't take his gloomy observations. She'd forgotten to address him as a professional. "Please, *Doctor*, share any factual or visual observations."

A few of the team chuckled, but they were nervous ones, shrill and uneasy.

"Yes, ma'am, of course," Reginald said.

He crept closer to her and muted his microphone. "Dr. Singleton, look, I know you don't believe in the spiritual realm, and the supernatural…"

"No, science can explain everything and if it can't, it will be able to in the future," she said.

"Yes, but listen, there is something not right about this jungle. It feels off, as if the air particles are flickering, like errant lights on the brink of going dark."

"The air particles?"

"Look." Reginald showed her the air quality monitor. "See the red bar here? It indicates the air has roughly fifteen percent pollutants, mostly carbon dioxide, which is five percent. But it also lists the humidity and the temperature. Nothing in this jungle should be producing this much carbon dioxide."

"What's the range?"

"Roughly seventeen square kilometers."

"It could be the area of the jungle we're in. Keep an eye on it." Nadya said. She unmuted her mic. "Team, we are picking up high levels of CO2. Do not remove your gear."

"That could've killed them," Leslie said. "At eight percent or eighty thousand ppm, the villagers would've experienced sweating, tremors, unconsciousness, and death."

"The drones didn't detect high levels of carbon dioxide," Cole pointed out. "It was one of the gasses they searched for when trying to figure out what happened here."

"And we're back to square one," Calhoun said.

"Not necessarily. Let's keep an open mind. The source of the high amounts of CO2 could've dissipated by the time the drones came through here for samples of the air quality," Nadya said.

The smell arrived just as they crested the hill.

Death.

The team found themselves on the edge of a small gathering of thatched homes. The isolated village spread out across the clearing, a swath of land the villagers had culled from the jungle. Stumps of felled trees jutted from various sections of the earth. Some had been adorned with what looked like offerings, and others remained withered by sun exposure.

This place had once been alive and teeming with life.

Now, it was a graveyard.

Why?

"All right, teams. I know we're fishing for information, but be careful," Nadya said. "You have your assignments."

She and Reginald approached the first home, crafted into the surrounding foliage. Shards of glass covered the ground. Nadya pointed to the direction the glass came from.

"There. Someone or something blew out all the windows here. Let's collect some and then try to find some trace of what it might have been."

"Sure thing." Reginald crouched down and opened his kit.

He used the automated hands to collect the shards. The robotic attachment protected his gloved hands and increased how much weight he could lift. One of the other scientists helped him get them on before he went to work. Definitely a two-person job.

Once that task was complete, Nadya and Reginald walked further into the village. The layout of homes and structures lacked identifying signage. The people who lived there must have known where to go. They didn't get many outsiders, thus signs probably weren't necessary.

She swept her torchlight over the area in front of her. Gamma Team worked to set up the lights so they could see what lay before them. They already had one set up and switched it on.

The illumination flooded the west section, revealing a dozen or so of what had once been people. The Noorbi had skin tones that ranged in colors from deep purple to bright pink—now those colorful skin tones bore blackened sections of decomposition. Their skin cells processed a variety of melanin. Leslie's team members were still studying it.

But when they died, the Noorbians' bodies did what human bodies do—deflate and dissolve in upon themselves. Indigenous insects and animals had descended on the cadavers.

"Dr. Francis, there's a body." Nadya pointed to a smoldering lump roughly twenty yards from them. "Francis!"

Francis followed her finger's direction. She squinted. "Maybe. Come on Tahinti."

Tahinti acted as Francis's research assistant. The young soldier hurried behind the scientist, his face shiny from sweat.

"So much evidence of suffering and fear." Nadya sighed, looking around. Children, teens, the elderly, no one was spared.

All around her were callous examples of the loss, a complete disregard for life. Whether it be biological or humanoid, it had torn through this village with a vengeance.

She and her team were embroiled in a major puzzle.

A dark shadow fell over her, making her flinch.

"Thoughts, doctor?" Marcelo asked.

Nadya swirled around so fast her fist was at his nose before he could breath.

"Regent?" Nadya huffed out an aggravated sigh.

"I didn't mean to startle you." The smirk curling his lips contradicted him.

"Tread carefully or you'll get more than you bargained for, Regent Duli." She lowered her hand. "What are you doing here?"

"We fixed the viewer. Funny thing, there didn't appear to be anything technically wrong with it. Just some film over the viewer's cameras. We cleaned it off, ran another few tests and all seemed well." Marcelo shrugged. "Williams checked with the other pilots and they found a similar substance on their viewers."

Nadya scoffed. "The same film was on all the shuttles' viewers."

"Yeah." Marcelo cocked his head as if confused.

Did he really expect me to swallow such an obvious lie?

Part of the technical prep and routine maintenance involved a cleaning the viewers' cameras.

"We'll need to get a sample of it. See what we're dealing with on that front. If we need to return here or send others to this location, we don't want them flying blind," Nadya said. "Literally."

Marcelo laughed. "Nice one."

No, it really wasn't. There's nothing funny about this situation at all.

But maybe she was being too hard on the regent. Some people used

25

humor to deflect or minimize stress.

She wandered over to Francis, and one of the deceased.

"Anything yet?" Nadya asked, putting her gaze on the surrounding jungle at the village's edge. She didn't want to look down at the liquefying body.

Francis looked up at her from her position crouched down beside the person. Her medical scanner and sample collection containers spread out around the larger tote bag.

"Well, this one, and probably all the others are already in the process of putrefaction. The heat doesn't help but accelerates decomposition, as you know. I have several samples from the skin, the nasal cavities, and hair. Without getting them to an actual autopsy lab space and opening them up, I cannot visually see any reason why they should be dead." Francis stood up and sighed. "There's some dried foam around the mouth. Could indicate a poison. Edgar!"

"Dr. Gupta can also confirm." Nadya looked down at the corpse. "What are we thinking? Something they ate killed them?"

Francis shrugged. "Too early to tell. I'll get Edgar to get a few samples and head back to start looking at them. I can tell you they didn't all die at the same time."

"How can you tell?"

Francis tested her hand on her full hips. "I'm not one hundred percent sure, but some of the bodies appear to be further along in the process. I'll need to inspect all of them."

There weren't any cups, food remnants, or indication they'd had a feast or festival.

"What are we missing?" Nadya said, more to herself than the pathologist.

Francis snorted. "We only just arrived. Trust the training and the teams. We'll figure it out."

"You're right."

Edgar arrived. "Dr. Francis. You called?"

Francis nodded. "Yes…"

Nadya turned away and walked back over to Marcelo, who had begun pacing back and forth at the village's edge.

A predator readying himself to pounce.

Hours later, Marcelo came from the far side of the village. "We'll need to set up camp and get these bodies bagged up."

Francis frowned. "I have and understand my orders, sir." With that she closed up her kit. "Tahinti, let's start analyzing from the samples we have."

"I agree," Cole said, joining them. Regret made his words heavy. They hung in the humid and sticky air.

Nadya's breath caught on all the things that could happen by staying over. That was the one thing she most certainly didn't want. The fact death lingered here and an unknown contagion did too, made her stomach return to its unsettled state.

"What?" Reginald shot to his feet. "You're not serious!"

"I haven't decided to stay here…" Nadya blinked sweat from her eyes.

"We haven't discerned the cause or origin of what happened here. We're not leaving until we do." Marcelo's rumbling arrogance made them all jump. "At this point, we're all carriers. We can't take it back to the complex."

"We're wearing protective gear." Nadya snapped, annoyed at the accusation.

"Yeah, but we can't filter out what we don't know, *Doctor.*" Marcelo turned away from her and said into his microphone. "We're setting up camp. Everyone collect your samples and findings. We'll use Alpha Team's clearing to erect the labs."

"Wait—" Nadya snatched his arm. "You're not in command. This is *my* mission, and use Beta Team's space. Most of the scientists are on that team."

"I'm assuming it." Marcelo shook her off and whirled around to face her mouth, a slash of how-dare-you.

Nadya wasn't a small woman, but he stood about three inches taller. And he stretched to make sure she felt the difference.

"No! The IO placed me in command of this investigation…" Nadya swallowed the rising anxiety and fury mix in her throat.

"Not anymore. I won't let you or anyone else potentially take a deadly agent back to our base and infect, not only IO soldiers and scientists but the Noobrian members!"

"We knew it was unknown when we flew out. We'd only just arrived. What are you doing?"

"Yes, I knew it was unknown, and I also knew we weren't gonna bring it back."

She opened her mouth, but he held up his fist.

There is it. This is why the council sent Marcelo. They wanted him to implement their secret orders in case things were as bad as they feared, or I was as incompetent as they believed.

He sneered. "I outrank you."

He did. His regent status notwithstanding, Marcelo's official rank of Senior Commander was two above hers as director. She had been afraid of this when he inserted himself into the mission.

"You were planning this from the start," Nadya said, the words like quick-fired pellets.

Marcelo chuckled. "I wish. No, this order came directly from Central Command in collaboration with the Noorbian Council."

Her blood went cold. *Of course with the Council. Nothing happened on this planet without their input.*

Central Command handled the higher clearance level operations and those off the official record. If Marcelo told the truth, then she and her team were in deep trouble.

"What order?" Leslie asked, standing up and walking over to the growing crowd around Nadya and Marcelo.

The sober and concerned faces peered through the protective face shields.

"What—what are you doing?" Leslie shouted at Marcelo. "Stop!"

The regent removed his facial covering and headgear, tearing it from his head.

"Whew! That's better! Even with the built-in fans, these suits are a hotbox." Plastered dark hair strands decorated his forehead. Marcelo licked his lips and looked around at them.

"What orders?" Nadya asked, her throat closing with the dawning horror of her suspicions being realized.

Marcelo raised his hands and snatched off his gloves. "We all took an oath to the Intergalactic Organization. We know there'd be dangers with each mission we undertake. It's part of the work. It's part of why many of you joined up."

"I get it," Cole said, pushing through to the front. "This is a suicide mission. Isn't it? We don't need the pretty words or the recruitment speech."

Reginald turned to face him, his mouth agape. "What?"

Cole shook his head. "You don't get it, yet. You're supposed to be the smart and brilliant ones."

"I *am* both brilliant and smart; however, I am *not* psychic," Reginald said.

Cole laughed, but it came out rough, like a cough. "True. I stand corrected, but what the crass regent here is telling us that the IO has dumped us here to find out what happened, and then abandoned us to whatever fate hit these poor souls."

"Left is what you mean," Reginald said. "They left us."

"Pilot Evergreen. Come in, please." Leslie looked over to Nadya, her eyes round in fear. "They're not answering."

"And they won't. They're gone, per orders," Marcelo said dryly.

"We're stuck here. I know I said I'm not a psychic, but Dr. Singleton," Reginald looked at Nadya, "we're going to die here."

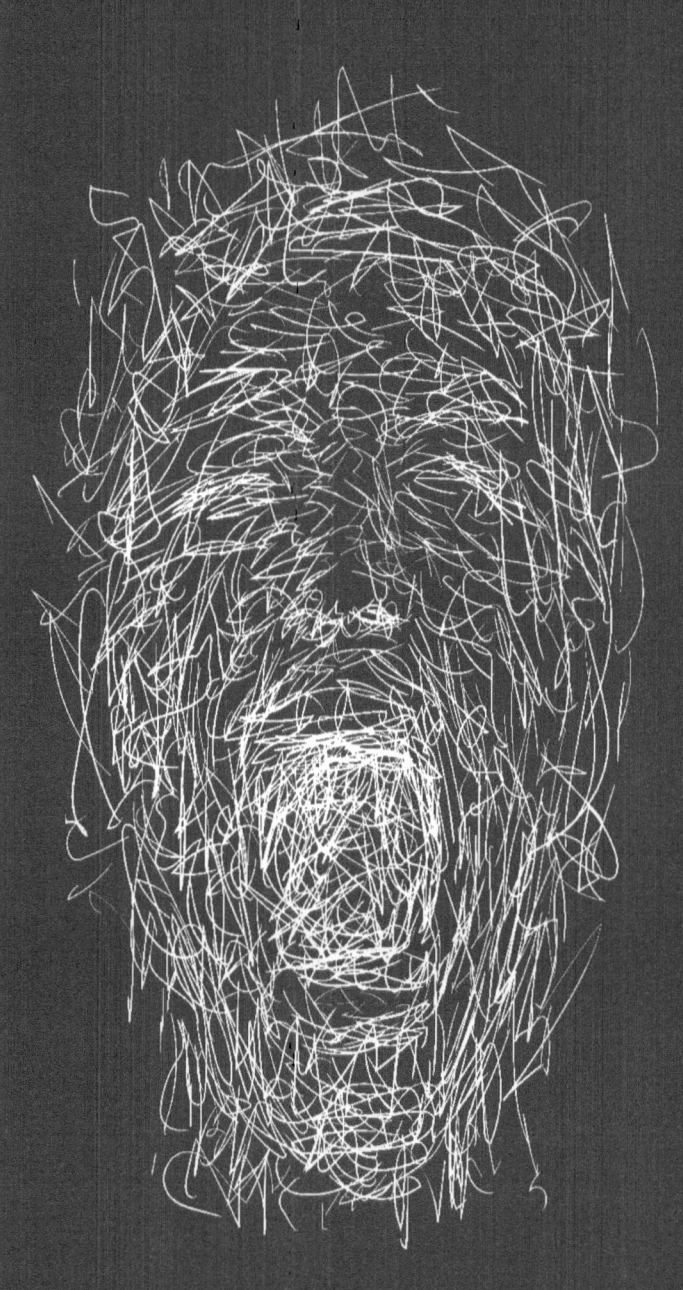

5

"No, we're not." Nadya pushed by Marcelo and went to Reginald. "We're going to find out what caused these people to die, and once we report it to the command, we're going back home."

She shot a look over her shoulder at Marcelo, daring him to disagree.

Instead the regent smirked. "Gamma Team, come on. Let's go get the camp set up. There's a mobile lab and everything, *Doctor.*"

"Of course there is, *Regent.* I ordered it for field tests." Nadya turned back to Reginald and held both his shoulders and lowered her voice. She muted her mic. "Reg, how long we known each other?"

"Since boots." He sighed heavily.

"We aren't gonna die here." She pushed confidence she didn't completely feel into her words. She needed everyone not to panic, and to focus on the work.

If Marcelo lied, she needed to be able to offer the commanders something tangible to ensure she and her team were able to return.

After the regent stormed off with Gamma Team, Leslie remained standing beside Nadya as the other scientists went back to doing their tasks.

When alone, Leslie said, "Nadya, what are we going to do?"

Nadya made sure her microphone was still muted. "We're going to find the answer and go home. The plan hasn't changed, no matter what Marcelo said. I haven't seen any official documentation of his supposed takeover."

Leslie grimaced. "No, but that would be the point of an off-the-books operation."

"There should still be some trail, something authorizing his command here." Nadya turned on her tablet and began to scan her messages.

"The pilots wouldn't take off without official orders." Leslie crossed her arms. "Nadya, seriously, we're going to die here, and before we do, I want to tell you…"

"No, we're not. I can't have that type of thinking now, Leslie, especially from you." Nadya squeezed the area above her elbow gently. "Come on. You and Reggie have got to set the example. This is not the time to quit."

She couldn't keep the quiver out of her own voice. When things got unstable or risky, she buried herself further in work. Now wouldn't be any different. She wouldn't spend time arguing with Marcelo. That would be a waste of energy.

"Let's go look at the communications station. The contact came from there." Nadya headed to the east, where a slender, one-room building sat in front of a thatch of trees. It was almost in the jungle itself.

Leslie followed, grabbing her kit and backpack as she did. Nadya entered the off room, careful to avoid the drag marks leading away from the door. Her torchlight sliced through the darkness.

"That looks like blood," Leslie said. "We haven't seen anything like that before with the others."

"No, we haven't." The hairs on the back of Nadya's neck stood. Thankfully, the suits stripped out some of the odor so it didn't make her gag. Nadya crept farther in, with her heart heavy. The small station had been ransacked. Toppled lanterns, shredded sitting pillows, torn robes and dresses.

Unlike the deceased others, this area screamed violence. She inched closer, heart galloping in her chest. Feet stuck out from behind the corner pillow pile. Her heart dropped.

"Nadya," Leslie called after her. "Let me take a look first. I'm a microbiologist, but I'm also versed in cadavers."

"I won't argue with you."

"You better not. You know what I'll do." Leslie winked at her, then with a somber expression, went to look. She gasped as she moved closer.

"Leslie?"

"By all things logical," Leslie whispered. "This is horrible, and you know, I've seen some things."

Despite her churning stomach and trembling hand, Nadya went to see for herself.

Regret was immediate.

Tossed like a rag doll, the village leader—as designated by their brilliant scarlet robe and necklaces—lay sprawled on the floor. A violent struggle occurred there, but who had wanted Agura dead?

"Who is it?" Leslie inquired. She stood beside her.

"Agura. They oversaw this village. There's bruising on the body, too. This looks like a beating, Leslie."

Nadya turned away from the grisly scene. "If everyone died, who beat them like this?"

"Could be the killer didn't want them contacting the IO," Leslie said. She bent down and searched the body's robe. "Here's a close contact wound. Someone shot her."

Nadya kept her back to Leslie. "One of ours?"

"I don't know. Let's get Francis to do an internal scan. The only certainty is that someone pressed a gun against their skull and fired."

"After a beating?" Nadya shook her head. "By all things logical."

Leslie stood up again and pressed her microphone. "This is Dr. Gupta. Dr. Francis please report to communications station. We'll need body removal and an autopsy. That'll be on you, Francis."

"Aren't they all on me?" Francis said back via comms.

"The body's in real bad shape," Leslie said. "And not like the others. You'll see when you get here."

"You got that right." Nadya met Leslie's worried gaze.

They went outside and waited for Francis and the rest of the assistants to help move the body.

The trees rustling reminded her of whispering. They witnessed the event but they kept their secrets.

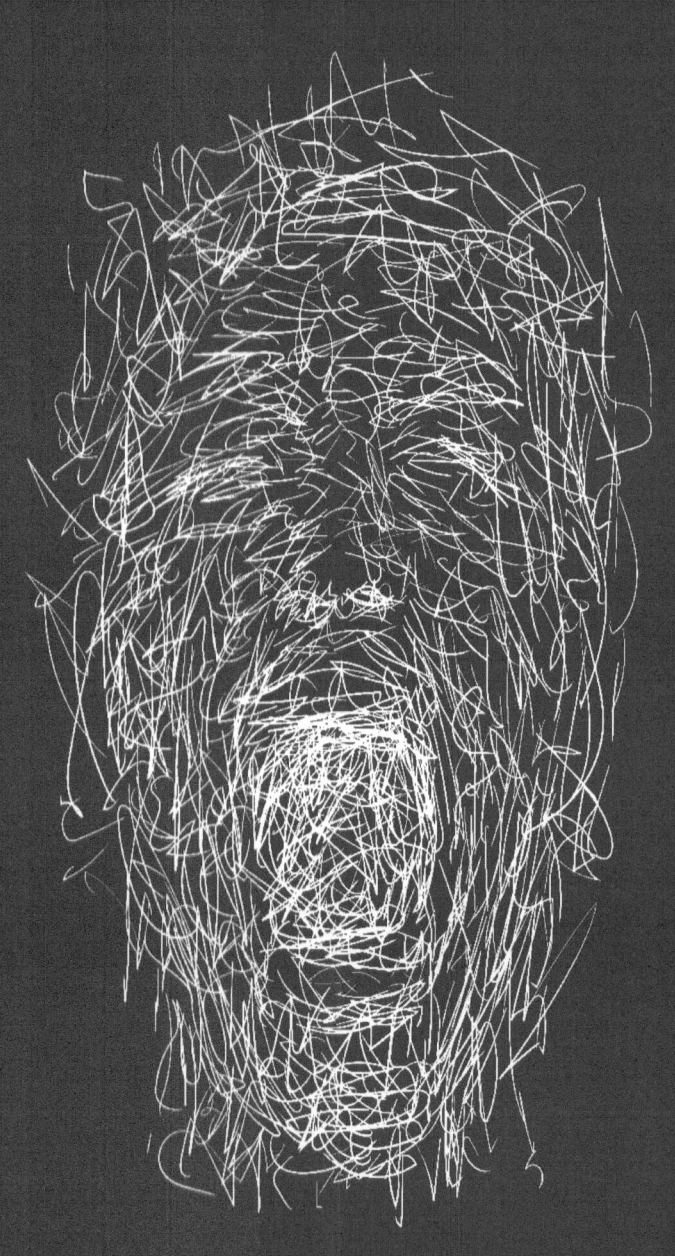

6

Marcelo reached the clearing where Alpha Team's shuttle had been. The large containers sat like metal sentinels guarding IO technology and the ability to unlock Noorbi's secrets. The southern hemisphere had long been a question mark for both the IO and the Noorbian Council.

Contrary to Dr. Singleton's assertions, there had been excursions here, several in the last two earth years. None of those dispatched returned.

No one came back—not the pilots, the soldiers, or the anthropologists.

It was as if a giant hole had swallowed them.

Comm links died. GPS failed.

Until the message from Agura. They had reached out.

Finally.

The IO answered.

"Did you mean what you said back there?" Calhoun interrupted his musings.

The older soldier had a stern expression he seemed to wear all the time, even when it didn't match his mood.

Marcelo paused. "Yeah."

Calhoun stopped too. His reddish face glared out from behind the protective gear. "We knew this might happen. Deep inside. You know?"

Marcelo nodded and resumed walking. "Whatever. We signed up for this."

"Speak for yourself! I'm a scientist, not an IO drone," one of the scientists, a man with a thin build and higher than average voice, said.

He didn't recall the pinch-faced man's name. In truth, he hadn't bothered learning it. Did the queen bee learn the names of worker drones? No.

"You're not Gamma Team, are you?" Marcelo said.

The man hitched his chin higher. "No, I'm a member of Beta Team. My name's Dr. Edgar Adu. Dr. Gupta sent me back to start reviewing samples."

"Right. I can see you're no soldier." Marcelo stepped into the man's path, blocking him. "Scrawny, whiny, but taking advantage of all the IO resources, like a fat tick."

"Sir! The IO gets to claim each new discovery and utilize our findings to enhance their positions in the planetary alliance and better the lives of billions." the scientist countered. "It's a symbiotic relationship. That means…"

"I know what it means, you tick!" Marcelo started toward the scientist, but Calhoun slapped him on the shoulder.

"Shush," Calhoun said, his face pointed to the west, left of the path.

"Don't you shush me!" Marcelo's annoyance landed on the veteran soldier. He snatched his hand off his shoulder.

"I heard something in the brush, over there." Calhoun nodded. "There it is again."

Marcelo calmed down at the seriousness in Calhoun's words. He lowered his night goggles and scanned the identified section. His infrared detector didn't show anything warm blooded in the darkness.

"What does it sound like?" the scientist asked.

"A whining, like an injured animal, but fast paced, like a panting." Calhoun shook his head. "I can't really explain it."

"Human or animal?" the scientist prodded.

"I don't hear or see anything—" Marcelo whispered.

"There is it again!" Calhoun's head jerked to the left. He inched off the path and into the tendrils of vegetation. "You can't hear that?"

Marcelo hurried over to Calhoun and snatched him by the backpack and guided him to the group.

"No, I can't hear it. Come on. We've got a camp and labs to set up."

Calhoun blinked repeatedly, and then said, "Yeah. Right."

"Are you alright, Cal?" The pinched-face man closed the distance between him and the soldier.

"He's fine," Marcelo snapped. *Damn scientists, always babying people, animals, plants.* "Let's go. Move it."

"He doesn't look fine," the scientist said.

No, he doesn't, but none of us are in great shape out here.

06:13 hours

Dawn broke across the horizon to greet them as Nadya emerged from the village path. She found the clearing filled with the containers converted to labs and a housing unit complete with portable attached bathing and toileting. Each shuttle carried one with enough space to house up to eight, with Gamma Team's ship being the largest as it had more members and more gear to transport.

The once empty field now contained several buildings and hummed with energy and machines.

"Where is everyone?" she asked when she reached the clearing. Marcelo sat in a fold-out chair in front of the housing unit, often referred to as a bunker box. He'd completely removed his protective outerwear. He appeared rested and washed.

"Where's Gamma Team?" she said.

He shrugged. "Gone to their site to set up for the rest of their team. We did manage to get the labs up. I think one of Beta's already in there."

Nadya followed his head nod to the square lab behind him. Sure enough, there was a light on and someone hunched over a desk. She couldn't make out who. Her body sang with fatigue. The muscles around her midriff ached, but she couldn't complain when this scientist toiled away, probably without any sleep. She understood that spark of discovery. It was a fire that burned beneath your nerves and tendons, forcing you to keep moving, searching, digging.

"It's looking like the cause may be environmental," Nadya said to Marcelo.

"Is it airborne?" Marcelo stood up, concern marring his usually handsome features.

"Not sure," Leslie said, joining them. Then to Nadya, "I'm going on ahead to sleep. Let's sync up tomorrow, well, later today, by that I mean tonight."

She squeezed Nadya's hand and drifted away. The longing in Leslie's parting gaze would fill oceans. Back at the complex, Leslie would crawl into her bed, or vice-versa, with Obe lying close by on his bed.

In the field, no such sleeping arrangement could be carried out.

Tearing herself away from staring after Leslie, Nadya put her attention back on Marcelo.

"We need to put someone on guard and take shifts."

Leslie shouted back, "Got it!" and waved goodbye.

"Why? What's happened?" Marcelo said.

Nadya told him about the leader's assassination and what Francis shared.

"Francis will do the complete autopsy later. She needs to rest."

"Fuck!" Marcelo wiped his face with his hand. "You're right. Cole, make sure Delta has someone on watch."

"I already briefed them." Nadya massaged her neck.

"Confirmed!" Cole replied via his communication link, as he too had made it a good distance along the route back to where Delta Team landed. He and several others disappeared around a bend in the landscape, toward their own camp.

Reginald didn't speak to Marcelo but went into the bunker. The automatic door hissed closed and then the loud whoosh of the disinfectant blower and lights commenced.

"Uh, yeah, I'll take first shift." Marcelo jerked down his jacket. He'd changed into his IO commander uniform. "I've had a nap. You lot look knackered."

She grunted in his direction and then went inside. She paused at the entrance, allowing the door to slide close and the decontamination sequence to begin. There weren't any windows, but three monitors surveilled the outer perimeter. Once done, the big button switched from red to green.

"Green means good," Reginald said.

"As far as we know," Nadya said then looked up.

"Two minutes is not enough time to enjoy a washup." He came from the shower's direction, naked as the day he was born except for a pair of underwear.

"You're not supposed to enjoy it. It's only good to get clean, like washing your hands but for your whole body. You don't linger."

The two separated stalls shared the same water source, one they brought with them, so the supply was limited at best. They could try to supplement it from a stream, but that would require them to install the fliters to remove the contaminents. If they stayed longer than a few days they would set that up.

Nadya closed her eyes and let the wave of tiredness crash over her in full.

Now inside the bunker and away from the village's carnage, she could start trying to decompress. From Marcelo's antics to the revelations they might have an actual humanoid killer and possibly an environmental contagion, all threated to send her into hysterical sobbing. She held on to her pride and the knowledge that if she broke down, Reginald would go with her. They'd been friends since bootcamp on Earth Station Four.

"Nadya, what are we going to do about Marcelo?" Reginald sat down on a cot, laid back and placed his hands behind his head to stare up at the ceiling. "You can't let this go."

Nadya's hands shook. "Not now, Reggie. I—"

"Not now? Not now!" He shot up to a sitting position. "We're stuck here! You're the leader. The director! Fucking *do* something."

"Shut up!" She closed her eyes to stop the bunker space from shrinking.

"…that incident with Brown and Kim-Lee on Delta Nine…"

Nadya's legs bolted, as if on their own will. She hurried down the center aisle, to the portable shower and potty.

Her eyes flapped open and she found herself in the wet stall. Tears raced down her cheeks.

I wish Leslie or Obe were here.

She slid down to the floor, her legs finally giving in to the familiar cold weakening her anxiety produced.

Too bad the shower can't last long enough to drown me.

Maybe her tears would help.

Later, when she exited the shower, she was surprised to see Reginald sitting up, waiting. He'd dimmed the overhead lights, but she could see his outline against the shadows.

"Nadya…" he started.

"Get some sleep. We're taking shifts. Marcelo is up first."

"Shifts?" Reginald said.

"Yes. Someone killed Agura." She gave him a quick summary of the murder as she put on her hair bonnet. "Someone's out there."

"*Something*, Nadya. *Something's* out there," he corrected.

7

12:00 hours

Despite the humidity, Dr. Edgar Adu, got up, dressed, picked up his collection kit and headed out into the bright, sunny afternoon. As a member of Beta Team and a botanist, Edgar liked plants. He would've been on Alpha Team with his colleague Dr. Perez, but the nature of this one placed him on Dr. Gupta's team. He didn't mind. His specialty was poisonous plants. He'd been fascinated by them since he was barely six years old. That's when he witnessed a hoger-ka consume a rather large pet while playing outside his home on Kreu. The viny plant had a trunk the size of most average tree trunks on earth, an oak or an ash, but it also had limbs that moved, like a human's. It was both strange and fascinating at the time.

He discovered later, Hoger-kas were against regulations.

The neighbors disappeared that night. He never saw them or the hoger-ka again.

"What are you doing, Ed?" Dr. Gupta's tone pierced through the quiet.

He'd made it as far as about the bunker box's end, when he paused.

"Even if you stay very still, I *can* still see you." Leslie walked across the grass to him. She wore a puffy metallic uniform and foamy dark boots. "We do have a guard on duty. I mentioned that we're taking turns."

"Yes, ma'am." Edgar turned to her. She didn't wear any protective gear now, and her hair had been tied in two long plaits on either side of her head.

"Any guesses who's turn it is?" Leslie smiled at him.

"Mine?" Edgar squeaked. His voice was tight with fear.

"Mine."

"Ah," he said, and gave a short, nervous laugh. "I—I like hiking in

41

the jungle, searching for new edibles and vegetables to supplement the bar rations. If lucky, I might discover some medicinal plants too. Maybe some poisonous ones?"

"I understand, but I gave orders to one, not go anywhere alone, and two, not without my permission. We need to know where everyone is at all times. There's a killer out here." Leslie stood with her arms akimbo, her face somber. "Let me get someone to cover my shift and we can go search together."

Edgar swallowed a groan. He liked the solitude of being alone to do his work, to avoid the questioning eyes of others who didn't understand his love of the profane, the grotesque, and violent foliage.

The doctor raced back to the bunker. Before long, he heard hushed talking, and then a few minutes after that, another scientist, Olivier, maybe, Edgar couldn't be sure. He couldn't quite make out the man's face from the distance and because the person rubbed their eyes. Probably wiping away sleep—their face was hidden.

Leslie raced back to him, her backpack on, and a manual face mask looped over her ears.

"For you." She handed him another face mask and nodded at his kit. "You have gloves in there?"

"Yes, I do." He placed the mask on, partially glad she couldn't see him scowl, and annoyed that she'd ruined his outing. When she looked at him, her eyes were tired and fierce.

"You must be exhausted from the night's activities. You should rest… I've done collections before."

She stilled and gave him a questioning look. "I'm well versed in your work, Ed. We do work at the same complex and even the same lab, just two doors down."

He forced a laugh. "Oh, yes, right, well, let's go."

When they reached the path to the village, Edgar went right and into the clustered jungle. The thick canopy kept the sun's direct light from them. The heavy air clung to them. It felt like walking through sap. With Dr. Gupta's presence, so close to him, Edgar sweated more, but it wasn't his body's attempt to cool down. This was a cold glaze produced by fear. Why was he afraid? He'd done nothing wrong.

After his run in with the regent earlier, he'd been unsettled around the others. His nerves had been smashed when he realized the pilots had all left and that they'd been abandoned to their fate. But the thrill of finding a new and strange plant eclipsed those frayed feelings.

Birds sang, and the strong odor of death and corn chips had lessened from earlier. It could be the wind had changed, or he'd grown used to the smell. He had no way of knowing which it was.

They hiked in silence. Edgar put his focus on the plants. The diverse and thick variety had many of the same spices as those up north but with minor adapted differences. The accepted theory was that the two continents probably used to be one, during the planet's developmental past.

"Are you searching for a certain type?" Dr. Gupta said. "I can help."

"I don't have a specific one. I want to document what's here and find any new species not currently in the IO database."

Dr. Gupta wiped her brow. "You couldn't wait until nightfall, when it's cooler?"

"Some plants bloom in the light and become active. If I only search at night, I may miss some."

Edgar couldn't believe she didn't know that, but then again, she was a microbiologist.

Branches snapped under foot as Dr. Gupta made her way behind him.

"Why don't you go toward the west," Edgar suggested. "We can cover more area."

"I wouldn't know what to look for, and our orders are not to be alone," Dr. Gupta said. "Why are you trying to get away from me?"

He stopped. "I, I'm not..." His cheeks burned.

She caught up to him. "Then we continue."

Edgar started again. "The Noorbians used this area for food and probably medicinal purposes. There's evidence of cutting and pinching on the plants."

Behind him the doctor grunted.

Edgar moved on, checking the moist base of the grounds around trees. The fungus he found must originate in the jungle. The villagers did some light agricultural farming, but most of their diet came from this rich source of food.

They moved slowly and deliberately through the thick vegetation. Low hanging tree limbs, flying insects, watched as creeping animals scurried across the ground cover.

Definitely more activity during the day.

"The Noorbians eat a mostly vegetarian diet. Do you think the same is true with the southern inhabitants?" Dr. Gupta stopped. "Oh look here— a Badda Blue Beetle! Oh! There's a colony."

Edjar let out a sigh of relief. He didn't enjoy small talk. He kept moving, leaving the team leader to conduct her own collection journey. Badda Blue Beetles were rare.

She might have called out to him, but he pushed on.

15:00 hours

"Dr. Singleton, come quick!" Marcelo said.

Nadya hurried outside the bunker box, her heart racing at the urgency in the regent's voice. Once outside, she winced at the sun's brightness. With her hand, shielding her eyes, she found a gathering of stunned and anxious faces.

"What's happened?" Nadya scanned the crowd. "Where's Les—uh, Dr. Gupta?"

"Missing," Marcelo said. "I just got the report."

A weary and upset Francis said, "I'd sent one of the assistants over to Beta team to fetch Edgar. The comms connection has been spotty at best. Anyway, when they got there, there wasn't anyone on guard duty, and no one had seen Edgar or Dr. Gupta."

"She, um, they could be at the village site..." Nadya offered.

Calhoun shook his head. "Already hiked over there. No one's there."

She spied Reginald. He wore sunglasses and munched on a rations bar. She'd been so soundly asleep, she didn't hear him get up, dress, and leave.

"Edgar found something yesterday, last night. He was excited about

44

it," he said.

"Do we know what?" Nadya asked, reeling from the news of Leslie's disappearance.

Where are you, Les? Did Edgar force you to go with him?

"No, but I'll go check his notes and samples to see what he left," Reginald said.

"I'm assuming you tried comms." Nadya looked at Calhoun.

"Yes. Only static," Marcelo said.

"But she had them. It means she probably left on her own free will."

The tight squeeze around Nadya's heart lessened.

"According to the team, she left Olivier on guard duty and went with Edgar," Cole said. "They are together."

"Or they *were,*" Calhoun added.

"We're going to search. We'll be available via comms," Cole said. "Don't worry. We'll find her."

"Both of them," Calhoun added. "They're probably a bit lost."

Nadya nodded, too numb to speak. She watched the group of four head off in the jungle's direction.

The remaining group members dispersed. Murmurs of conversations buzzed. A thin layer of fear threaded through them, tethering them together, even as they parted.

"Let's go see what Edgar found," Nadya said to Reginald.

"I was heading that way."

They walked across the clearing and into the jungle. The shadowy space under the thick overhead canopy was instantly cooler. She followed Regniald, who in turn followed Beta Team members to their camp. On most missions, the camps were together, not spread out. This arrangement left them vulderable to attack. She'd considered they would be in this type of danger, but not from a killer.

"Aww! Freakin' spider webs!" Reginald's arms whirled like a windmill. "Off! Get off!"

Nadya laughed. "There goes a brave IO soldier."

"I'm a botanist!" Reginald shouted.

"We're all many things," Nadya said, suddenly somber.

It sparked a thought, an idea.

"What if we've been looking at this the wrong way?"

Ahead, Reginald hopped over a puddle. The damp ground cover hinted at an underground spring or water source.

"What do you mean?" He huffed.

Nadya jumped over the water. "Francis said the villagers hadn't all died at exactly the same time, as initially reported. What if they died over a series of days? When Agura realized the growing epidemic, she reached out for help."

Reginald nodded. "That follows..."

"The remaining villagers disagreed, and a violent attack unfurled. Agura is killed and the villagers die, like the others."

"Where's the weapon? Did Francis find weapons on the bodies?"

"No." Nadya sighed. "I did say it was a theory."

"Okay, but it supports what we found so far. It doesn't answer what killed them."

Nadya didn't need him to tell her. "It's either environmental or a deliberate mass poisoning."

"Either means nasty business." Reginald lifted a low hanging purple line. "And possibly hard to prove."

They reached Beta Team's camp. The mobile labs gleamed in the afternoon sun, Several members went into the labs and resumed work.

"Now, let's see what made Edgar's heart race." Reginald entered the first square lab on his left. Cool air and the disinfectant routine greeted them. Reginald was first. He secured a mask and gloves before asking one of the fellow scientists, "Which one is Edgar's?"

"There," a large, brunette woman said and nodded at the empty microscope station across from her.

Nadya and Reginald went to the clean desk. There, a computer woke and the botanist went to work. "Let's see here. Yeah, he found some fungus on the villagers' lips. The ones with the foam around the mouth."

"A fungus?" Nadya read over his shoulder. "It could be something they ate or touched."

"Or both, and all the villagers would've had to ingest and touch it," Reginald said. "I don't think it's contagious, but I can't rule it out."

He placed a slide under the microscope and hummed. "Give me your secrets."

While he worked, Nadya drifted over to the other Beta Team member. At this station, the woman had several colorful leaves arranged in vertical lines.

"What are these?" Nadya pointed at them.

"Leaves from several trees located around the village. They contain fecal matter from the area bats. Sometimes a virus jumps to humans," the scientist said. "As I'm sure you know, Dr. Singleton. When they're stressed, they shed at an accelerated rate."

"You're thinking a possible spillover event or transmission could explain why people died." Nadya agreed, but so close together? "It was one of the theories we wanted to investigate to rule either in or out."

The scientist nodded. "Yes. Dr. Gupta assigned it to me."

She sighed and hesitated, glancing quickly at Nadya before looking back at the leaves. "I hope they find her."

"They will," Nadya said with more confidence than she felt.

"Nadya…" Reginald waved her over. "It's not out of the realm of possibility, but I'd put my currency units on this…" He stepped back from the microscope for Nadya to look.

Nadya peered in. "Mold?"

"Yes, and it's a particularly nasty bit of growth. It's fast. Look, Ed collected this roughly twelve hours ago. It's already reproduced, growing to twice its size."

"What's it feeding on? This tiny bit of material here?" Nadya asked. "What's this, the pink bit?"

"Us," Francis said from the entrance. "The fungus feeds on flesh."

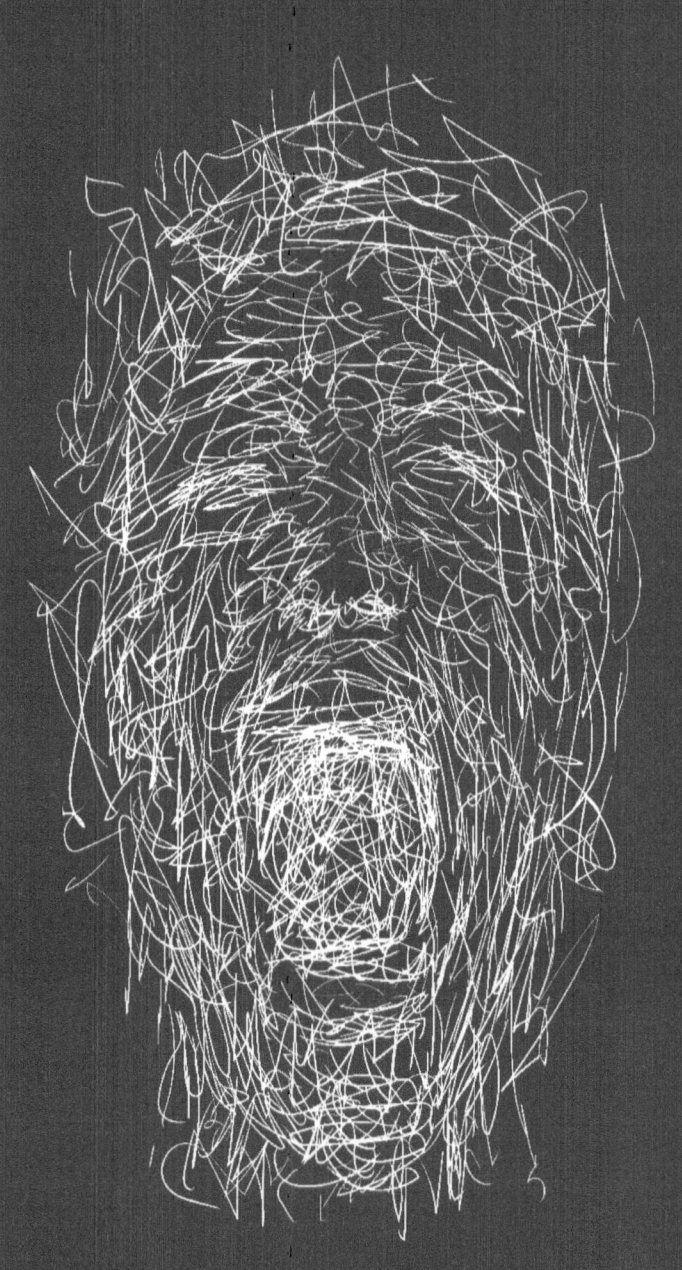

8

Later, all the team members not out searching for Leslie and Edgar met outside Beta Team's mobile lab. Nadya rubbed her hands on her uniform, but she couldn't wipe off the anxiousness crawling over her skin, like a hundred ants, circling the area between her elbow and fingertips.

Francis stood beside Nadya, facing the others. "There's still no word from Cole?" she asked, low enough for only her ears.

"No, not yet."

The longer the silence went on, the more nervous she became. Marcelo hadn't checked in.

"They'll find them. They're probably lost." Francis gave her a small, reassuring grin.

"Come on, let's start." Nadya swallowed to wet her dry throat. "Okay, team. It's been about eighteen hours since we landed. Let's see where we are and what we've found. Dr. Francis?"

She went to stand with the crowd as Francis cast a projection from her tablet onto the lab's wall.

"As Dr. Singleton mentioned, it's early days, yet. We haven't completed autopsies on all the villagers but from the seven we've done so far we've noted some commonalities. Our preliminary findings are as follows."

She swiped and an image appeared of a deceased Noorbian. "As you can see here, there's a white, waxy foam on this victim's lips. We found this on the other villagers, too. Every single one, even children and babies. At first, I thought it was part of the decomposing process of the Noorbians. That was until I autopsied the sampling group."

Nadya waited with bated breath.

"I found it throughout the cavity," Francis said. "Even in the stomach contents. I believe the fungus, as Dr. Adu identified it, was ingested and then began to sprout, sending these spores…" Francis swiped and another image appeared. Oval, black dots littered the lab's outer wall. "…via the bloodstream to all organs."

"It looks like black mold," Reginald said, stepping forward. He stood on the opposite side of the projection. "But this one is carnivorous. It's unlike anything we've seen before on this planet. The fungi isn't in the IO database, either. We speculate that once it reaches those major organs, it attaches to them and begins to feed."

"Is it contagious?" Tahinti asked, eyes wide, lips trembling.

"If the spores are airborne, then maybe," Reginald said. "But it looks like the villagers consumed it."

"That's based off the small sample we've autopsied so far," Francis interjected.

"Early days," Reginald added.

"What we don't know is if it is breathed in and attacks the lungs, can it stick to bronchial tubes, filling the cavity causing death via suffocation." Francis finished.

Silence.

Then everyone started talking at once.

Nadya walked to the front. "Thank you. Does anyone have any additional findings to share? Theories? We are keeping an open mind."

Tahinti said, "Dr. Francis is running toxicology taken from the sample group. So far the findings haven't revealed anything of note."

"Thank you, Tahinti." Nadya clasped her hands together. "Let's start again tonight about twenty-one hundred. Until then, rest. Eat. I want to start with clear eyes and rested minds."

They dispersed.

Francis collapsed the projection. "You should rest too."

Reginald scoffed. "She won't."

Nadya glared. "I'm standing right here."

They exchanged looks and laughed.

Nadya folded her arms. "Francis, I want to review the autopsy notes."

Francis nodded. "No problem. I'll grab a coffee and bar rations and

I'll meet you in the bunker box."

Reginald said, "I'm going to get back to the mold. Edgar's notes are brief but I want to do some more tests."

Nadya watched Reginald disappear into the lab. They were on track to getting answers.

Then why did she feel so scared?

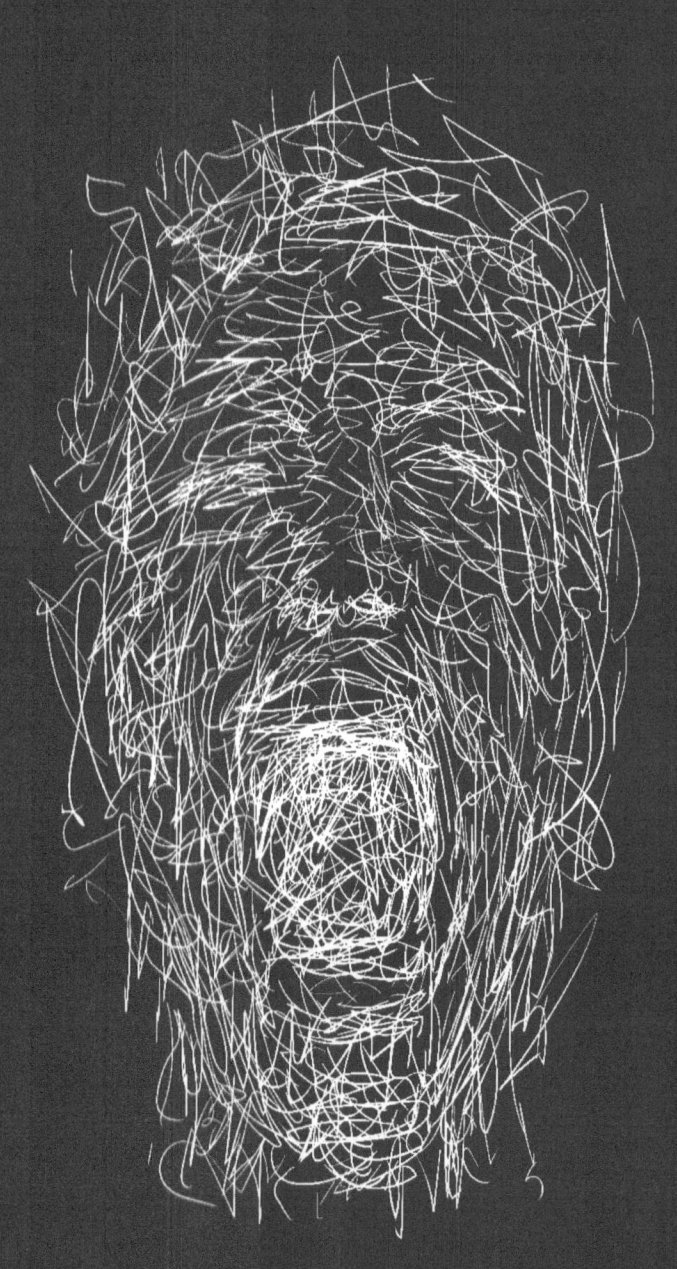

9

Leslie called out to Edgar. She couldn't believe he'd run off and ditch her, deep in an unfamiliar jungle. She had to admit, the botanist had a one-track mind. When he focused on something, he hyper did it. His behavior told her he wanted to get rid of her and when the opportunity presented itself, he did.

The brush embraced her as she continued through snapped trees, torn overhead canopy, and across the damp ground. She adored fieldwork, and it had always given her joy. It fed her, entertained her, and allowed her to be herself. Nature didn't demand anything in return, except respect. Honeysuckles scented the air and tickled her nose. She moved slowly, but with purpose. Edgar left a trail as he pushed through the jungle.

Overhead, the midday sun lumbered toward dusk. Insects buzzed, and birds sang sweet temptation to eligible mates. Scurrying animals darted through the shrubbery and trees.

Gradually, the landscape changed. Broken limbs, brunt debris, and deep gouges in the earth spoke to something unnatural.

It grew quieter.

She came upon a wreckage. "What happened here?"

Leslie touched her ear to activate the comm link. "Come in, Dr. Singleton. Come in, Nadya. Cole? Anyone?"

A rush of static answered.

"Damn it." Leslie inched closer to the downed shuttle. It didn't appear to be recent, but it was an IO vessel. The registration code and identification all pointed to the InterGalactic Organization. Vegetation, a lovely orange, had reclaimed the hull. "It's down, but not completely totaled."

Could this be where their mystery assassin came from? Could there be survivors?

The door had been wrenched from its hinges, leaving a gaping hole in the shuttle's rear. With her curiosity getting the better of her, she went on board. The interior reeked faintly of burnt rubber. Broken glass scattered across the floor and crunched beneath her boots. She squinted against the gloomy inside. The room illuminated once she came further in, spooking her. *Motion sensors.* It couldn't have been abandoned too long ago.

Two bucket seats, scorched and knocked off kilter, lay on the flooring. The craft appeared to be abandoned. She didn't see any hits of recent activity.

Suddenly, a shrill blaring ripped through the craft. A loud voice declared: "Intruder! Intruder!"

Leslie put both hands over her ears. The alarm's bellowing voice couldn't be drowned out by her hands, only muffled.

She hurried over to the navigation console and pressed a few keys, but nothing happened. With her mind whirling, she shifted over to the copilot station, when the blaring noise and flashing red, warning lights suddenly ceased. Leslie breathed a sigh of relief. She hadn't realized she'd clutched her jaw and balled up her fists.

"Whew." She made herself relax in the stunned silence. She welcomed it.

"What. You. Doing?" a voice like crushed glass yelled.

Across from her—a person, a man? He looked like a walking contagion. The left side of his face and upper torso was covered by a waxy foam-like substance. It crept down his face, around his collar, and down his shoulder on the left side. He didn't wear an IO uniform, but a pair of threadbare pants and what looked like the remains of an undershirt.

He smelled strangely of corn chips.

He stomped toward her. A reddish, mucus-thick saliva dribbled from the corner of his mouth.

Leslie fell back a step until she hit the console's edge, the scream lodged in her throat.

She glanced down at her wrist. It had scanned the individual, but didn't find any biometrics, no barcode scan, nothing. He didn't even come up as human.

"I—I'm Dr. Leslie Gupta of the InterGalatic Organization. We're here on a fact-finding mission, to investigate the incident at Uzuri…"

He roared, spewing spit and foam bits from his mouth. Leslie covered her face with her arm, to protect her eyes and as much as possible. He already had a mask and gloves on.

He leapt at her, and she dodged him, her heart racing, her feet moving on their own. She scurried out of the shuttle and into the small clearing the damaged ship had crafted in its crash.

She looked back over her shoulder to find the man stumbling out of the shuttle's opening and giving chase. This forced her to move faster, but running blind through an unfamiliar area didn't sound like a great idea at the best of times.

He probably knows this area better than I do.

Leslie tripped and fell face-first on a hard, above-ground root. She tasted blood and pushed herself back up to a standing position. After three steps, a shadow fell over her and the rush of body odor, decomp, and corn chips yanked her attention.

Her attacker's arm shot out and grabbed her right arm. He snatched her backward so hard, her feet flew out from underneath her.

She didn't scream or yell. Instead, she took her free hand and punched him in the face, using the momentum, albeit unbalanced, to land it with greater impact.

Stunned, the man howled and let her go.

Not wasting any time, she scurried out of his arm's reach, this time careful of the moist ground cover's pitfalls. His heavy panting followed her, closer than she liked.

Who is this? Why is he attacking me?

For the briefest of moments, she thought she'd stop and explain she wasn't an enemy, but she wasn't sure he could understand her. The fungal growth on his body might have damaged his brain, or he could have head injuries from the crash or both. She sprinted along, moving not in a straight forward path, but zigzagging through the thick vines and colorful leaves.

Her forehead burned where some of the man's spittle landed. She tried wiping her face with her gloved hand, just that spot so she didn't end up spreading it all over her face. She wanted to use a disinfectant but there'd been no time.

She remained on her feet. She'd dare not sit or stop to rest. Once an opportunity presented itself, she needed to act.

Edgar, if I live through this I am going to kill you!

Meanwhile, Edgar squatted down on his haunches and peered with his magnifying glass at the round, black-capped mushrooms growing at the base of a large, ancient-looking red tree. The fungus resembled little grim reapers, blackened cloaks with no face. It would be fitting, since he suspected these small fungi killed an entire village.

The tree itself seemed to be as big and as wide as a retrieval shuttle, which was one of the reasons Edgar believed it had been there first, or at bare minimum a long, long time. It may have been one of the jungle's founding members.

The spray of fungi dotted the area, not overcrowding each other, but definitely reproducing at a good rate. Edgar suspected they didn't have any natural predators or, if they did, they'd died out.

He stood back up and opened his collection kit. He already wore the mask and gloves, but now he slipped on his face shield. The last thing he wanted was for one of the mushrooms to erupt with spores and he get a face full of them. That would be horrible.

He took out his paring knife and began cutting pieces of one of the mushrooms from its base. The entire specimen would be best. It would give him more material to test with. The latex stuck to his hands. His heart beat rapidly as the first one slid into its glass container. They weren't bigger than his index finger.

Then movement caught his eye. Between the tree's wooden fingers-like exposed roots, an insect lay on its side, belly up. All he could make out were the antenna as they wiggled in slow, sluggish jerks. The rest had been blanketed with a waxy, white foam, not unlike what he'd found in the villagers, but this time, he found some of the blackened caps around the insect's mandibles. The mushroom bits had clung on to the sharper, more pointed parts. He could see the foam oozing from the fungi, eating through the shell and dissolving muscle and tissue as they feasted. Watery pink fluid leaked from the insect, and it fidgeted on its back, unable to move or halt the assault.

"It must've been hungry, decided to eat these, and turned the tables." Edgar smiled. "Brilliant."

"You know what isn't brilliant? Ditching Dr. Gupta and the team," came a voice that brought goosebumps along Edgar's skin.

Marcelo.

Edgar looked up from his magnifying glass and turned to see three men standing behind him. Cole and Calhoun wore amused expression, but Marcelo looked like he could spit acid.

Not now. I just got to the good part.

"We got separated," Edgar said. He didn't lie. They did. "I'm sure she's close by here. It wasn't that long ago."

Cole nudged Calhoun, "Go see if you can find her, but circle back tight. Not too far."

Calhoun nodded and drifted backward into the shadows.

Marcelo took in a deep breath and released it. "What are you doing?"

Edgar rose up on his knees. "I believe I found the origin of the fungus that killed the villagers."

"Already?" Cole said, not bothering to hide his shock. He frowned in confusion. He glanced at Marcelo.

"Well, it wasn't that hard. It had to be a species that was plentiful, and due to the nature of the specimen I looked at, I knew it had to be some type of fungi spore." Edgar wiped his face with his sleeve. "I've been out here for hours and have inspected roughly sixteen different mushrooms."

Cole blew out an "Oh."

Marcelo smirked. "You really found it?"

"I will need to test," Edgar said. "I also need to collect a few more samples."

"Fine." Marcelo turned away. "Cole…"

Shrieking, loud and shrill and dripping with terror erupted, tearing through the muffled buzzing and insect chittering.

"That sounded like Dr. Gupta," Cole said. He pressed his ear piece. "Calhoun, you got eyes on Gupta?"

His blue eyes met Edgar's. "Nothing. Static. Calhoun. Report!"

Marcelo shook his head too. "I got the same thing." He looked down at Edgar. "You, get the samples and get your narrow ass back to camp. Do you understand?"

"Yes, of course."

Cole said, "Ed, seriously, don't dwindle. Whatever's out there may be coming this way."

Edgar sucked in a breath and nodded at Cole. He'd always liked the soldier. Cole respected him, tried to be transparent, and above all professional. He took his duties seriously and was thoughtful in his interactions with the scientist. Cole was no alarmist.

So it was great disappointment when he saw Cole take off and Marcelo stayed behind, lingering.

"Uh, aren't you going to go help them?" Edgar asked in a tiny voice. It sounded small. That was how he felt.

Marcelo peered at him with a wide, cold grin. "Yeah. I'm going to go help."

Edgar's eyebrows rose, but he didn't respond. He shuddered when goosebumps spread across his arms.

He was very worried about Cole.

10

Leslie wasn't sure what happened. Everything went by so fast. One minute she had managed to put distance between herself and the mass of oozing corn chips, and the next she was flat on her back, with scraps on her palms and a gaping puncture in her calf, bleeding profusely. Thanks to adrenaline, she must've blacked out.

"Dr. Gupta! Leslie! Wake up!" Cole shouted, gently shaking her. His words seemed to come from the other end of a long tunnel. "We've got to move!"

She blinked, trying to send the sharp stabbing frontal lobe pain away. She nodded she understood and immediately regretted the action. *Damn, I might have a concussion.* At her feet, Calhoun tied a tight bandage from his med kit around the wound and got up to his feet, gun in his right hand. He replaced the kit with one smooth motion into his backpack. The gun remained trained on whatever approached.

"Come on." Cole hoisted her up without waiting for her to say ready.

He, too, had a weapon out.

Wow.

Her head ached, and she felt the spot that burned. Her gloved finger came away with a waxy, pink fluid.

"Fuck," she said.

Cole raised an eyebrow. "Never heard you curse before. What's wrong?"

"We need to get going," Calhoun said.

"You can walk?" Cole asked her.

"Yes." Leslie didn't know for sure, but she wouldn't be the one to slow them down. "You saw it?"

"The walking fungus monster? Yep," Cole said, as they started walking through the jungle.

"I suspect he used to be a healthy IO soldier or scientist," Leslie grunted.

Calhoun placed his gloved index finger to his lips. "Shhhh."

Cole nodded.

Leslie swallowed the pain, pushed it down. It hurt. Every step. The terrain didn't make it easy either. The non-leveled brush and debris tripped her up, made her injury sing in glorious pain to the point that Cole ended up having to support her with his body. His free arm wrapped around her waist to steady her, as if they were both in a three-legged race.

A roar, both animalistic and human, gelled and echoed throughout the space around them. She couldn't focus well enough to know what direction it emitted from. *Thanks head injury.*

But she could smell him.

"He's close to the right!" Leslie shouted. Cole and Calhoun both turned to the direction she indicated.

The vines shimmed and then exploded as the attacker shot forward, mouth wide, hands like claws high in the air, ready to pound them or rip them from limb to limb.

The smelly menace's hands ripped through the thin air, missing Calhoun's forearm by less than an inch. Fast, the damn beast was *fast*. Calhoun and Cole didn't waste time watching.

She held the anguish inside, shoving it deeper into the well of adrenaline surging upward through her.

Cole released her at once and fired. Calhoun did too. The bullets landed but did nothing to stop him from coming. He swiped at Calhoun and managed to punch him in the ribs. The blow knocked him back several feet.

"Cal!"

She'd never heard Cole sound like that before— afraid and furious. Chills skated down her back.

Leslie fumbled with her own pack to see what she had that could help.

The monster lifted Calhoun from the ground as if he didn't weigh over two hundred fifty pounds. Calhoun continued to unload his weapon into the being. One of his shots hit the monster square in his face and he felt it.

He looked at them with a confused expression and shock before throwing back his head and howling. He fell backward a step and slung Calhoun to the ground so hard, Leslie heard a *crack*. Well, it was a series of cracks.

Cole was busy reloading so he didn't go to him.

Leslie did. She limped across to a crumpled Calhoun. Blood dripped down the corner of his mouth and nose. He wheezed, and his breathing was labored. His eyes moved but he didn't shift his body or his head. Leslie steadied herself.

"Doc…"

"Shush. Don't talk. Save your strength. We're gonna get you out of here," Leslie said. "We aren't losing any one."

She quickly took off her old gloves and put on a fresh pair. With fast hands, she took the disinfectant from her kit and poured it on a swab. She dabbed it on his facial injuries and along the scraps around his abdomen, switching out swabs as one became saturated with blood.

"You've broken some ribs," Leslie said, watching the battered bones shift beneath his skin when she applied the disinfectant. "It's going to sting."

Calhoun laughed and then winced in agony. "Don't…make…me…laugh."

"Okay. I'm sorry." Leslie patted his knee and it slid at her touch.

Her insides quaked, and she wanted to vomit. Adrenaline made everything sharp and acidic.

"Fuck!" Cole stumbled backward, tripped over Calhoun's outstretched and booted foot. "We gotta get outta here. The bullets aren't stopping him. It's pissing him off."

Leslie closed her kit and replaced it in her backpack. "Cal isn't going anywhere. He's got broken ribs, a broken leg, and his knee's busted."

With wide eyes, Cole looked down at Calhoun, who gave him a bloodied grin. "You…look…scared…boy."

Cole frowned, his cheeks flushed. "I told you not to call me boy, old geezer."

Calhoun choked out a laugh and then spat a scarlet wad into the dirt beside him.

Leslie watched the trees for movement with a lump in her throat. They couldn't move Calhoun, not like this. She had only one good leg. If the monster continued to track them, only Cole stood between them and certain death and infection. Heck, they might already be infected.

She looked over at Calhoun. Sweat beaded across his brow and above his bloodied lip. They sat on top of the dried cranberry color, making his upper lip look glossy with lipstick.

A sharp pain stabbed her in the forehead and she reeled over and vomited.

A concussion.

Great.

She wiped her mouth and snatched off the gloves. Through slits, she spied Cole frantically reloading.

The creature staggered forward, but he swayed on his feet.

"We may not be out of options yet," she said to Calhoun. "Stay with us."

11

Night had fallen, cooling off the atmosphere. Leslie, Cole, and Calhoun had taken refuge at the base of a large purple tree with glorious deep violet leaves. Her hip ached from the wound to her muscles and tendons at the lower calf. It was all connected, and the small of her back joined in to lodge their complaint, too. With the tree's massive trunk to their backs, they kept their eyes trained on the area in front of them.

Cole wore his infrared glasses. Seated beside Leslie, he drank water from his synthetic waterskin. He passed one to her and one down to Calhoun who sat slumped on the other side of Leslie. His shallow breathing twisted his face in discomfort.

"You didn't come prepared. That's not like you," Cole said.

Leslie winced as she smiled. "I thought I'd be back before dark. I hope Edgar's got back to the camp."

"I'm sure he did," Cole said, after a quick swig of water. "You know, Nadya's sick with worry."

Leslie's heart ached. "Yes, I'm a bit worried myself."

She gently shook Calhoun. "Cal, what's your mother's name?"

Calhoun roused, pink-faced and bruised, he tried to smile. "Uh, Goff. Her name's Goff."

"How's your leg?" Cole nodded at the bandages around Leslie's knee.

"Healing. The nanos are doing their job repairing muscle. It stings."

"Good. You know it's working." Cole touched his earpiece. "Come in, Dr. Singleton. Alpha Team, come in. Marcelo?"

"Still can't get the comms to work. What in the world could be blocking it?" Leslie said.

Cole shook his head. "I'm not sure."

"And Marcelo?"

"Same answer."

Leslie rubbed her forehead with her fingertips, careful not to touch the raw area of her face. She closed her eyes, resting them from the constant strain and tension.

Then, the wind shifted.

A now familiar but pungent odor bowled over them seconds before the creature smashed through the hanging vines and tree limbs.

Cole was on his feet at once, firing both guns, emptying them into the raging man. Furious howls held pain and agony, but the bullets' impact pushed him backward, as if a giant finger poked his hard in the shoulders. He growled, tried to grab something for stability, found only air and crashed to the ground.

When he gained his composure, the fungus man seethed, rising up on his knees, but no farther.

"He's hurt, Cole!" Leslie shouted, despite the hot stabbing pain behind her eyes.

While the creature struggled, she dug out her med kit. She found more gauze and then she removed her bandage from her injury. Next, she poured alcohol on the now knotted ball of gauze.

"Doctor G. Go. Get. Out," Calhoun wheezed. With clenched teeth, he pulled himself to a standing position, largely supported by the tree's trunk. His non-injured leg quaked from bearing his almost full weight. Flushed, sweaty, and shaking with pain, Calhoun raised his gun, not far above his waist, and fired.

"We have orders not to leave anyone behind." Leslie wrenched out a lighter. "You don't read the briefings. Do you?"

Cole glanced over to them. "Hey! You're not gonna do what I think you're gonna do!"

"Yes, I am!" Leslie shouted.

"You'll set the entire jungle on fire!"

"Only if I miss," she replied. Fungus didn't like fire.

Cole reloaded his guns. "Last ones."

"Y-you crazy," Calhoun choked out another laugh. Bright red blood shot out across his hand.

"You just now realizing that?" Cole yelled back but he smirked.

Ahead the wounded creature moaned, rubbing his chest; his thick fingers glided through the rash of foaming fungus, burrowing into his skin, his muscle, him. He slung the slop of it off and onto the ground, his face twisted in terrible agony and wet from sweat.

An eerie quiet fell.

Only the man's low moaning broke the cautious silence. Cole looked from him to Leslie and Calhoun and back again. He didn't lower his weapons, but he inched closer.

"Careful!" Leslie said. "He's still dangerous!"

Beside her, Calhoun slid back down. His strength gave out. He groaned and panted heavily, his tongue out. His face shone with agony.

Leslie put her ball and lighter down and limped over to him. "Here. Drink.?"

Don't die on me. I'd be devastated, but Nadya would be destroyed.

Movement snared her attention. She looked over to their attacker. She didn't want to kill him. Part of her heart pinched in pity. He didn't ask for this to happen to him, and they would probably use him to find a cure. The flesh-eating fungus ravaged the left half of his body, but he still was alive.

Her comm beeped. "Cole. You hear me?"

"Yeah! Where the hell have you been Marcelo?" Cole said.

Leslie watched as the regent emerged from the area behind the crumpled soldier, his weapon drawn.

"Around, but I'm here now." Marcelo put his attention on the downed man. "Looks like you didn't need me, anyway."

"Secure him!" Cole shouted, gesturing at the soldier. "Before he gets back up."

"Oh, that's not going to happen," Marcelo said. "Right, Daniels?"

"Daniels?" Leslie said. *How does he know the man's name?*

The man growled, a deep back-of-the-throat rumble. He lifted his head and turned to Marcelo. Confused, he said, "Who. You?"

"I'm no one important," Marcelo said to Daniels and then to Cole. He walked around the fungus man, not securing him. "We found Dr. Gupta. Mission accomplished."

Cole swore. "Sir, secure the threat! Use your restraints!"

"Daniels isn't a threat, well, not anymore. Thanks to you, and Calhoun." Marcelo waved his gun at them. "The threat now, you three, have seen too much…"

"You can't be serious. He's a fantastic specimen but more than that, he could help develop a cure." Leslie clawed herself to a standing position.

It dawned on her what Marcelo meant.

"You knew! You knew about Daniels, the fungus, the origin of the spores, and why those villagers died." Leslie's anger fired. "You could have saved valuable time!"

Marcelo shook his head. "No, I didn't. I only learned his name because I found the downed shuttle."

Cole seethed. "You went to investigate while we almost died! Hell, Cal might still die!" He closed his eyes and swore again, before opening them. "What kind of Regent, screw it, soldier are you?"

"A good one." Marcelo smiled.

Daniels groaned and struggled to stand.

"What are we going to do about him? We can't leave him." Leslie pointed at Daniels.

"You just want your specimen." Marcelo walked over to crouch down by Calhoun. He put his weapon into its holster.

"Yes, I want a specimen that has survived, but he's also an IO soldier," Leslie explained.

Meanwhile, Cole marched over to Daniels. He put his guns into their holsters and removed the restraints from his backpack.

"No…" Daniels flinched and leaned away from Cole.

"I'm not going to hurt you," Cole said, gently.

Marcelo chuckled. "Didn't you load a bunch of bullets into him?"

"Do *you* know how to help?" Leslie asked, only half joking.

"He may not, but I do!" Edgar's whining voice said as the man himself emerged from the west.

They all looked at him—stunned.

"Where did you come from?" Marcelo laughed.

Edgar spied Daniels. "Oh! Y—you got him."

"Yes. We'll need to get him back to camp," Leslie said.

"No. Daniels won't be leaving and neither are any of you," Marcelo stood, drew his weapon and fired.

Cole grunted, uttered a "Doc," before drawing his own gun, blood gushing through his fingers.

"Cole!" Leslie screamed.

Edgar started for him. "No, no, no, Cole!"

Daniels caught a second wind and roared to his feet. He rushed Marcelo, bowling the regent over as he ran off into the dark jungle.

Leslie huddled close to Calhoun who, startled by the commotion, had drawn his weapon too.

"What—what's…"

Leslie yanked the gun from his hand. She spun around, just in time to see something unexpected in a day already brimming with the extraordinary.

Edgar's shaking hands were wrapped around a gun, most likely Cole's.

Leslie wanted to call out to him, but she didn't want to startle him and make the botanist accidentally shot someone.

Cal chuckled next to her. "He…gonna…shoot…him…self." A rack of wheezing forced him to double over, clutching his chest.

"Stop, Marcelo!" Edgar shouted, his thin voice a higher octave then usual. "You—you've done enough! You hurt Cole, upset Dr. Singleton, got Cal damaged…"

"It's okay," Cole said from beside him, holding his shoulder. "Dr. Adu…"

Marcelo guffawed. "Put it down. You're not a soldier. Remember?"

"You first!" Edgar shot back, but he sounded close to tears. "How dare you shoot Cole?"

"If it's any consolation, I'm going to shoot all of you…" Marcelo said.

And while his attention remained focused on Edgar, Leslie sat up straight, aimed Calhoun's gun at Marcelo.

And fired.

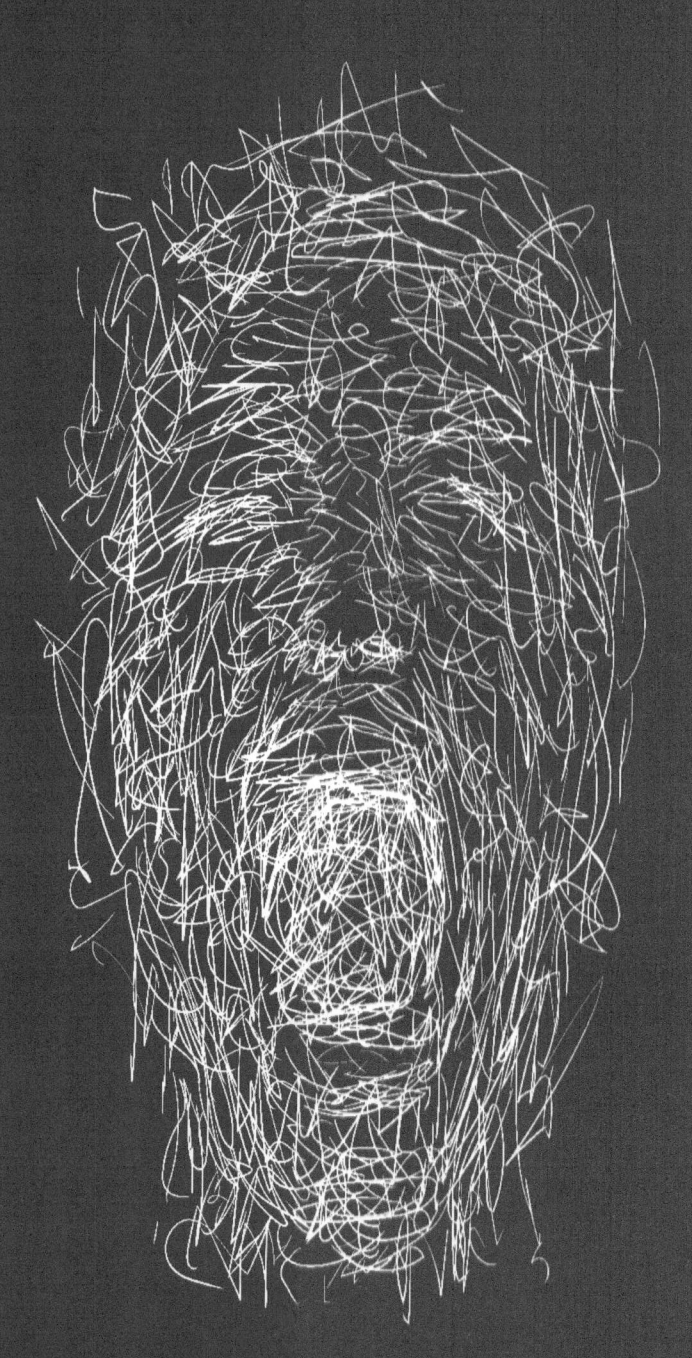

12

21:00 hours

"Did you hear that?" Nadya spun around, wearing her night-time, infrared glasses. She scoured the surrounding dark.

Reginald nodded beside her. "Gunfire."

"This way." Nadya's heart swelled, encouraged by the hope that Leslie and the others were alive.

But for how long if someone's shooting?

They hurried as fast as they could farther into the jungle's mass. They used their torchlights to cut through the thick darkness, but it would conflict with the infrared glasses, so Nadya switched between them. The hushed quiet surrounding them reminded her of the first night they arrived. It felt like forever ago, but it had only been thirty hours.

Behind them, four other soldiers from Gamma Team carried supplies like water, ration bars, and medical supplies. Two of them were medics. Nadya wanted them to come in case—well, she blew out a breath.

I can't even think it, let alone say it.

Reginald's arm swept out in front of her. He put a single finger up to his lips. Behind them the others stopped too.

No one moved.

Waiting.

Listening.

Reginald relaxed. "I thought I heard something."

Before he took a step, Nadya said. "Stop! Corn chips!"

"Huh?" Reginald said.

The odor grew stronger and before she could answer Reginald's question, a large man ran toward them. Immediately the six of them got out of the way, scurrying around the jungle trees. Nadya watched as the man ran

69

out of steam, waved like a leaf in the wind before falling, face first, into the ground.

"Who is that?" Reginald asked and looked at Nadya. "Did you say corn chips?"

"I did," Nadya said.

She inched over to the man. He didn't move. His massive chest rose and fell, but other than that, she couldn't determine if he was awake or passed out.

"What are you doing?" Reginald whispered. "We need to keep going."

"We do," she said.

Leslie and the others had been missing for more than eight hours. With Noorbi's heat, that could mean death. Still, her curiosity got the better of her. As she approached him, the odor became more pronounced. It came from him.

"Oh!" she fell back a step once she spied the fungus, white and foaming, actively ingesting the flesh on his face. No, not the skin. It had worked well beyond the surface and down into the pink muscle and white bone.

Reginald shouted. "Are you okay?"

No.

Instead she said, "Yes. This, uh, man has the fungus on him."

She swallowed as she scanned the rest of the man's body. Her torchlight revealed more horrors. Dried, crusted blood streams and splatter decorated his back. He had a few what looked like bullet holes in his clothing.

"Reggie, he's got bullet holes." Fear skated up her back, casting chills in its wake. *Leslie.* "There's been gun play, and judging by his body, a lot of it."

"Let's move," Reginald said and waved the others to join him. "Let's go the way he came."

Unable to speak, Nadya forced herself to look away from the grotesque being in front of her, and back to the inky darkness.

Please, Leslie, be alive.

13

Nadya heard her before she saw her, and her eyes watered immediately.

"Leslie!" Nadya shouted, hurrying forward in the blackness to the sole light she knew, the only source of comfort, and peace through the galaxy. "Leslie!"

"Slow down! Wait!" Reginald called after her.

He didn't understand, couldn't understand the desperation clawing at her insides, nails digging out gouges of hope and discarding them. No, Nadya had to see her partner, now. The delay had been enough torment.

Hope blotted everything out.

She rounded a corner, where the trees curved as if by some foreign hand, and there in a tiny clearing, they were. Her torchlight met another one. Twice the illumination revealed Leslie, being held up by Edgar.

"Leslie!" Nadya raced to her partner and swept from Edgar's hold into her arms. She rained kisses onto her face.

"Ow, ow! Naddy. Ow! Yes, love, it's me." Leslie laughed, despite her complaints. She hugged Nadya back, clutching her so tight, as if to blend together. Then they'd never be apart.

"Hey, we're alive too," Cole said. He had one arm draped around Edgar's shoulder. "Good to see you too."

The medics raced forward to Cole, and Edgar gently gave him over to them.

Reginald looked around, counting them. "Where's Cal?"

Cole didn't speak, but his face burned.

Edgar sighed. "We left him to come find help and aid."

Leslie released Nadya enough to talk to the others. They still held each other loosely around the waists. "Edgar can take you to him. He's going to need a transport. He can't walk. He'll also need a blood transfusion…"

Three of the soldiers nodded. "Understood."

Edgar said, "Follow me."

Reginald meet Nadya's watery gaze. "Marcelo?"

Nadya looked at Leslie. "What happened?"

"He's over there by Cal, at the big tree." Leslie released her and hopped back. "I—I'm exhausted. Can we do the debrief later?"

"Yes, sure, of course." Nadya caught Leslie as she fainted. "Medic!"

Two of the other soldiers hurried over to Leslie and laid her down on the ground. They began working on her, inserting an i.v. for fluids. The same as the one Cole had.

Cole said, "She shot Marcelo, Dr. Singleton."

Reginald frowned. "She what?"

Cole nodded, his face somber. "She shot him to she save us."

"Did you encounter the man with the flesh-eating fungus?" Nadya struggled to put together what happened. She couldn't imagine Leslie firing a gun. But the evidence spoke to a lot of gunfire.

"Tell me what happened." Nadya crouched down beside Cole. "Start from the beginning."

Cole sighed and swayed.

"Dr. Singleton, he's in no condition to keep going. He needs rest," the medical soldier said.

"It's the same for Dr. Gupta, ma'am," the other medical personnel said. "I'm sorry, but she's unconscious. We'll need a transport for her too."

"Damn it. Whatever happened must've been awful." Reginald touched Nadya's shoulder. "They're alive."

Nadya swallowed the knot of relief. "Yes. You're right."

"Dr. Singleton, what about him?" the third soldier asked, pointing down at fungus-ridden man.

"Secure him using the preventative protocol. He's a biohazard," Nadya said.

"We're going to need help getting them out of here," Reginald said.

"I know." Nadya pressed her earpiece. "Comms have been so touch and go."

"Anything?"

"No. Static."

Reginald sighed. "There's got to be something in the atmosphere that's blocking our ability to use the comms."

Nadya nodded. She crouched down and held Leslie's hand in hers.

I'm sorry for letting this happen. I am an incompetent leader. Marcelo was right. They were all right.

She wiped tears from her face. Reginald stood over her with the torchlight.

Leslie opened her eyes at Nadya's touch. "Don't do that."

"Do what?" Nadya wiped her cheek. "What's this on your forehead?"

Leslie licked her dry lips. "Fungus."

"What?" Nadya got the medic's attention. "Disinfect this and utilize the antifungal medication."

"Yes, ma'am." The medic put on gloves and grab the items from her kit.

"Dr. Singleton? This is Pilot Williams and Reyes, ma'am. Are you there?"

Nadya stood up, her heart-pounding in disbelief. "Uh, yes, I can hear you, Williams!"

"Great ma'am. We're about four hours out, but we're on our way to you with a medical team."

Reginald's face lit up. "By all things logical, we're saved!"

The soldiers broke into applause.

"How did you get through to us?" Nadya asked.

"We received an urgent message from a downed shuttle on an outdated frequency. We've mapped to its coordinates." Pilot Williams explained.

"Why did you leave?" Reginald asked, taking over the conversation.

Silence.

"Williams?" Nadya said.

"We had orders, ma'am, to drop you off and return to base." Pilot Williams sounded sad, no, guarded.

"By who?" Nadya asked.

"Regent Duili ma'am."

Marcelo!

"We'll arrive by 0100 hours, ma'am," Pilot Williams said.

"See you then." Nadya met Reginald's glare.

73

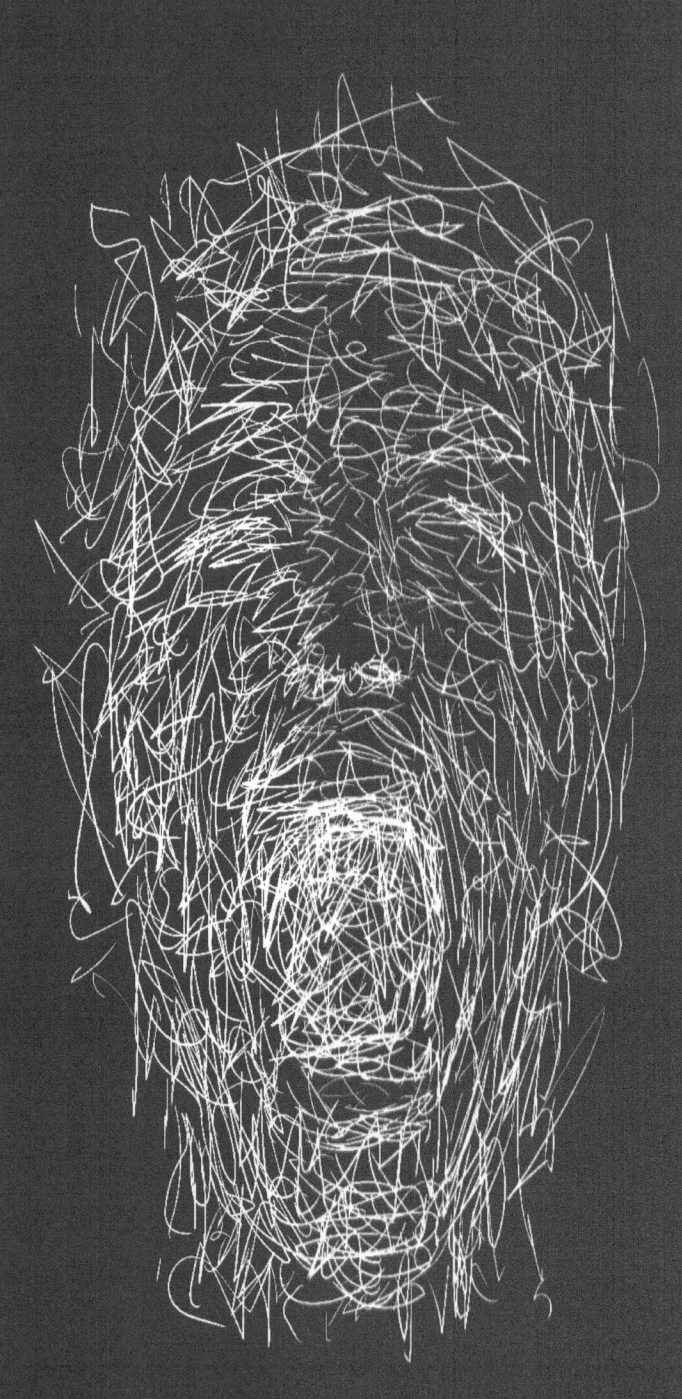

Epilogue

Two weeks later

Obe's bright glowing made it hard for Nadya to sleep. Instead, she sat up and watched Leslie give her usual lyrical snore routine. Her partner had begun to recover, but the fungus had left a scar—a reminder of her close encounter with death. She'd escaped, but only just.

Nadya hugged her knees and sighed. She'd nearly gotten her entire team killed.

You cannot know what is not revealed. Obe said, his yellow eyes opening and turning to look at her. *The mission was successful. Your team discovered the cause of the villagers' deaths and found a missing officer.*

True, but Leslie and Cole and Calhoun! Cal is still in the medical ward.

They are alive. You returned everyone. Obe countered.

Edgar found the mold's origins, Leslie stopped Marcelo, Cole and Calhoun stopped the infected soldier, and I did nothing. Nadya sighed and hugged her knees tighter. *I didn't do a damn thing but stand around.*

From what I have seen of humans, a good leader stands back and allows her team to succeed. She steps forward when things are bad. You did. Yes?

Nadya sighed. *I-I did. Didn't I?*

You saw death, faced it, and survived. That is success. Is it not?

It is…

Then rest.

Nadya smiled at Obe's mothering. She could hear warmth in the shared thoughts.

You're right.

I am a chumba. We are always right. Obe rolled over onto his side. *Give us a scritch.*

The End

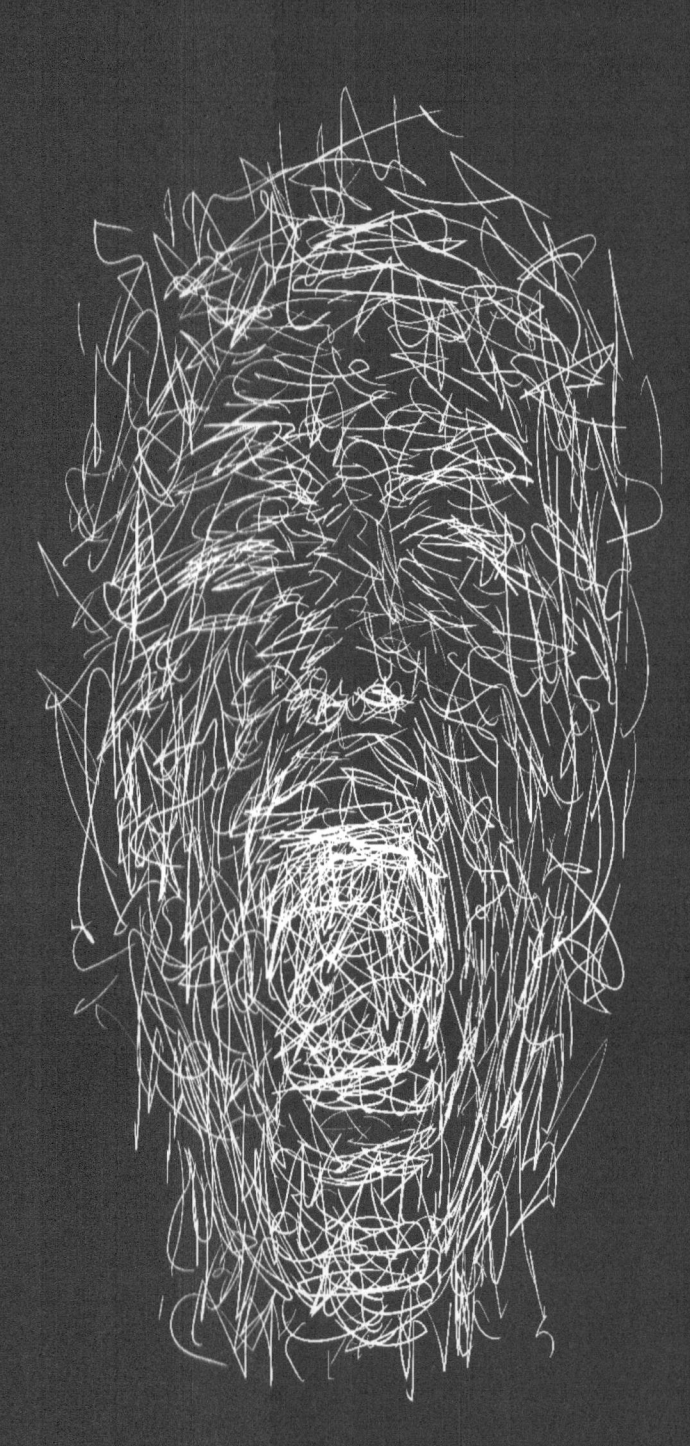

Scavenger Hunt

By Michael G. Williams

Part 1 of 5: Before Beginning

First, my name is Roderick. Please, do not call me "Rod" or "Roddy." My name is Roderick and that is what you shall use.

Now, before we speak of Key West in 1984, let us speak of Seattle in 1969.

When I finally regained conscious thought after becoming a vampire, I found myself greedily sucking crusted blood from the carpet in my father's living room. It was November 4, 1969. The sun had been down for hours, and I did not recall the four days (or nights) prior to that moment. My last memory had been of October 31—Halloween, yes, but also my birthday.

My father's long-dead corpse lay nearby, his throat torn open, and it was his blood I greedily—shamelessly, even—suckled from the rug. I was dressed in bellbottoms I'd managed to rip in the exertions with which I killed him. The floral shirt I last recalled wearing was nowhere to be found. I was half naked, covered in my father's blood, and burying my face in the hideous gold shag he'd had installed six months before to seem hip. I possessed no recollection regarding what led up to that moment, nor any idea what I had become. My every sense screamed at me of hunger: the deep and empty hunger of days, the dull ache of a stomach that once knew steady satisfaction and now stands denied, the flared nostrils of a nose that can smell the stench of a little more blood locked in those rancid fibers. My skin itched all over like a white-knuckle drunk who quits cold turkey. My brain buzzed.

Every nerve ending in my body cried out for more, *more*, MORE, not some day, but *NOW*. The starvation I felt was not merely an empty belly, it was a demand from every cell of my being, every iota of who I was. I did not *want* more blood, I *needed* it, the way a person *needs* to kick out the window and escape a car as it sinks in a lake. I could—would—have killed anyone in that moment, would have devoured an army, and I knew deep in my heart that I could fill myself on the blood of a hundred of my father and it would never be enough.

Too bad I'd only the one.

It is important you understand this from the outset: I became who I am— physically, psychically, *carnally*— in a state of ignorance and with none to guide me. That is no way to enter the world, but such are things for many of our kind. (Here, I mean both vampires and homosexuals.) Yes, Key West is to be the focus of this conversation—I realize this does not seem the time, but there are things we must discuss and choices you must make—but we must begin, as they say, at that blood-soaked, shit-stinking, rain-drenched beginning.

A magnificently violent rainstorm scoured Seattle clean that night of November 4. As I returned to myself, I sat back on my haunches and wiped from my cracked lips my father's blood and a scrap of ragged flesh I gnawed from his throat to get at what pulsed inside it. In that moment lightning shattered a street lamp at the end of the block. With the eyes of a vampire, I watched in slow motion as it twisted itself apart. Its metal arms melted to slag in a single blow from that angry sky. A hundred yards distant, I heard it sizzle as it splashed against asphalt.

Amazing. I was reborn as something altogether and unmistakably terrible, and at the same time recognized my new self as what I waited all my short life to become.

My most recent conscious memory was of inviting a stranger into my father's house. The man was older, well-dressed, and exuded an air of trustworthiness and calm. He told me he was a business partner of my father's there to meet with him. I knew little of my father's work, even at the age of nineteen, even as I relied on it for *almost* every penny I could put my hands on. He did something in "business" but did not speak endlessly of its significance the way a siding salesman or an investment banker insists, and so I vaguely assumed he had criminal connections. That would certain explain some of the few "business associates" to whom I was exposed in childhood and his reticence regarding how he put bread on the table. Had I been made to guess, I would have said he laundered money for the mob: something unsavory but not directly dangerous. That same phrasing would describe my father to a tee.

My point is, it was not unusual for him to receive visitors after dark for private meetings. Neither was it unusual for me to receive visitors after dark and in private: how else do you think I earned the pennies I did not take from my father? But for me to *receive* one of my father's associates was quite another matter. This man seemed uncharacteristically charming compared to my father's usual flavor of suits and goons. This man complimented my "athletic figure." I offered to make him a drink. Four days later I woke up dead. My father's "associate" was nowhere to be found. He never so much as told me his name. I have never again seen him.

I know you feel alone in this moment—terribly, and perhaps unexpectedly—but I intend to show you that awful solitude contains the seed of our community. You must be patient, however. I promise I will arrive at the meat of the matter—the murders, the mayhem, the way I came to know my purpose—but first we must speak of winters, and of weather, and of men who help and who harm.

Part 2 of 5: Of Winters and of Weather

That story happened the last night of 1984, a year in which America elected a demented entertainer to a second term as President on his threat to slash our government while ignoring a pandemic, and I was on the prowl. I had just turned thirty-four, looked nineteen, and told people I was twenty-six. Such are the little white lies a vampire tells when living in a place like Key West. But first we must discuss what brought me there.

To begin with, I was merely wintering in Key West in 1984. I did not live there full time and had not, at that point, ever considered anywhere other than Seattle to be "home." But that oh-so-literary year it rained in Seattle ten of the first fourteen days of September, and they called for an even rainier October, and for some reason I could not articulate I found it impossible to face the thought of cold rain on my thirty-fourth birthday. I suppose early middle age had arrived, though I no longer thought of myself as having gotten any older. It is both a blessing and a curse that our age is arrested at the moment of our becoming the undead. We never watch crow's feet creep in, to be sure, and one does not require laugh lines to scoff at small ironies, but I sometimes wonder if our inability to acquire the outer reminders of the passage of time makes us slower than others to achieve those inner hallmarks of wisdom and self-awareness.

Key West—a few dozen square blocks of two- and three-story guest houses, boutique hotels, bars, restaurants, shacks slinging key lime pie, and an historic army fort, one part pastel-shaded seaside escape littered with feral chickens and tourists, and one part a tiny New Orleans five minutes before or five hours after Mardi Gras—had by 1984 become a major pilgrimage site for gay men and lesbians. (I do not seek to exclude other members of our queer communities by that statement, but I confess in 1984 I was much younger, less experienced, and frankly rather bad at recognizing the blessed diversity of identities we now enjoy.)

You may wonder how Key West, a dot at the end of a long ellipsis of islands on the tip of the dick that is Florida, had become important to us and the answer is simple: because it was so remote no one would look for us there. It was a place to which we could get away at a time when escape had become important to our survival. Plus, we had power there and in multiple forms.

First, Key West allowed us political power: the city had just elected its first gay mayor. Second, it recognized our cultural power: Tennessee Williams still owned a home there when he died the year prior. Truman Capote, who passed away just a few weeks before my trip, had long been among the gay literary lights of Key West.

That gay writers could live and work there would have been enough on its own. Words – stories – are important to us in a way I do not believe others experience or comprehend. Plenty of straight people write, of course, but they have other ways to leave a legacy. Ernest Hemingway may still be remembered mostly as a novelist, but he also fathered three heirs whom he could raise or neglect as he saw fit.

We do not bear the burden of progeny, but we still feel called to "raise" those who come after us. Our culture is not one conveniently handed down from grandparent to parent to child, a generational bucket brigade of trauma and celebration passed hand to hand, reinforcing fingers brushing against one another, the social euphemism called "values" directly conveyed and enforced.

No. We, unlike the heterosexual child who grows up in a prison of examples of how to live and die, must find or fashion our own. Each of us must turn the dials of our mind and appetite until we find something that inspires us to sing along.

This makes the few means and rare opportunities we have to speak *directly* to one another, to use our stories as a means of clasping hands across the divides of space and time, all the more critical to gay continuation. Key West had developed a reputation as a place not merely welcoming of us but *important* to us. It was where our unrelated forefathers had gone to set down words for future generations, even – especially – words the straight world refused to publish and so often seeks to remove from libraries and bookstores. That is very special to us. It is very precious. Key West's role in the collection and preservation of sacrilege had made it sacrosanct to the damned.

Key West also stood out as one of the handful of places of *actual* power for homosexuals: money. Key West businesspeople formed the nation's first gay travel association and tourism bureau, and there is no greater, more valid, more respected, more pursued, more readily exerted form of power in America than money and its aesthetic accoutrement.

My travel agent back home was a yuppie named Tony I first met while cruising for blood, dick, or disco in the homophile bars of Seattle's Capitol Hill. Tony knew me as an impossibly baby-faced late-ish-twenties-ish-something partying my inheritance away. He commented once on my being "apolitical," and when I asked why he said that he replied, "Well, I've never seen you at the Pride picnic, and I think I would have noticed a boy like you." I told him I take a close interest in politics and in the cause of gay liberation, but I also have delicate skin, so much so that a picnic would mean too much sun on a Saturday in June even under Seattle's famously overcast skies.

Tony said he liked delicate men. I said I liked men, *period*. We slipped off to the back bathroom and within six tidy minutes had consummated our professional relationship in quite personal ways. I left the bathroom feeling momentarily sated in more than one manner. He left it feeling temporarily lightheaded from orgasm and blood loss. After that he always met my travel needs with vigorous enthusiasm. Money is the blood of America, and in that sense we *all* love its taste.

It is worth noting I am not an attractive man. I have stringy blond hair hanging limply just past my shoulders and skin so pale it is almost gray, with no beard, no moustache, no muscles. As a bird-chested waif, I was doomed to flunk the Disco Era, which had eyes only for lumberjacks in denim jeans and broadcloth shirts. When I died to daylight I had been a strung out, acid-headed hippie coming off a four-day bender with no one to teach me what I'd become or how to survive. (Did my father's "associate" make me a vampire? I have never known and doubt I ever will.)

My point is, I died looking like hell and thus every night for eternity I will look no better. Makeup can help, but I must choose my lighting carefully if I wish to pass among the living without looking like I'm on a binge or a bender. That would make life difficult for many, but I can be quite persuasive when speaking one on one thanks to certain gifts this condition grants me. It helps that social acceptability and access have value in America and thus can be priced and purchased. I did exactly that, and in the bargain cultivated Tony as a conversationalist, a business associate, a sexual partner, and a meal.

On September 14, 1984, I slipped a note through Tony's travel agency's mail slot saying I wished to winter in Key West for a change of pace. I asked that he find me an apartment I could rent or an amenable host at one of the city's dozens of gay guest houses who would let me stay for the season, ask no questions, and obey my every command. The next night, I rose from my daily slumber to find a response waiting on my answering machine: he'd gotten me an apartment two blocks off Duvall, the main drag. It came with a houseboy to empty the trash and do the washing two days a week and a golf cart for my personal use. For twenty extra bucks in each pay envelope the houseboy would happily provide an alibi or run interference with the outside world should I ever require it. Tony didn't ask why someone with such delicate skin would visit the Sunshine State. We are, as a people, skilled at knowing what questions to avoid.

I left messages with Tony and my attorney—a delightfully mean lesbian who mostly represented wives and widows in divorces and estate law, but still always found room in her schedule for her fellow queers—to sign whatever was required. I would pick up the apartment keys at Key West International when I arrived. I paid the lawn boy in advance, filled out a mail forwarding request, packed two small bags, and cancelled my subscription to *Seattle Daily Times*'s afternoon edition.

Three nights later, I boarded the first of an absurd sequence of nocturnal flights, the patchwork of strung-together airlines and timetables required to cross the continent without seeing the sun. For the final leg, Miami to Key West, Tony had to charter a Provincetown-Boston Airlines prop plane which, let me tell you, cost a pretty penny and was loud as an orgy in an earthquake. Worth it, though, and so much better than driving. Driving might be easier logistically, and the meal service more varied, but I am one of those creatures for whom immortality has not cured my native impatience.

I hate waiting to get somewhere. I like to hurry up and arrive.

I had read Key West just might be heaven, and on arrival realized it was as close as I hope ever to get. By sunset on Winter Solstice in that city I was getting nearly thirteen hours of dark every night, with low temperatures of 73 Fahrenheit and highs of 79. The men were friendly, the cops mostly subdued, the town *excessively* gay, and the streets awash with tourists every night. The tiny airport, with its one gift shop and its snack machines, vacuumed up the human refuse remaining at the end of a week of dingy revelry and replaced them with fresh-faced, red-blooded travelers eager to taste something sinful and strange.

I was only too happy to oblige.

The good times lasted for three months, two weeks, and three days.

Then I met my first serial killer, and Key West became briefly complicated.

Well, my first *human* one, at any rate. Naturally I have met many among my own kind.

At last we should speak of murders.

Part 3 of 5: Men Who Help

Predators are of course always attuned to their prey, but something you may not realize is we are even more sensitive to the presence of another predator.

It makes sense: another who stalks the same victims as we may scare those victims off. They may even serve as an evolutionary pressure, causing game to become progressively better at realizing when dangers await them. The rabbit who learns to spot a trap makes a poor meal, as they say.

They do say that. Somewhere, anyway. I am certain of it.

Lean closer to me and repeat after me: *they do say it*.

Thank you. I am glad we agree.

Now, that particular night, the thirty-first of December, New Year's Eve, I had gone out among the revelers in search of a feast. I know vampires who eschew mortal holidays and other times of excess. They regard it as tacky to walk the streets on Halloween with their fangs out and a ghoulish grin.

I do not regard such things as tacky *at all*. I think them delightful. What a joy it is to be one's truest self among those who should most fear us! If fundamentalist missionaries are allowed to stand in front of stores and ring their bells for five weeks between Thanksgiving and Yule, broadcast their beliefs on television, and threaten young women outside abortion clinics, and none may complain, then I certainly am going to insist on participating in the one night when I might go about as myself rather than as whatever mask I must don to go window shopping.

Every year I go out in costume, some variation on "vampire wastrel," as that is what I will always be, and every year I take great pleasure in the compliments I receive on my very realistic fangs and reddish eyes. There is no better hiding place for the wolf than amongst the flock. We have all heard the phrase "wolf in sheep's clothing," but when the sheep think they have spotted a sheep in *wolf's* clothing, and offer it a high five, *that* is a taste I *relish*.

We are locked in an eternal contest with mortals, mark my words. We may live next door and play nice and wave the flag on the Fourth of July, but we are not the same and we never shall be. They can sense that sometimes. I am certain of it. I have *felt* the realization register in the soggy porridge of their minds, that dim awareness I am something other than they, and the alarm they subsequently experience is all I will ever need to know they will never *quite* accept us.

Their loss.

New Year's Eve in Key West has a certain Halloween-ish cast to it, but mostly in the sense people go out and drink and dance and make love to strangers and fuck their closest friends. There is a bar in Key West that blocks off the street outside that a drag queen may slide down a giant shoe at midnight while the crowd counts backward from ten, and it is one of my favorite variations on the "ball drop" we all know from television and New York. When I tell you Key West had already become exceptionally gay, this is what I mean: homosexuals were running city hall, we were running the bars, we were running the restaurants, the hotels, the little huts that sell key lime pies, and we were running the holiday parties. We had precious little to fear, not even the law.

1984 was a particularly bad year for the Key West police department, whose leadership were almost entirely arrested by the Federal Bureau of Investigation in a cocaine sting. The feds called the KWPD a "criminal enterprise" in the media. It made some cops sheepish, but others became even more aggressive when circumstances allowed. It was a matter of statistics: a handful of police officers standing on a street corner where five hundred people—a thousand, two thousand, who knows—pour one another shots and take each other's clothes off simply do not stand a chance. Their mere *presence* became a joke, much less their efforts to put the kibosh on unruly celebrations. But find yourself alone with a policeman in Key West, especially as a homosexual, and very bad things could happen. Even in Key West, where money could purchase power, what mattered more was *authority*.

1984 was also, however, a particularly bad year for street celebrations in general. There was (and is) a long tradition in Key West called Sunset Celebration: street performers, musicians, jugglers, the usual flavors of carnival trade, gather in Mallory Square each evening. It is a large, flat, open space on the western tip of the island with a perfect view of the Gulf of Mexico. Locals and tourists alike go there to watch the sun sink behind the horizon, toss spare change into open guitar cases and upturned hats, and get high. It was (and is) not unlike the old small town tradition of the general store or the public green, but with more varied intoxicants, the sort of place community gets made and maintained, and the city government—gay mayor and all—wanted to get rid of it to build a bigger dock for cruise ships.

I had escaped the rains of Seattle only to arrive in a Key West where many of our kind felt the city had chosen to rain on their parade. By the time New Year's Eve rolled around, the tension in the city was ramping up. People spoke openly in bars and on sidewalks about how they hoped holiday celebrations would be a chance to blow off some steam, reduce friction, and renew the ties of pleasure and commerce that bound neighbor to neighbor as they have in every tourist town since the dawn of time. Many of us had come to Key West to dance and get fucked, not argue local politics, and thus after a dreary couple of weeks of newspaper editorials and heated debates most people positively ached to go out and get wild.

I found my first victim of New Year's Eve on the dance floor of the Copa (destroyed by fire a decade later—I still have a matchbook with their logo, I think there's magic inside it). The building Copa called home had been a dignified local theater in the early part of the century, then a porno palace in the '70s, and by '84 it had become the sort of bar where the sexiest, raunchiest things could be done and seen on their high class stage. They retained the façade and the marquee of the old theater, but inside it was wall-to-wall darkness, spotlights, a wood-topped bar, and hormones so thick you'd need to wipe your glasses. The place was enormous and had no cover charge most nights. A thousand horny men would get dressed up in their tightest jeans and ringer tees and go there to spend much of the evening taking them off.

I *adored* it.

I got to see Vicki Lawrence sing "The Night the Lights Went Out in Georgia" on a random Friday in November, which is quite an experience when there are couples fucking against the back wall. That is the sort of club it was.

On New Year's Eve we had the pleasure of watching Divine do her new tour show, one part glamourous drag and one part foulmouthed gross-out jokes. *Hairspray* had just come out, and she lived in Key West at the time. She did two sets that night, and in the hour between I had the good fortune to find myself half-crushed between two of those musclebound types whose popularity persisted long after disco died. I wore tight jeans, a crop-top tee shirt with a can of Crisco on it, and the beaten-up sneakers so inexplicably popular as club wear at the time.

The man in front of me wore most of a biker outfit. The man behind wore unbuttoned flannel and khaki shorts with pleats. *Pleats,* I kid you not. Duran Duran's "Wild Boys" beat its fists against our eardrums on the dance floor. I had my face pressed to that magnificent canal of hair and supple skin between the pectoral muscles of Mr. Motorcycle while Pleats ground against my back and groped my bony ass. Above and around me, they made out. How could I resist? I *required* the pleasure only blood affords.

There are large veins and arteries on either side of a man's chest, leading to and from his heart. It was nothing to nuzzle my face beneath the flap of Mr. Motorcycle's leather jacket, taste his flesh, and slice a tiny gash with my fangs. That perfect, blood-gorged organ in his chest pumped a hot spatter of his precious life across my tongue and I knew—I *knew*—his hopes, his fears, his dreams, his lusts. I could taste the very essence of who he was, the life he lived. I could taste the youth he worried he had shed despite being merely thirty-one. (I could taste his birthdays to count them.) We do not drink a victim's blood, my friend. No, we drink their *life*. His spilled out inside me and I spent two unpleasant seconds fighting down the urge—present in each transaction of this sort—to drain him dry on the spot and damn the consequences.

It is a horrible thing to leave a prize like that alive. But it is also a necessity if we are to pass among them without detection.

I feel I should note humans do not suffer when we feed. The man— his name was Joshua; Jewish; native of Savannah—already had an erection that could have driven a railroad spike and the moment my fangs broke the skin and I took what I so desperately needed, he enjoyed an orgasm so explosive he would spend the rest of his life remembering it as one of his best. He clamped his kissing partner tighter, who in response ground himself against me in returned enthusiasm, and I reflected had I been human they might have suffocated me in their passion. What a way to go, if go one must.

The wounds we leave are tiny and heal in short order, and thus though I smelled the blood trickling hot-to-cold down his rippling torso, the wound had closed by the time any became visible along the waistband of his overstuffed jeans. The Brawny man in back reached down, grabbed me by the sides of my thighs, and lifted me bodily off the ground with one arm like a doll he'd won at the fair. With his other hand he took Mr. Motorcycle by the bicep. In that manner he carried and dragged us off the dance floor toward one of the darker corners. I looked forward to spending a timeless twenty minutes in their enthusiastic embrace—minutes in which I could siphon off whole years of their lives if I wished it—and had just gotten down to some serious fun when I looked up to see we had an audience.

Some twenty feet away a stringy young white man with dark hair and dark eyes was being courted at a small bar table by a middle-aged fellow whose every mannerism screamed "cop."

Police were even more dangerous to us in those nights than they are now, even in a town where they had been humiliated and diminished as they had in Key West. In this instance, by "we" I mean queer people. Gay sex was an illegal act. People still sometimes got arrested for it. Those charges could prevent them from getting jobs, apartments, car loans, you name it. Newspapers would print lists of people locked up for "sodomy" and "indecency" just to harass them. You may think that unlikely in such recent times, but it was generations ago and the Jerry Falwells of the world had long been at their wicked work of whipping up society against us. HIV and AIDS had handed them a second excuse for their hate, too. People thought they could get AIDS from mosquitos, and they thought it was our fault.

We have a knack for spotting our enemies. And now by "we" I mean both queer people and vampires. Oh, I knew everything about what was happening at that table. That cop had come here alone. Perhaps he had even come here hoping to get laid. But once he found himself in the den of sin he himself sought, he felt overwhelmed with shame and disgust and wanted to get revenge against us for "tempting" him. He couldn't take us all on at once, of course, and he couldn't call in backup and launch a raid—it was Key West, after all, and in many places the smarter cops still feared sparking another Stonewall-sized riot—so he would find one of us on whom he could vent his self-loathing. He and his victim would watch me savor extracting from my companions the satisfaction we all required, then he would take his victim back to his car, slap handcuffs on him, stuff half a joint in his shirt pocket, arrest him for "drugs," go home, and jerk off.

It happens every night somewhere in America, I assure you. Even now. Perhaps *especially* now.

The cop locked eyes with me as I did some of my best work.

They, too, are good at spotting enemies.

He smiled the way a predator does.

I brought the Brawny man to a tidy climax between huffing groans, then surreptitiously took my sustenance straight from one of the bigger veins of his inner thigh while he drifted in post-orgasmic ecstasy. Mr. Joshua Motorcycle of Savannah, Georgia, swore in enthusiastic admiration. He had no idea I drank the Brawny man's blood, of course, but he applauded my other skills. I was only too happy to favor him with them for his "round two," as they say.

The cop watched the entire show we put on, and he spent it groping the crumpled-up twenty-something at his side.

By the time my new friends and I wrapped things up, Divine was about to come back out on stage, and we had less than two hours to midnight. I thanked my partners with sincere gratitude for helping me start the night off so well. The Brawny Man wanted my phone number. I told him if it were meant to be he'd see me around. They each waved to me with one hand, their other arms around each other, as I backed away and into the crowd. I like to think they got together after that. I like to think they remembered me fondly. Nevertheless, I had not finished my hunt and needed to find fresh prey.

Call me what you will. I waste no time on social obligations.

You may wonder how I spotted the guy as a cop, what gave him away. It is sometimes difficult to describe. I have occasionally pondered that it works in much the same way as gaydar: we just *know*. There is some subtle tell in a person's body language, their mannerisms, the tone of their voice. In the time in which I write this, it has all been obscured by social media performances of dominance: deep voices giving commands, and so on and so forth. And to some degree our native sense for police officers had been befuddled in the 1970's and later by the Tom of Finland types standing around the bars with their thumbs in the beltloops of their leather trousers.

But with an honest-to-gods cop, there's something extra behind it: it is clearly not playful. What I am about to say is not true of *all* police, but it is true of *some*, which is that they may wish to control the people around them for the joy of doing so. If he had restricted his manhandling of the young man he'd caught in his fishing net, I'd have decided the cop was simply a leather daddy on the hunt. But the way he stood, the way he sometimes flexed to twist the young man's arm subtly as they watched me take a little life straight from the source of the two men I had just entertained, the way he set his jaw as he observed: it all added up. I do not know how else to describe it.

And when I saw him half-drag his date toward the back of the theater, the front of the bar, I knew he was about to spring the trap and ruin this young man's life. I could not let that happen. We must stick together in such times. And so I slipped between the re-congealing crowd as the music started up for Divine's second set, and I got my hand stamped on the way out so I could come back in, and I followed them out into the street.

I had no idea *what* I would do, but I would do something. I could not let the night swallow this young man up to satisfy some perverse closet case's frustrations with himself.

Part 4 of 5: Men Who Harm

There are automobiles in Key West, but in comparison to the average American city or town, the vehicles are few and far between. In part this is because so few persons in town at any given moment are locals and in part because it is such a pain in the neck to get a car there: hours and hours of driving on long bridges do not an exciting road trip make. The streets, especially Duvall or Union or any of the other roadways where the bars and restaurants cluster, are often given over entirely to pedestrians after dark and especially so on holidays. I had expected to have my certainty of the cop's profession finally confirmed by seeing them climb into a vehicle, probably the one unmarked car the Key West Police Department had that was not seized by the FBI earlier in the year. (Everyone knew it. Even with the naval air station nearby, there were low odds so many white men with crew cuts would be sharing the same '76 Mercury Monarch. One might have thought they would have spent all that cocaine money on something better.)

The two of them, to my surprise, made their way down a side street, and then into an alley between the backs of two buildings. I wondered whether the cop was going to have his way with the young man right there against a dingy brick wall. I am often happy to play voyeur—every vampire is, we see more of the world from a surreptitious shadow than we ever do from the spotlight—but that night I approached the task of finding a suitable viewpoint with a professional interest rather than a personal one. There is nothing worse than a homosexual who hates himself so much he hurts others like him. I could not allow that. I would have to seek my opportunity to interfere and do so with caution.

Sure enough, Officer Fuzz had placed his stringy, strung-out twink so that the boy had his back to the literal wall, the cop facing him, one beefy arm extended over the young man's shoulder to place a hand against the bricks. The cop had lured his prey away from the herd and now would make a meal of it. I considered my options, and decided stumbling headlong into the alley under the pretense of being a wobbly drunk looking for a place to puke was probably my safest bet. The cop would recognize me from the Copa, of course, given the close attention he'd given me as I gave close attention to Mr. Motorcycle and The Brawny Man, but it would provide enough disruption for the lad to make his escape, and I would be alone with the cop to nip his problem in the bud in my own highly effective way.

Just as I lifted one worn Adidas to affect a stagger and begin a stream of indecipherable babble, I heard the sound of a spring-loaded knife and saw a flash of metal. There was a sound of high, pinched surprise, and the unmistakable pop-slap of a blade breaking skin with surprising force.

The cop leaned forward as if to kiss his beef-jerky prey, then sagged, then stepped backward with one hand to his belly.

The twink, knife in hand, studied the cop's face with the calm eye of a scientist or an orchestra conductor. He shifted the knife in his grip and plunged it into the cop a second time, closer to the heart. The twink murmured something as he did so. A mortal never would have caught it, might not even have seen the boy's lips move, but a vampire's ears are tuned for such moments.

The boy whispered one word: *hypocrite*.

Then the twink yanked his blade free one more time and used it to slash at the cop's neck. Glistening ruby-red life spilled from the older man's neck and splashed against the boy's chest and shirt. He flinched at the impact, but only barely, and kept eye contact with the man for anguished seconds.

I felt the life go out of the cop. His eyes took on the unfocused quality of the dying.

The next moment he collapsed against the ground.

The twink looked up at me.

"*Well*," I said aloud. I crossed my arms and tried not to smile. The evening was taking an unexpected turn, and I usually savor such moments. "Sex *and* violence in the same night? But my birthday was *months* ago."

He ran at me, knife out, and I confess I laughed with delight. I had enjoyed a relaxing season, but the sight of one mortal spilling the blood of another made me realize I had started to get bored.

No mortal, not even a murderous one, stands a chance going toe-to-toe with a vampire. I stepped to the side faster than his eyes could have seen, slipped an arm around his shoulders as he lunged in slow motion toward where I had been, and used my other hand to stop him short. The force knocked all the air out of him, as though he had run chest-first into a steel beam. He folded up around my arm and then staggered backward. From his perspective, I imagine I simply blinked out of existence to reappear draped around him. It is a pity we cannot watch ourselves work.

"Now, now, that is surely no way to greet a new friend," I said. He looked at me in confusion and then tried to take a roundhouse swing at me with the knife in his fist. I wrapped my hand around his and held him fast. "I appreciate that you may not be in a conversational frame of mind at the moment. Bloodlust does that to a person. But I assure you I am not your enemy."

I am not telepathic, I cannot force my mind *into* another's and give commands, but I can certainly press against it and make suggestions. I do not invade a person's brain so much as I elbow-wrestle them for the armrest of agency between us in a way they sometimes find persuasive and sometimes find unnerving. (Often it is both.) I did so now, leaning my will against his and giving it an uncomfortably intimate and stifling hug, like swaddling their decision-making capacity not until it smothers but until it ceases to struggle.

"*I am not your enemy*," I repeated. I felt his psyche relax the tiniest bit. I said it again and expanded on it. "*I am not your enemy* and in fact I could be open to becoming your *friend*." I put special emphasis on these ideas, and I could feel them take hold.

I considered drinking from him right there. It makes humans more cooperative in the long run. But I decided his blood probably rang with the hormones, pheromones, and other chemical signatures of stress and fright as much as it would with those of pleasure and relief. After killing, a person

94

feels thrilled, terrified, perhaps a tad disappointed. It takes little time, if any at all, to start wondering what one should do next and how long until the deed is discovered. Such worry sours the blood. I did not need to feed myself that sort of garbage, especially not in a city full of men so eager to feed me pleasure instead.

The boy eventually—a matter of thirty or perhaps sixty seconds, an eternity when passed with idle hands but not so long when one holds a trembling young man fresh off a kill—stopped holding his breath between gasps. He let out a breath, then drew another and let it out again more naturally, and I nodded up at him—he stood perhaps five foot ten, and I am five-five in boots with heels—and offered him a soft smile.

"Good boy," I murmured. "Now how were you planning to get the body out of sight, or are you hoping he'll be discovered?"

The boy blinked at me, eyes dull, but eventually information made the circuitous trip from his ears to his brain and steered a response to his lips. "Leave him there." His voice was barely a whisper.

"Okay, you were planning to have him discovered. Well, fine by me. It means a lot less blood all over this shirt and I am quite fond of it." I let go of the boy's knife hand and took my other arm from around his shoulder blades. "My name is Roderick. What is yours?"

The boy relaxed a little more. Perhaps "relaxed" is an incorrect statement. He became a degree less tense and found his voice. "Archie."

I repeated his name back to him with a big smile. I showed lots of teeth. "Archie. A good name. A solid name. I read those comics as a kid. Still do." I stepped a half-stride away to give him some room to breathe. "So do you kill here often?" I allowed myself a little chuckle at my equally diminutive joke. I find mortals sometimes benefit if we are the first to break the tension.

The blood drained from his face, but he tried to keep his cool. I had not meant to embarrass him and felt a small pang of guilt.

"My apologies," I said, "back to talking shop. If your intent is for him to be discovered here, at the scene of the crime, we should make our way elsewhere with some haste. But you surely must have other clothing nearby. That shirt is, no pun intended, a dead giveaway." I gestured at his chest and torso, aromatically stained as they were. Blood loses its appeal to us fairly quickly after the victim's death in most cases (my father's carpet was an exception of which I am not proud; no one is in their right mind immediately upon being reborn). This was fresh enough still to hold some appeal, but as its temperature dropped I found it stymied my appetites rather than rousing them.

"I didn't—" Archie stumbled over his words, or more accurately over the thoughts running helter-skelter through his mind. "I don't know."

I stepped back and took a closer look at him. "You have a lovely physique, Archie. Take off your shirt." He blinked at me and I snapped my fingers. "Now. Hop to it. You have heard the old adage about a criminal returning to the scene of the crime? Well, it is even easier to be caught if one lingers and never leaves. Off with the top, kid."

He wore the gay uniform of that era, a white ringer tee and jeans. He began tugging the shirt up over himself from the bottom hem, apparently in the habit of taking his shirts off inside out, but I stopped him. "No, not like that. You'll wind up with blood all over your face. Lift from the neckline." He did as commanded, and with some delicate assistance from me he managed not to smear evidence all over himself. There was a fair amount on his torso, but once he handed me the shirt, I folded it up and used it to mop him close enough to clean. I handed it back to him and he stared at it in his hands.

"Should I leave it here?"

Good gods, had I gained a *student*? I had come to Key West to spend a few months free of responsibilities, not burdened with more. I took the shirt again and pointed at his crotch with it. "Active or passive?"

"What?"

I repeated myself and indicated for him to turn around. "Active or passive? Would you rather people think you want to get—wait, have you never heard of the hanky code? In *Key West*?" My disbelief could be explained by any casual observation of a crowd: almost every man in the city who went cruising for sex indicated his goals and aspirations by use of colored handkerchiefs tucked into one or both of his back pockets. I will spare you the color key and simply say each shade indicated a given adult activity, and which pocket indicated whether they wished to be the one *doing the doing*, so to speak, or the one to whom the doing is done. In modern times it sounds far too complex compared to simply installing an app on one's device, but at the time it was the lingua franca of gay sex and it saved an absolute *ton* of time. One could look around the dance floor and spot everyone who might be interested in the same sort of congress as one's self. It was, in fact, how Mr. Motorcycle and Brawny and I had found one another earlier the same night: we'd all had robin's egg blue hankies, mine in the right hip pocket of my trousers, theirs in the left.

I stepped back from him and made a small sound of surprise. "Are you not a homosexual? Well, I certainly will be damned." I narrowed my eyes. "So do you seek to kill homosexuals?" My voice took on its most dangerous possible edge, a fully conscious choice on my part. A vampire is every bit as good at communicating our intentions as we are at masking them. I used all the subtle harmonics of a decade and a half of practice. I knew exactly how to set my voice to put someone at ease, and I could just as effectively terrify my prey instead. I wanted this young man to know, were it the case he sought to hunt my kind, that his career would be over before it started.

The anger of youth flashed across his features. "Of course I'm gay!" He sputtered a bit as he spoke. "Why do you talk like my grandpa? And why are you standing here helping me instead of, I don't know, screaming and running away?"

I, in my surprise at the conversation unfolding, had not considered that he might ask what the fuck I was doing there and why I had not fled. I tried not to laugh, and failed: a single, stifled chuckle, and then I placed a fist on my hip and shrugged. "Because I love surprises." It was my most honest answer of my entire tenure in Key West thus far. "And because I have to assume you are new at this or you would have planned better."

"Aren't you worried I'll kill you?" Archie put his height advantage to full use in his attempt to loom in menacing fashion.

I waved one dismissive hand and used my limpest wrist to do it. "Not particularly. But come, we must away. Tuck the shirt in your pocket like a handkerchief and get his wallet out of his pants."

"I'm no thief."

I turned down the corners of my mouth and crossed my arms at him. "Archie, child, listen to me. If the police think someone murdered one of their own for no reason, they will assume it was *because* he was the police. If you take his wallet, you get his money, and they are left to wonder. Trust me, that is preferable. And be quick about it. We must go somewhere and speak. Somewhere public, so none who might notice us can say we slinked away to hide, and somewhere loud that we might converse without eavesdroppers."

Archie defied me yet again. "No. Let's go to Southernmost Point."

"Fine, whatever, wherever, but we must depart. We may argue along the way."

He tucked the folded tee into his left pocket and I thought, *Oh, I'm just so sure*, then offered me his right arm. I slipped my hand into the crook of his elbow and he gasped at how chilly it was compared to the warmth one might have expected. "Sorry about my clammy hands," I sighed. "My circulation is simply dreadful."

Together we stepped from the alley and onto the empty side street, then strode some dozens of yards to reenter the flow of foot traffic along Duvall. As the crowd sealed up around us like a puckered wound, I leaned closer and spoke toward his ear. "Southernmost Point will have far too many people."

"It's nearly midnight," Archie countered, "they'll all be too busy checking their watches to care what we say."

I laughed and clasped his bicep with my other hand. Again, he shuddered at the touch. "So you aren't *completely* new at this. Or at least have thought about it?"

"I know where to go in public so most people won't notice me but the right people will," he said, and he didn't sound thrilled about the memory of learning that lesson.

I made a small sound of *aha*. So that was the problem with the cop: Archie was a hustler. I wondered how often the cop had extorted sex from him, to have become the prey in Archie's first kill.

Southernmost Point is a concrete buoy overlooking the water. In 1984 it had just, the year before, been erected by the city as a tourist attraction. There had always been a wooden sign declaring that specific spot as the southernmost location in the continental United States, but the city wanted to make it more photogenic. Next to it was the old telephone and telegraph hut that used to connect Florida to Havana. In the old days there was a sign with an arrow pointing over the water and the phrase "90 Miles to Cuba." It remains a fun—if slightly cheesy—spot that tells an enjoyable lie (it is not the southernmost point in the nation) where one might take a selfie with friends. The old "Conch Republic"—too lengthy a digression even for me—is remembered there, with tables and tidy rows of conch shells placed around it.

Plenty of tourists had gone there to count down to midnight. The bars were filled with the gays, and Southernmost Point played host to the straights who were not comfortable going to the bars. Archie—a shirtless young white man with hair black as tar on his head and in the center of his chest—and I stood out somewhat, but this was to our advantage. The straights did not know what to make of us so they kept their distance. These days they might be altogether too eager to perform their comfort by making sure we were in the background of every snapshot. Back then, they gave us plenty of space.

Archie told me his life story in a tidy three minutes: a Midwestern childhood, dropping out of trade school, washing up in Atlanta as a rentboy and being whisked away to Key West by a client who promptly dumped him there. Archie suspected the man had a wife and kids at home and may have taken him to Key West specifically to abandon him there, knowing Archie would have no way back. The man had flown them down first class, bought Archie two new outfits, left $500 in cash by the sink in their room at a guest house, and vanished. At the time, Archie thought the man had done him a great favor. Now he was no longer sure. Archie faced greater competition in Florida. In Atlanta he had been a commodity. In Key West he was just another wild hen wandering the street. (Have I mentioned the feral poultry that wander Key West? There are many. They are a signature feature of that strange and wonderful place.)

As Archie began to tell me of his life as a hustler in Florida, I put a finger to his lips.

"I get it," I said. "I have heard it before. I have even lived parts of it. But something happened, Archie. Many of us turn the occasional trick in our youth. Few of us do as you just did."

Archie's eyes sagged a little and he looked momentarily crestfallen. I could see—could *feel*—he had been spinning a grand and tragic narrative with himself at its center and my question had burst his bubble, pulled him off the stage and out into the pressing crowd. People around us looked at watches and talked each other out of popping the corks early on their champagne. They paid us no attention. I pushed against them with my mind to make them turn away, to look elsewhere, to listen to one another and not to us.

"I had a lover." Archie barely whispered, and his voice still hitched at the end. Speaking of love in the past tense can do that to a person.

I put a hand as cold as night against his sternum and ran my fingers through new hair that still smelled faintly of blood. "I am sorry. Did the police hurt him?"

Archie blinked back tears and put his left hand over mine where I rested it against his chest. "He used to touch me here, too. Just like this."

I waited. In moments like these, when a young man begins to speak the truth, everything is fragile. The slightest breeze can shatter it.

"He got arrested. He was trying to catch some fresh johns. He had been up in Mallory Square, hoping for some action from the cruise ship crowd. He was hot. He had good luck up there. But one of his new 'friends' turned out to be a cop. And that cop died six months later. He died of lung cancer, but a rumor went around the other cops that he'd died of AIDS and he got it from busting hustlers. Johnny'd spat on the guy when he was getting arrested, and the pigs decided Johnny gave the guy AIDS that way. It was crazy. It didn't make any fucking sense." Archie whispered all of this to me, so softly he probably was not himself certain I could hear him, but the ears of a vampire hear all things. "They tracked him down. They arrested him. Three days later what was left of him washed up on the beach at Fort Taylor. They had to identify him by dental records. It was that bad."

I leaned close and nuzzled my face against Archie, a mimicry of easy intimacy while we had the hardest conversation of his short life. "And that was recent." It was a statement, not a question.

"Thanksgiving Day."

In October of that year, the *New York Times* had run a story stating scientists believed AIDS could be transmitted through saliva. We now know that is not true. At the end of 1984, however, people were altogether too ready to believe whatever gave them permission to hate us.

I smiled a little to myself. I had felt Archie shudder when I blinked and my eyelashes tickled his chest. His mind might be trapped in the horror of his lover's murder, but his body was in the here and now. Life is funny like that sometimes.

"So now you want to kill the cops who killed Johnny." I leaned away and looked up at him. Archie looked down at me in return, and it was easy for me to imagine a boy of nineteen or twenty, naïve as any other yet already calloused by life on the streets, falling in love with those eyes. I did not, mind you. But I could understand it happening. They had been two castoffs from the world, pushed away from the pack and left to scavenge, and they had found one another. People fall in love for worse reasons every day.

"No." Archie did not smile as he said it, but I felt him take the sort of breath one takes when one wishes to sigh. "I want to kill *everything*. I want to kill the *world*. But I'd make do with the cops who hurt him."

I wrapped my other arm around Archie's comfortable waist and spoke into his collarbone. "Do you know for sure that cop was involved?"

"I know he works the vice squad," Archie murmured. "And they're the ones who busted Johnny."

I leaned away again and reached up to tousle his thin, straight hair. "It was more than that. I suspect he mistreated you as well sometime."

Archie blinked at me but did not speak. I needed no further confirmation.

"There is no shame in defending yourself," I said. "And frankly I see no shame in revenge. The world is turned against us, Archie. If we must carve a space of our own, a knife is as good a tool as any to do the carving."

"You really aren't freaked out by this?" Archie studied my face. He had no misgivings about making eye contact. It surprised me when he looked over and around my face otherwise, though, as if seeing it for the first time. I wondered if he pondered how old I might be?

I have said I looked nineteen, and that is true. I will look nineteen forever. But one carries age in more than wrinkles. One carries it in the set of a jaw, in expressions of experience and determination, in eyes that are hard or soft as needed.

I nearly laughed again but contained it. The boy had built himself up to the moment of his revenge, the launch of a campaign of violence against the monsters who killed the love of his life thus far, and the first person to know of it acted like it was an interesting hobby no more remarkable than the collecting of rare stamps.

"I am not. I've seen worse. I've done worse, certainly."

"Bullshit." Now he smiled, and it was the first time I'd seen it. He had charming dimples. In another life, he would have been the face on television selling something wholesome from the store.

There was no time like the present. As I smiled back, I let my fangs descend. None of the people around us would see it. Archie certainly did. I felt his body tense in fright. He did not speak, did not cry out, but I felt the terror paralyze him. Everyone has watched old movies. Everyone has read old books. Every human has heard of vampires, and on some level they *know* the stories are real. It's why they keep telling them.

I slid my fangs back out of view and kissed Archie on the chin. "To answer the most common questions: yes, they are real; no, I will not turn you; no, I do not kill often; yes, I do *love it*. My hope is that you will make the intellectual and emotional leap required to realize I understand you better than most and harbor you no ill will. I feel we have much in common."

Archie licked his lips and studied me and then nodded. It took him a few moments of staring out over the water, then he nodded again, this time to himself or to some unseen other out there, between here and Cuba, some dark spot with water in all directions and no conscience or culture to stand in the way of his thinking. Then he looked back down at me and said, "Okay. So you can tell me what to do. You can teach me."

I rested my chin along his neckline and the breath I moved to speak tasted of blood and flesh. I could tell it had been some time since he had enjoyed intimacy like this. For me it was largely mechanical. Oh, I took pleasure in it, to be sure, but Archie was not my usual sort of trade. Give me the lumberjacks and leather men any day. Archie was what at the time we called "chicken" but now we call "twinks." He was handsome enough, and I would have said yes had he propositioned me in the back room of a bath house, but I would not have pursued him on my own. He looked too much like me. I prefer variety in my diet. Yet when I whispered my reply I meant every single word.

"Archie, *mon cher*, I can *help* you. But when we go after them, we do not start with the cops. We go after his pimp."

Archie hesitated, then relaxed a tiny bit. I took that as the moment he agreed. His next question was one part assumption, one part plea. "What? When? I'm guessing we need to let things cool down after what just happened. Right?" What I heard in that question was simple and very human: *I've had a big night, and now I've blown my nerves. I need time to work back up to it before I kill again.*

I relished the malice in my own reply. "No, quite the contrary. We strike while the iron is hot."

Part 5 of 5: An End and a Beginning

I of course have no objection to those whom we now call sex workers. In 1984 we called them rentboys, hustlers, prostitutes, gigolos, and any number of other terms, each said with disdain I do not share. I offer no moral judgment of the work they do—after all, I did it myself in 1969. The public hungers for their service, and they provide satisfaction. It is that simple. In this age of fan sites and content creators, it may be difficult to believe the opprobrium with which their career path was once greeted. I assume it often still is, of course. But it is much easier now for one to find a corner of our culture in which such work is respected or at least not as disrespected.

At the time, despite it being the "greed is good" 1980s, a time when profit motive outweighed all other considerations, the era of leveraged buyouts, hostile takeovers, and endless capitalist excess, performative morality was everywhere. Mothers covered children's ears when rock came on the radio and shielded their eyes in movie theaters. So-called "family values" grew and spread like black mold in the culture's crawlspace. To be a sex worker in 1984 was to be looked down on from all sides. To be a gay one was to be a monster.

It was the other side of the oh-so-appropriate metaphorical coin: if anyone was allowed to do anything as long as they did it for money, something had to be off-limits, and sex fit the bill. Further, gay sex was the worst thing imaginable to most people's minds. It was not merely distasteful, it was regarded as *predatory*. I cannot overstate that. There were neither adorable but neutered gay best friends in sitcoms nor horny gay soap operas on cable television. Queers who fucked were an embarrassment, a moral danger, and a threat to society. They treated us like a plague. That some of us had fallen victim to a literal plague was considered the proof.

A part of me will never forgive them. *Never.*

Point being, I have nothing but respect and good wishes for those of our community who turn tricks to get by.

Pimps, however, are another matter entirely.

Among gay sex workers, pimps often present themselves to their staff in the same way as straight pimps—as protectors and benefactors, there to keep them safe from johns who would do them harm—but they couch it in "we're all in this together" rhetoric that does little more than sweeten the poison of their abuse. A pimp is a human trafficker, pure and simple, and no handy lie or false camaraderie can cover that up.

Johnny's pimp, a man named Randolph, lived upstairs in the back of a grand old home subdivided into five small apartments. The building was well-kept, and Archie said Randolph was a man who would mind his p's and q's enough to stay out of the public eye. The steps up to his apartment were freshly painted for the winter season, and the porch light by his front door shone bright and had been kept free of cobwebs. Milkmen were a thing of the past by then, of course, but grocery delivery still existed in the better metropolises, and Key West was among them. By the front door to Randolph's apartment was a basket from a corner store two blocks away, set out for the next delivery boy to collect when he returned. It was all very tidy, very domestic, and very anonymous. It was the sort of apartment few would ever see and none would ever notice. When you look on a row of homes, the ones that are quietest harbor the worst excesses. Trust in that. Look at me: in Seattle, I live in a *very* quiet neighborhood, and my home is the tidiest and quietest of all.

We had stopped by my apartment on the way there—I had naught to fear from some mortal boy knowing my address, killer or no—that Archie might dispose of his bloodied shirt and wear one of mine. It read PRIDE

PICNIC '82 in fading yellow letters against green fabric, and it was a favorite. I had been given it by a charming young man back home in Seattle. I did not tell Archie this, but my lending it to him was, for me, a token of kinship. I had made acquaintances in Key West, people who asked after me and after whom I had asked, that we might nod at one another from opposite ends of the bar. I had savored many a strapping man, too, in dark booths and crowded rooms drenched in blacklight where I had played the pipe organ of their flesh and been thanked in blood and more. But I had met no other *killers*, no others who would taste the piping hot life of a man like Mr. Joshua Motorcycle from earlier that night and think to himself *what a shame to leave this creature alive.* To lend him—likely to *give* him—my favorite shirt in all the world? That was as close to brotherhood as I might ever know.

Archie worried that if Randolph spied him through the peephole that he would not let Archie in: he knew of Johnny's relationship and may have feared the arrival of infuriated or tearful melodrama at his quiet door. He stayed at the bottom of the steps, out of sight, and I touched the buzzer to get Randolph's attention.

"Can I help you?"

"I hope so," I said, and via that small conduit of communication I pushed my mind forward. I pictured a spare but tidy apartment, nothing too extravagant, nothing too grand, and the sort of man who might abuse another to get so small a payoff, and then I pictured clawed and gnarled hands extending from my forehead, through the lens of the peephole, and driving their talons into the man's skull. I visualized those ferocious claws tearing a rent in the mental shadow of his flesh, grasping each side of that ragged wound, and ripping it wide like a split melon. And when that image was complete, I said, "I need help, Randolph. *Open the door.*"

I could hear his hands shake as he undid the chain, twisted the deadbolt, and turned the lock in the knob. The door opened. He stepped back. His eyes were toward me but not *on* me. He had started to drool.

"Come on up," I said softly over my shoulder.

Archie stood by my side in a flash.

I made Randolph tell me the names of the cops on the vice squad who worked with him. Randolph had, of course, been feeding the police boys from his own stable every now and then to keep them off his back. It happens more than one might think. A hustler gets too old, or too familiar, too frequently seen on the streets. The local johns grow weary of him and the cruise ship trade prefer fresher faces with fewer lines. What better way to dispose of washed-up talent than to send them to jail and get them off the streets? It can be a tidy system. What are the lives of a few young homosexuals when there's money to be made?

Archie did not want to hear it, but I made Randolph confirm that he had done this to Johnny. Slurring, his mind irremediably shattered by the things mine had done to it, Randolph told us that Johnny had refused to put out for him one night—not refused to work but refused to service Randolph himself in order to demonstrate his submission to his pimp—and so Randolph fed him to the boys in blue to teach the rest a lesson. "I didn't mean to hurt him," Randolph had groaned, struggling to produce words from the other side of a million miles of pain and psychic spiderweb.

"No," Archie said. "You meant for *them* to hurt him."

I admit, doing all this, dragging the story out of Randolph right there on the spot and making sure it hurt Archie to hear it, had been intentional. Archie had killed, yes, and had even explained to me why he did so. In his mind, this was *mostly* an unerasable mark, a permanent new feature. I think he wanted to think himself A Killer, and wanted to believe doing so would make him too strong for others to hurt. He wanted a defense against a world that was hostile to him on all sides. If he was known as a hustler, some gay clubs would deny him entry. If he was known as a homosexual, most of society would do the same. I think Archie wanted to graduate up to being the one who did the hurting for a while, and I could not hold that against him.

I will never know what, if anything, I said to my father before I killed him, but I know that when I came to my senses and realized I had murdered him, spilled his blood, and then sucked it from the very carpet, that I also realized I had hated my father far more than can be measured. I knew vampirism had not *made* me take his life. Vampirism had *allowed* me. I had wanted to be the one who made others hurt for once, and it had felt grand.

But Archie was no vampire. He might have *believed* he wanted to hurt others, but what he really wanted was not to hurt anymore. That is a different thing. He wanted to end the suffering already inflicted on him. He could never kill enough Randolphs to bring Johnny back, and sooner or later he would realize that and his actions might feel hollow. Were he to get revenge, he would have to do it *now,* before wisdom or restraint had time to damp the flames. If he did it again—and again, and again—right now, while it was all still fresh, perhaps the seed would take hold. Perhaps he would quench that thirst for revenge and give himself time to consider whether there were other Randolphs, other vice cops, other abusers, others who hurt boys like him, and boys like Johnny, at large in the world. Perhaps Archie could blossom into monstrosity. Perhaps he could live up to that desire to bear an indelible mark on his mortal soul.

And so I made sure Randolph told him everything, every detail, even relished the times when Johnny *had* serviced him as an act of humiliating subservience. It was no act of cruelty. It was one of kindness. More importantly, it was *necessary.* I could not let Archie walk away from the opportunity before him. Before him knelt the pathetically begging mortal who had raped his lover repeatedly then abandoned him to the brutality of police who raped him again before murdering him. I looked back on my own first remembered night as a vampire and I knew—and still know, so many decades later—the only heat I found in a life of cold sorrow and numb resentment had been anger.

I needed Archie to hate as I hated. I needed Archie to realize the wrong that had been done to him and make the choice to correct it the only way that would matter because it was the only way that would *last.*

I urge you not to consider this some lame repetition of trauma in mimicry of that bucket brigade of parent and child. This was an act of *education.* We do not become aware of the harm inflicted on us by accident. We do not choose to fight back by chance. We must teach one another. No one else will do it. None other *can.* We must be the ones to point to each other's anger and say *there, my friends, we shall craft our own salvation.*

The vampire who made me, saved me. And as Archie unfolded the crumpled wad of his life story to me that night, I realized I bore—and still bear—the responsibility to do what I can to save others.

As Randolph blubbered and babbled at my command, the litany of his many sins against Johnny spilling out of his mouth as does pus from an infected wound, I saw Archie take it in and realize for the first time the true horrors Johnny had endured at the hands of Randolph and other terrible men. Archie's expression showed anger, and then sorrow. He shed silent tears, but soon they dried. The blood drained from his cheeks. His puckered lips drew thin and flat. He lifted his chin and gazed down on Randolph not in pity, and not in the heat of fresh anger, but as through a whiteout blizzard of cold hatred. With every detail, Randolph surrendered his own humanity in Archie's ever-narrowing gaze. Randolph went from being the man who had hurt his boyfriend to being a *thing* to be destroyed.

I could see the flame of anger flare in Archie's gleaming eyes, and it made me smile.

Archie waited three or four seconds and repeated what he'd said before but with different emphasis. "You meant for them to *hurt* him. You sorry son of a bitch."

And then the knife—*the* knife—was in Archie's hand, a flash of mirrored steel, and Randolph's life began to spill out of his sliced-open neck.

The shock and pain shook Randolph free of my mental grasp, and he clapped a hand to his throat to hold the blood in. "Oh fuck," he gurgled, "Fuck you *you fucking*—" but Archie flipped the blade around and slashed again in the other direction. Now Randolph's eyes nearly bugged out, and he wrapped both hands around his own split flesh as though choking himself. His tongue lolled out, and his mouth opened as he tried to speak.

Words did not come out of him, only blood.

I tell you, I *felt* when something shifted in Archie's young and malleable mind. I *sensed* it. This was Archie's iteration of that moment when lightning plunged my street into darkness, and I knew I had become something both *new* and which I had *awaited*. And so I grinned with fanged abandon when Archie raised the knife again, high overhead, grabbed Randolph by the chin and forced the bastard to meet his own terrible gaze, then drove that knife, over and over, right down Randolph's throat and out the other side, through his spinal column. I saw the bloody tip of Archie's blade burst through the skin at the back of Randolph's neck, heard the pop and tear of his spinal cord as vertebrae were wedged apart on the point of Archie's anger, and clapped my hands together in jubilation when the light left Randolph's eyes. Archie kept stabbing, kept thrusting bloodied steel through Randolph's dead flesh, the weapon Randolph had used to wear his lover's life down to a nub before snuffing it out, and very nearly decapitated the man's corpse before he stopped. Archie caught himself at last, the knife held aloft for one more stab like sharp-edged lightning, but the boy waited, blinked, and slowly realized Randolph was dead.

Archie had done it. He had become something *new*, something he had waited his whole life to become.

I studied Randolph's corpse as it sagged, then folded, then fell backwards onto the hardwood floor of his modest abode. I think he lived long enough to really *feel it*, and that, I believe, had mattered.

Archie drew panting breaths, shallow, faint, rapid-fire, and I worried he might collapse. When I looked at him, his teeth were gritted in a snarl, his mouth open, the corners stretched back and down. Spittle bubbled in the corners and I wondered if he were having a seizure. His whole body trembled. He began to produce a sound, vocal but not verbal, wordless, not a scream or a yell but a tiny, soft, high-pitched whistle or whine like a tea kettle about to cross the boundary into boiling. I tried to feel his mind, but it was like trying to know the inside of a walnut: hard, opaque, unguessable. Whatever was in there rattled around but gave up no secrets.

I waited thirty seconds, and eventually Archie closed his mouth, worked his tongue around inside it, and swallowed whatever it had unearthed. He stared at Randolph the entire time. Once he began to relax, to move again, to breathe slightly more steadily, he looked at the knife and at his hand. His thumb and knuckles had blood all over them, as though he had just won a prize fight. His face turned in on itself, and he started to cry.

I put my arms around him. Now we had blood on both of us, hardly a tidy first lesson, but he needed a friend more than to wash himself. He needed to know he was no longer alone. Archie leaned into my embrace, let me rub his back and stroke his shoulder. He strangled on his own tears, choked, coughed, then began to weep, then to sob. I had to hold him tight to keep him from making so much noise someone might notice and wonder. I walked him over to the center of the room, away from the outer walls, and I murmured reassurances in his ear as he washed my shirt in tears. When we become something new, a part of us necessarily dies. We mourn on that occasion. It is only natural to weep as we say goodbye to the person we used to be, who is, in fact, a person we never really *were* to begin with.

Archie and I stood like that for fifteen minutes. In the street outside, people began to count backward from ten.

At nine, they were laughing.

At six, they were shouting.

At one, they were rushing so much they stepped on each other.

When midnight struck, they all cried out as one. The city of Key West rang with celebrations. The '80s were one year closer to being over.

It was 1985, and Archie and I had work to do.

And that, my young friend, is the story I felt I should tell you. Oh, I know, it is shocking. You do not believe me. It is, I confess, entirely incredible as such tales go. I can see from your expression you do not trust me. I do not blame you. I have caught you in a moment of great personal compromise, and you are worried what I might do or say. But let me tell you, my friend, I can also *feel* that in your mind you *want* to believe me. You want to think you are not alone, and I am here to assure you that you most certainly are not.

Archie was my first but certainly not my final pupil in the way we sometimes must protect ourselves. That, it turned out, is my purpose: to teach those among us who have had enough. We get pushed around. We get spat on, shoved aside, called names, made scapegoats. They—you know exactly whom I mean, you could probably give me a list of names from your own life—tell us over and over again that we are monsters. Looking around the room in which we find ourselves now, at what I just watched you do, I would say you, too, have grown weary of being targeted. The shame they speak at us too often takes root. It poisons the soil of our souls. It convinces us we are unworthy. But you, my friend, are worthy. You deserve joy. You deserve happiness.

You deserve revenge.

You deserve to be the person you have always waited to become.

And if you let me, I can show you how to find them.

The Case of the Haunted Tiara:

A Zombie Cosmetologist Story

By J.D. Blackrose

"The tiara is missing, and Donald is dead!"

The play's prop master, Livvie Sunshine, skidded into my art studio as if on roller skates, her red face swollen from crying and shock. And yes, that was her real last name. When she'd moved to Hollywood from Yukon, Oklahoma she became one of the rare people in this show business town using her given name.

She looked anything but sunshiny now.

"Waylon?" Livvie sobbed. "Did you hear me?" She carefully checked the floor and stepped around wet red spray paint. I was working on a life-size model of a ghoul.

"I heard you, Liv, but I don't think I'm following. Is this a major script change?" I considered the "dead" part. "I love doing cadavers. I'm shocked they'd kill their leading man, but making Don dead will be super fun. How dead will he be? Like a day or a week?"

I didn't mention that I loved doing cadavers since I essentially was one. She'd never believe me, and besides, barring a lack of a heartbeat and breathing, I seemed perfectly, Hollywood-wacky normal.

As the play's makeup artist, it was my job to make sure each actor looked the part, and this movie had a lot of special effects that required rapid aging of actors, fake blood, and the appearance of grievous injuries. Not being a movie with an unlimited budget and CGI, the producers and director of *The Case of the Haunted Tiara*™, let me call the shots.

I blabbered on. "I'll research the amount of swelling the body would have, depending on how long he's dead. Oh! And fluids. They're going to leak everywhere. Out of eyeballs, ears, the skin—"

"No, Waaaaaaylon!" She dragged my name out in exasperation. "Donald is dead. Like, someone killed him. And the tiara is missing too."

I turned on my swivel stool and wrinkled my nose at her. "The tiara's been stolen?"

"Did you miss the part about Donald being dead?"

I topped my spray paint and put it carefully on a table. "Are you serious? The Muskrat is actually, truly, physically dead? Not just morally and spiritually? Because he's been dead those ways for a long time."

Livvie collapsed onto a chair next to me before I could tell her I'd spray-painted it yellow only a few minutes prior.

"Uh, Liv…"

"Don't interrupt me," she said, holding up a finger. Her entire sleeve was yellow, but I mimed zipping my lips.

She inclined her head. "Thank you. Now, I'm trying to tell you that I walked into the prop room fifteen minutes ago and I found Donald John Tingsley, movie star, leading man, and pervert, and, yes, privately known among his colleagues as the Muskrat, dead as a doornail in front of the open cabinet where the tiara had been stored."

I hummed Captain and Tenille's "Muskrat Love," the source of Don's nickname. He was a total prick and came on to any human with two legs, and at least one time, a veteran with only one. He didn't understand the word, "No," and his agents had buried more scandals than cemeteries had dirt, but he persevered in Hollywood because his fans loved him.

"Who did you tell?"

"You."

"I mean, who else did you tell?"

"No one. Just you."

Holy fuck. I'd been alive since the Battle of Shiloh, and my life hadn't been as big a mess as it had in the last year. Between the deaths, the crimes, the police, and masquerading as Tigger in Disney World, I hadn't had a second's peace in ages. "Liv, my darling girl, why did you tell me? Why didn't you pick up your cell phone and call the police? In fact, you should call the police right now."

Before she could respond, squeaky sneakers preceded the arrival of our red-haired, freckled assistant to the deputy stage manager. Reggie's job was to hold the coffee of the deputy stage manager while she held the coffee of the head stage manager, who had a horrifically complicated job and needed a lot of coffee.

Unsurprisingly, given Livvie's adorable button nose and petite but curvy figure, Reggie had a huge crush on the prop master.

"Waylon! Oh, Livvie, you're here! Thank goodness—"

A tiny tan cockapoo scrambled in, nails tapping on the concrete floor, followed by a giant man with a huge beard who looked like a Viking and was appropriately named Erick.

"Buster," Erick wheedled. "This is not a safe place for you. You'll get paint on your widdle paws."

"No, he won't," I said, hoping Liv didn't stick to the chair. "Come here, Buster. Let me get you your treat."

"Treat!" Erick, Buster's owner and handler, bellowed. "I knew it! You've been sneaking my tiny sweet'ums caloric snacks. That's why he's up two ounces."

"They're small snacks. For small dogs." I stood and walked to a cabinet at the far end of the room, next to one of the sinks. We had three for washing makeup brushes, paintbrushes, and hands. I removed three tiny snacks and gave them to the obedient dog at my feet, who'd sat and offered a paw to shake without having to be asked.

"Here you go, boy. Eat up."

The dog gobbled them down just as Erick scooped him up and cuddled him to his massive chest. "Waylon, he can't have treats. He's the star of this movie. He must watch his figure."

"He's barely bigger than a hamster. No one will notice."

"The cockapoo is the clue to what happened to the haunted tiara! Everyone will notice. He performs live, you know. It's not a movie. We can't take weight off him in post."

"Well, speaking of the play," Reggie said but then trailed off as Livvie let out an enormous shriek.

"I'm yellow!"

Damn. Guess she noticed.

"Only a little bit," I said, giving a weak wave in her direction. "And it's a pretty color."

"Oh, my God, Waylon!" She sloshed over since her pants were soaking wet and sticking to her skin. She grabbed me by the collar. "Why didn't you tell me?"

"You sat down before I could!"

"People!" Reggie yelled loud enough to capture our attention. Even Buster peeked his head out of Erick's flannel shirt to see what was going on.

"Mario wants to see us right now. Especially you, Livvie."

"What about?" I asked.

Reggie folded his hands in front of him as if in church. "Don is dead."

Oh. Right. I kept forgetting that.

"The Muskrat died?" Erick asked. "Of what? A perpetual hard-on? The clap? I bought him a new box of condoms last week."

Reggie flipped Erick the bird. "No. He was"—Reg lowered his voice to a, you should excuse me, stage whisper—"murdered."

Livvie, Erick, and I ceased our chatter. Buster cocked an ear but didn't bark or even beg for another treat. It was if time stopped.

"Livvie," I started, unsure how to approach this subject. "How did you know Donald was dead?"

"Wellllll, Waylon," she said with as much sarcasm as possible, "By the axe in his head."

I leaned against the counter, unable to believe my bad luck. Why was I always falling into murders? "Are you kidding me? You didn't think to mention this first thing?"

"You were too busy thinking about how to make him look like a cadaver, not that he is actually in real life, now a cadaver."

I sighed and whirled my finger in the air. "Roll up, team. Let's go see Mario and find out who didn't love the Muskrat."

The entire play's cast and crew met on the stage. The set design folks had worked overtime to create a creepy castle complete with bats, cobwebs, and multiple hidden doors. I didn't even know where most of the doors were. The plot required characters to enter and leave by mysterious means, so we had trapdoors, bookcases that opened into hallways, and even a wire rig to mimic levitation.

Hundreds of people gathered in small huddles wondering what this was about.

"Are they shutting down the play?"

"Is Mario quitting?"

"What about Octavia? Maybe she's threatening to quit if she isn't paid more. I heard Donald is getting twice her salary."

Mario Bianchi, our director, paced in the center of the stage. His flamingo-pink pants sparkled in the LED lights, and his open white-sequined shirt fluttered with his frantic steps. Rumors said he'd had an affair with the Muskrat that had ended badly, but I didn't know the details. I'd been traveling with an elite zombie military team infiltrating an international beauty contest at the time.

Octavia DeVeene, the film's ingénue, filed her nails in a chair off to the side She wore white stockings with a white garter, a matching white bustier, and a filmy white robe over the whole ensemble. She'd slid her feet into some transparent high-heeled mule slides with faux rabbit fur over the peep toe. She looked like a very tall, statuesque, 1950s Hollywood pin-up girl. Even her hair fit the theme. Her hairdresser had tightly curled it and pulled each side up with elaborate hair pins.

She sat next to Brody Connor, the twenty-something actor with two first names who had the supporting actor role. He leaned against the wall next to a gargoyle sconce, looking studly in his carefully ripped jeans, tight black T-shirt, and perfectly wavy shoulder-length black hair. That stupidly sexy hair had won him several million followers on social media.

I hated him on principle.

The murmuring continued until two uniformed officers sauntered in with a man dressed in a fugly brown suit and maroon tie, who I guessed was a plainclothes detective.

The trio stood center stage with our agitated director. Mario held up his hand and we fell silent.

Voice warbly and thin, Mario announced the bad news. "I'm afraid I have terrible news. Our male lead is dead."

Gasps and whispers greeted this news.

"But there's more," Mario continued, in much the same manner Reggie had used to tell us the news. "Donald was…" He took a deep breath. "Murdered."

I watched the crowd as he delivered this doozie. Octavia flicked her eyes up in surprise but didn't otherwise show an outward reaction. Pat, our casting director, just about fainted, falling into a nearby dilapidated chaise that was a part of the castle set. Brody came to attention, head tilted as if listening especially carefully, lips pressed and eyes tense.

Beside me, Livvie muffled a sob. Before I placed an arm around her I surreptitiously tested the yellow paint with my pinky and it was tacky but not wet. Risking it, I placed an arm around her and hugged her to my side, hoping she didn't notice my body temperature was a little less than a normal human 99.8. In other words, I ran cold. It happened when you were dead.

Erick whispered words of reassurance to Buster, who had fallen asleep in the big man's arms and clearly didn't give a fuck what had happened to the Muskrat. Reggie clicked and unclicked a pen until I grabbed it out of his hand and threw it across the room.

The plainclothes cop stepped forward and turned in a circle, both hands raised, calling for quiet.

"People! Pay attention. My name is Detective Robert Newland.

This," he said, jerking his thumb to the two uniformed cops, "is Officers Jones and Murphy. We're going to ask everyone questions, so no one leaves, not even for a coffee break. This is a serious crime, a serious matter, and we're going to treat it seriously. Everyone understand?"

I elbowed Livvie and whispered. "I seriously do."

She snickered.

"You!" Newland barked. "You find this funny?"

I looked around to see who he was talking to, and then realized it was me.

"Me? Ah, no."

"Then what were you laughing at?"

Livvie, the traitor, shuffled away from me.

"N…nothing. You used the word 'serious' a lot."

Newland strode over and poked me in the chest. "What's your name?"

"Waylon Jenkins."

"What do you do here?"

"Makeup artist."

"I'm interviewing you first. Follow me." He walked away from me, and I hung my head as I followed. Whispers tracked my progress, and I knew that I was going to be the butt of many jokes later.

We walked backstage and he indicated we should go down a level. The lower section housed the dressing rooms, bathroom, the prop room, and my studio.

As we made our way, Newland chatted at me. He tried for a "just two friends talking" tone but only achieved "detective sussing out information."

"Waylon, I'm a little surprised to see you here, but Captain Perkins has told me a bit about you. You do seem to be in the middle of a lot of murders."

Ugh. Captain Perkins was the head of the Malibu/Lost Hills station of the Los Angeles Sheriff's office. We had a love-hate relationship. He knew I was a zombie though.

"I'm sure most of the things he's told you are true, Detective," I said, going for nonchalant and utterly failing. "But not everything."

"Look, because the captain vouched for you, I want you to see the crime scene. I hope you don't get sick to your stomach easily," Newland said.

This was a rather timely warning because he took me down the steps to the prop room and made me stand outside of the open door, which was cordoned off by crime scene tape. A forensic team wearing full protective gear worked the room and a tiny woman leaned over the corpse studying the horrific axe wound.

There was an awful lot of blood. An awful lot. Plus, brain spatter. But all I saw was the tiny lady leaning over the body.

"Sorya?"

My girlfriend, who was also the chief medical examiner, looked up and smiled with unmitigated joy. I smiled back, sharing that emotion. This woman was the best thing that ever happened to me.

"Waylon!" Sorya jumped up and waved. "I thought this was your play."

Sorya moved and talked as if she was running downhill after drinking six espressos. She moved fast. She talked fast. She fell asleep as soon as she closed her eyes and woke up with a start the next morning. Everything with her was speed and split-second timing.

"It is."

"Well, your star is dead, and not mostly dead. All the way dead."

"I guessed that."

"Jenkins." Newland frowned at us. "You know Dr. Sang?"

"She's my girlfriend."

"Dr. Sang, a suspect is your boyfriend? This is a conflict of interest. You must recuse yourself from this case."

Sorya took off the head gear and pointed a gloved finger at the detective. "You go to Captain Perkins with that request, Newland, and get yourself laughed right out the door. And Waylon isn't a suspect, you ninny. He was nowhere near this room."

"How do you know that?"

"I have wig samples from every hairpiece, and hair samples from the victim and eight other people from this crime scene. I promise you that none of them are Waylon's."

"That doesn't mean anything."

"Since you're such a forensic expert, why don't you come on in here and take a good long look at this dead guy's brain and nasal cavity. And when you get home, tell Tammy I said hi and ask if she made the cookie recipe I gave her."

Newland balked. "You know my wife?"

Sorya smiled sweetly. "I know everyone."

"You gave her the snickerdoodle recipe?"

Sorya smiled sweetly. "I did."

Newland backed off in a hurry. "Okay, Dr. Sang, carry on. Jenkins, let's go into this dressing room."

The dressing room belonged Octavia, so it was filled with lingerie, hats, headbands, high-end cosmetics, and piles of shiny gewgaws and baubles so deep that I couldn't tell you what they were. It was a mess.

She wasn't a diva but doing Octavia's makeup was difficult. She thought she knew better than I did what "worked for her face," and maybe she did for every day. But this was stage makeup, and I had to make the look consistent from scene-to-scene and performance-to-performance so I couldn't allow her to randomly apply whatever she wanted on any given day. Getting her to understand this had proven challenging. The director wanted a certain look, and I kept a record of every product we used, a picture of her face for each scene, and detailed notes about application. I'd often come in this room and find her doing her own makeup, which I then, after much fuss, had to remove.

The detective sat in Octavia's chair, and I sat in the only other one in the room.

"Now, Mr. Jenkins, you laughed when you heard Mr. Tingsley was murdered. Is that how you often react to violent death?"

In my head, I thought, *Well, not really, but I've seen so much of it that it doesn't affect me anymore. I mean, what's one murdered man compared to the Civil War?*

Out loud, I said, "I didn't laugh at the murder. I laughed at how many times you used the word 'serious.'"

"Wouldn't you agree this is a serious matter?"

"Of course. Which is why I told Livvie to call the cops as soon as she found the body."

Newland sat up straight. "Livvie Sunshine found the body? We were told the janitor found him."

Uh oh.

"Livvie found the body first, I think, and she came and told me. I told her to call the police but then Mario called us to the stage, and you were already here."

"I will have to talk to Miss Sunshine." Newland pierced me with his gaze. "Why would Livvie tell you?"

"I'm her friend."

"Sure, and maybe she thought you had something to do with it and wanted to warn you the body had been found."

"Not at all. I had nothing to do with this."

"Where were you at two o'clock today?"

I motioned with my head. "Down this hall, in my workshop."

"What were you doing there?"

"Painting a ghoul."

"Don't be a smartass."

I was out of patience. "I do makeup but also special effects. I was painting a life-sized ghoul for a particularly gory scene. In the beginning of the play, Brody's character kills a lot of people and some turn into ghouls. I need a few bodies to throw around."

"Brody Connor isn't the hero of the story?"

"No. Donald was."

"Interesting. Maybe Brody killed Donald to get the lead part."

I shook my head. "Unlikely. The lead is an older man, and I'm pretty sure Brody and Donald were sleeping together."

"An affair, you say?"

"There are always theater romances."

Newland scoffed. "And you know all the details, right?"

"Of course. I'm a makeup artist. People tell me things." I shifted, uncomfortable with this topic. "I hear the gossip."

"Who, in your opinion, would want to hurt Donald?"

"I have no idea. He had a string of ex-lovers, and it didn't always end well, but I think you're missing the most important part."

Newland leaned back in his chair. "And what would that be?"

"Why steal a prop tiara made of fake crystals?"

"Because it wasn't." The detective tapped his fingers on the chair's armrest. "Because the tiara was on loan from the Paranormal Museum."

"The wha—?"

"The Paranormal Museum features exhibits on vampire lore and the paranormal. It's in a small town in Pennsylvania."

"I've never heard of this museum."

He chuckled, a wry sound, not mirthful. It was a sound that said, *I was going to home to a nice bourbon on ice and now I have to deal with shit.*

"Neither did I until I caught this case. But the tiara was on loan from the museum. It contains fifty carats of diamonds and is set in platinum."

"They used the real tiara for the play?" I whistled. "Who knew this?"

"I'm taking that you did not?"

"No way. I thought it was just a pretty, fake bauble."

"Mr. Bianchi knew the truth, but I don't know who else. So, you are going to help me find out."

"Me?" I said, pointing to my chest. "Why?"

"Because you hear the gossip, Mr. Jenkins. You're a makeup artist. People tell you things."

I crossed my arms. "There is such a thing as client/cosmetologist confidentiality, you know."

"Not when it comes to murder, Mr. Jenkins. Not when it comes to murder."

"And theft?"

"For a two-hundred-and-fifty-thousand-dollar tiara? No, it doesn't exist there either."

The next person Newland wanted to talk to was Livvie, so we marched to the stage and looked for her. She sat on a stool with her yellow back against a wall lined with a tapestry supposedly showing the main character, the vampire Count of the castle, who was supposed to be played by the late, great Donald John Tingsley, riding a black stallion to the king's palace to claim his bride, played by Octavia DeVeene.

In the movie, he steals her away and woos her until she falls in love with the dashing and mysterious Count, who is good to her even if his incisors are too long. He says she is his fated mate and his one true love, and she swoons over his tragic past. Meanwhile, her legally betrothed, played by Brody Connor, raises an army to murder the count and rescue the princess, who by now doesn't need or want rescuing. The count gifts the princess a tiara as he watches the army come up the hill.

It's a tale as old as time. Emotionally tortured boy kidnaps princess. Princess falls in love with said boy, thus healing his deep-seated pain. Frat boy leads an army to claim what he believes is rightfully his, ignoring her stated wishes.

Everyone dies and the tiara magically (abracadabra presto!) becomes haunted with the princess's soul. In Act II, hundreds of years later, an archeology team, who look shockingly like the original characters (read: exactly like, the actors play both roles) finds the tiar and the whole story plays out again.

Except this time, there's a twist. The lead archaeologist, played by Donald, and his assistant, played by Brody, are the ones who fall in love.

The local young woman, played by Octavia, wants Brody's character for herself and is the sorority mean girl of this version.

It is a tangled web and sort of a stupid plot, but I got involved because I appreciated the openness about gender roles—and Livvie begged me.

That'll show me. Talk about no good deed goes unpunished.

"Hey, Liv? Detective Newland wants to talk to you about finding the body." I wince as she opened one closed eye to glare at me.

"I told the truth! Don't be mad."

She sighed and stood, wiping her hands on her thighs, adding dusty streaks to the ruined black pants. "I'm not, Waylon. Whaddaya want to know, Detective?"

"Let's go someplace where we can have some privacy, okay?" Newland motioned for me to follow as well. We were headed back to Octavia's dressing room. As we made our way across the stage, a flicker of movement coming from the set wall caught my eye, but when I looked more carefully, it was gone.

"Theater ghosts," I muttered to myself.

This time, Livvie sat in Octavia's chair, Newland sat in the guest chair, and I stood awkwardly.

"Miss Sunshine, when did you find the body?"

"A little after two o'clock."

"What did you see?"

She shivered and rubbed her arms. "Donald on the ground, an axe buried in his skull, blood everywhere, and the cabinet, which is always locked, wide open. That is when I noticed the tiara was gone."

"Did you know the tiara was made of real diamonds and worth a lot of money?"

"I sure did," Livvie said, nodding hard. "Mario told me. I didn't want such an expensive item in the prop room, but he said no one would think it was the real thing. He said Don wanted it to add 'verisimilitude' to the play." She rolled her eyes at that statement.

"I told him I didn't want to be responsible, but he insisted so I put it in the only cabinet that locked and stored it that way after every rehearsal. I asked to see proof of insurance, but he said it was in his office, and he'd show it to me later. He never got around to it."

A soft pitter-pat caught my ears. It came from within the walls. I inwardly moaned. We had rats. Old theaters often did, and rodents could be a serious problem. They chewed on wires and left droppings everywhere. I'd have to tell the lighting and sound directors so they could hire a pest control company. Honestly, it would be more effective to get a couple of stray cats. Poor Buster, as a cockapoo, wasn't much of a mouser and frankly, the rats might outweigh him.

I brought my attention back to Livvie and Detective Newland. Newland pointed at the weapons corner. "Are those real?"

"No, of course not. They're props."

"Any idea where the axe that killed Don came from?"

Livvie shook her head. "I don't know, and don't look at me like that," she added when Newland gave her the stink eye. "I know this looks bad for me, but I didn't kill Don. If I was going to commit a murder, do you think I'd be dumb enough to do it in my own prop room with a real axe?"

"I don't know. Are you that dumb?"

I stepped in. "Detective. Really?"

"Sometimes the easy explanation is the right one, Jenkins."

"Maybe we could hurry this along?" I asked.

"Fine. Livvie, what were you doing before you found Don?"

Newland asked.

Livvie blushed. "I'd rather not say."

"Are you refusing to answer?"

She squirmed in her seat. "It has nothing to do with the murder."

"I'll be the judge of that."

Livvie let out a frustrated humph. "Fine. I was heading to the bathroom with Reggie."

It took Newland a second, but then he got it. "Ah, and I'm assuming Reggie will corroborate this?"

"Of course," Livvie said, flouncing her hair. "We only had a few minutes, so it was going to be a quickie."

"Going to be?"

"We got in there and Brody was taking a shower, can you believe it? What are the chances?"

"I couldn't guess. Before the uh, intended quickie, where were you?"

"On stage, talking to some of the set design guys. But then Reggie came over and gave me that 'look.' You know the one," she said with a quick lift of the eyebrows and a grin. "So, I snuck off with him."

"When the bathroom break didn't work out, where did you go?"

"To the craft table. I was starving. I needed a sandwich. They have a good pesto chicken."

"Did other people see you there?" the detective asked.

"Several people."

"Okay, after your pesto chicken?"

"To the prop room, which is when I found Don."

"Okay. Stay here please."

He crooked a finger at me, and I followed him. He pulled me into an alcove.

"Does everybody have sex with everybody else?"

I shrugged. "Ever work in the theater?" He shook his head, so I continued. "Look, showmances are a thing. We're all open about it. If all parties are consenting adults, it's no one else's business. Except as a source of gossip, that is." I winked at him, which he did not seem to appreciate.

He rubbed his eyes. "Go get Mr. Bianchi, will you?"

Mario sat on the edge of Octavia's director's chair, one foot on the ground, the other balanced on the wooden frame, right on the X in the front where the struts met. His bent knee bounced a mile a minute.

"Mario," Newland said. "How many people knew the tiara was real?"

"Just me and Livvie." He scrunched up his face. "And Don. Maybe Octavia because she and Don were, well, you know. And Brody could have because Don was sleeping with him too." He chewed the inside of his cheek. "Pat could have known. We share an office."

Newland's face drained of all color. "So basically everyone."

"Except me," I said. "I didn't know."

"So much for everyone telling you everything."

"That is odd. I'm insulted." In fact, this did gnaw at me. Was I losing my touch? Had I gotten a reputation as a cosmetologist/makeup artist no one could trust?

"Here's another question, Mario. What's up with wanting a real tiara worth a small fortune on the set?"

Mario blew out a breath hard enough to send his coiffured bangs floating. He leaned forward and whispered. "Look, I need this play to be a success. My last film flopped, and this is my last chance to have a hit before the studios and producers think I've lost my touch. If I become unbankable, my career is over."

Newland raised his eyebrows. "What's that have to do with the tiara?"

Mario's eyes grew wide. "The tiara is actually haunted! The museum says that a ghost follows the tiara wherever it goes, and when I heard that, I knew we had to have it. The tiara's spirit will bring a level of creepiness, a spark of authenticity, that nothing else can. The tiara and the plot work together, you see. Their energies work in synergy." He interlaced his fingers. "They work in tandem to add Truth to the story."

He said "Truth" with a capital T. I heard it in his voice.

Newland just stared at him, not understanding the director's artistic speak. He cleared his throat and gave a tiny head shake as if throwing off a level of stupidity he couldn't quite grasp.

"Did you insure it?" he asked Mario. "You told Livvie that you had the documentation was in your office."

Mario burst out laughing and then veered into tears. "Insure it? Of course not. Who could afford that? I showed the museum a forged insurance certificate." He rubbed his hands together in a repetitive motion, Lady MacBeth style. "We locked it up. We were real careful."

"Not careful enough. It was stolen and your lead actor is dead."

Mario shrunk into himself, his face crumpling. "Well, when you put it that way." He wiped his face. "Our backers are going to kill me."

I thought he might be right.

Octavia flounced into her dressing room, her face a mask of disapproval. "Couldn't you find someone else's dressing room to use for your interrogations?" she asked. "Why must I bear the indignity of being kicked out of my only private place? You could have used Don's dressing room."

"It's considered part of the crime scene," Newland explained. "We're examining it for clues. Maybe Don left some evidence in there about who wanted to kill him."

"Oh, heavens!" Octavia threw an arm in the air and covered her eyes. "Poor Donnie! Lost to us at such a young age. What a tragedy!" Big, fat tears dripped down her face.

"Your mascara will run if you keep crying like that," I warned her.

She stopped weeping on a dime, whirled to study her face in the mirror, and quickly blotted her cheeks with powder.

After powdering, she turned to the two of us. "Look, Don owed at least two bookies money, had a raft of jilted lovers, and was a piece of shit sometimes. Except to me, of course. We were," she sniffed and shot us a coy look, "involved. He adored me."

Her face grew sly, and she leaned forward to whisper conspiratorially, "But—and I hate to throw shade, but I must be honest. A dastardly crime has been committed after all." Octavia threw a hand up to her forehead. "A devilish wrongdoing, indeed."

"Just tell us what happened," Newland said, digging into his pocket.

She glanced right and left as if looking for spies. "I heard him yell at Livvie just last week. She'd misplaced a cloak he wears in the second part of Act I. She found it lickity-split, but you know Don. He's—I mean, he was—a tad spicy."

"Did he yell at a lot of people?"

"Yes," I said.

"Sometimes," Octavia said.

Newland removed a small bottle of ibuprofen from his pocket and popped three dry.

"Where were you at two p.m. today?" Newland asked. He slumped a little in the chair, completely exhausted by her dramatics. I leaned against the wall and watched the scene.

"Speaking with Mario. It's imperative that a director and the lead actress are in sync."

Oh, no. We were back to synergy.

Newland rubbed his eyes. "What does that mean?"

Octavia examined the backs of her hands and reached for lotion. "I was unhappy with my death scene at the end of Act II. Don had a meaty death in Act I when Brody's character kills him, cutting off his head with an axe. Waylon here had to make a fake head for Don."

I nodded. "It's true. I had a special effects sculptor help. Super talented."

Newland held up a finger. "Don was supposed to be killed with an axe in the play?"

"Of course," Octavia said in an easy-breezy tone. "He was supposed to be the first vampire. How else would you kill him?"

Newland blinked at her. "A stake through the heart? Like Mr. Pointy in Buffy?"

"A stake is cliché and boring. The axe is so much more dramatic. Blood everywhere."

"Okay," Newland said. "What's the problem?"

Octavia's voice rose, warming to her subject. "In the second act, when my character dies and the archaeologist and his assistant ride off into the sunset, I fall off a mountain. A mountain! Off stage! How boring is that? All I do is fall backwards onto a large mat and yell."

She demonstrated by wailing as she leaned her head back. A mirror fell off the wall behind her and shattered, revealing a poorly patched hole in the wall. I was certain someone had placed the mirror there to hide the crappy repair job.

Great. Rodents, a crumbling theater, a dead lead actor, and a missing diamond tiara.

Things were going so well.

"Waylon, how well do you know Livvie?" Newland asked.

"I've known her for years," I said. "We've worked on both plays and movies."

"What movies?"

"Well, she worked on the last Jason Teague one."

"Didn't he die on that set?"

"Maybe not a good example, but you know Mitzi?"

Newland looked at me like I was stupid. "Everyone knows Mitzi." His eyes widened. "Did you work on *All Schoolgirls Go to Heaven*?"

"I did. So did Livvie."

Excited, he flapped a hand at me. "Could you get me Mitzi's autograph?" He caught himself, regained his composure, and said, "You know, for my wife."

No hetero female that I knew of had enjoyed All Schoolgirls Go to Heaven, but the men did. And the lesbians. Oh, the lesbians! They loved that movie. It had become something of a cult film for them, and Mitzi was a huge supporter of the LGBTQIA community, so she adored the attention. She'd been paid a ton of money, too, which helped.

"I'll see what I can do."

Newland adjusted his tie. "Yes, well thank you. I'm sure she'll appreciate it. In the meantime, your friend Livvie is the most natural suspect. She had means, motive, and opportunity."

"Oh, don't be silly, Detective. Livvie wouldn't hurt a fly."

"That's what everyone says about every murderer, ever."

"You seriously like to repeat every word."

"What?"

"Never mind."

Reggie met us outside Octavia's dressing room and refused to go in. "Have you been in there? Oh, of course you have. Stupid question." He pointed at the door. "It's a pigsty. I constantly tell her to clean it up, but does she? No. She wants a production assistant to tidy after her, and I refuse to ask anyone to do that, so I do it myself, but does she thank me? No." He finished with a little humph.

"Okay, fine," Newland said. "Where else can we go?"

"My studio is available," I said. "Just don't sit in the yellow chair. It's probably dry, but I can't promise. I did two coats."

We tromped down to my studio and Newland took my chair, frowning at the ghoul next to him. Reggie wisely ignored the yellow chair and pulled over a stool. I leaned against the sink and listened, again. This was becoming my go-to move.

Newland radioed one of the officers and asked him to stand watch at the door while he conducted the interview. Once done, he removed a small pad and a pen from his pocket. "Where were you at about two p.m. this afternoon?"

"With Livvie."

"Where?"

"In a bathroom."

"Right. For the quickie."

Reggie drew up at that comment. "For lovemaking."

"Okay, Romeo," Newland said, barely keeping the snark out of his voice. "You two were planning a private interlude. A quick one."

"We didn't have a lot of time, and I knew that," Reggie admitted. "But she's amazing. The things she can do with her tongue—"

Newland held his hand up. "Stop right there. We're good."

Reggie had the good graces to flush in embarrassment. "I'm just saying we're meant for each other." His eyes grew dreamy. "Forever." He shook himself. "But it didn't work out because Brody was in there taking a shower."

"Is that unusual?"

"No. Anyone can take a shower or use the facilities. I was surprised he didn't lock the door, but once we realized he was in there, we hightailed it out."

"I think I follow," Newland said. He scribbled something in his notebook. "After you left Livvie, where did you go?"

"Mario had texted me while I was with Livvie." Reggie pulled out his phone and showed Newland the text. "I went in search of him, but I didn't find him at first. It took a while."

"And you found him where?"

"In his office, but I had checked there, and he wasn't there. I must have missed him, and we sort of circled each other."

"Okay, so when you finally found him, did he tell you Don was dead?"

"No. That came later. The custodian found Don and ran to tell Mario. I was there when Mario learned."

"And then what happened?"

"Mario asked me to round everybody up and bring them to the stage. He knew I could get around quickly using the tunnels and false entrances. I've worked in this theater before and know all the shortcuts."

"I didn't realize there were tunnels."

"Mostly just hallways behind the stage and below to help actors get from one place to another quickly."

"Interesting. Okay, how was Mario when you left him?"

"He was very upset. He almost fainted. I had to help him to a chair and bring him a glass of water."

Newland studied the young man. "Reggie, I'm going to tell you this in confidence and out of respect for your feelings."

Reggie frowned. "Tell me what?"

"Livvie is my prime suspect."

Ugh. I knew this technique. I'd seen Perkins use a few times. The captain would pretend to take a person into his confidence and bait him to see what he'd say or do. I guess it was a time-honored police trick, but I disliked it. I made a point of frowning in Newland's direction. He saw it and gave me a small, unconcerned shrug.

"Livvie?" Reggie's jaw dropped. "What? Why?"

"She's in charge of the prop room, had access to the murder weapon, and Octavia told us that she heard Don yelling at Livvie about a cloak."

"The Muskrat yelled at everyone."

Newland wrinkled his nose. "Who's the Muskrat?"

"Don." I cleared my throat. "It was a nickname."

"Not a very nice nickname."

"He wasn't always a very nice person." I grimaced thinking about it. Don hadn't been pleased with his fake head, but I told him too bad, so sad. Not that I was going to mention that to Newland.

Newland was confused. "But everyone was sleeping with him or had been. Octavia. Brody. Mario."

"I guess Don was good at something."

"Geez, ick. Anyway," said Newland. "Livvie had a reason to resent Don, if what Octavia said is true. That's a slam dunk case."

"What about the forensics?" I asked.

"Livvie was in the prop room. We know this. Forensics can't tell us anything."

Reggie, red in the face, popped to his feet. "She's not tall enough!"

Newland stopped talking.

Reggie continued, loud and agitated. "Ask your medical examiner. Someone tall had to have swung that axe down on Don's head. Livvie's short. Perfect for me, but not tall enough to have killed Don."

Livvie stumbled around the corner, pushing a surprised Officer Murphy out of the way. "Reggie, are you calling me? You keep yelling my name."

Reggie threw a protective arm around Livvie and pointed at

Newland with the other hand. "This...this...inept detective thinks you killed Don!"

Murphy reached out to escort Livvie out, but Newland waved him away.

Livvie covered her face with her hands. "I told you I didn't. I'd never hurt a fly. I'm a vegetarian, for heaven's sake."

Newland's voice was mild. "Vegetarians commit murder too."

"Not this one!" Livvie said, thumping her chest. "And again, I ask, why would I? Don was my meal ticket."

"He was upset about the missing cloak."

"I found that cloak in two seconds, and he was the one who misplaced it." She looked from me to Reggie to Newland. "How did you know about that?"

Newland flipped his pad where he'd obviously scribbled some notes. "Octavia said she heard Don yelling at you."

"Don yelled at everyone."

"So, I've been told, but Octavia seemed to think this upset you more than normal."

Octavia had never said that, and I wondered again why Newland was fishing. I was about to butt in when Livvie let out an ear-splitting shriek.

"That bitch! I'm going to kill her!"

"Ah, Livvie," I said, alarmed. I sprinted to her and grabbed her bicep. I leaned down into her ear and whispered, "Not the right time to be making threats like that."

Livvie's eyes grew wide. "I was kidding. Only joking. But I am upset that she'd say something like that. It's not true. She's trying to frame me."

Newland raised his eyebrows and shrugged. "Just sharing what I've been told."

"Well, actually, Octavia didn't—" I started, about to protest again, but was cut off this time when Octavia clip-clopped into the room on her high heels. Her blonde hair was down and in loose waves, and she'd changed into a flowy housecoat topped by a loose kimono.

"What in the name of our heavenly playwright William Shakespeare is going on here?" She flipped her hair, Mitzi style, and I glowered at her. Octavia shouldn't even try to step into Mitzi's curlers.

"What's going on?" Livvie ranted. "What's going on is that you're trying to frame me for Don's murder when I didn't do it. You should mind your own business you old biddy. We all know Don was going to leave you."

Octavia gasped. "No, he wasn't!"

Livvie took a step toward Octavia, but Reggie and I held her back. "Yes, he was. Maybe it's the cellulite he didn't like. Or the crow's feet. Or the fake boobs."

Oh, no. She went there. Rule one of theater, showmances don't count. Rule two, don't mention plastic surgery.

Octavia went ballistic, screeching at the top of her lungs. "How dare you? You talentless shrike! We all know you wanted to be an actress like me but couldn't hack it. Props is the like the fallback fallback's position. It's the thing people do when they can't do anything else but are desperate enough to want to stay in show business."

Mario stomped in just in time to hear this last part and he grabbed Octavia by the shoulders and restrained her.

He looked around, bewildered. "What the hell is happening?"

Octavia yanked herself out of his grasp. "Livvie killed my one true love!"

"Oh, stop it." Livvie balled her fists. "I didn't kill anyone, you B-list hack."

"I'm an A-list, award-nominated actress," Octavia said, her hand to heart.

"You aren't a good enough actress for a college horror flick. And that award you were nominated for was a hometown hero award from Akron, Ohio, and you lost to a football player."

Now Octavia lunged and Mario had to drag her from the room. "I'm taking her to my office," he announced. "Enough of this."

Reggie murmured to a crying Livvie while I stalked over to Newland. "Do you see what you've done? Why did you egg this on? You know Octavia didn't say that Livvie appeared 'more upset that usual.'"

Newland gave me a partially chagrined look, but mostly he was amused. "I wanted to see what would happen."

"You started World War III. Good going."

"I don't regret a thing. I've never been so entertained in my life," Newland said. He stood and dusted off his pants. "Livvie, stay here in Wayland's studio." He picked up his radio. "Officer Jones, please come to the art and makeup studio and spell Murphy for a while. He deserves a break from guard duty."

Livvie sobbed and sank into the yellow chair. I really hoped it was dry.

Newland and I were back in Octavia's dressing room while Octavia had a nice cup of tea, with a splash of whiskey, in Mario's office. The detective brought in Brody and the handsome, young actor sat in the hotseat while I once again leaned against the wall with no place to rest my elbows and a crick in my back. I noticed that someone had replaced the mirror over the rough patch job. This time they'd used a heavy, ornate brass oval mirror that looked like it weighed a ton. I really hoped it would hold.

God forbid the Lady Octavia had to look at spackle.

Brody sat with his head in his hands, his voice so low it was hard to hear him.

"When did you last see Don alive?" Newland asked.

"On stage, rehearsing. We were reviewing the beheading scene."

"I understand you were having an affair with Don?"

Brody wiped a tear away from his cheek. "Yes. I loved him."

"If you don't mind me asking, what did you see in him? Multiple people have told me he yelled at folks regularly." Newland tilted his head with this query, like a curious parrot.

Brody sighed a big body sigh and leaned back. His wet eyes and ruddy cheeks made me realize his emotions ran deep. Brody was mourning Don.

"He was… He was…charming. I know he yelled on set or here in the theater, but privately, we hit it off. He taught me a lot about acting and cultivating a following, which is a requirement these days. Social media runs the world. When he hugged you, he hugged you." Brody hugged himself tight to demonstrate. "I never felt out of place, or like the weird gay guy when I was with him. He never made me pretend I liked girls like my agent does. He was openly bisexual, and it made me think I could be myself, my real self, and have a career."

"Did it bother you that he was also sleeping with Octavia?" Newland asked.

"Not really. I knew his preferences before we got together."

Newland checked his notepad. "Rumor has it that Mario was very jealous of Don's other relationships."

Brody sniffed and I handed him a tissue. "Thanks, Waylon." He blew and threw the tissue in a trash can. "You must understand, Don was mesmerizing when he wanted to be. But he and Mario didn't work out and both liked to gamble. Don was up to his eyeballs in debt and not to nice people."

"Interesting. Do you gamble?"

"No. Sheesh. I have enough debt. I'm still paying off Juilliard."

Newland startled. "Julliard. Wow. That's impressive. I didn't know you classical training."

Brody waved the compliment away. "It was great while I was there, but I should have come out to California first instead."

"Why?"

"I dunno. It's just a feeling." Brody shrugged, a listless motion that mirrored his subdued mood. "Maybe I'd have more connections? I've always wanted a movie career. New York schools emphasize plays. I can still recite all of Romeo and Juliet."

"How did you meet Mario?"

"At a house party he hosted. A friend of a friend brought me."

"What would you say your relationship with Mario is like now?"

"Okay. I did spend time at his house a couple of weekends ago. He made a fire in his huge stone fireplace, and we drank wine and talked about the play. It was nice. He gave me advice on what to do next. He has an amazing house in the hills. He owns several acres with lots of trees. It's a massive fire hazard given the lack of rain, but it's gorgeous. I'd love to afford a house like that one day." He scoffed. "But first I have to pay off college."

"Broke, huh?"

"Well, yeah. I live in Los Angeles. I share a two bedroom with three other actors. I couch surfed when I first got here."

"That's nothing to be ashamed of, Brody," I said. "It's tough for everyone when they are starting out. This play could be very good for you."

"If we go on. Don's understudy hasn't shown up for rehearsals the last two days."

"Why not?" I asked.

"He got a hemorrhoid cream commercial." He pretended to hold up a tube of medicine. "When the go hurts, cream it!"

"I don't know what's worse," Newland said. "That tag line or that I know exactly what the packaging looks like."

"That's it," Brody said, touching his nose. "Branding is everything."

Newland left to confer with the two officers. Jones still stood guard, and Murphy was interviewing other cast and crew members. Brody departed with a warning from Newland not to leave the theater.

That left me alone, depressed and anxious. I couldn't help but ask myself what would Hercule Poirot do? He'd piece together the clues, but did we have any clues? I was left with the question, "Why would anyone want to kill Don?"

I mean, stealing the tiara was one thing. It was worth a fortune, although I doubt you could fence it. You'd have to sell it to a collector. But murder? An entirely different kettle of fish.

A cold breeze blew through the room, followed by a musty smell. I stood and whirled in a circle trying to identify the source. I saw nothing but I heard the creak of a door or an old cupboard.

"Who's there?"

No response.

I was hearing the theater ghosts. Every theater had ghosts, and this one was no exception. Many dramatic, passionate actors had traipsed these halls, and I believed that some stuck around after death, far too full of themselves to abandon the stage, even after their time had passed. Many people didn't believe in ghosts, but they also didn't believe in zombies, and yet, here I was.

"Okay, ghosts, enough fooling around. I'm going to sit here and paint. Don't—"

There was a loud thunk and the walls shook. My ghoul paint can flipped and poured Blood Red pigment all over the floor.

"Dammit, dammit, dammit!"

I thought I'd closed that paint can tightly, but the growing puddle belied that thought. I sought a bucket of rags we kept under one of the sinks and just as I stuck my head into the sink to fish around for the pail, the lights went out. All of them. The entire theater sank into darkness, and an eerie howl rose in the air. There was a glimmer of light in the hallway as the backup generator kicked on and emergency wall lights illuminated.

Goosebumps rose on my arms and the back of my neck crawled as a chill passed through me. I crept backward a foot and rose to my full height, holding the pail in my right hand. Another howl, this one closer.

A shadow stood in the studio's doorway, and it was so big I thought it was a yeti, a sasquatch, an abominable snowman—anything but human. If I'd had a heartbeat, it would be hammering out of my chest; as it was, my voice came in a choked whisper.

"Who's there?"

The shadow loomed closer and in terror, I swung the pail as hard as I could. It bounced off the creature's head, who shrieked with surprise. A howl of protest followed as the rags flew hither, thither, and yon.

"Waylon? What the hell are you doing?"

"Erick?"

"Of course it's me! Ouch! What was that?"

"A bucket."

"Why are you slinging buckets?"

The lights returned with a hiss, and I blinked at Erick and Buster, who had a rag on the top of his head. Erick's beard and hair stuck out at all angles, and Buster looked terribly aggrieved.

"Sorry, little buddy," I said to the dog as I removed the wayward rag. Erick rubbed the left side of his face which was puffing up nicely. Even his eye was swelling shut.

"Oh, dear," I said. "I'm so sorry. I freaked out and thought you were a monster. Maybe the killer. You know, you're very tall. How tall are you?"

"Six-five."

"And Buster, wow. Who knew he could howl that loud."

"He got scared when the lights went out." He held his hand to his head. "Can you get me some ice?"

"Sure!" I hopped to it. "Sit down there but be careful of the—"

"Ahhhhhhh!" Erick took a wrong step backward, slipped in the puddle, and fell on the floor. Buster leaped from his arms and managed to jump clear.

"—the paint."

"Wayyyyyyylon!"

"I'm sorry! That's why I was getting the rags."

Erick hauled himself up and took a deep, cleansing breath. "It's fine. I have spare clothes in my car. They're in a red and black gym bag."

He handed me the keys. "It's the green Jeep."

"I'll get right on it. Wait here."

I snatched the keys out of his hand and hurried to the theater door.

"Where do you think you're going?" Newland asked me, hands on his hips.

I tried to explain about Erick and Buster and the paint, but it was a jumble.

"Forget it," Newland said. "Just come right back."

"Got it."

When I returned with the gym bag, Newland was waiting for me.

"What made the lights go out?" I asked him.

"Someone tripped a main breaker. We don't know how or why but everything is working again."

"That's good. I must get these clothes to Erick and clean up the floor."

Newland shook his head. "This place is a zoo."

"Yeah, but it's our zoo, and you're locked in with us."

The cast and crew were all abuzz and everyone gathered on the stage and in the auditorium to chatter about what had happened. Newland and his officers used the opportunity to talk to crew they hadn't interviewed yet.

"What was that bang?" I asked.

"Oh, the new mirror fell off my wall," Octavia said.

"It looked heavy."

"Solid brass. What a poor choice."

I still had the heebie-jeebies. I decided to shake off the creepy vibe by finding Erick, apologizing again, and, if he would let me, petting Buster.

I found them smack in the middle of the stage, shooing people out of the way.

"We're training," Erick said. "Buster needs routine to calm his nerves."

"I'm really sorry about before."

"It's okay." He rubbed his face. "Ever play baseball? You've got quite a swing."

His face was still swollen but his eye was open, and the redness was down. I expected a purple and yellow bruise to develop later. I had a magic face cream I'd give him later to help with that. It was Reborn Luxury Cosmetic's Rescue Remedy, and it had bits of zombie cells in it. Mitzi swore by it, but she didn't know the truth.

Erick placed Buster down in the middle of the stage and issued a command. "Tiara."

Buster trotted off, weaving around people.

"What are you doing?" asked Newland.

"Even though the play is on hold, maybe cancelled forever, Buster likes to train. He's a working dog."

"He's the size of a large squirrel." Newland's voice dripped disbelief.

"So?" Erick drew himself up to his considerable size. "Are you size shaming?"

Newland picked at a cuticle. "No. What is it he is training for?"

146

"Well," Erick said, immediately warming to his subject. "He's the best at playing fetch. I can show him an object, be it a ball, a stick, a frisbee, or in the case of the play, a tiara, and he will find it."

"Wait," Newland said, holding up a hand palm out. "He fetches the tiara?"

"Fetch is a poor use of the word in this specific case. I hand him the tiara backstage, and he carries/drags it out on stage during the last part of the second act. That's the clue to the archaeologist about what is happening. The archaeologist knows the story of the tiara and figures out that the ghost is manipulating circumstances to re-enact her story. That's the big clue that solves the mystery."

"What is Buster looking for now?"

"I have a fake tiara that I use for training. He's retrieving it from shelf I leave it on." Erick frowned. "He should be out by now."

We waited some more.

No Buster.

"Buster!" Erick called. "Come back."

Still no dog.

"I wonder what happened?" Erick's voice trembled with worry. "Buster!"

When the dog still didn't return, Erick tromped off after him, and Newland and I followed. We walked off stage right, through the partially parted black curtains, and Erick stopped at a bookshelf.

"Look. The practice tiara isn't here, but neither is Buster." He scanned the floor. "Buster! Buddy! Where are you?" When the dog didn't appear, he grabbed my arm in a panic. "Oh, no, Waylon. Do you think he got dognapped? Or...or killed by the murderer? Don first, Buster next?" Erick's lower lip trembled as he tried to hold back sobs.

I was more concerned Buster got carried off by a couple of

unusually big stage rats, but I didn't say that. Instead, I patted him on the shoulder. "I'm sure he's around here. Maybe someone offered him a treat."

"You're the only person that gives him treats, Waylon. Everyone else respects his dietary needs." Erick whistled for his pet.

Newland and I scurried around the room, looking under chairs, in between the folds of the curtain, and any other place a small dog might hide.

Erick's calls grew increasingly frantic, and he drew everyone to him.

"What's going on?" Mario asked, flinging his hands out in some kind of supplication. "Can we get no peace?"

Octavia sauntered out arm-in-arm with Brody, which was a new development. I eyed them with suspicion. They'd both been sleeping with Don the Muskrat and now they were besties? Excuse me if I threw up in my mouth a little.

Livvie followed, and as usual, skidded around the corner as if she was on a skateboard, arms flailing. Practiced at this by now, I reached out to steady her. What I was not prepared for, however, was to see the bookshelf shift all on its own and open towards us with a high-pitched squeal. Darkness loomed from the space behind the shelf, except for a small glow that bobbed up and down. The stomp, stomp of footsteps echoed as someone came towards us.

We all jumped back. Octavia screamed, and I yanked Livvie away from the possessed bookshelf. A squeaking sound raised my hackles.

"Oh, my, god," I whispered. "The rats have figured out how to move furniture." I grabbed a nearby broom and held it at the ready.

"What rats?" came a voice I recognized.

Reggie emerged from the blackness, and he held something in his hand.

I scrunched my face at him. "Where did you come from?"

"Remember, the stage is full of back corridors and shortcuts. I was looking for Mario." He took two more steps, and his sneakers squeaked on the old wood floor. Then he checked his watch. "I've been looking for ten minutes."

Okay, I told myself, *the squeaks came from his sneakers and the glow from his watch. Those were not rats with their beady eyes. I'm okay. I'm okay. I'm okay.* I fought to make my breathing even.

No one noticed my distress because Erick poked Reggie's arm and Reggie yanked it away with an offended, "Hey!"

"What's in your hand?" Erick demanded.

"You mean this?" Reggie held up a tiara. "I found it on the bottom shelf and thought maybe we could rescue the show by using this one. The show could go on as planned, and if the show was successful, we'd make enough money to pay back the owner."

"That's my training tiara!" Erick said. "I can't find Buster. Was he in there with you? He was here a minute ago. I sent him to fetch that exact practice tiara and when he couldn't find it, he must have wandered off, searching for it."

Ignoring Erick, Mario shook his head at Reggie. "It's a nice thought, Reggie, but I doubt we're going to make any money, given that we don't have a leading man and his understudy finished the hemorrhoid commercial and immediately got a new one for dandruff shampoo."

"I could take his place."

Octavia laughed, an obnoxious hee-haw that contradicted her glamorous exterior. "You?"

"Yes, me," Reggie said, drawing himself up to his full five-foot-eight. "I know every line."

Mario's voice was gentle. "I'm sure you would be great, Reggie,

149

but we need a big star to make this play work."

"Why is everyone forgetting about my dooooogggg?" Erick wailed. "My baby!"

I raised a hand and everyone looked at me. Newland cleared his throat. "Yes, Waylon?"

"If Reggie had the practice tiara, and it wasn't on the shelf, Baxter couldn't fetch it. Where would he go next?"

"I don't know," Erick said, tugging his hair. We all looked at each other, eyes questioning, but each of us shrugged an "I don't know," and I swore we looked like The Three Stooges doing a baseball schtick.

"Let's spread out and look for him," I said, because what else was there to do? "Erick, do you have any treats?"

He shook his head. "Not on me. I'll go get some."

I waved him off. "Don't bother. I have some in my studio." I pushed past everyone and said, "BRB."

I walked around the side stage and down the steps. I had to walk past all the dressing rooms to make it to my workspace, but I stopped, distracted, as snuffling and small barks echoed throughout the long hallway.

"Buster?"

I followed the yipping to Octavia's dressing room and found Buster barking and scratching at the repaired wall that now held a newly restored mirror.

"Erick!" I yelled. "I found him."

For such a big man, Erick could move fast when he wanted to. He stormed down the steps into the backstage hall and burst into the dressing room. Livvie followed, directly on his tail, her little feet pitter-pattering behind his big clunky ones.

Erick came to a sudden stop and Livvie, being too close, slammed into his back. While she was small, she had a lot of momentum, and the impact hurtled Erick forward until he crashed into the wall. The mirror once again fell, this time cracking into multiple pieces. Erick, in a medal-worthy gymnastics move, scooped his beloved dog up as he plummeted forward, and cradled the small canine to his chest.

Livvie tumbled with him, and all three—giant man, petite woman, and teeny dog—slammed into the poorly patched wall.

Which broke open like an egg.

Buster scrambled through the hole.

"Buster!" Erick called to him while pushing Livvie off and trying to stand. He bled in several places but didn't look badly hurt. Livvie rolled off Erick and cradled her knee, swearing like a sailor.

"Goddammit, that dog! My goddamn knee is tweaked. Motherfucker!"

Erick rolled to his stomach and belly crawled closer to the broken wall. "Buster. Come on, big boy. I need you. Come on out."

A tiny, muffled bark came from the wall and then Buster's itty-bitty head poked out, holding—

The tiara.

He dropped it at Erick's head and sat, tail wagging.

"Is that? Is that the real one?" Livvie asked.

Octavia pushed past me into the dressing room, which was now seriously crowded. "What has that dog done?" She looked down at the sprawling Erick and staggered when she saw what lay on the floor in front of his face.

"The tiara!"

Mario arrived, and he also pushed his way into the dressing room, forcing us all to turn sideways to accommodate the extra bodies. He stared at Buster, the tiara, and Erick, and instead of looking relieved and happy, he went gray.

"Erick," I said. "Can you get up?"

"Yeah." Erick pulled himself to his knees, picked up Buster and the tiara, and stood. I held out my hand for the tiara.

"Look in that hole and see if anything else is there."

"Like what?" he asked.

"Just look."

He pulled the thin drywall out of the way to make more room and, after shooting me a confused glance, shoved his head in the opening.

"Oh, my God," he yelled.

"What?" Octavia asked.

Mario tried to slip past me, but I grabbed his elbow and shook a finger at him. "No, you don't."

"Newland?" I call.

A distant, "Here," came from outside the room. "What did you find?"

"The real tiara and the murder weapon."

"Everyone out of my way!" Newland ordered.

"No!" I hollered back. "Go find Brody."

"It's crazy," Erick said as he stepped through the wall into the hole. "There's a labyrinth back here."

"Those are the tunnels Reggie told us about," I said, elbowing Octavia so I could force Mario into a corner.

I held him in place with my forearm, leaning my weight into it, the tiara in my other hand. "Why?" I asked. "Help me understand."

"He left me for Brody and Octavia. And I was supposed to just sit by and take it?" Mario hissed.

"You mean this whole time you meant to murder Don?"

"Not at first, but he flaunted his new relationships in my face."

"So, you killed him and took the tiara?"

"No!"

"What?"

By this time, Octavia and Livvie were listening in. Octavia hopped up on the makeup counter to make some more room. Erick held Buster from inside the hole in the wall, which he was steadily making bigger by tearing out chunks of drywall.

I glared at Mario. "You just said you killed him."

Mario shook his head. "No. I brought in the axe from home and placed it in the prop room, replacing the fake axe. I wanted Don killed on stage in a violent, public 'accident.'" He wiggled his fingers to place air quotes around the word "accident."

"Besides," he added, "think of the publicity!"

"Oh, we'd be sold out for months!" Octavia cooed from her perch.

"But Don would be dead," Livvie said, as confused and horrified as I was.

Mario tutted. "We'd find someone to replace him. There are a ton of aging leading men out there."

Newland returned, squeezing into the center of the small room with Brody in tow.

"Give me the tiara, Waylon," the detective said, holding out his hand. I gave it to him, and he radioed for one of his men.

"Where's the murder weapon?"

Erick stepped back, sinking into the darkness of the tunnel beyond. "In here. I haven't touched it."

Newland stuck his head inside and as he turned his attention from Brody to the axe, Brody tried to make a run for it, breaking for the door.

Just as I reached out to grab his sleeve, Officer Murphy stepped into the doorway and blocked his path. "No, you don't."

Newland stepped inside the hole, and he talked to Erick, as well as someone else. When he emerged, he wore gloves and carried an axe with a wooden handle. "It's a camping axe good for splitting small logs," he remarked. "We'll get prints off it, unless someone wants to confess."

Erick squeezed out of the hole and now we all stood in the tiny dressing room shoulder-to-shoulder. Behind him, Reggie slipped out of the tunnel into the room, but he was so slight he hardly took up any space. He ducked under Erick's arm, slid past Newland, and pushed his way to Livvie.

"Honey, you okay?" he asked. "What happened?"

Newland lost his patience with being packed in like sardines. "Everybody into Waylon's studio! Now!"

We had more room in my studio, but I warned everyone about the red paint on the floor.

Officer Jones cuffed Mario, who sunk down the wall onto the floor, head hanging. Officer Jones held Brody's arm with a strong grip.

Newland tossed the questioning to me. "Waylon? What have you figured out?"

"Brody told me that he'd gone to Mario's house, and they'd sat by the fire. That's why Mario had an axe."

"Okay, but Mario says he didn't kill Don. He only *planned* to kill Don."

"Right. I think this was all about money."

"Explain."

"I suspect that Don couldn't pass up the chance to steal a $250,000 tiara. He knew it was in the locked cabinet and that Erick had a replica. He most likely saw a chance to steal it and pay off his gambling debts, which Brody told us were extensive."

Everyone looked at Brody, who studied the floor.

Newland motioned for me to continue. "So, what happened?"

"Don tried to steal the tiara. Brody discovered him in the act." I turned to the morose young actor. "You want to tell us what happened next?"

"I didn't mean to kill him!" Brody shouted with a sudden burst of energy. "He was stealing the tiara, and I found him doing it. I wanted the tiara for the same reason he did, to get out of debt. My debts weren't as extensive as his, but still, I'll never get out of my two-bedroom, three-roommate apartment if I don't pay off my student loans."

He seemed to lose all his energy and slumped against the sink ledge. "But Don got to it first and I didn't want him to have it. He got into debt from gambling. It was all his own fault. I got into debt seeking an education. They're totally different reasons."

He petered off and I nudged him.

"You didn't mean to kill him."

"No. I didn't know the axe was real. I thought it was a prop, so I picked it up, heaved it hard and hit him on the head. I thought I'd stun him or knock him out, or something. Can you imagine my surprise when all this blood came flying out? It was disgusting, and it got all over my clothes and shoes."

Newland asked the next question. "What did you do next?"

"I left the tiara where it lay and dropped the axe. Then I peeled off my clothes except for my underwear and fled to my dressing room next door. No one saw me. I shoved the clothes in a plastic bag, wrapped myself in a robe, and—"

Livvie gasped. "And took a shower."

"Right. I was in such a panic I forgot to lock the door."

Newland paced. "Let me get this straight. You," he said, pointing at Mario. "You wanted to kill Don and brought in the murder weapon, but didn't kill him."

Mario nodded.

"And then, you," he said, pointing to Brody, "didn't mean to kill him but did so by accident when you tried to steal the tiara and found Don getting there before you."

Tears streamed down Brody's face.

Octavia spoke up. "How did the murder weapon and tiara get into my wall?"

This one I could answer. "The wall rats."

"What?" Octavia jumped onto the counter and searched the floor for rodents.

"Not real ones, although I thought we had rats because I kept hearing squeaks from within the walls, but it turns out it wasn't rodents at all. It was Reggie."

Reggie threw his hands in the air and sunk into yellow chair. "It's true. I didn't see the murder, but when I couldn't find Mario, I decided to look in on Livvie and see if he was with her. Instead, I found this grisly scene and immediately knew Livvie would be blamed for it."

Newland stared at him, hands on his hips. "You didn't think to call the police?"

Reggie squirmed. "I did, but I was worried for Livvie."

"What did you do then?" Octavia asked, chin on her fist, fascinated by this tale. She looked as if she was watching a who-dun-it dinner show.

"I brought them into the tunnel system, but then I tripped holding the heavy axe and knocked a hole in your wall, Octavia. You didn't notice because I patched it with drywall and hung a mirror there. You never cleaned your dressing room, and I did all the picking up, so I was confident you'd never notice the change or care."

"No," Octavia said. "I just liked the mirror."

He rolled his shoulders as if he could lessen the stress of the moment. "And I was right to worry because you, Octavia..." He said this with so much malice it shocked me. "You, Octavia, threw Livvie under the bus by telling the detective about how Don had yelled at her, never mind that you knew full well that Don was over his pique in a minute."

I thought about how I'd heard scuffling behind the wall when Newland interviewed Octavia. That had been Reggie.

Reggie blew out a frustrated breath. "I was going to move the tiara and the axe later but there was all this hubbub on stage about Buster going missing, and I knew I'd have to wait. I never expected that meddling dog to find the real tiara."

Erick stroked Buster and whispered, "You are such a good dog."

Newland motioned for the cops to arrest all three men. Livvie jumped in front of Reggie. "No. You can't. He didn't kill anyone. He was trying to protect me."

"Sorry, Miss Sunshine," Newland said. "He interfered with a

murder investigation and tampered with evidence. But you can bail him out later."

Reggie kissed Livvie even as his hands were handcuffed behind his back. "Don't worry, doll. We'll figure it out."

Livvie cried as the officers took him away. Brody and Mario stumbled out, both with hangdog expressions. I figured the play was toast so I'd better clean up my things and go home. Sorya wasn't going to believe this.

Don murdered. The director, the co-star, and the assistant to the deputy stage manager all implicated in the crime. Someone, I thought, should write a play about it.

7734

By Jason Roach

1

There wasn't much time to converse after the plane landed at JFK airport. Once given the all-clear, passengers immediately exited the aircraft in a single-filed fashion - like pigs lining up to be slaughtered. Greg and John were waiting outside the jetway when the others emerged. No one bothered to look at their tickets to see where to go next. John immediately took charge, leading the way to the next gate. Greg hung back to check on Reid as Ethan stayed close to John.

"Hey, buddy. How you holding up?" He said, placing his arm over Reid's shoulder.

"I'm ok," Reid quietly replied. "Thanks for checking. Ethan gave me some kind of sedative. Truth be told, I think it was a painkiller of some sort cause I can't feel a damn thing. I passed out before we even took off. Slept through the whole flight and still a bit groggy, though."

"Damn, man. That must have been some good stuff," Greg remarked.

"Ha! I'm just a lightweight, but I'm glad we don't have to go back through security cause they would truly think I was high as a kite." Reid wobbled a little while trying to walk with Greg's weight hanging on him.

"Nah! It's New York City! I'm sure they are used to people being on all kinds of medications when flying," Greg stated. "But, hey, on a brighter note, at least we all get to sit in the same row this time. First class to

Switzerland was even too much for John's budget. It will be great to catch up with you. That is, if you're not passed out again."

"I may be, but we've got the whole week and the train ride... where we will be on solid ground and can't fall out of the sky for no apparent reason." Reid chuckled as he tried to make a joke that he immediately realized wasn't funny at all.

"People fly all the time. You're gonna be just fine," Greg comforted.

"Yeah, I've done my research. I've basically taken an online crash course on survival techniques for just about any type of disaster you could possibly imagine," Reid shared. "Though I hope I'll never get the chance to use any of it."

Greg rubbed his hand over Reid's back, trying to assure him everything would be ok. There were times when Reid's anxiety got the best of him, but if there was anyone who would be able to save them in a disaster, it would be him.

"Everyone's so eager to fly across the pond, I see," Greg said as the four of them reached the gate desk. John turned to the group, ushering them into a corner next to the jetway.

"They're gonna start boarding soon, so there is no point in sitting down and getting comfortable," he explained. "Let's figure out the seating. The Airbus has three rows of three. One of us is going to have to sit across from the others."

Greg quickly spoke up. "Why don't you volunteer us as tribute? It will give you some space."

"That didn't take much thought," John murmured under his breath, but everyone seemed to ignore the tension building between the two. "So, we'll have Ethan, Reid, and Greg in one row, then I'll sit in the seat across from you all," he continued. "Oh, let's make sure the snacks are overhead so we can get to them easily. Ethan, do you think you can handle that?"

"Sure thing!" Ethan replied.

"Here we go," Greg mumbled to Reid. "He's gonna get on another one of his power trips again."

John again mumbled something under his breath, but Greg couldn't make out what it was. At least he wouldn't have to sit beside him for nearly eight hours and listen to him gripe and complain as he'd done on the previous flight. Truth be told, he was more excited about sitting next to Reid than the person who was supposed to be the love of his life. There was something about Reid that intrigued him, though he couldn't quite put his finger on it.

The announcement echoed over the loudspeakers, saying that Flight 7734 was ready for boarding, and Greg snapped out of his internal self-evaluation. He extended the handle on his carry-on, joined the cluster of others, and proceeded towards the jetway. He'd once again found himself inside his own head, justifying all the reasons John was the way he was, though it didn't seem to be working in the grand scheme of things.

Boarding was smooth, and they quickly found their row parallel to the wing. They placed their carry-ons overhead. Greg watched John roll his eyes as Ethan struggled to get the snack carry-on into the overhead compartments. It was only a backpack and shouldn't have been too hard to squeeze in there, but not everyone can do everything flawlessly like John can, and Greg told himself that's completely okay.

Taking their seats, Ethan slid in first to grab the window seat, then Reid and Greg. In the adjacent aisle, John took the seat across from them. He immediately reclined the seat and buried his head in his hat. Maybe it was nothing, or perhaps it was him trying to "Stick it to him" for suggesting they be the couple to split the aisle. Who knew? There was no telling with him, but Greg pulled his mind of conglomerated thoughts together and buckled in for the long haul.

"Good evening, passengers," the pilot spoke over the intercom. "Thank you for joining us on Airbus 340 Flight 7734 from New York City to Zurich, Switzerland. The time is now approximately 10:00 pm— 4:00 am in Zurich. We have a roughly eight-hour flight from here to Zurich, and we should arrive around noon Central European Time. It is snowing heavily in Zurich right now, which will cause some extreme winter weather conditions towards the end of our flight path tonight, so please pay attention to the fasten seatbelt sign. Everything should be fine, though, a little turbulence here and there should be about it. We want to thank you again for flying with us. Sit back and enjoy the flight."

Immediately following the message from the captain, a flight attendant stood at the front of the economy section, going over safety protocols. Greg looked down to see Reid clenching the armrest at the mention of turbulence and extreme weather, and he placed a hand over Reid's to try and calm his nerves.

"You'll be fine, I promise," he reassured. "Ethan and I will be right beside you the whole time."

"Unless the tail falls off, and it sucks you out the back of the plane," Reid replied with another one of his not-so-funny jokes. "No… really. There are so many things that can happen in extreme winter conditions. I've studied them all: power outages, icy runways and railroad tracks, blizzards, avalanches, below freezing temps… I mean, the list could—"

"Now you're being paranoid. Here!" Ethan interrupted. Reaching into his pocket, he pulled out two little blue football-shaped pills. "When they come around with the trolley, get some water and take this."

"Ethan! What are you giving him?" Greg asked. "Can he even mix this with what you gave him before?"

"It's just a little Xanax. He'll be fine," Ethan responded.

"Don't I get a say in this?" Reid spoke up. "Maybe I'd like to be coherent during this flight. No matter how scared shitless I am."

"Here. Just hold onto it." Ethan stuck the pill in Reid's hand. "You'll have it for when you need it. I'm going to get some rest during the overnight flight."

The two of them watched as Ethan popped the other blue football into his mouth, swallowed, and snuggled up against the window.

"Damn, I wish I could be like that. Not a care in the world," Reid said, tucking the little blue pill into his pocket for safekeeping.

"Don't we all," Greg agreed. "I can't, in good faith, allow myself to be that way. If something's gonna hit me in the face, I'd prefer to be coherent and awake enough to see it coming."

"Same." The plane gave a jolt as it reversed from the airport and started its way down the tarmac, and Reid let out a. "Oh, boy. Here we go."

The cabin bounced as the wheels hit every possible pothole on the runway. Greg pressed his head against the seat and closed his eyes, trying to stabilize the whiplash in his neck from the roughness. Then, all of a sudden, he felt someone's hand land on top of his and squeeze tightly. He opened his eyes wide enough to see Reid's hand clenched to his.

Things started to get much smoother as the plane lifted into the air.

Reid's grip loosened, allowing the circulation to flow back through Greg's hand. After a few minutes in the air, though, things became a bit more worrisome. There was a little bit of vibration, and the cabin started to jerk violently. Passengers began to scream. Even Greg found himself letting out a "Fuck me!" as he braced in his chair. Reid was digging to find the Xanax. Just as he'd pulled it out of his pocket, the plane dropped suddenly, and the pill hit the floor, rolling under the seat. Greg's stomach dropped as the plane continued to jolt. It felt like he was on the steep decline of a rollercoaster. Nausea set in, and he grabbed Reid's hand, hoping to calm both of their nerves. John, however, seemed to be unphased by what was going on. He and Ethan both.

Beep! "Attention, passengers. This is your captain speaking. Our apologies for the unexpected early turbulence. We should be through the worst of it for a good while. Though I expect things to stay a little bumpy along the way. Everything will start to smooth on out shortly. We will leave the seatbelt signs on throughout most of our flight. Please try to relax and have a great time aboard Airbus 340 Flight 7734."

"Jesus Christ! That scared the shit out of me," Reid whispered. "And I lost my damn pill!"

"Yeah, same here, man!" Greg looked around on the floor for the pill, but it was nowhere to be found. "I don't see it anywhere. Not sure you'd want it after it's been on this nasty-ass floor anyways."

"The five-second rule still counts," Reid replied. "Even if it is in an airplane."

Greg turned to John, tapping his arm to get his attention. "You okay?"

"Yeah, I'm fine. Why?" John snapped as if he were being bothered. "It was just a little turbulence. Nothing to be worried about. Now, let me rest."

"Okay…" Greg leaned back in his seat, letting out a sigh. "Might be about time for the attendants to put the alcohol on heavy rotation."

"No shit!" Reid immediately followed. "I need something strong to relax me after that."

"I'll see if I can't flag one down and get us both something to drink," Greg said, waving his hand to get the flight attendant's attention.

"Can I help you, sir?" the attendant asked.

"Is it possible we could get my friend and me something to drink? Something a little stronger than a soda?" Greg asked. "You see, he's just really nervous about flying."

"Sure. Sure. What would he…?" the attendant said.

"A rum and Coke, please," Reid jitterily interrupted.

"Sure thing. I'll be right back. Anything for you, sir?" the attendant asked.

"I'll have the same. Thank you," Greg responded.

A few minutes later, the attendant returned with two cans of Coke, four miniature bottles of rum, two small ice-filled plastic cups, and a hand-held card reader for payment. Greg glanced at the total— nearly forty dollars— before inserting his card. John was gonna have a shit fit when the charge came out of their bank account, but if it helped calm the nerves, that's all he cared about. Act now, and ask for forgiveness later. He'd deal with the argument later. Pouring and mixing the drinks proved to be a bit challenging, but once all was said and done, he passed one to Reid and held his up in the air in a toast. Quoting his version of his favorite Bette Davis line, he said, "Fasten your seat belts, Reid. This plane is going to be a bumpy ride."

2

Ding! "Attention passengers. We've started our descent into Zurich. The weather is quite heavy here. It will make the landing a bit bumpy, but nothing to worry about. The time is currently 11:31 AM Central European Time, and we should be docked by 11:57 AM, getting you there a few minutes earlier than planned. Please remain seated while we descend, and thank you for choosing American Airlines Airbus 340 flight 7734 for your travels."

The captain's voice over the intercom awakened Greg enough to comprehend what had been said, but he was still in a daze from the exorbitantly potent amounts of alcohol. He opened his eyes, squinting against the brightness of the cabin lights, to find himself snuggling up to Reid. The rum and Cokes must have done their job because he barely remembered falling asleep, let alone getting all warm and cozy with someone else's man. He nudged Reid enough for him to shift to the other side of the seat, landing on Ethan's shoulder, who was also still passed out against the window. He glanced over at John, who hadn't appeared to move the whole flight— still under his hat.

Greg stretched to his left, trying not to wake the two guys between him and the window. Ethan mumbled something, adjusting in his seat, giving him access to raise the visor covering the porthole. He'd hoped the view would be spectacular, like a Thomas Kinkade painting of snow-covered Alps, but all he could see was a grayish-white hue. Even with the plane gradually lowering its altitude, the ground below was lost to the thick fog, nimbostratus clouds, and the pelting of heavy snow.

Ding! Ding! The passengers waited for a new message from their captain, but nothing followed. Greg noticed the flight attendants rushing towards the front of the plane. Something didn't feel right. He leaned over in his seat to see what all the commotion was about.

"Excuse me, sir!" one of them urgently said as they swiftly brushed past him.

He jolted back into the upright position of his seat to keep from a full-on collision with the attendant.

"Something's wrong…" He paused, leaning back out into the aisle once it was clear.

"What? What do you mean something's wrong?" Reid started to question as he awoke.

"Great! Now look what you've done, Greg. Can't we just land this thing and get off so we don't have to deal with his hysteria?" Ethan groggily noted, as if Greg's comment was solely responsible for sending Reid into another tailspin of worry.

"No. Really. Why are they all rushing to the cockpit?" Greg questioned.

"Just chill out," He heard John say from across the aisle. "It's probably something related to landing protocols. Maybe an end-of-flight meeting or something. There's no need to get everyone else in a panic."

"You're probably right. That's all it is," Greg said, trying to calm himself down. If he could succeed at that, Reid might calm down as well. But it wasn't long before a loud sound of metal screeching against metal came from below and reverberated through the aircraft. The entire plane shook. Terrified screams echoed through the fuselage, and passengers trembled in fear as they gripped onto the person next to them. As the plane continued rock, Reid let out a petrified sound—

"Oh, God, get me the fuck out of here!"

"Okay! Now you see! What was that?" Greg's panic kicked in, which, as expected, gave Reid an even more reason to get worked up.

"Oh my God! We're gonna crash! I knew—" Reid panicked.

"We're not going to crash! Just shut up and listen to what they have to say." Ethan snapped and handed him another pill. "Here, take this."

"Stop! Stop drugging him every time something is wrong." Greg yelled over the roar of the panicked crowd.

"Then you deal with his crazy shit cause I'm about sick of it!" Ethan turned towards the window, disassociating himself from the situation.

Ding! "Attention, passengers. Once again, this is your captain with a little bit of news. Now, I want you all to remain calm as we have the situation under control, but there has been a slight issue with the front landing gear. We will brace for the possibility of an emergency landing. Please stay seated and follow the flight attendants' instructions as they make their way back to their sections."

"Oh my God! We're gonna crash! We're gonna fucking cra—" Reid panicked.

"I can't with this shit. Just take the God damn pill." Ethan barked.

A rumble of panic filled the entire cabin as fear of the unknown set in. Someone in front of them clenched the cross hanging around their neck and started reciting the Lord's prayer. Others were grabbing their loved ones, tears pouring down their faces. Screams accompanied each turbulent bounce of the plane as if it were the end.

"Everyone, please! Please settle down and listen," a flight attendant yelled over the intercom, trying to regain control of the situation. "Please listen to the other flight attendants as they come around. At this time, please stow all personal belongings under your seat, fasten your seat belts, and get into the crash position— leaning forward, hands over your head."

"Oh shit! This is real," Ethan said, his own nerves starting to get worked up. He struggled to get his backpack underneath the chair. A moment later, a flight attendant reached between the three of them, taking his back. "Wait! That's my bag! Give that back!"

"Sir, if it won't fit below your seat, we'll need to put it overhead. It will be right up here if we land safely," the attendant said, slamming the overhead compartment.

"Safely? What the fu—" Reid yelled.

"If?" Greg chimed in.

Ding! "Listen up everyone! Get into crash position NOW! Lean forward! Heads down! Hands over your head! BRACE! BRACE! BRACE!"

Greg tightened his seatbelt once more for safe measure, his hands shaking in fear with every movement. The plane shook in the air like it was going to fall apart with each vibration. As the three of them leaned over and covered their heads, Greg's mind ran with questions. *What was going on? Were they really going to crash? Was it really going to end this way? How far were they from the ground?*

He rose up and peered around the seat to see what was going on. The flight attendants were scurrying around, assisting the other passengers and quickly working to get everything secured. It wasn't long, though, before one of them brushed past him, yelling "Heads down, sir!" and he felt the palm of their hand force him back into he crash position.

"BRACE! BRACE! BRACE!"

The plane suddenly made a hard right upturn, and everything left unsecured shifted. Petrified screams could be heard coming from all directions inside the fuselage. A trolley filled with snacks and drinks broke free and nearly fell over. One of the flight attendants quickly stepped into action, keeping it from crashing into one of the passengers.

Ding! "Attention passengers. You know who I am by now. Apologies for that sharp turn back there. According to the tower, they have cleared space for us on the tarmac with emergency response. We are preparing for our final descent. Cabin crew, prepare for landing. Good luck to us all, and God bless."

"BRACE! BRACE! BRACE!"

"God bless? The blessing would've been for the landing gear to work in the first fucking place. And would they stop fucking screaming! We get it!" Greg mumbled aloud as he leaned forward, tucked his chin to his chest, and placed his hands over his head— his elbows rubbing against Reid's. The rumbles of people around him saying their *I love yous* poured out like it was the last time they'd ever get to say it. He glanced to his right. Beside them, the top of John's hat was barely visible, his fingers tightly intertwined over his head. He felt so far away, yet so close. If only he could reach out and touch him one last time.

It's crazy the things your mind will process when faced with death. They say your life flashes before your eyes, but that didn't seem to be the case for Greg. Instead, the things he'd never get to finish, the things he'd never get to start, the things he'd never get to achieve filled his mind. His head turned and locked eyes with Reid, and despite the safety protocols they were supposed to be following, the two immediately grabbed each other's hands in a death grip.

"I don't wanna die. I don't wanna die."

Reid sobbed over and over as the plane wobbled back and forth in the air just before the back landing gears touched the ground. There was a hard bounce, jolting the entire fuselage before lifting back into the air. Everyone screamed. The second attempt felt more successful as they could feel the vibration from the wheels churning across the runway. Now, the moment of truth. Would the pilot lower the nose without the gear failing or plunge the nose into the ground? The passengers of flight 7734— strapped to their seats and their heads folded into their laps— sat dreadfully awaiting their fate.

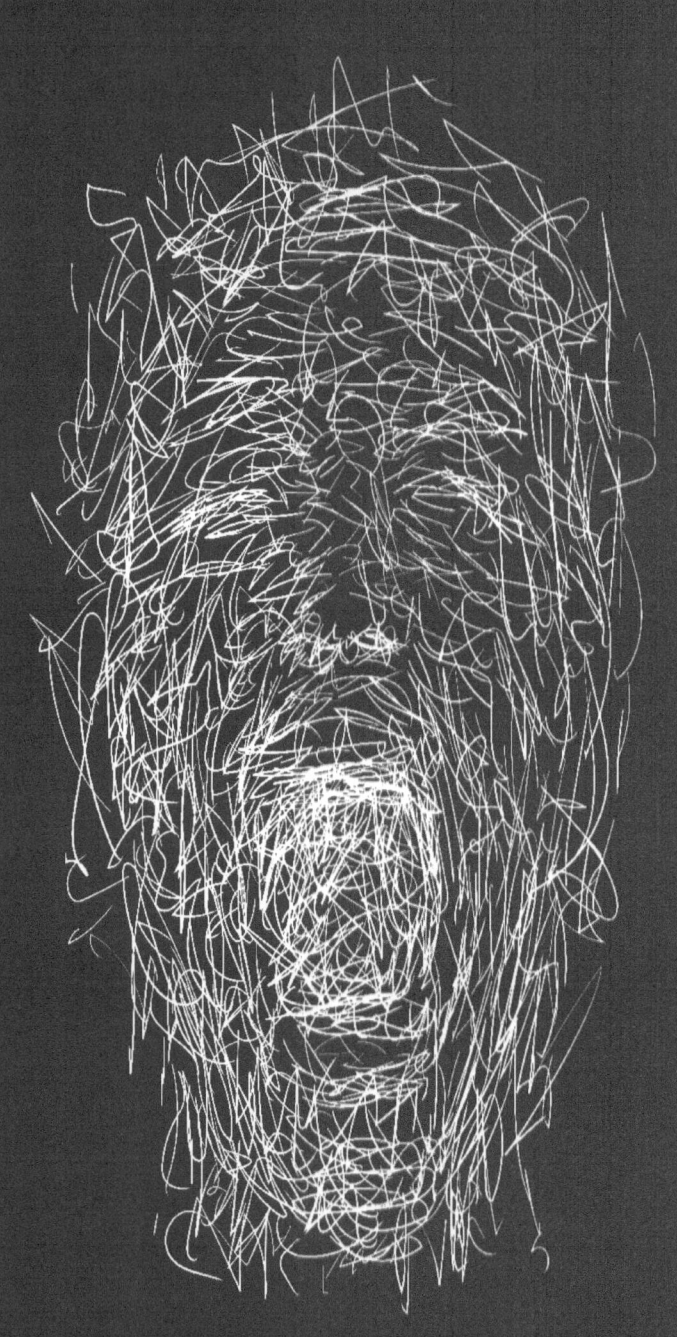

3

In the blink of an eye, things took a turn. The plane was no longer shaking, the cabin lights weren't flashing, and the people weren't screaming. In the sudden silence, it was as if he'd lost all hearing. Greg opened his eyes and looked around. Everyone was still hunched over as though they were frozen in time. *Was he dead? Were they all dead? Was he stuck in a never-ending warp destined to spend eternity on this God-forsaken plane?*

Ding!

"Well, folks, this is once again your captain speaking. Looks like we made it! Our sincerest apologies for the scares, and a big thanks to our cabin crew and the professionals on the ground at Zurich Airport. We'll be docking in just a moment, and everyone will be free to go about their day. We wish you the best from American Airlines, and thank you for flying Airbus 340 Flight 7734."

"What?" Reid questioned, looking around. "We made it? Oh, thank God."

The sound of Reid's voice brought him back into reality, and Greg shook off his premonitions of death and tried to pull himself together.

"No, thank the pilot as you get off the plane," Ethan said.

"Either way, I'm ready to get off this damn aircraft," Greg said. "At least the train will be on the ground."

"Yeah, the ground. That's much safer, for sure," Ethan chimed in from across the way.

"Don't be so sure about that," Reid whispered to himself.

Even though they were all eager to get off the plane, John had the bright idea of letting everyone else get past them before trying to pull all carry-ons out from overhead while people were trudging to get past them. It did make them the remaining few to get off the plane, but that was fine. They still had to go through customs, get to the baggage claim for the rest of their luggage, and figure out the transit system to get to their destination. As they exited, each one thanked the pilot who was standing at the door as they trudged by. Reid paused as he was walking out.

"Is there any other way for us to get back other than flying?" He asked the pilot.

"I'm afraid not, sir," The pilot responded. "But I promise we'll take good care of you on your way back."

"What about a boat?" Reid suggested, trying to find any other solution rather than gettting back on another airplane.

"Then you'd just sink like the Titanic," Ethan quipped. "Now, move along so we can get on with it."

"Ethan, you're such an ass sometimes," Greg snapped at him. "You could be a little more compassionate and understanding. If you don't wanna deal with him freakin' out, stop antagonizing him all the damn time."

An awkward silence filled the group as they all glanced up at the captain, then dropped their heads in embarrassment as they hustled out of the jetway.

The Zurich Flughafen train station was located directly below the Airport Centre, which made it easily accessible from the baggage claims. The platform had a futuristic feel to it. Blue and purple-hued lights hung from the ceiling as if the train station had just transformed into a nightclub. The walls and overhead screens were designed to match this aesthetic. Railways lined each side of the curved platform for trains going in and out of the station.

From here, they would catch the next train out— the first stop would be in Bern, then on to Zurmatt. The train ride would take them through the center of Switzerland, where charming towns and stunning landscapes sit at the heart of this beautiful country. It's what the whole vacation was for— to see this gorgeous beauty with the naked eye. What they didn't plan for was the winter storm of the century choosing to pass through during their trip. One part of their journey had already been plagued with troubles due to the storm, and as they sat waiting for the next part to begin, they all hoped that this one would be more fortunate.

The adrenaline had drained. The lack of a good night's sleep and a touch of jet lag was already catching up to them, and everyone was feeling somewhat lethargic. Greg glanced up at the television screens while he sat snuggled up with his oversized coat. A rather sexy young man in a suit stood in front of a weather map on one of the overhead screens. His hands gestured over the Switzerland map, which was covered in multiple shades of dark blue indicating heavy amounts of snow either had or was expected to be fallen. A red banner with white German lettering ran across the bottom of the screen. Unfortunately, the only Bernese German he'd managed to learn in preparation for the trip was how to say hello. Other than recognizing a few names of towns he'd read about in brochures, and roughly how many meters of snow had fallen, he had no clue what else was being said.

The excitement of the train entering the station perked everyone up as the next part of their journey began. The group patiently waited for others to exit the train before entering the long tube-like space bullet. They entered single file, depositing their luggage onto the holding racks by the doors before taking a seat in the available double-seating on each side of the train. Unlike the plane, each couple sat together. The open picture windows provided an awe-inspiring yet snow-covered view of the city as the train pulled out of the station and into the city proper.

"Man! This is going to be amazing!" Greg said. "Aren't you excited? I can't wait till we get into the mountains."

"Yeah, it's gonna be nice," John replied, reclining his seat and pulling his hat down over his eyes."

"Really?" Greg sat up, turning to face him. "Look, if you're not gonna pay attention, will you at least switch seats with me so I can sit by the window? We've only got about a three-and-a-half hour ride…"

"And that's three-and-a-half hours I'm gonna catch up on some rest, considering I lost most of it because someone can't land a plane without a scene." John interrupted. "Now, if you're not going to let me rest, get over here so you can see, and I can sleep."

Greg stood up and moved into the seat next to the window as John slid underneath him.

"Shit!" he whispered, as he fell back into the reclined seat.

John chuckled a bit saying, "That's what you get."

"Don't be an ass," Greg quipped back. "You know this trip could be the end of us if you don't stop treating me like shit."

"You wouldn't dare leave me. You can't afford it. Now stop playing around, watch your window scenery, and let me rest." John buried himself back into his hat.

He glanced back between the two seats, checking on the others who were off in their own little worlds, or just ignoring the fact of John being John— a complete and utter asshole. Either way, as he'd always done, he'd try to make the best of it. At least he had his window seat with a view to die for.

He folded his winter coat up as a pillow, placing it against the window before resting his head against the glass. The grayish sky, snow-covered grounds and buildings, along with the heavy flakes falling from the clouds created a near whiteout. However, it blended perfectly with the gorgeous medieval architecture peeking out from underneath. It reminded him of a spectacular, picturesque landscape painting.

The outlines of the mountains could barely be made out in the distance. At some point, the train would be passing through them, powering on, despite the weather outside. If they were still in the States, all of North Carolina would've been shut down, roads salted just enough to melt, then freeze, and grocery stores devoid of bread and milk. It was interesting to see how other countries handled weather, even those more accustomed to the heavy poundings of snow in the wintertime.

The time passed by even quicker than he'd expected. Before he knew it the train had exited the mountainous area and was hurling towards the city of Bern. The weather had lightened up a bit in the area, and things were easier to see. The river Aare was covered entirely in a thick layer of ice as they crossed the bridge into the center city. Many of the older buildings were covered with graffiti, which saddened him a bit. *If these stoned walls could talk,* he thought.

The train pulled into the station, coming to a complete stop, allowing those traveling to the city to depart and others to board. Greg had forgotten about the short layover in Bern, but the roughly thirty minutes gave him a chance to observe the locals, though the people he could see turned out to be mostly tourists who were lost and trying to find their way. In some sense, he could totally relate. His brain pondered how he would navigate being in an unknown city if he were here alone. His sense of direction wasn't the greatest, and if he'd ever gotten lost, the only thing he knew from Boy Scouts was to look for the North Star. Supposedly the brightest star in the sky, it didn't do any good if his ungodly vision prescription and astigmatism caused every star to appear the brightest. And what if it were daylight? He pictured himself lost in the woods, staring up at the sun through the over-towering trees, trying to figure out which direction to go. He'd be useless. Greg's daydream came to a jolting end when the train thrust into reverse and began exiting the station. He knew at least from looking at a map they would be heading south, continuing toward their destination. John was still passed out, oblivious to the fact they had even stopped.

Zermatt was only another hour and a half away, and soon they'd be checking into their hotel. While he loved the traveling and the scenery, it was definitely time for a nap, though he'd never admit that to John. He took a quick glance behind to see what the others were doing. They were all passed out. Behind them, Reid was against the window, and Ethan hunched over on the aisle-side armrest. *Oh, well… their loss*, he thought, turning to glare out at the snow-covered mountains, vineyards, and countryside; his breath leaving little patches of fog on the window as he exhaled.

The train whistle sounded to signal the station approaching, and Greg's eyes popped open. Even he'd drifted off to sleep at some point. The last thing he remembered was looking out over the ice-covered Gornera River that'd followed them most of the way down into Zermatt. He observed the commotion of everyone moving around on the train, gathering their luggage and whatnot, before the train eased into the station. In usual fashion, John must have already ordered everyone in the group to stay seated till the last minute, but then he realized John was nowhere to be found. He poked his head between the headrests.

"Where's John?" he asked the guys behind him.

"Oh, he got up a little bit ago and said he was going to wander the train," Reid replied. "Not really like him though, considering he told all of us to stay seated as he walked off."

"Yeah, that's John for ya," Ethan chimed in from two rows back. "Maybe he went to the restroom. God knows I could piss."

"That's actually not a bad idea. I think I'll do the same before we get off." Greg laid his coat on the empty seat next to him and headed towards the door with a black sticker label on it marked "WC". The light above the door was lit up red to indicate it was in use. As he approached, a younger guy, slender and quite attractive, exited the bathroom. Shortly after, John appeared from the same door, flashing a quick smile as he walked past Greg. It wasn't until he'd entered the tightly spaced, one-toilet bathroom that he realized what'd just happened.

"Really? Here? In the goddamn train?" he said aloud, shaking his head. He'd gotten used to John's extramarital affairs over the years and turned a blind eye when they became public knowledge, but this was supposed to be their vacation. Their time together. Ever since this trip had started, he'd been nothing but an asshole, and now this! *No wonder he told everyone to stay in their seats. He'd slipped away to play while I was asleep.* Well, that was it. Enough was enough. So much for the happy vacation. He'd do his best to remain calm in front of the others, but the next time they were alone, well, he'd just better be ready. War was coming.

4

Greg bottled his anger as he took in the beauty of the hotel. He knew they'd splurged on accommodations, but he didn't expect such elegance. The outside was nothing compared to what they were standing in, though that could have been due to them barely being able to see with the snow pelting them in the face. The inside was the sheer example of sophistication. He was going to make sure he took every advantage of this he could. After all, he'd probably never get to stay in a place like this again.

"Isn't it gorgeous?" Reid asked, coming up from behind and placing his arm around Greg's shoulder.

"Yeah, I can't believe it. It's like walking into heaven," Greg replied.

"If there's one thing I can do, it's find a damn good place to stay," Reid boasted. "Our rooms are supposed to have a perfect view of the Matterhorn. You know, we saw it from the train on the way in. It's known to be the world's most dangerous mountain."

"Oh, that's awesome! Think we'll still be able to see it in all this snow?" Greg asked.

"I overheard someone going outside say it's supposed to clear off overnight, which will be perfect for the Glacier Express tomorrow!" Reid answered.

"How was the train ride with Ethan?" Greg posed a question he probably already knew the answer to.

"Eh, the usual. 'Here, take this. It will knock you out.' I'm so used to it by now, I forget how often it happens. Truth be told, I'm still a little shaken up from the plane. I hope nothing happens while we're on the Glacial Express. I really like to enjoy that one." Reid said, letting the excitement he'd once had drain from his face.

"Yeah, me too actually, among other things." Greg sympathized. "At least the trains on the ground. What could possibly go wrong out there?"

The reassurance of ground travel perked Reid back up. "But guess what! We're gonna have a blast this week. Look at this amazing place! It's gonna make everything okay. At least for the time being."

"Damn, right it is," Greg said, watching Ethan stride over from the reception desk.

Ethan walked up to make a grand entrance to the conversation. "What y'all over here talking about?"

"Oh, nothing. Just admiring the beauty of this place," Reid said. Proud of himself yet again for landing them the most magnificent hotel.

"Well, you may have found it on Google, but I did all the work getting it booked," Ethan let out an evil laugh.

"Yeah, yeah… that's just the logistics." Reid flashed a smile.

"When do we get our rooms?" Greg asked. "I'm dying to see what the rest of this place looks like."

"And for a hot shower," Reid added.

"John has your room keys," Ethan replied. "Reid, here's yours. Now quit star-gazing over here and come on. After all that travelin', I need something to eat."

"Yes, we know you are not yourself when you haven't eaten," Reid quipped. "Do you need a Snickers?"

He flashed them the "Go to Hell" look they always expected to get whenever he disapproved of their teasing. "Come on, children." He pivoted and walked back over to John, leaving the two of them alone again.

"Hey, thanks for checking in on me." Reid's free hand took one of Greg's. "You know we both deserve a chance at something better."

Greg watched him turn and walk back to Ethan, letting his hand slowly slide out of his. "No problem," he muttered, then walked up to John. "Can I have my room key?"

John handed him the key without a word. Greg grabbed his snow-soaked luggage and strolled off to find their room. The rest of the gang followed suit, agreeing to meet back down in the hotel restaurant in two hours for a luxurious dinner. The large rectangular room was filled with a king-size bed, armoire, and multiple other amenities and led to a balcony overlooking the city. He snuck a quick glance to see if what Reid had said about seeing the Matterhorn was true. Sure enough, there it was. Still visible through all gray skies and snow. No wonder it was one of the top iconic mountains in Europe.

While he could never tire of the view, Greg turned around to see the rest of the room. He decided it would be the perfect time to go ahead and shower, getting the whole experience of the lavish bathroom. With a thrust, the suitcase landed on a nearby chair. He was pleased to find that while the exterior of the luggage had taken on water, the contents inside remained relatively dry. Grabbing his toiletries, he mentioned to John he was going to shower, but there was no acknowledgement he'd even spoken.

After about thirty minutes of sheer relaxation in the tub, the water had started to cool. He finished washing up and got out, unfolding the parka-shaped towel, patting himself dry, then wrapping the towel around his waist. When he exited the bathroom, he found John lying on the bed, nearly asleep, and his anger unbottled.

"Really?" he asked. "Have you not had enough sleep? Or did your extracurricular activities on the train exhaust all the rest you've had up until that point?"

He dropped the towel, fishing through his suitcase for his boxer briefs.

"I don't know what you're talking about," John snidely replied. "I'm on vacation. I'm here to rest and get away from the hustle and bustle of life. Just let me do that. Lord knows the plane ride from hell didn't let me."

"Whatever. You're not going to ruin this trip for me. I wish I'd just come alone. I don't even want you here right now!" Greg's voice rose as he slid on a pair of pants. "If you think I'm going to sit back and watch you parade your junk all over Switzerland, you've got another thing coming. You don't think our friends know what's going on? You don't think they noticed you disappeared to the back of a train? You don't think they see what it does to me on the inside I…"

"Are you done?" John interrupted. "These walls are old and probably paper-thin. Everyone's going to know our business if you keep yelling. You're just on edge because of the plane. Why don't you go hit up Ethan for one of his little pills? They work great for Reid, keeping his mouth shut. You know, truthfully, I liked him better when he was Reese. He was meeker and more tolerable then. That…"

"Really?… Really? You're going to be a bigot on this trip, too? Why would you say that? I swear, it seems like I don't even know who you are anymore. That is my friend. I don't go around talking shit about all your little fuck buddies, so just shut the fuck up, John! And for your information, I'm not on edge because of the plane. I'm on edge because of you!"

Greg pulled a hoodie over his t-shirt and walked towards the room door.

"What is your issue? I was just making a joke. Where are you going?" John interrogated.

"My issue is you! I'm tired of fighting to keep this marriage together when all you do fuck around, stay angry at the world all the time, and tear down good decent people who deserve some damn respect in this world. And if you must know, I'm going downstairs to get away from you. If you decide to come to dinner, be sure to lose that 'I'm better than you' condescending attitude."

Greg swung the door open and walked out, slamming it behind him. As it closed, he could hear John whining, "But you didn't kiss me." *Fuck that. If he wants a kiss, he can kiss my ass.*

The hotel lobby was quiet this afternoon with the occasional newcomer checking in. The weather had tapered off, leaving the overhead gray gloom to dim towards nightfall. Greg sat in one of the leather chairs by the fireplace, listening to it crackle and watching the screen above the mantle as it showed the local news. Another red bar with the words "Lawine am Piz Medel" was running across the bottom of the screen. He got distracted from it when another guest walked up and asked to join him. The two of them sat in silence, watching the screen.

"Oh shit!" He heard her say as her attention fixated on the news anchor.

"What's wrong?" He asked. "I can't speak German, so I have no clue what they are saying."

"This can't be good," she said. "Those poor people."

"What? What is it?"

It only took one word for his stomach to sink.

"Avalanche," she said with bated breath.

"You're right. This is *not* going to be good," he said. "Where is it at?"

"It's around Piz Medel. Says three hikers are missing and presumed dead," she explained. "How sad. I hope they find them."

"I'm sorry. We just arrived here a little while ago. Where exactly is that?" Greg asked again, trying not to sound like a pompass unsympathetic ass, but still wanting to know more.

The lady walked up to the television and pointed to the location of Piz Medel. "Right around here, you see. The tracks are here. Just north. So many high mountains in that area. The snow could move off any one of them at any moment."

"Thanks! I'm going to join my friends. Maybe let them in on this. Do stay safe and have a good trip." Greg started walking towards the restraint. His mind was running with how he was going to explain the news to the rest of the group. His first immediate thought was not to tell Reid, but that would mean having to get Ethan and John alone, and that was something he didn't care to do. He decided it was best not to discuss the avalanche unless one of the others brought it up. They'd been through enough with the plane. Why add more fears on top of that? The Glacier Express was to be the highlight of their trip. Eight hours of scenic beauty through the heart of the Swiss Alps, and then a returning trip the next day back to the SCHLOSS. It was the epitome of stress relief. Why ruin that for everyone? Besides, what else could possibly go wrong on this trip?

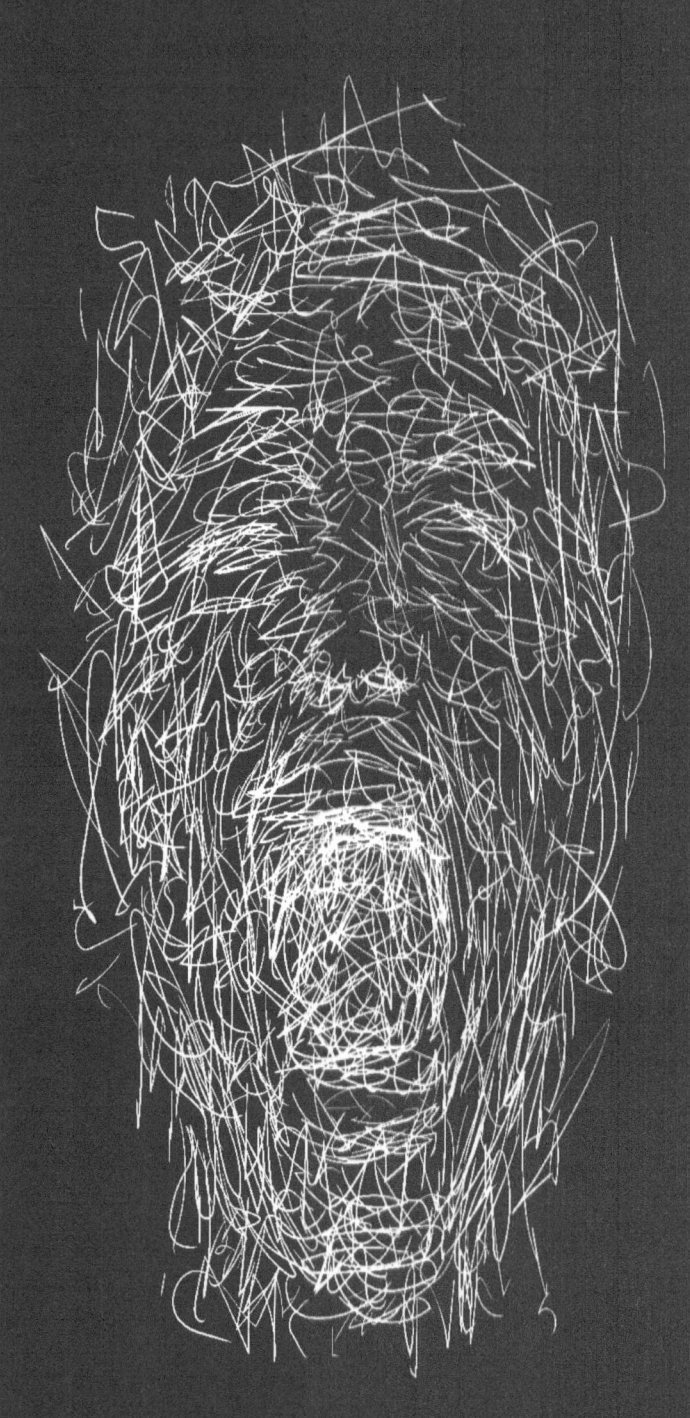

5

The red engine with the red and white railcars behind it pulled into the station. The Glacier Express had a strong resemblance to the underwater tunnels in an aquarium. The sides and top were all glass creating a hundred-and-eighty-degree view of the sites around them. They'd yet again splurged for the Excellence Class, which featured an integrated multi-course gourmet culinary experience along with exclusive fine wines and a private bar. Each pair of tickets came with a cozy place setting for two next to a panoramic window.

Greg's stomach started feeling a little queasy. He couldn't tell if it was from the excitement of the upcoming ride, having to sit at a table for eight hours with John, or the fear of some form of impending doom while on this train. Stomachs have a way of letting people know things, and he's always lived by the trust your gut motto. But this time, he had no clue what it was trying to say.

The gang loaded in, tossing their overnight bags into storage before taking a seat at their tables. John and Ethan immediately hit the bar. Greg, on the other hand, found himself gazing out the window. His stomach eased when Reid sat down across from him.

"This is going to be so awesome!" Reid said. "Just think about all the exciting things we are going to see. And thankfully, the storm cleared out. Now we have clear skies and snow-covered mountain tops."

"Yeah, do me a favor and try not to take any of Ethan's stash," Greg said. "We don't want you passed out and missing the whole trip."

"He'll be at the bar most of the time, but for real! Unless I really need them, that is. I've learned to hide them under my tongue or in my hand, then dispose of them when he's not looking." Reid pulled a plastic baggy out of his messenger bag full of random pills he's been stashing.

"My God! How long has this been going on?" Greg asked.

"Oh, at least for the last year. It started when I had my top surgery," Reid explained. "I didn't take all my pain meds, and he got into them. I don't know where he is getting them from now. Sometimes they help me, so I don't mind. I guess, too, it's partly my fault for letting him get into my meds."

"No! Do not put that on yourself. Some people out there have a harder time admitting they have a problem," Greg said. "You can't carry the weight of his problems on your shoulders. Besides, you have so much more to live for."

"Do I?" Reid raised his head, looking into Greg's eyes.

"We both do. Look at this amazing view we get to enjoy because we're both alive to enjoy it… together."

Greg gazed off at the magnificent peaks towering over them as the train slowly passed through a valley. The trees around them crystallized and weighted down with snow. A pond next to the tracks, completely frozen over, provided a picturesque view for ice skating. It truly was a winter wonderland. "This is truly breathtaking, isn't it? I can't believe we're finally on this train. Seemed like we'd never get here."

"Right! I could sit here all day and just stare out the window," Reid replied.

"Well, you're going to for the next two days at least," Greg quipped, turning his gaze back to Reid, and the two of them broke out into a bout of laughter.

"I'm filing for divorce when we get home."

"Whaaaattt?" Reid said in shock. "Oh, honey, I'm so sorry."

"Don't be. It's been a long time coming," he continued. "I just don't know who he is anymore. We have nothing in common, he's always somewhere else, and I'm left all alone. I just don't know how I'm going to afford to do it."

"I can't say I'm surprised, though," Reid said, placing his hand on top of Greg's. "We all kind of saw it coming. We were just waiting for you to figure it out on your own."

"I should have done it a long time ago. I just felt trapped. I still feel trapped, but I've got to do this for myself. Even if it takes everything I love away from me." Greg's emotions got the best of him, and a tear started to slide down his face.

"Oh, don't cry, baby," Reid scooted closer to him, wrapping him in a big hug. "You're not going to lose us. We'll be here every... Wait, did you feel that?

"Feel what?" Greg asked.

They sat very still, and Greg's stomach dropped. Immediately, the news broadcast came rushing back into his mind.

"That! There! The vibration," he tried to point out.

"It's probably just the train," Greg said, trying to justify the situation.

"This train only goes twenty-four miles per hour, and the last four hours or so has been smooth." Reid jumped up, looking out the window. "Something's not right."

"What do you mean something's not right?" Greg asked. "We're going over a bridge. That had to be it, surely."

Reid walked to the empty table adjacent to them to get a view from the other side. His body was starting to tremble, and little beads of sweat started to form on the top of his forehead. His mouth dropped as if he were about to speak, but nothing was coming out. Greg stood up beside him— the pit in his stomach sinking farther.

The vibration had gotten much worse, shaking the entire railcar. Greg grabbed onto his shoulders to brace himself. He took Reid's clammy hand into his. The rumbling overtook the sounds of the train. Through the window, the two of them saw the most horrifying thing imaginable. A large cloud of white dust was rolling down the mountain and barreling directly towards them.

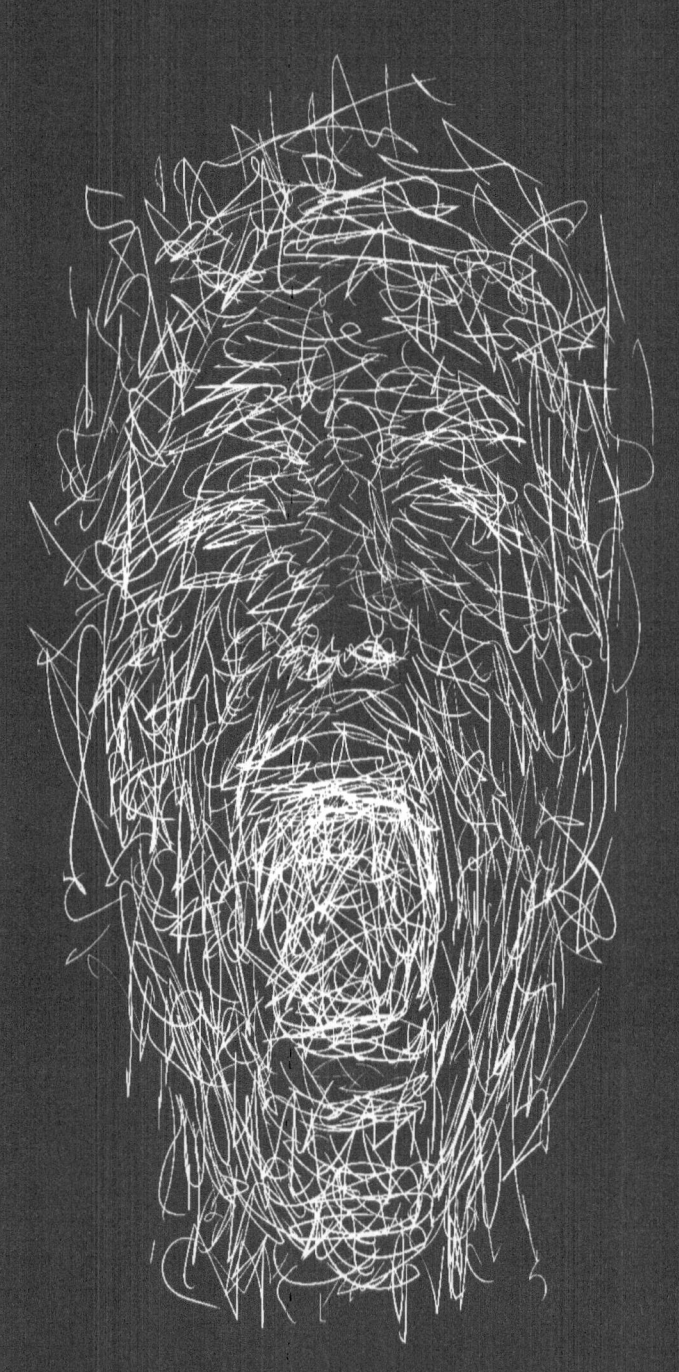

6

Greg and Reid embraced tightly. There was a brief moment where Greg wondered where John was, but the snow plowing into the train pushed the thought from his mind. The sound of screams pierced their ears. Shards of glass scraped across their face. The screeching sound of metal ripping apart filled the air. Clangs and clatters sounded as the rail car hit the ground and bounced down the mountain. The two of them lost their grip on one another as they tumbled against the tables. Colliding into each other, pain ripped through their bodies as if they were being ripped apart.

The car stopped rolling. Now it was sliding to the foot of the mountain at high speed. The surrounding glass was nearly gone and chipping away more and more by the minute. With the car on its side, Greg hung from one of the window seals to keep from being dragged against the ground. He didn't know how much longer he could hold on. His hands, burning from tiny cuts and the cold, were starting to give out. A jolt and sudden stop knocked him loose, and he fell into the railcar, his head heavily landing on one of the uprooted tables.

"Greg! Greg wake up!"

He could feel a hand on his shoulder, shaking him. As he came to, immense pain shot from the back of his neck and through his skull, landing behind his eyes, throbbing more and more. A loud ringing in his ears made it difficult for him to tell who was calling his name. He was wet. *Why was he wet? What had happened? Where was he?* Forcing his eyes open, he saw the table his head was resting on surrounded by snow, and feet attached to two legs towering over him. It all started to rush back to him, filling his mind with the replay of events. Each image pulsed through with yet another throb of pain.

"Wha…What happened? Where are we?" he asked.

"There was an avalanche. We're somewhere towards the bottom of the mountain. Are you hurt? Can you move?" The voice responded.

It wasn't until he slowly lifted himself off the table that he saw Reid standing over him. As the ringing faded, it was replaced with the sound of screams in the distance. Dizziness filled his head as he attempted to stand. Nearly losing his balance, he braced himself against a metal rail. Pain shot through his arm as the open wounds on his hands stung at the touch. More pain radiated through his leg. He looked down to see a shard of glass protruding from his right calf.

"Jesus fucking Christ!" Reid yelled.

"Where's John? Where's Ethan?" he asked, taking deep breaths, restoring oxygen to his brain, and doing everything he could to ease some of the pain.

"I don't know. I think the cars got separated as we rolled down the mountain," Reid answered, his voice becoming more frantic.

Greg nodded lightly in agreement. He pulled himself together as best he could and propped up against a table.

"Here, let me," Reid said, as he knelt down to examine the bloody calf. "We have to pull it out."

"I know, but we're gonna need something to wrap it with once the shard is gone. Check over there. See if there's anything we can use." Greg pointed to one of the suitcases buried in the snow.

"There's a scarf! Will that work?" Reid asked as he held it up.

"We'll make it work. Now, give me a moment to— GOD DAMNIT! MOTHER FUCKMMMMM!

Without warning, Reid had yanked the shard from his leg. Blood poured from the wound, and he quickly began wrapping the scarf as tightly as he could. He grabbed a handful of snow and pressed it against it, trying to numb it as best he could.

"A little warning would have been nice." Greg winced as he tried to reposition himself.

"Sorry," Reid replied.

"We've got to find John and Ethan."

Greg reached into his back pocket for his cell phone— surprised it was still there— when Reid said.

"There's no service out here. I've tried mine already."

"Then we're gonna have to go out there and look for them." Greg started frantically searching around the car, opening every compartment he could hobble over to.

"What are you looking for?" Reid asked.

"More clothes. We can't go out there dressed like this. We'll freeze to death in no time," Greg answered. "Find our overnight bags...our coats...something."

Reid sprang into action, searching for anything they could use for protection against the cold. Greg realized he hadn't checked on him. He watched as he dug around looking for the bags but couldn't see anything wrong other than a few scratches here and there. A moment of relief came over him. At least one of them wasn't injured. Two overnight bags were all they could find. They layered as many clothes as they could, then wrapped themselves with as many of the blankets found in a closet. Reid kicked the railcar door— now turned sideways— open.

Reid stopped in his tracks. "I don't think we should be going out here."

"Why not? We've got to find the others,' Greg said.

"Well, with everything I've researched on just about any type of disaster that could possibly occur—" Reid paused. "You're not supposed to leave. You're supposed to stay put and wait for help to come. Also, you're not really in any position to be hiking up a snow-covered mountain. What if another avalanche comes? What if we cause one while we're out there?"

"We're going! I have to find him," Greg asserted.

"Okay. But we're not wandering far." Reid said as he stepped out into the cold.

They'd been slightly blocked from the elements inside the railcar; now the wind hit them in full force as they exited, stinging as it hit their faces. Tiny particles of loose snow still flew around in the air; the sun blinded them as it reflected off the white-covered mountain. The freezing temps intensified as their feet sank into the foot or more of snow.

Once their eyesight adjusted, the actual horrors revealed themselves. Their railcar had been stopped by a tree just before going over a cliff.

Thankfully, the entire car was still on solid ground. The edge dropped off into a snow-covered forest down below. There didn't appear to be any immediate indication of a cataclysmic disaster down below, though it couldn't be completely ruled out. They turned around to face up the mountain. In front of them was a debris field scattered at least three football fields in length on a vertical incline— pieces of luggage, clothes, large metal pieces from the train, and what possibly could be identified as other passengers were partially buried in the snow. Two other cars could be seen in the distance.

"You sure you're up for this?" Reid asked.

"No, but I've got to. We'll take it slow." He grabbed a handful of snow and pressed it onto his injured leg. He nodded his head when he was ready to go.

Unaware of how stable the snow was, they started their hike, carefully placing each step to keep their footing. One wrong move, and they could create another avalanche, sending more snow down the mountain and the empty rail car off the cliff. Greg recognized one of the bags as he started to climb up the mountain and tossed it over his shoulder for safekeeping. Before he could tell Reid, he heard him scream out.

"Hey! Over here! There's someone over here in the snow!"

Greg carefully navigated his path to Reid, who was standing over a body lying face up in the snow. He quickly recognized the person as one of the stewards who'd delivered their lunch not too long ago. He bent down, placing two fingers on the carotid artery. Nothing. A few more feet in front of them was another body. This one, a child. Nothing. And another…nothing…and another…nothing.

The further they progressed, the more the incline proved even more challenging to traverse. The pain in Greg's calf was starting to radiate into his thigh. By the time they'd reached the first car, he was crawling across the snow, dragging his injured leg along with him. As they approached, they realized the car was on its side. Reid climbed over the bottom of the railcar to inspect the interior. There was an unrecognizable person smashed up against the wall, but he could tell it wasn't John or Ethan by the clothes. No one seemed to be alive as he looked down from above. A slight shift in the car caused him to lose his balance, but he managed to brace himself on the window framing to keep from falling through the open hole in the car.

They pressed onward, passing well over ten different passengers and railway workers buried in the snow— their lifeless bodies beginning to freeze into solid slabs of meat. The hopes of finding John and Ethan alive were starting to dim. Surely, they weren't the only survivors. Someone else had to have made it out of this horrible tragedy. And if the train had seven cars, where were the other four? Were there survivors with the other cars? Because it wasn't looking very hopeful at this point.

Greg collapsed on the ground. The emotional state of the situation was getting to him, and he wasn't sure how much more he or his injured leg could take. They'd been out here for at least two hours searching for John and Ethan— or any survivors. It was all seeming very worthless. He wasn't even sure how he'd react if they found John dead. It hadn't even crossed his mind until now. Yeah, they'd had their issues, and he was a complete ass. But he didn't want him dead. His thoughts were interrupted when Reid arrived by his side to check on him.

"You ok?" Reid yelled over the wind.

"Yeah, it's just all a bit much right now. My leg is fucking killing me, and what if we don't find them? Maybe we should just go back and wait for help." Greg leaned his head into Reid's chest as he felt his arms wrap around him.

"You were the one who was so headstrong in wanting to come out here, so we're going to find them," Reid comforted. "We'll find them. I promise.

The comfort and reassurance from Reid's embrace didn't last long. He felt Reid patting him on the back and saying, "Hey… Hey, hey, hey. Look!" and he took off running.

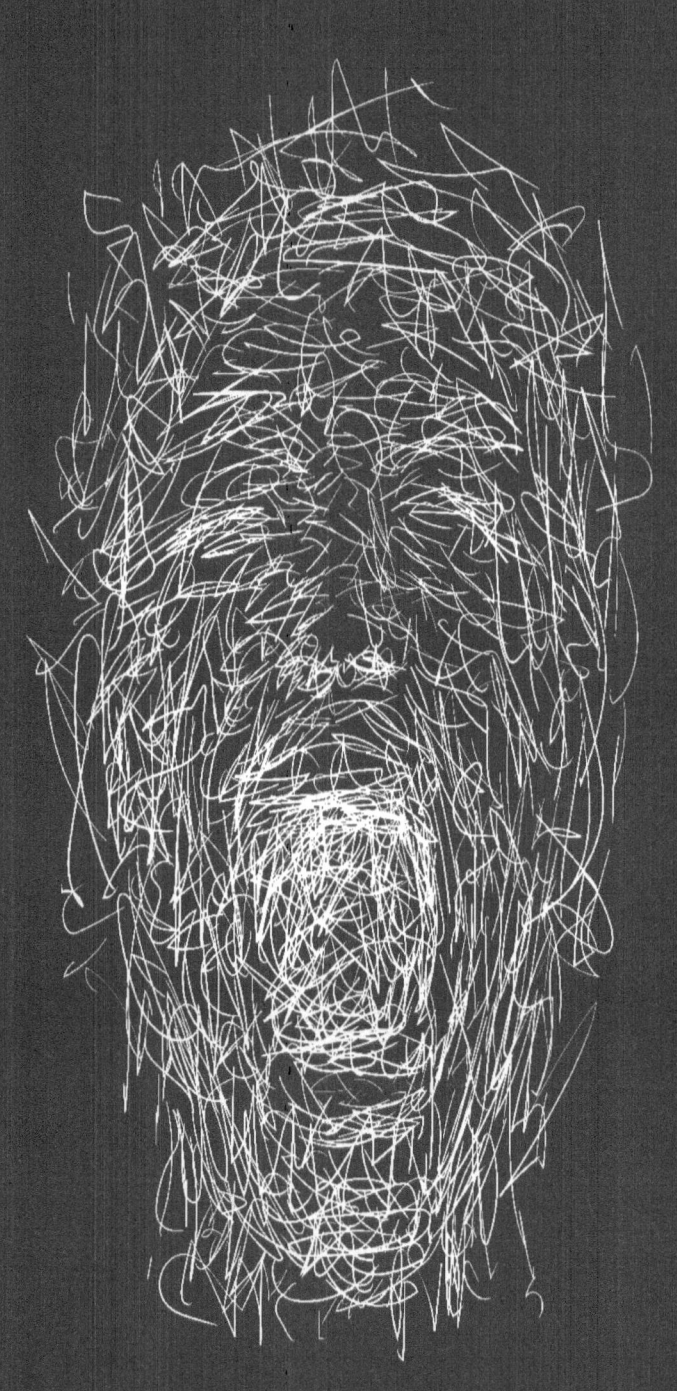

7

Greg looked up as Reid took off up the mountain. *What was it? Another dead passenger?* He must have seen something Greg obviously couldn't. Something that mustered every bit of energy he'd had left in him to take off as fast as he did. With the sun's reflection blocking his view, he crawled his way up the mountain to follow him.

Greg reached the spot where Reid had collapsed in the snow, hurriedly digging around the outline of a body lying next to a tree. It was Ethan. Not only had the frigid temperature started to blacken his air-exposed skin, his legs were bent in the most unnatural position. His gut wrenched as he reached down to check his pulse. As he'd suspected, there was nothing.

"Reid...Reid. Come on. We're too late," he said, pulling him back.

"No! Let go of me!" Reid sobbed. "Not like this!"

Despite his protest, Greg took him in his arms, holding him tightly. Reid sank into Greg's chest. It made him question how he would react when, and let's face it, it was a matter of when, they found John in a similar situation. Would the tides be reversed? Would he be the one lying on the ground crying his heart out while Reid comforted him? Only time would tell. They were running out of daylight and needed to push forward. He left Reid sitting with Ethan's lifeless body, granting him his wish to be left alone.

The last of the railcars was just ahead. It'd split in two, with one half disbanded into pieces around them. Various bottles of alcohol and polished pieces of wood were scattered across the debris field. It was apparent this was— or what was left of— the railcar bar.

Greg approached the now wide-open end of the car, his stomach in knots at the thought of what he'd find. There was a part of him ready for all this to be over. He'd had enough death surrounding him for one day, but the other part of him didn't want to see John's perished body slung out all over the snow. He closed his eyes, rubbed them with his damp gloves, inhaled, and let out a deep breath. It was now or never.

He looked inside. At first glance, there wasn't anything noticeable, but the sun going down reflected off a tiny sliver of metal sticking out of the snow. He crawled in further to investigate. It was John's Gucci G-Flat watch attached to an arm buried in the snow. There was a sinking feeling in his gut. The time he knew would come was here. An icy feeling came over his eyes as tears started to form and run down his cheeks. Emotions started to run high, but he held them back. He'd already mourned the loss of their relationship and what could have been left of a friendship a long time ago. And while he didn't deserve to die, he told himself he'd shed the last tear over this hateful man. He reached out, taking the nearly frozen hand sticking out of the snow. While he wasn't religious, he bowed his head for a moment, then let go.

"Hey, buddy. You okay?" Greg asked when he returned to Reid.

"As good as can be expected," Reid looked up and noticed the emotion in Greg's face. "Oh, God, no. I'm so sorry."

"It's fine. I'm fine. We've got to get a move on," Greg said. "The sun's gonna be gone soon, and we've got to find some shelter. We haven't made it that far, and our car is the only one mostly intact. We should head back down for now. If or when we get out of this, we'll make sure they get a proper burial."

Reid jumped up and tightly wrapped his arms around Greg. Their long embrace produced barely enough body heat to knock off the chill of the wind, which was starting to increase in strength as the sun went down on them. Before leaving, Greg grabbed a couple bottles of alcohol from the ground and tossed them into the bag he'd found earlier.

"Maybe we could gather a few sticks for timber on the way down," Greg suggested. "We're going to have to find a way to stay warm tonight. There's no way we're getting out of here in the dark."

"That's a great idea," Reid agreed. "I can build a fire to keep warm by. We can burn some of these stray clothes as well."

"I'm not sure I'm going to be much help carrying things," Greg said. "But let's take as much as we can back down with us. Just be careful of what and how we pick things up," Greg said. "We don't want to cause another one of these damn things. It'll send us off the mountain this time for sure."

Going up the mountain was a lot easier than going down. They had to make sure they didn't step on anything that would cause them to lose their footing— and Greg was already struggling with trying to stay balanced. One wrong move and all bloody hell could break out again. By the time they'd reached the bottom of the cliff again, dusk was on the horizon, and the temperatures were dropping fast. They entered the railcar and collapsed on the ground. Greg pulled the bag off his shoulder and dug out a few Snickers bars.

"You found the snack bag!" Reid said with excitement. "How did I not notice that?"

"Indeed. And I grabbed a couple bottles of alcohol to help keep us warm throughout the night. We're gonna need it if we're gonna hike out of here in the morning," Greg said.

"The only thing that alcohol is going to do is burn like hell when I pour it on your frost-bitten leg," Reid quipped. "And there's no way we are marching out of here in the morning. You're not going anywhere. That leg needs rest. When the train doesn't arrive at its next stop, they'll send someone to look for it. If we wait long enough, help will arrive. Surely, there are protocols in place for when disasters like this happen. We should wait."

"Yes, sir, Mr. Take Charge," Greg mumbled under his breath. "What do you suppose we do in the meantime?"

"We wait! And try to stay alive. Now sit down and rest that leg." Reid started going through the overhead compartments.

"What are you looking for?" Greg asked.

"A first aid kit," Reid replied. "There's got to be one around here somewhere."

"Check the closet again. It's probably in there." Greg used one of the dislocated seats to prop himself up against what was once the floor of the car.

"Did you ever hear about the Andes flight disaster?" Reid asked, continuing to search.

"You mean the rugby soccer team whose plane crashed in the mountains? Yeah, I've heard of it," Greg answered, chowing down on the last of the Snickers he'd pulled from the bag. "If you think I'm going to go out there and eat someone to stay alive, you've freakin' nuts."

"Then you better make that snack bag last, cause that's all the food we have," Reid snapped back. "And my point was they stayed put because help was coming."

"But didn't two of them hike out of the mountains to get help?" Greg rebutted.

"Okay, eventually, yes, they did," Reid agreed. "But that was after seventy-two days of fighting to stay alive at the crash site.

"So, we have to wait seventy-two days before we can hike out of here?" Greg was starting to get defensive. The events of the day, the immense pain, and the fact that Reid was starting to sound like John were starting to take a toll on him. He cracked open one of the bottles of vodka and took a big swig.

Reid knelt down next to him and removed the bottle from his hand. "And this is going to dehydrate you quicker than you know it. Now, I'm not trying to sound pompous, and I can tell you are frustrated. I promise I'm not trying to take John's place, but I've studied natural disasters my whole life—" He unwrapped the scarf from Greg's calf. "It's what I do. So I know how to survive in them if I need to. And, yes, it's also the reason I have so much anxiety—" The skin was starting to darken, and Greg winced as the fabric pulled away from the wound. Reid reached for the bottle of vodka. "Now, this is going to burn quite a bit, but we have to clean it. I want you to focus on me. Listen to my—"

"God Damnit!" Greg screamed and squirmed as the cold alcohol ran over the wound, and Reid tried to hold him in place.

"There, there," Reid said, trying to comfort him by rubbing the back of his head. "It will stop stinging soon. Let's rewrap it."

He removed some gauze from the small travel aid kit he'd found, placing it tightly on the wound as he wrapped the compression bandage around it. Once finished, he placed one of the random luggage bags underneath to keep it elevated, then wrapped him in a few of the extra blankets from the closet. Greg sat bundled up and useless as he watched Reid drape one of the blankets over the open window hole in the top of the car to block out some of the elements. He left one side open for ventilation as he started to work on the fire to keep them as warm as he could. He stepped outside the car. When he returned, he was carrying the pile of sticks he'd brought down from the mountain. Placing them in the center of the car, he then piled some of the scattered clothes on top and sprinkled them with some of the vodka.

"I need a lighter. Do you have a lighter?" He turned and asked Greg.

"Check the snack bag. John always tossed an extra one in there," Greg replied.

Reid dug the extra lighter out of the bag and flicked it against a piece of clothing. It took a few tries, but it ignited. An initial blast of heat filled the car and then exited through the vented areas. The fire itself wouldn't be enough to keep them warm, though. Navigating the frigid temps was going to be difficult. It would require the use of multiple layers of clothing, every single passenger blanket from the train they could find, and a good supply of body heat from each other. Greg noticed him looking around the car again.

"What are you looking for now?" He asked.

"Some kind of metal tin or bowl," Reid replied. "We need to melt some of this snow so we have water to drink."

"Well, you just think of everything, don't you?" Greg chuckled.

"Again, you wanna stay alive?" Reid cut him a look that said *bitch shut up*.

A few minutes later, Reid's makeshift snow melting contraption was in place, and Greg adjusted himself to make room for Reid to join next to him— equipped with more blankets. The two of them rested their heads on each other, both letting out a sigh. Even with the touch of heat, their breath formed a fog in front of them. They sat, doing everything they could to stay warm. Hoping they would both survive the cold temperatures of the night.

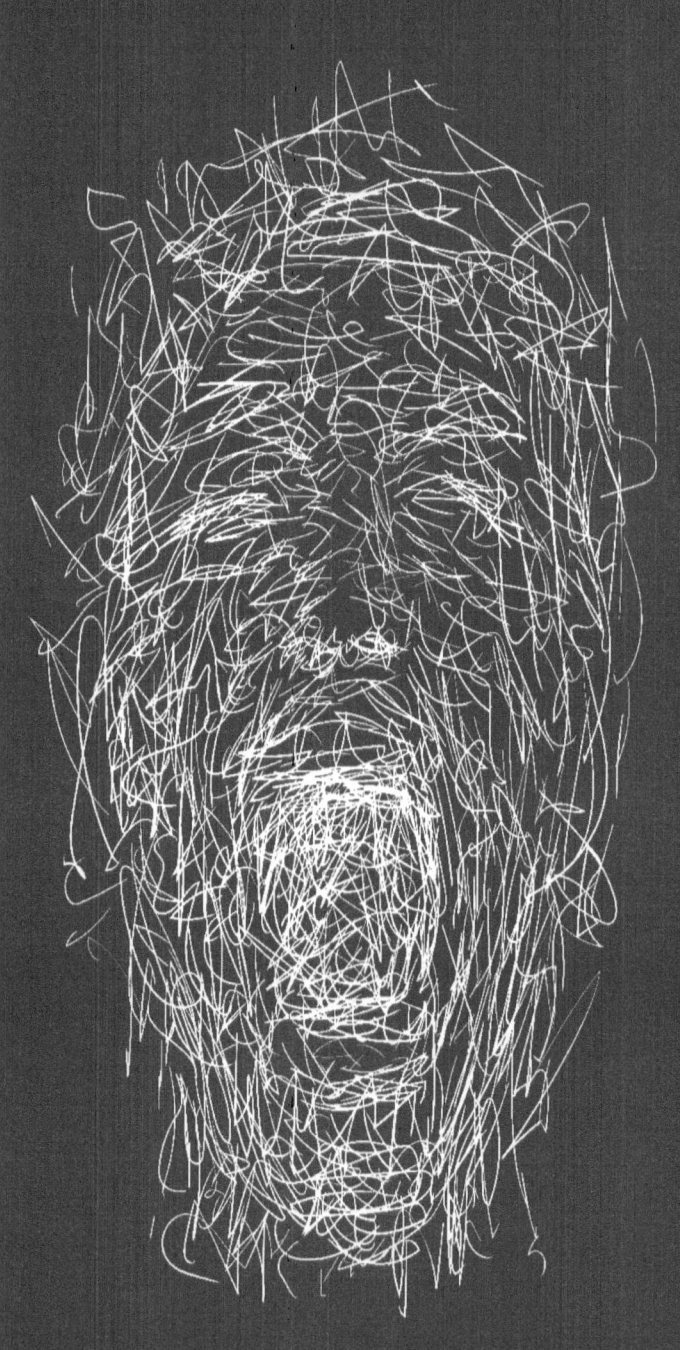

8

The cold chill of the morning awoke Reid in shivers. At some point during the night, the fire had gone out, and their heat supply was cut off. He raised his head from Greg's shoulder, wiping the frozen drool from his mouth. Sliding out from the blankets, he tossed a few more spare clothes onto the fire area, but when he went to grab the bottle of vodka, it was gone.

"What the hell!" He said aloud as he started looking around, though it didn't take long for him to find the empty bottle snuggled tightly in Greg's arms.

"Greg! Wake up!" He yelled, standing over him and slapping his face to get him to respond.

His chest was moving up and down, so he was conscious, just drunkenly passed out. Greg started to mutter something as he came to, then leaned over, letting out a spew of vomit that splattered all over.

"See! That's what happens when you don't listen to me. Do you want hypothermia?" Reid scolded. "You need water. You're gonna dehydrate."

Reid turned to see his water contraption had refrozen after the fire had gone out. He beat it up against the frame of the railcar to break it up, then shoved a piece of ice in Greg's mouth. He handed him the bowl with instructions to keep eating the ice while he looked for the other alcohol bottles Greg had brought down from the bar car. When he found them, he popped one open and poured just enough on the pile to get the fire going again. Smoke billowed out the open parts of the car.

Digging through the snack bag, he found some Slim Jims and passed them over to Greg. "This isn't going to mix well with the vodka, but hopefully most of that is out of your system and all over the ground. It will at least give us a little bit of protein for the time being."

"Thanks! Hey, I'm sorry I didn't listen," Greg said. "I couldn't sleep last night and needed something to dull the pain— emotionally and physically.

"Look, I get it. We've been through a lot these past twenty-four hours. But you have to take care of yourself if you want to get out of this alive," Reid sympathized. "I can only do so much for the both of us."

"You're right. I'm just not so sure I want to get out of this alive," Greg responded. "I'm all alone, and I'm probably going to lose my leg if we make it out."

"Now, see, we're not gonna have that kind of talk. You are not alone. We're getting out of this, and we're going to do it together." Reid turned to face Greg. "Despite the things we have lost, we've got a lot to live for. We still have each other."

"Yes, I guess that's true," Greg agreed. "We do have each other, and I probably wouldn't be alive right now if it weren't for you. So, thank you."

"I'm not looking for thanks," Reid said.

"Well, you're getting them," Greg tossed another ice cube in his mouth as the water contraption worked to turn more snow into water. "So, we just sit here all day and wait?"

"Wait! What's that?" Reid said.

"Oooohh Noooo! The last time you said that, we nearly died," Greg snapped.

"Shhhh… Listen!"

The sounds of a chopper rang throughout the sky. Reid looked over at Greg who was sucking profusely on the ice chunk saying:

"I told you help would be coming. Stay here. I'm gonna see if I can flag them down."

"Can't really go anywhere," he yelled as Reid ran out the sideways door.

Once outside the car door, he jumped, screamed, and waved in hopes he or the smoke rising from the fire would be able to catch the attention of whoever was piloting the aircraft, but it seemed his efforts were going unnoticed. Then Reid saw something out of the corner of his eye.

He took off running to grab a scrap piece of metal from the debris. He knew without a doubt this would work. Using one of the sunbeams shining through the trees, he held up the metal sheet, catching the ray and reflecting it back into the air, signaling they were down there. Now he just needed the chopper to acknowledge they'd seen it. There was a loss of hope when there was no apparent signal from the aircraft above, but surely, they'd seen the smoke rising from the fire. And the debris field surrounding them. He returned to the inside of the car with a look of worry.

"Did they see you?" Greg asked.

"I don't know," he replied. "Hopefully. If not, there's probably going to be more coming. Could have been a news chopper covering the avalanche or the missing train. There's no telling. We just have to wait."

"Seems to be the story of our lives here lately," Greg grumbled, adjusting himself to a more comfortable position. "Wait to get on the plane, wait to get on the train, wait to be rescued, wait to die."

Time seemed to be passing at a snail's pace. The two of them had lost track of what day it was, but it seemed like they had been stranded out on this mountain for an eternity. There was no indication of a rescue, and the last sign of life they'd seen was the chopper a few days ago. Daily activities were becoming more habitual and mundane: wake up, find things to burn, restart the fire, clean the wound, find something to redress the wound, redress the wound, take a nap, portion out meals. The food supply was becoming another issue. It was starting to run low. There was only so long a bag full of granola bars, Slim Jims, and Goldfish would last. Reid was starting to get worried. There wasn't an endless supply of wildlife around to feast on, and it was starting to look pretty dim. He knew what the last resort would be to survive, and Greg wasn't going to go along with it. Once the food was gone, and hunger started taking over— if nothing else could be found— well, there was a whole meat freezer laid out on the mountainside. But could he actually do it? Could he bring himself to even suggest cannibalism? Would it be best to starve to death? The decision would weigh heavily on him when and if the time came.

The sky was also looking rather angry. Gone were the sunny blue skies. Gray overcast filled with dark clouds was starting to roll in, and Reid felt sure another winter storm was about to hit. There would be no chance of survival should another storm hit. The fire wouldn't stay lit, it'd be impossible to stay dry, and the wind and below-freezing temps would take them out in less than a few hours, if that. He figured with as fast as the clouds were moving, it'd probably hit just before nightfall, and that didn't give him much time to prepare.

"What are you doing now?" Greg asked, seeing him eye the partially covered open hole where a panoramic window used to be.

"Trying to figure out how to cover this hole better than a blanket and a few sharp shards of glass holding it in," Reid replied.

"Why do you want to do that? Not like it's going to help," Greg mumbled. "I've gotta go to the bathroom. Can you help me up?"

"Sure," Reid said, kneeling down to help lift Greg off the dislocated seat they'd been using to keep themselves off the wet, melting snow beneath them. It was probably one of the few things that was keeping them from getting full-on hypothermia. Helping to prop up Greg proved to be more useful than one would expect. While outside the car, he remembered a large sheet of metal close to the first car they'd stopped at when they were searching for Ethan and John. If he could get it down to where they were, He might be able to use it to help block some of the elements from the incoming storm. Once Greg was situated back inside, he took off up the mountain to retrieve it.

The sheet was heavier than expected, but he somehow managed to get back down to the railcar with only a few minor cuts on his hands. Though any cut, anywhere on the body at this point, could prove problematic down the road— especially cuts from metal. There were still a few screws still in place around some of the outer edges. If he could find something to use as a hammer, he might be able to use the screws as nails, making a halfway decent attempt to secure it to the new top of turned over railcar. Getting it up over the side was tricky, but once he had it in place, he used a broken piece of the window seal to attempt beating the screws down into the red fiberglass. A few hours later, everything was set.

"That should give us a little more protection for the night," Reid said as he dropped down through the remaining open area.

"You really think we are going to still make it out of this?" Greg asked.

"Hey, at least I'm not giving up." Reid pulled the last two packs of Goldfish out of the snack bag and tossed it to the side. Passing one to Greg, he said, "Here's dinner. Make it last."

After stoking and replenishing materials for the fire, he sat down next to Greg, snuggling up as close as he could and burying themselves under the mound of blankets. They both let out a sigh, holding each other tightly as the wind started to howl around them. Droplets of sleet started to rattle the tin roof, slow at first, then the hammering down started. Despite the shielding they had, it still managed to smack them in the face as the increasing wind speeds swirled. They pulled the blankets up over their heads. Pieces of the fire dislodged, some blowing over the cliff. The situation was going downhill fast. Reid squeezed Greg even tighter. He laid his head on Greg's chest, closed his eyes, and spoke, "I love you."

A large white spotlight shone down over the wreckage. The heavy pounding of snow reflected off the light as if it were some kind of space travel. A six-foot-tall man with a stocky build harnessed up and checked the safety cables attached to his harness and waist.

"We've gotta make this quick. You're sure this is where you saw him?" One of the operators said over the headphones.

"I'm positive!" the guy replied.

"Then let's do this. We don't have much time."

The operator dropped the rope ladder, assisting the man down into the harsh elements. The wind caused the ladder to sway, making the descent rather difficult, but once he was down on the ground, he got to work.

"Hello! Anyone alive down here?" a deep husky voice shouted, but there was no response. It was possible no one could hear him over the sounds of the engine that hovered above him

"Hello!" He shouted louder, approaching the overturned railcar. He opened the door, shining his flashlight into the car.

Noticing the two bodies bundled up in the damp pile of blankets, he escaped the pelting elements, entering the railcar. He pulled the blankets back to expose the bluish colored faces of two individuals. He checked their pulse— while it was faint, it was still there— though both appeared to be unconscious. He reached for his radio and alerted the operator.

"I've got two live ones down here! Gonna need two long boards lowered down immediately. Make sure they're tightly secured to the rig. And hurry!—" He continued examining the bodies. "Toss a couple fleece banked on there too! Looks like we've got some hypothermia going on. —" He lifted the blanket to expose the bottom half of their bodies. "And we have an open wound with severe frostbite."

He met each long board that came down with each of the bodies he'd dragged out from under the blankets, rewrapping them in the new, warmer blankets before giving the thumbs up. As each one rose, the gurneys spiraled in the air with the force of the wind. He hoped they would make it all the way up before the line snapped.

9

Three Months Later

Greg sat on the front porch drinking a nice, cool glass of freshly made lemonade. The breeze in the air helped to regulate the beating heat of summer. He'd completed all the chores around the house, and now it was time for a rest. The days and months had flown by since they returned from Switzerland, and aside from dealing with hospitals, funerals, and legal matters, this was the first time he and his friends had been able to get together and just chill.

Looking out over the open wheat fields ready for harvest, he noticed the gray SUV approaching. As the car came to a stop in the driveway, Reid hopped out, arms full of party supplies. He reached for his crutches and hobbled over to help him.

"What is all this?" Greg asked.

"Stuff for the party! It's going to be the best party yet. Especially, once we announce the big news," Reid answered, grabbing a huge bundle of balloons from the back of the SUV and passing them off to Greg. He leaned in for a quick kiss before taking off into the house.

"Would you like some lemonade? I just made a fresh batch," he offered.

"That would be wonderful," Reid said. "It's hot as balls out there."

"I wouldn't complain about the heat too much. Be thankful it's here and we're not still wrapped up in blankets, lying at the bottom of a mountain." Greg quickly reminded him of the hell they'd escaped not too long ago.

"True dat," Reid agreed. "But let's also not forget, honey, that a large part of that survival was due to me being a complete anxious wreck, causing me to learn the survival skills of just about every natural disaster that could occur."

"That is true, and I love you for that," Greg stated. "And while, yes, I'm thankful for the heat. I don't care if I ever see another snow in the south again."

"Here! Here!" Reid said, holding up his glass of lemonade in a cheer. "So, what time are people arriving? Trying to pick the perfect time and place for us to tell them."

"Most will be here around six, but I think we can play that by ear," Greg answered. "Let's just let the night flow. For once, we can have a party that won't have every move dictated by someone with a superiority complex."

"Sure thing, babe," Reid said. "Anything you say. Why don't you go rest up? I'll finish up with the decorating, and you'll need your strength tonight."

"Thanks, I think I'll take you up on that," Greg hobbled to the doorway, then turned to look back at Reid. "Getting up the stairs is getting easier, but I can't wait till I can get this prosthetic leg. It's going to make getting around so much easier. I'm sure it will take some getting used to, but I promise to work really hard. We'll be walking down the aisle together in no time."

The End

Family

A Skeeter the Monster Hunter Short Story

By John G. Hartness

Dedicated to the memory of W.T. Sims

I parked my Beetle in front of a neat two-story house on what passed for a Main Street in Lockhart, South Carolina, and got out, my shirt instantly sticking to my back as the muggy April air banished the cool air conditioning of my car to a distant memory. "I hate the South sometimes," I muttered. The Bluetooth earpiece I wore picked up when the car sync cut out, so my boyfriend (and on this case, my tech guru) Billy could be with me virtually no matter where I went.

"Why, babe?" Billy asked. "The humidity, the homophobia, the gerrymandering, or the racism?"

"E, all of the above," I said, then stepped up onto the wide front porch, complete with swing hanging from the ceiling. This place was the absolute picture of small-town Southern life. It could have been transplanted onto the set of *The Waltons* and no one would have noticed. I knocked on the screen door and heard a rustling inside in response.

"Hang on a minute, I'm coming!" a woman's voice called out from the other side of the door. I saw a curtain twitch, and a few seconds later, the front door opened and I got my first look at our client, a white woman in late middle age with wisps of gray hair trying valiantly to escape from a bandana tied around her curls.

"Ms. Carter?" I asked. "I'm William Jones, from the Department of Homeland Security." I held up my credentials for her to examine through the screen. I grew up in the small-town South. And more importantly, I grew up Black in the small-town South. So I knew better than to open the door to a white lady's house without her express permission, especially when I couldn't see both her hands. For all I knew, she had a pistol in the one behind the door.

But her face lit up at my words, and she shoved the screen door open so fast it almost smacked me in the face. "Agent Jones, thank you so much for coming! Please, come inside, come inside. It's God's own hot out there, and between the humidity and the pollen, I swear it's like I can't even walk to my truck without getting painted yellow! Let's get you a glass of tea and I'll tell you all about our troubles up here. And please, call me Lila Grace."

The smile made her look twenty years younger, and it reached all the way to her eyes, putting aside a lot of my concerns. I followed her into the house, taking note of her worn blue jeans, scuffed work boots, and the dirt around the hem of her shirt. It seemed like I'd interrupted her gardening. She was definitely dressed for mucking around in the dirt. I was sporting what I called my "professional outfit," an emerald-green polo shirt tucked into my newest blue jeans, and a pair of Rockport hiking shoes that I'd picked up on our last trip down to Atlanta. Billy was always pushing me to dress better, but so far all he'd managed to get me to agree to was better shoes. My normal attire was still baggy gym shorts and t-shirts. But since I was seldom out of my home office, nobody but the two of us ever saw it most days.

She turned and headed back into the house at a brisk walk, leaving me to follow. So I did. I stepped into the neatly appointed living room, which was a mix of new tech and old decor, with a flat-screen television sitting on top of an old Zenith set. There was a small desk set up in the corner of the room with a laptop on it, and a pair of recliners facing the TV. I filed that away for future reference. Her email hadn't mentioned a husband, but there was obviously a man who spent some significant time in her house, judging by the copies of *Guns & Ammo* and *Sports Illustrated* on the coffee table next to *Southern Living* and *Reader's Digest*. I gave myself a little mental slap. Women were perfectly capable of reading gun and sports rags, even though breaking gender norms was much more rare in small towns. I told myself to keep my mind open, but I still looked for more signs of whoever the second recliner was for.

"It's my boyfriend's," Lila Grace said without turning around. "You can sit there, Willis won't care. Hell, he won't even be home until after suppertime. He's got a case hunting down bootleggers in the woods off Highway 49, and there ain't no way he's getting done with that until it gets too dark to walk through the woods."

She kept walking, leaving me alone in her living room as she walked through a visible dining room and through a swinging door. I saw a refrigerator as the door swung shut behind her, leading me to assume she was fixing that tea she mentioned. I sat on the love seat, not wanting to mess up Boyfriend Willis's butt groove in his favorite recliner. I sat in Bubba's chair once, and he didn't shut up about it for a month.

"I ever tell you I hate haunted houses, Billy?" I said into the air.

"Um…didn't you specifically tell Bubba you wanted to handle this one, babe?" Billy replied after a moment's hesitation.

"Yeah, but every time we start a case, Bubba finds something inane to whine about and says he always hates whatever the inane thing is, despite it being nothing he's ever mentioned disliking. I was just trying to keep the vibe…you know what, never mind. It's stupid. I'm glad you're my G.I.T.C. for this one. I let Bubba run my overwatch for a job a few years back and it took me a month to get my office back right after his giant ass sat at my desk for a few days."

"I'm just happy to help. You know this is the first time you've actually let me see what goes on when y'all do these missions. I'm kinda honored, if I'm being honest," Billy said, and I flushed a little bit.

He and I had been together for a year and change, but he was right, I'd kept my work life and personal life as separate as possible. What we do isn't pretty, and a lot of times it's dangerous, and I'd seen close up what could happen when a Hunter's love life got too close to his heart. It took Bubba a lot of years to get over his first love dying at the hands of a monster, and I didn't want to lose Billy that way. But I didn't want to shut him out of such a big part of my life, either. Ergo, time for him to start helping out if he was willing.

"Just one question," he said.

"What's that?" I replied.

"What's a G.T.C.C.?"

I laughed. "*G.I.T.C.* You're the Guy in the Chair. Like they said in that Spider-man movie. Every hero needs a guy back home sitting in a chair running the tech and making sure he has the backup he needs. You're my Ned. Except not bald."

"And a little slimmer," Billy replied. He wasn't kidding about that. Ned in the movies was an adorable chunky boy, but my Billy was very much not. He had the body of a swimmer, all lean muscle and wavy hair, with eyes that melted my heart when he smiled at me. "But I'm happy to be your guy in the chair. And on whatever other furniture you want me on."

"Cut that out," I said. "I'm sitting in this lady's living room and don't need to start blushing and stammering because my boyfriend got me all hot and bothered."

A minute later Lila Grace came back through the swinging door with two glasses of ice, a pitcher of amber liquid, and a plate of ginger snaps on a silver tray with a lace doily that I reckoned was older than both of us put together. I love old Southern ladies, they can make a glass of tea and some dollar-store cookies look like high tea at Windsor Castle. I took a glass and poured myself some tea. It was sweet enough to make me worry about my next physical, but it hit the spot. "Thanks," I said. "This is great."

"Glad you like it. I don't hardly ever get to make tea my way anymore.

Willis is a Yankee, so he doesn't understand that is the spoon don't stand up in the pitcher on its own when you're stirring, the tea ain't sweet enough."

I ate a cookie, then decided that was all the time I could donate to propriety. I had a boyfriend to get home to, and while I didn't think Lockhart, SC was still a sundown town, I didn't feel like I needed to take any chances driving home late at night through the backwoods. "What makes you think there's a ghost, Lila Grace?" I asked.

"Well, there's always been tales about that stretch of Sutton Springs Road being haunted, but most folks thought it was just something the old folks said to scare their young'uns away from the deep woods back in there. But recently, there's been a lot more sightings, and even some physical manifestations. Then I went out there last Thursday night to see for myself, and I did. There's a spirit there, and it's *angry*."

I took another bite of cookie and another sip of tea. "You saw the ghost? With your own eyes?"

Lila Grace glanced over my right shoulder, as if asking confirmation, or permission, from someone there, then said, "Yes. I saw the ghost. I tried to talk to him, but he was too mad. I think he's been there a long time, and I think whatever chained him to that place was...well, horrible feels like an understatement."

"You're..." I trailed off because I wasn't sure if I was looking for "psychic" or "crazy." She didn't *look* crazy, but Bubba didn't look like a liberal, either. Looks could be deceiving.

"I think most people prefer the term 'medium'," Lila grace replied. "I don't know what to call it, but I've been able to see—and talk to—the spirits of those who have died and not moved on ever since I was a little girl." A shadow crossed over her eyes, a wistful look that made me think that however she realized she had this ability, it came with a price.

I took a long drink of tea, then refilled my glass. This was not what I was expecting. "That's a new one," Billy said in my Bluetooth earpiece, jarring me out of my reverie. I saw a little of why Bubba found it so distracting.

"There wasn't anything in the file about her being psychic, was there?"

I didn't reply, but Billy was right. When we got the case from the Department of Homeland Security's Paranormal Division, it didn't mention a medium. It just said there was a potential malicious spirit in rural South Carolina, and the nearest DHSPD team was particularly unsuited to handling it. Which made sense, now. Quincy Harker was only about an hour and a half from here, but he would *not* be the best person to send to meet Lila Grace Carter. Harker was prickly at his best, and a downright prick at his worst. And Bubba thought ghost hunting was stupid, so I volunteered to handle the job. And now I was sitting across from a sweet old lady who said she saw dead people. Go me.

I made a snap decision to accept her words at face value. I mean, my best friend was part faerie and we'd been in a knockdown drag-out battle a year ago alongside Count friggin' Dracula, so who was I to say that people couldn't see and talk to ghosts? I'd seen actual wizards fight, so nothing should be off the table anymore. "Okay, Lila Grace. Tell me more about the ghost. Is it a man or a woman?"

"It's a Black man. He looks to be in his late forties, and judging by his outfit, I'd put him to have died somewhere around the early 1900s or maybe as late as the twenties. He's well-dressed, but he can't speak, just scream. Most of the time he's inaudible, but it seems like the first time he appears in a night, he can be heard, and if he gets particularly agitated, he has the ability to move things."

"Well, I'm a pretty far cry from a ghost expert," I said. "My team mostly handles monsters, but you…seem to have a lot of experience."

Lila Grace smiled at me. "I know, honey. I'm old."

"That…that's not what I meant. I mean to say—"

She cut me off with a wave a hand and a laugh. "I know, sweetie. I'm just messing with you. I don't get too many visitors that aren't local, so it's fun for me to poke at a new person now and then. But yes, I've been talking to ghosts for at least fifty years now, and this man is the angriest I've ever seen.

I tried to calm him down, to get him to speak to me and maybe help him move on, but he just screams and screams. And if he stays manifested too long, horrible wounds open up all over his body. Bullet holes, stab wounds, an incredible array of bruises…whatever was done to this poor man, it was terrible." She shivered despite the muggy day. "Even my team of subject matter experts didn't have any information for me."

"Subject matter experts?" I asked. I thought that's what I was supposed to be, but I was starting to feel way out of my depth.

Lila Grace waved a hand around the room. "My assistants. I have several ghosts of town matriarchs who help me if there's a difficult encounter. They call themselves The Dead Old Ladies Detective Agency." She pointed to three spots around the room. "Frances, Faye, and Tot were pillars of the community in life, and they have refused to move on from this world because they can't stand the thought of missing even the tiniest bit of gossip." She laughed. "Oh, hush. You know I'm telling the truth, Tot."

I sat back on the love seat, feeling the world shift around me a little bit. I wasn't just investigating a haunting. I was sitting in a medium's living room as she told me she used ghosts to investigate other ghosts, and to help them move on to the afterlife. I was having to seriously reconsider my religion, right there on a slightly ratty sofa sipping sweet tea. "What is it you want me to do, exactly? It sounds like you're usually the person people call when they have ghost problems."

"I am, but this is one I can't handle. That's why I called in the big guns. You know it's got to be serious when somebody from the first state to secede from the Union calls the federal government for help."

She had a point there. My home state of Georgia had no love lost for the government, but rebellious roots ran even deeper in South Carolina. "But what exactly do you want me to do, Ms. Carter? I've read the rituals for banishing spirits, but I don't—"

"No," Lila Grace said, cutting me off. "A lot of those rituals are violent, and we don't even know if all of them help spirits cross over to their eternal rest, or if they destroy the soul entirely. This man, whoever he is, has suffered enough. We need to find a way to communicate with him, make some kind of connection, and send him to his rewards without harm. And we need to do it before he hurts somebody badly, or maybe even kills somebody."

So I had a vengeful spirit, a helpful medium, a trio of friendly ghosts, and a mandate to do no harm. I reckoned it was a good thing I hadn't let Bubba come on this little adventure after all.

Lila Grace wanted to wait until dark to go visit the scene of the haunting, so I took my laptop over to the library and set up to do some research. Bad idea. Apparently, Lockhart, South Carolina is not a place where fiber optic internet is widespread, or even existent. Once I realized that I had more computing power in the trunk of my VW, I found a local coffee shop, lugged my backpack over to a table in the far corner so I wouldn't be in anybody's way, and got to work.

My first search, for "lynchings" and "South Carolina" provided a depressing and nauseating number of results, but when I narrowed it down to lynchings in Union and the surrounding counties between 1890 and 1920, that cut the numbers down to something manageable. If you consider the murder of sixteen Black men by lynch mobs over thirty years "manageable." Then I remembered the road Lila Grace mentioned, and found it in nearby York County, between the town of Sharon and the county seat of York.

That got me where I needed to be, or where I never wanted to be, if I'm being honest. But I thought I'd found my ghost. Or at least, I thought I'd found who my ghost used to be. Apparently W.T. Sims was a local pastor who had managed to enrage both the Black and the White communities. One by speaking out against the use of the draft to fill the ranks of soldiers in World War I, and the Black community by allegedly misappropriating funds from the Baptist church where he was a pastor.

Thus it was that late one night in 1917, a group of angry men of both races surrounded the home where he was staying and enacted a very rough, and very final form of justice and attitude adjustment upon Mr. Sims. He was found the next morning by the owner of the home with bruises, welts, cuts, and bullet wounds, but he was still alive. He was taken for medical attention by the two men who owned the property across Sutton Springs Road from where he was shot, but he died before a doctor could arrive.

I let out a low whistle, attracting the attention of the "barista," an older white man in a white dress shirt with a newly trimmed gray beard.

"You find what you were looking for, son?" he asked.

I looked over to him, but since there wasn't another soul in the shop, it was pretty obvious he was talking to me. "I'm sorry?"

"You just been typing on that laptop for a solid hour, and then you leaned back, breathing like you just run a marathon. I was wondering what you could have been studying that got you so worked up is all. Don't pay me no mind, I'm just a nosy old man." He went back to polishing coffee cups.

I walked over to the counter. "Sorry about that," I said. "But since you asked about my work, can I ask you a couple questions?"

He leaned on the counter, grinning at me like this was the most excitement he'd had in a month. Although, given the level of commerce and how stale the pastries looked, my sitting in his shop on my laptop for an hour might have *been* the most excitement he'd seen in a month. "Go for it, son. I've lived here seventy-three years. Anything you want to know about this part of the world, I probably know it, or I'm probably kin to somebody that knows it."

Just what I needed, I thought. I tapped my earpiece to make sure my mic was on, so Billy could hear everything I heard. It drives me up a tree when Bubba shuts off his mic just when something interesting is about to happen. It's why I've bugged his belt and his shoulder holster, too. "You said you've been here all your life?" I asked, waggling my cup at him for a refill.

"Yep," he said, topping up my coffee. "Refills are a dollar."

I fished out a five and laid it on the counter. "Keep it," I said. "Call it rent on the table. Have you ever heard anything about ghosts up on Sutton Springs Road, on the other side of Sharon from here?"

He scratched his chin, then shook his head. "No, can't say that I have. But I don't go up that way much. But let me call my cousin Arlene. I think she's got a cousin on her mama's side that lives up there."

He picked up an honest-to-God rotary phone and dialed a number from memory. That's a skill that I've lost since cell phones became such a part of my life—remembering phone numbers. The old man talked into the phone for a moment, then hung up and turned back to me. "You talking about the ghost of that Black preacher they lynched up there? I heard that was a Klan thing. Arlene said it was a big story when she was a kid, something mamas and daddies told their kids about to keep them from messing around back in them woods after dark."

"From what I can find, it's more than just a story. There does seem to have been a man murdered out there back around World War I."

"Well, I hate to admit it, but that wasn't a good time to be Black in South Carolina. A dangerous time, if you know what I mean."

"Is it all that much better today?" I asked.

"Well, they ain't burning crosses in nobody's front yard, but it still ain't great. Especially for folks like you or me, no matter what color our skin is."

I raised an eyebrow at him. "Like you and me?" I asked.

"Gay, son," he said, slapping the counter. "Don't tell me your gaydar is so bad you didn't spot me for an old queen the second you walked in!" He laughed. "Lord, my Michael would laugh himself silly if he heard I managed to make some big city queen think I was straight!"

I laughed. "To be honest, um…what was your name again?"

"Darrell," he said, and stuck out his hand.

"To be honest, Darrell, I hadn't given it any thought one way or the other."

"Well, good. Because I'm taken. So don't go getting any designs on this vintage chassis," he slapped himself on the rump and we both laughed.

"I'm…I'm taken, too," I said, feeling myself blush. I hadn't told too many people about me and Billy. Mostly because I work from home, and everybody I work with already knows. But it felt nice to tell a stranger that I was with someone.

"Damn right you are," Billy said in my ear. "And don't you forget it, hot stuff."

I reached up and tapped my earpiece, suddenly understanding *exactly* how distracting it can be to have someone talking in your ear. "But you're right," I said, sobering. "It's still not great to be like us in a small town. And worse when you can't hide who you are from the worst of them." I rubbed my forehead. "Nope, still Black."

"Yeah, I reckon it was about as bad for that preacher back in the day. Did you find anything else on your machine there? Was it a Klan thing?"

"I don't think so," I said. Seems like the mob that killed him was made up of Blacks and Whites."

"Damn," Darrell said. "That's a shame. Seems like he didn't have nobody to help him when he needed it most."

And then I had it. He didn't have anybody to help him then, but he had Lila Grace and me now. Maybe we could do today what nobody was willing to do more than a hundred years ago. Maybe if we spoke for him, we could find him some peace. I shook Darrell's hand and said, "Thank you. You've helped me more than you know."

"Well, son, I don't have any idea what I mighta done, but I'm glad to have done it. You always gotta help family, and no matter if we've known each other all our lives, or if we just met this afternoon, we're family."

There might have been a tear in my eye as I packed my bag, or it might have just been sweat. The air-conditioning in that coffee shop couldn't quite keep up with the heat, after all.

"I think I know who our ghost is, and I'm pretty sure I know how to give him peace," I said when I barged in Lila Grace's front door, skidding to a stop as a big White man hopped up out of the recliner and grabbed a pistol that had been laying on the side table next to him.

"Willis, don't you shoot Skeeter!" Lila Grace yelled from the kitchen. She stuck her head through the swinging door. "He's here to help me with the ghost up on Sutton Springs Road. And I told you to lock that damn pistol up when you're in the house! What do you think, the damn zombie apocalypse is going to break out in the middle of an HOA meeting or something?"

"You been reading them weird-ass books again, Lila Grace. We ain't even got an HOA," the man said, de-cocking the pistol and walking over to the mantle. He moved a painting, pressed his index finger to a biometric lock, and put the gun in the safe. Then he walked back over to me and put his hand out. "Willis Dunleavy. I'm the Sheriff around here."

"Skeeter James," I said. "Department of Homeland Security."

"Sorry 'bout the whole gun thing," Dunleavy said.

"I'm a Black man walking in unannounced into a White lady's house in South Carolina," I replied. "I should have expected worse."

Willis had the good grace to look ashamed, and the good sense not to argue with me about it, just mumbled "sorry" again and motioned for me to sit on the couch. I did, and a few seconds later Lila Grace walked backward through the swinging door with a pitcher of iced tea and three glasses on a tray. I didn't bother asking if the tea was sweet. It was South Carolina, after all. Unsweetened tea is considered a graver sin than salt on grits around there.

"What did you find out, Skeeter?" Lila Grace asked, pouring the tea and handing out glasses.

I told her the whole story, or as much of it as I could find from century-old news clippings badly scanned into archives. "So it seems like Mr. Sims died for nothing, or at least partially nothing. Investigations into the church's finances revealed no embezzlement, so that part of the mob just murdered him for, well, nothing."

"And the ones that shot him down for speaking out against the draft were most likely the white men who would have killed him no matter what he had to say behind his pulpit," Lila Grace added. "Shameful."

"The more I learn about the history down here, the more it feels like some of the dark shit that went on in Chicago back in the day. I mean y'all had a different way of handling elections down here than we did up there," Willis said.

"Yeah, down here it was more 'vote once and get your Black ass lynched,' as opposed to 'vote early, vote often,'" I said, not even hiding the bitterness in my voice. "It's better now, somewhat, but still not like it should be."

"No, it ain't," Lila Grace agreed. "But maybe we can help Mr. Sims find some rest and put closed at least one chapter of our state's dark history. That's about the best we can hope for today."

I thought about that for a minute. Was it enough? Sure, we might help this ghost find peace, but what did that do for the living? Was closing this chapter really what we needed to do? That was a tomorrow question. Tonight's question was—could we help him find rest at all?

"I hate tromping through the woods in the middle of the night," I muttered as we did just that some five hours later.

"Now that is something I believe you actually *do* hate," Billy said in my ear. "Despite living up here in basically a mountain paradise, I don't know that I've ever seen you go for a walk in the woods for pleasure."

"That's because the woods is where all the snakes are, Billy," I said. I caught Lila Grace looking at me sideways, so I turned my head to her, showing her the Bluetooth headset. "My boyfriend, Billy," I said by way of explanation. "He's back home running tech for me on this op."

"Oh, we're an 'op?'" she asked. "How exciting. I've never been an op before." I got the suspicious sense that she was making fun of me, but I let it go. She didn't. "So, how long have you and Billy been an item?"

An item? This woman was not *that* much older than me, maybe twenty years, but she talked like a Nick at Nite TV show sometimes. "We've been together a little over a year. We met on a case, hit it off, and we've been together ever since."

"That's kinda how me and Willis met. He moved down here to be the new sheriff, I helped him solve a murder, and then we kinda fell into bed. And in love, but that came later."

"Us, too," Billy said in my ear, making me blush even more. I wasn't sure what I wanted to discuss less, my sex life or Lila Grace's, but neither one was on my list of Things I Want to Chat About While Dodging Copperheads by Moonlight.

"How far are we from where you first encountered the ghost?" I asked, pulling an EMF meter from my backpack. It showed nothing yet.

"It's just up ahead. Do those things really work?" she asked, pointing at the meter. "I've seen them on them ghost hunter shows, but I've never needed any fancy hardware to find ghosts. Usually I can't get them to leave me alone." She shot a snarky glance off to one side, and I wondered if her trio of geriatric busybodies were following along with us. I kinda wish I was the incorporeal one, with how many stickers and thorn bushes I was pushing through.

"They seem to do a good job of finding paranormal activity, but most of the time I'm not the one in the field. And we don't usually let Bubba handle expensive tech. He's…not the most delicate of flowers, you could say." Billy snorted through my headset and Lila Grace gave me a smile.

"I've seen pictures. He looks like the kind of man who shoots first and thinks never," she said.

"That's not quite fair," I said, leaping to defend my best friend since middle school. "Bubba's a good soul, but he's not what anybody in their right mind would call subtle. This is definitely more my speed than his." I didn't add that if he had met Willis Dunleavy, the pecker-measuring contest between the Georgia redneck and the Chicago lawman would have been epic, and probably spectacularly hard on the furniture.

"We're here," Lila Grace said.

I looked down at my meter. Nothing. I looked around the woods. More nothing. "You sure?" I said.

"Skeeter, I have been traipsing around the woods in this part of the country since before you were born. I sat on that stump over yonder and called out for Mr. Sims, although I didn't know his name at the time. He appeared right in that clearing over there to the left and made it very clear that he didn't want me there. He's nowhere to be seen right now, but this is the spot where I first met him. I'd bet my favorite china on it."

I knew full well that to a Southern woman, that was way more serious than staking her life on something. "Okay, then. Let me set up some equipment and then you can call to him again and maybe we can help him rest."

"I don't think you're going to need much in the way of equipment," Lila Grace said, pointing off between the trees. "Because he's right there."

I looked up and sure enough, there was a hazy outline of a man gliding between the pines. The ghost of W.T. Sims had arrived. He was a thin man, dressed in overalls with a long-sleeved, brown-checked shirt and a large hat. His battered work boots skimmed the ground, but he moved with the slow plodding walk of a man who had worked a long day only to come home knowing that tomorrow brought nothing but more toil. His hands were huge, with long fingers and thick, knobby knuckles. That struck me more than the anger on his face—those heavy workman's hands that in life could fix a wagon, saddle a horse, or plow a field. Those hands that were nothing like my soft ones, but that carried some of the same scars. His were just easier to see than mine.

He stopped about twenty feet away and glared at us, his head whipping from me to Lila Grace to a spot off to her right shoulder, where I assumed her trio of spirits stood. He turned his attention to me, and his lip peeled up in a sneer. He didn't speak, but I felt his judgement nonetheless. This man could see deep into me, and he found me wanting. The more he stared, the more I found myself lacking, too.

"Mr. Sims," Lila Grace said, holding up a hand. "We want to help you move on. You're scaring some of the people here, and they ain't gonna let you stay here forever. Besides, isn't there somebody you want to see on the other side?"

His head whipped to her, and the disdain on his face for me turned to pure rage at the sight of Lila Grace. He opened his mouth, and the most godawful howl I've ever heard came out. It sounded like a tornado siren married to a bull horn with a side of jet engine, and Lila Grace dropped to one knee, both hands clapped to her ears. I stepped in front of her, both my hands out in front of me trying to hold back the sound like it was a physical thing.

"Stop it, Uncle!" I yelled, instinctively slipping into the honorific Black men use for older men in our community. "Please! She ain't here to hurt you. Neither one of us are. We want to help you. We know what they did, Mr. Sims. We know, and we can make sure everybody knows how wrong it was. You didn't steal nothing, did you?"

The roaring let up a little bit, and I could almost make out a mournful "no" in his moans. I took a step forward, both hands still outstretched. He looked more solid now, and I really hoped Lila Grace was right and he couldn't manifest fully. The last thing I needed was a raging ghost that could kick my ass in the physical plane as well as scream like a banshee. He reached out as if to grab my wrist, but his hand passed right through me. His touch was cold, like dipping my hand in ice water, and when he tried again, the chill stole my breath.

But I kept my hands up. This man had been brutally murdered for nothing more than speaking his mind, and nobody had raised a hand to help him. If I could help him now, it wouldn't make up for all those years he was abandoned and forgotten, but it might ease his passing at least a little. So I let him grasp at me again and again, until my hands shook with the cold and I could barely hold my arms out any longer. Finally, his screaming faded, and he stood there, staring into my face for a long moment.

He opened his mouth again, and I flinched, expecting another ear-splitting shriek, but the only sound was a whisper, barely louder than the wind. He looked at me, sadness of a century carved in the lines of his face, and said just one word before he faded out. That word, that one name, floated on the air as I knelt beside Lila Grace to check on her and make sure she hadn't blown an eardrum.

"What did he say?" she asked. "Right there at the end. I couldn't make it out." A trickle of blood ran down her nose. Whatever Sims had done, it definitely hit Lila Grace way harder than me.

"All he said was a name. He said 'Bob.'"

I dropped Lila Grace off at her house and drove the fifteen miles to a Quality Inn in Union. They definitely should have put "quality" in quotes on their signage, but it wasn't the worst place I'd ever stayed. I only felt like I needed to wedge one chair under the door, and the bathroom was clean. The whole place smelled like cigarette smoke, despite asking for a non-smoking room, but I was pretty sure that was going to be the case at any godawful crappy motel in a tiny town nowhere near an interstate. So I picked up some Lysol at a nearby Piggly Wiggly, unpacked my laptop and WiFi hotspot, and settled in to see if I could figure out who the ghost had been asking for.

"Are you okay?" Billy's face popped onto my screen unannounced, and

I almost fell off the bed in surprise. Then I remembered that he was sitting in my office, hooked up to all my computers. He had enough hacking power at his fingertips to bring major corporations to their knees, but all he wanted to do was check up on me. My heart swelled a little at the consideration.

"I'm fine," I said. Then I shook my head. "No, I'm not. I don't know what it is about him, but the ghost struck me as really sad. And lonely."

"Aren't most ghosts sad?" Billy asked.

I thought for a moment, then shook my head. "Not really. Usually if someone can't move on, it's anger that keeps them stuck to this plane. But while Mr. Sims seemed angry, too, right there at the end he… I don't know, it's silly."

"Tell me, babe. What is it?" Billy asked.

"It was like he recognized me. And I felt it, too. Like I recognized something in him, and I…I think I *felt* his sadness, somehow. It was weird."

"Not really," Billy said. I cocked my head in an unspoken question. "Look," he went on. "You're empathetic. That's part of who you are. How you've managed to hold on to that running around a big goofball like Bubba all these years, I'll never know, but you are. Maybe you're a little tiny bit empathic, too."

"What, like I can feel other people's emotions? I've never noticed being able to do anything like that."

"Maybe you've never been around emotions as strong as this ghost's before," he replied.

I leaned back against the rickety headboard and pondered this for a second. "You might be onto something, babe," I said. Just then, my stomach growled. "And if I don't get onto some dinner, I'm never gonna get to sleep tonight."

"Okay, then. Get some food and get some rest. Is anything still open? It's after ten."

I looked at the corner of the screen. "Shit," I said. "I think I saw a Sonic and a McDonald's on the way into town."

"Well, get the Sonic. I know you love their chili dogs, and I don't want you bringing that gassy shit into our house," Billy said.

I laughed. "You got a deal. I'll have a chili dog tonight, and all the farts should be gone by the time I get home."

"They better. I didn't sign on to sleep with Bubba. I picked the pretty one of the team. Love you."

"Love you, too." I closed the laptop and ventured out in search of food, because if I was going to unravel the mystery of who "Bob" was, I needed some fuel. And a chili dog sounded perfect. As long as I could crack a window in that hotel room.

I was standing on Lila Grace's porch the next morning as Willis walked out to go to work. "Mornin' Skeeter," he said. "You gotta pee?"

I might have been bouncing on my heels a little. "No, I'm fine," I said. "I've got a lead. Is Lila Grace up?"

Willis laughed out loud. "Up? Hell, son, she's already fixed breakfast, washed the breakfast dishes, done a load of laundry, and is out back hanging clothes on the line to dry. She is not a woman to lie abed all day, no matter how often I try to persuade her to do just that."

I laughed and patted him on the shoulder. "I'm leaving that one alone," I said, watching the big lawman blush a little as he realized his unintentional entendre. "I'll head on around back."

"Have a good day, Skeeter," he said, not meeting my eye as he walked off the porch and headed to his patrol car.

Lila Grace was struggling with a fitted sheet and clothespins as I opened her back door. I hurried down the concrete steps and grabbed one end. "Here, let me help."

She gave me a grateful look, and we made short work of the rest of the laundry. "Thank you," she said. "Some things I used to could do with one hand tied behind my back feel like they need four arms nowadays. I reckon I ain't as young as I once was." Then she chuckled. "But I'll never say that when them three old ladies are around. They'd never let me hear the end of it."

"I kinda wish I could hear them," I said, and meant it.

"Oh, most of the time I love having them around, but every once in a while, I wish they'd mind their own beeswax. Usually when they start giving me relationship advice." She pursed her lips, then smiled at me. "But you didn't come over here this early to hear about an old woman's love life."

I tried not to let on exactly how little I wanted to hear about her love life, but from the smile in her eyes, I wasn't very successful. "No, that wasn't the main reason for my trip. I think I figured out who Bob was."

She looked confused for just a second, then she snapped to it. "Bob! The name W.T. Sims said to you at the end last night. You know who he is?"

"Was," I said. "And I'm pretty sure it was Robert Burris, the man whose house W.T. was staying at the night he was killed. I don't know what kind of connection there was between them, the paper just listed them as friends, but I expect that's who Mr. Sims was calling for." *Or mistaking me for*, I left unsaid. I'd seen a grainy photo of Robert Burris in the newspaper's online archives, and while I didn't think there was much resemblance, he seemed to be about my height and weight, and both he and Sims would have been about my age when the murder took place.

"Well, that's something for sure," Lila Grace said. "Come on in the house and let's give this a think. There's got to be something keeping W.T. tied to Robert Burris after all these years…" Her voice trailed off as she picked up a laundry basket and walked indoors, stopping in the mud room to deposit the basket and an apron full of clothespins she had tied around her waist.

Five minutes later we were sitting at her dining room table with glasses of iced tea in front of us and a set of dusty high school yearbooks spread out in front of us. "I'm pretty sure I went to school with a bunch of Burrises. They're pretty thick on the ground around here. Not as bad as Comers. Lord, you can't swing a dead cat without hitting half a dozen Comers. I've never understood that saying, have you? Why would you want to swing a dead cat around anyway? Don't make a lick of sense. Here he is!"

She turned a yearbook around and pointed to a picture. I didn't need too much help picking Donald Burris out of the group, since there were only two Black faces on the page, and the other one was a girl. There was a slight resemblance to the photo I'd found online of Robert Burris, but this photograph was actually clear.

"Do you know him?" I asked. "Is he still around here?"

"I knew him to say hello when we were in school, but we weren't in many of the same classes. And we didn't run in the same circles outside of school. It was...a different time, back then." She looked away, but I knew what she meant.

Desegregation came slow to a lot of the South, and even slower in small towns. Even after the schools were integrated, some forcefully, the children still tended to stay with "their own kind." It was better by the time Bubba and I were in school, but Lila Grace was a bit older than us, and in the South that was the difference between going to kindergarten in an integrated school, and starting school under segregation.

"I get it," I said. "It wasn't that much different growing up in the mountains of Georgia."

"It's shameful, but it's all we knew as children."

"All we can do is try to be better adults than the ones that came before us," I said.

"I wish more people thought that, Skeeter, I really do."

We sat there for a long moment, lost in our thoughts, until I finally broke the silence. "Is Donald Burris still here? Can we maybe talk to him?"

"I don't know," Lila Grace replied. "But we rode the school bus together, and I think I still remember where he lived. Want to go take a look?"

"Let's do it," I said, pushing back from the table and taking our glasses through the swinging door into the kitchen. Maybe Donald Burris could help us unlock whatever was keeping W.T. Sims here, and we could help this poor man get some rest.

"Lila Grace Carter, is that you?" The wizened little man sitting on his porch looked like a California raisin in overalls, which I was beginning to think was the uniform for Black men in upstate South Carolina. Although, most of the White men I'd seen except for Sheriff Dunleavy had been wearing bib overalls, too, so maybe it was just what everybody wore in these parts. It was not a fashion trend I was interested in following. I might not be the stereotypical gay fashionista (that's Billy), but if I was seen in honest-to-God overalls and not on Halloween, I'd have to burn my Stonewall commemorative t-shirt.

"It is me, Donnie," Lila Grace said, stepping up onto the porch and putting her arms around the man's neck. Looking at the two of them, it was hard to believe they were the same age. Donald Burris looked at least twenty years older than Lila Grace, with the few hairs clinging to his shiny pate snow white, and his shirt and overalls hanging loose on his emaciated frame. "What's got you so skinny, Don? You ain't sick, are you?"

He let out a reedy laugh. "Lord, no, Lila Grace. I'm healthy as a horse. Except for the emphysema. And my old friend Arthur. He come to visit when it's gonna rain or when it gets cold. But that ain't no thing this time of year."

"Lord, I know about Arthur," Lila Grace said, rubbing her knuckles. "I can't handle snapping a bushel of green beans no more. Not like when we was kids. You remember that?"

The old man laughed, which turned into a cough, then he fished a flask out of the front pocket of his overalls and took a sip. He extended the flask to Lila Grace, who shook her head. "Do I remember that? Of course I remember! I remember my gran threatening to tan both our hides if we didn't quit eatin' more beans than we was snappin'!" They both laughed, and after Donald took another pull from his flask, he squinted at me. "Who's this? He look like some long-lost cousin. Tell me that ain't Reggie's boy come back to see his people!"

Lila Grace shook her head. "No, Donnie. This here's Skeeter. He's…well, he's a federal agent."

Donnie's eyes got wide and he tucked his flask away. "He's a G-Man? Like Eliot Ness? What he want 'round here?"

I held up my hands to show I was harmless. "No, Mr. Burris. I'm not like Eliot Ness. I'm…well, I'm not like him. Besides, wasn't he White?" I looked down at my arms. "I been accused of a lot of things in my life, but I ain't never been accused of passing." The more time I spent around the people of Lockhart, the more I sounded like my family. I'd beaten my accent mostly into submission in college, but it never takes more than half an hour around somebody with a thick Southern twang, and I sound like I've never left my mountain. Of course, I still live on that mountain, so I guess I earned the accent.

Donald Burris laughed again and fished out his flask. This time he offered it to me, and I took a sip. Then I was the one coughing, as fire rolled down my throat and exploded somewhere around my bellybutton. Whatever the old man was drinking, it was *stout*. I passed it back, wiping my mouth with the back of my hand and swearing, not for the first time, to never again drink anything that I didn't know exactly what was in it. Except Baja Blast. Nobody understands what's in that shit, but it is *amazing*.

"Donnie, I hadn't heard about you havin' emphysema," Lila Grace said. "I sure am sorry to hear that. Do the doctors think they can do anything?"

He waved off her sympathy. "Oh yeah, they told me if I quit eatin' red meat, smokin', and drinkin' that I could live another ten years. I told 'em if I gave up steak, cigarettes, and corn liquor, I'd think I was already dead. So here I am, sitting on my porch waiting for the undertaker to come one last time. But he ain't here yet, and you are. And you a damn sight prettier, too. Now sit down in that rocking chair and tell me why you brought this federal agent up on my porch."

Lila Grace did just that. There were only two chairs, so I grabbed a cinderblock from beside the house, turned it on end, and sat on it like I used to at family cookouts. "We're here about W.T. Sims, Mr. Burris," I said.

He looked at me, confused. "Who?"

"The ghost up on Sutton Springs Road on the other side of Sharon. His name was W.T. Sims," Lila Grace said.

"What's that got to do with… Wait, is this about my great-grandpap Robert? He used to live up that way."

Bingo. "Mr. Sims was apparently staying with your great-grandfather when he was killed," I said. "We were wondering if you knew what the connection between the two men was. Were they friends? Did Mr. Burris work for Mr. Sims at his church? Or what?"

Donald leaned back in his chair, seemingly deep in thought. After a long moment, he said, "I don't know nothing about that. I'm sorry. Pap was gone before I was born, and Granddad moved down here soon as he got home from the war. We ain't had no people up there long as I can remember."

I was about to get up and head back to the car, thinking this was a bust when I saw Lila Grace motion me to stay still. She was subtle, but I could tell from the distant expression that she was getting advice from one of her trio of ghostly assistants. After a few more seconds, she asked, "Do you have any of your great-grandfather's things, Donnie? Any pictures, or letters, or anything like that?"

The old man's face brightened. "I don't know," he said. "I might. I know there's an old Bible in yonder that my mama used to keep old family papers

230

in. Dang thing ain't never closed, there's so many loose pages stuffed in there. I'll be right back." He stood up, swayed a little, then steadied himself on the back of the chair as he toddled into the house.

"Is he okay?" I asked as soon as I thought he was out of earshot.

The look Lila Grace gave me was a sad one. "He's dying, Skeeter. The girls tell me he probably doesn't have much more than a few weeks left, if that. He talks a big game, but he's dying, and he's scared, and he never married, so he's probably going to die alone."

I blinked away a tear. "That's sad."

"It is," she agreed. "I'll try to come see him some more, so he doesn't get lonely. Maybe I can get some of the less irritating ladies from my church to come by, too."

I couldn't help but laugh. "You think the women in your church are irritating?"

"Half those bitches spent their whole lives looking down their nose at me because I was poor, and the other half crossed the street so as not to share a sidewalk with the crazy woman who talks to ghosts. Like they don't ask their dead grannies what to wear every year to Homecoming Sunday."

"So why do you go to church with them?" I asked.

"It's a small town, Skeeter. If I didn't go to church, I wouldn't have a social life at all."

I thought about that, and decided she was probably right. If it weren't for Billy, and Bubba and his crew, I wouldn't have any kind of social network. Then I'd probably end up sharing a pew every Sunday with people who'd look sideways at me all service, just waiting for me to burst into flames. Fortunately, Donald came back out carrying a massive family Bible stuffed full of old papers, along with a smaller book that looked equally old.

"They tell me Pap got this Bible and this journal from a friend who used to preach out of it back in the day. Reckon that might be your Mr. Sims?"

"I expect it probably was, Donnie. Can I take this with me? I want to look through these papers, but I don't want to waste all your day. I'll bring it back tomorrow or the next day, I promise," Lila Grace said.

"That's fine, Lila Grace. That's fine. I reckon I might go on in the kitchen and fry some bologna for lunch. Y'all want some?"

"No, thank you," I said. "We really need to get this research done."

"Well, alright, but I tell you, boy, I make a mean fried bologna sandwich. Put a little Duke's mayonnaise on it, and a slice of fresh tomato, and it'll do you right."

"I know it would, sir. I know it would." For the first time since I was about sixteen, I didn't bristle at someone calling me "boy." Anybody else doing that, there would be words or worse exchanged, but this kind old man? He could call me whatever he wanted, for however long he had left.

Lila Grace and I got in her battered old pickup and rode back into town. We had a long day of research ahead of us, and I felt sure we'd find the answers somewhere in that old Bible.

"I hope this works," Lila Grace said as we pulled off the road in the same spot we'd stopped the night before.

"I do, too," I said. "If it doesn't, I don't know what might help him rest. And if I'm wrong, then…"

"Then things being what they are, he might be more angry than ever?" Lila Grace asked.

I looked over at her, this unlikely ally on a bunch of levels, and said, "Yeah, he might very well be. But it's the best idea we've got, and if I'm reading this journal right…"

"Then you know why he's still so hurt and angry after all these years."

"Yeah, I definitely know that." I opened the door with a loud creak and slid out into the tall grass, trying very hard not to think about snakes or anything else I might be stepping in or on. These weren't my best shoes, but they were still nicer than anything that I needed to be wearing while I traipsed around in the woods after dark. I tapped my earpiece. "You there, babe?"

"I'm your guy. And I'm in my chair," Billy replied. "But your reception is a little scratchy."

"Cell service in this part of South Carolina isn't what it could be," I agreed. "I don't think we'll need backup, but…"

"But if you're out there, I want to be on the line," Billy said. "I'm so glad you let me be with you on this, even over comms. I have to admit, I get a little tiny bit jealous sometimes, always being the one who doesn't get to save the world."

I'd never even considered that. I always thought I was keeping him safe, never considering that he might not want to be safe. "Then when I get home, we'll get you trained up and the next time I have to go save the world, you can have my six."

"If that means I get to be the one behind you, I'm there. I like the view." I blushed bright enough that I'm sure Lila Grace noticed, even in the dark. I was never letting my boyfriend hang out with Bubba again. He was picking up all kinds of bad habits. I'd heard my best friend say the same exact thing to his fiancée more times than I could count.

"You behave," I said, not even trying to do an Austin Powers impression. I motioned for Lila Grace to lead the way into the woods, hoping and praying that a ghost would come along and save me from dying of embarrassment.

We walked for about ten minutes in the light of her flashlight, one of those big yellow plastic things with a huge square battery, the kind that was on every back porch in America in the '70s. It wasn't near as bright as the new LED ones, but the damn things never die, so I bet there'll be a million of them still shining merrily along well after humanity has done something so stupid we give the planet back to the roaches and the fungi. We stepped into a clearing, and I instantly recognized it as where we'd encountered Mr. Sims's ghost the night before. But there was no ghost to be seen.

"You think he's off haunting someplace else?" I asked. "Is that even how it works? Can he do that?"

"Some ghosts can," she replied. "Some are tied to a place, some are tied to a person, and some can wander wherever they want, like my Dead Old Lady Detectives. They can pretty much go anywhere they feel like, but they stick close to Western York and Union Counties for the most part. I don't know enough about Mr. Sims to know if he can move around, but if your guesses are right, I expect he'd stay pretty close to home. Or where he died, rather."

"Well, I reckon you're right," I said, pointing at a flicker through the pines. "Because unless that's a will-o-the-wisp or a truffle hunter, I think he's here." The flicker solidified into the now-familiar form of W.T. Sims, and I looked over at Lila Grace.

"Oh no, honey, this ain't my tale to tell. If anybody can relate to him, it's you."

She was right, this one was all me. Or it could have been, a century ago. And could be again, if certain people had their way today. Well, it was wrong then, and it's wrong now, and if I was going to make the world better for the living, I had to start by helping lay our dead to rest. "Mr. Sims?" I called out, my voice a little tremulous thing, like a field mouse who'd just seen an owl's shadow fly over.

"You got this, babe," Billy's voice in my ear straightened my spine. "I'm right here with you." And that was what all this was about. He was here for me, and I was here for W.T. Sims.

"Mr. Sims, my name is Skeeter," I said, my voice stronger now.

"Bob?" The ghost glided toward me, stopping about ten feet away.

I stepped closer. "No, sir. I'm not Bob. I'm sorry to tell you, but Bob Burris passed a long time ago. He's... Well, sir, he's not here anymore."

"Bob?" He asked again, and his voice seemed more agitated, but not angry. More like a sad, confused old man. Lila Grace had told me that as ghosts lingered, they lost more and more of themselves until they became nothing more than revenants, traces of powerful emotion with no real consciousness. Those were dangerous and couldn't be reasoned with, and had to be banished by whatever rituals we had to use. She felt, and it seemed to be true, that Mr. Sims didn't have long before he would lose those last shreds of himself and become nothing but rage. This might be our last chance to help him move on. To help him see Bob again.

"No, sir, Bob's gone," I repeated. Then I held up the small journal Donnie Burris had lent me. "But he left something for you."

"That…that was Bob's?" Sims drifted closer, almost within arms' reach now, and I held out the book. His fingers passed right through it, but I saw a glimmer of a sad smile dance across his face, as if some remnant of Bob Burris lingered on the pages that he could feel.

"Yes, sir. This journal belonged to Robert Burris, the man whose house you were staying in when they came for you."

His face darkened at the memory of the night he was killed, and I hurried on before the rage could overtake him. "He wrote something in here, after you were gone. I'd like to read it to you if I can. It might… Well, sir, I think it might help you feel better."

Sims drifted back and hung there in the air, his ethereal feet an inch or so above the ground, looking at me. I walked over to a tree stump and sat down, Lila Grace standing over me with her dim flashlight on the pages. I flipped through the journal gingerly until I came to the page I'd found that afternoon, the page that I thought explained everything.

"William," I began to read. "I am sorry. I am so sorry for not helping you when them men came. I was scared if I said anything, they'd take me too. I should have said something. I should not have let them take you like that and do all that to you. I am sorry, William. I failed you like you never failed me, not even once. I hope God in Heaven can forgive me, on account of I can't forgive myself for letting you down. You were—" something was scratched out that I couldn't decipher, but I went on past the mark. "—my best friend in my life, and I let them take you. I can't never forgive myself for that, and now you ain't here to forgive me. So I hope God will forgive me for not saying nothing when they come for you. I'm sorry, William. I miss you and hope you are in the loving arms of our Savior Jesus Christ, and I hope when I pass on, that I can see you and we can walk together again and go fishing in Bullock Creek in the springtime sunshine again. That's my Heaven, just sitting next to you with our toes in the water, not catching nothing, just watching the sun dapple on the water all day. I'm sorry. I miss you."

I took a deep breath and dashed a tear off my cheek with the back of my hand. "Your first name is William, isn't it?" I asked the ghost.

He nodded, and in the gloom I could see the tracks of ethereal tears running down his face.

"He wasn't just your friend, was he?" I asked.

The ghost shook his head.

"I know what it's like," I said. "I know what it's like when you think your whole life you ain't gonna find anybody to be with, that you ain't ever gonna get the happiness you see other people get, and I know what it's like when you finally find that. It's the most beautiful thing ever, ain't it."

William fell to his knees, like his incorporeal legs could no longer support the weight of his sorrow, and buried his face in his hands. I got off the stump and knelt down in front of him, passing the journal off to Lila Grace, who clicked off her flashlight. This wasn't a moment that needed any artificial sun. The moonlight through the trees was all we needed. That, and the glow around Sims' ghost, flickering like its own full moon.

I put a hand out, knowing I couldn't touch him, but knowing how important even the attempt was right in that moment. "William," I said, my voice soft as the wind through the pine needles.

He looked up at me, this forlorn man trapped by sorrow and rage for so many years. His mouth opened, and in a voice barely audible over the breeze, he said, "Bob?"

"You can go see Bob now," I said. "He's been waiting for you for a long time, and he's right there, on the banks of that creek, sitting in a sunbeam with a fishing pole. Can you see him?" I pointed off in the distance, and as I did, the moonlight seemed to coalesce into a shape, a shimmering pool of light floating in midair, shining like a beacon in the night.

"I see him." William's words were a whisper, just a breeze in the night, but they came to me clear as if he was in the flesh. The ghost rose, and as he moved toward the light, he became more and more solid. He sank a little until he was bending the grass beneath his with every step, and as he approached the glowing pool of light hanging in the air, a man stepped through, hale and hearty, a Black man in overalls and a blue chambray shirt, with a smile wide as Christmas morning. The man held out his arms and William stepped into the portal, wrapping his arms around the love he'd thought lost forever. The two men stepped through, and as the light began to fade, W.T. Sims turned back to me, smiling for maybe the first time in over a hundred years, and said, clear as a bell, "Thank you."

Then they were gone. I could feel it as the portal closed. The ghost of W.T. Sims no longer haunted that patch of woods. He was gone to be with his love, in a way they never could be in life. He had finally, after so many years of loneliness, found peace.

Lila Grace put a hand on my shoulder. I looked up to see tears running down her face. "How did you know? I read that same passage and never picked up on it."

I chuckled, and heard Billy doing the same over my headset. "No offense, Lila Grace, but you wouldn't. I recognized the coded language for what it was, and knew that William and Bob were more than friends. And I knew that they could have never let on to that, and if Bob had tried to stop anything that happened to W.T., he would have been killed, too. But that didn't stop Bob from regretting it the rest of his life."

"But now they can be together again. And you did that, Skeeter. I never would have been able to give him rest, because I wouldn't have known what he went through in life. Thank you for your help on this. I really appreciate it."

"I like you, Lila Grace, but I didn't do this for you. I did it for William, and for Bob. Because it's what you do for family. Somebody told me yesterday that you gotta help family, and it don't matter if we've known each other all our lives, or it we just met yesterday, we're family."

"I like that," Lila Grace said. "Well, thank you, Skeeter. You going back to your motel tonight? You could come have a late supper with me and Willis if you wanted."

"No, ma'am," I said, feeling a broad smile creep across my face. "I'm going back just long enough to grab my stuff, then I'm hauling my narrow ass home. I've got family of my own to get back to."

"Damn straight," Billy said in my ear. "Hurry home, babe. I love you."

"I love you, too," I said. Then I smiled, clicked off my earpiece, and headed back to Lila Grace's truck. It was time for me to go home, and maybe tomorrow I'd find myself a creek and sit on the bank with my toes in the water and my hand in Billy's, and not give a damn if I caught a single fish.

The End

Author's Note

W.T. Sims was a real person, and he really was murdered by a mob in 1917 in York County, South Carolina. The facts of the murder were as described in this story—a mob of White and Black men dragged him out of the home of Bob Burris, where he had been staying. He was whipped, beaten, and shot, then left for dead. He lived until the next morning when Burris sent for help, but he died before a doctor could arrive.

News accounts indicate that he was killed largely on suspicion of mismanagement of funds from a church where he was the pastor, and for speaking out against the draft of World War I. Two men were arrested for the murder, one White and one Black, which marked the first time in South Carolina that a White man was arrested for the murder of a Black man. Neither of the men were convicted.

W.T. Sims's spirit has long been said to haunt that stretch of Sutton Springs Road. It is my hope that he can someday, somehow, find peace.

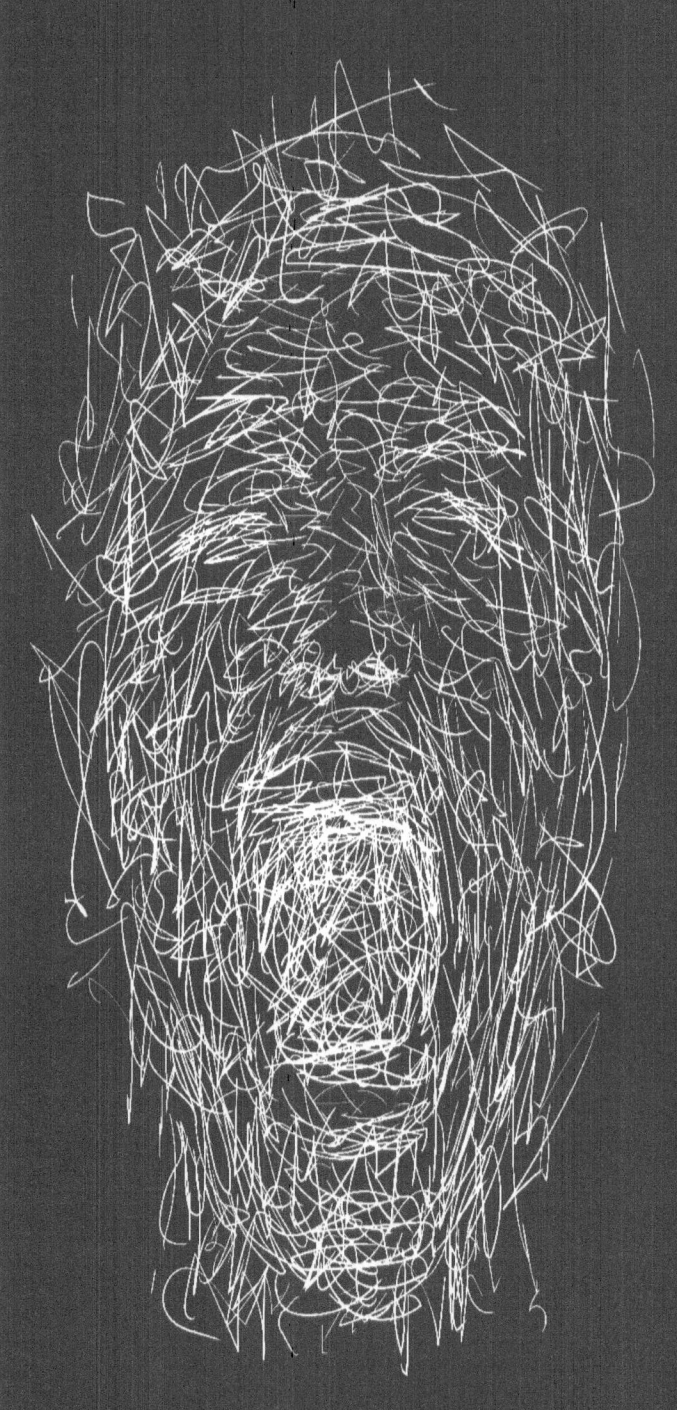

Epitaph for the Burning Times

by Rachel A. Brune

The Twenty-Second Month of the War

The smell of salt from the downriver marshes sat heavy in the fog that hovered over the river. In the pre-dawn shroud, the dipping of the oars made ripples in the water that slapped, almost inaudibly, against the wood that creaked under the weight of the silent passengers.

Talla huddled in the bottom of boat, shivering. Her wool cloak, once a pretty deep green, was now covered in mud and droplets the heavy mist left along the coarse fabric.

"Don't worry, little mum." Above the dark cloth swathing his face, the man's eyes crinkled around the corners. "Ol' Towser'll have you right across before you know it."

The girl smiled hesitantly, clutching her beads to her chest. She shrank back against her mother's skirts, unable to look away from the uniformed figure slumped in the prow.

"Never mind him," Towser whispered, his hands steady on his oar. He winked.

"Talla, look to me." Her mother drew her in, facing her away from the figure. It didn't matter, just as it didn't matter that he was now bound and gagged, his face bruised from the beating the smugglers had dealt him. Talla

241

could still feel his fingers on her throat, the weight of him bearing her down, the hatred that twisted his face as he snarled at her. *Witch. Witch. Burn the witch…*

She could hear it even now, circling through the thin streams of his mind as the small craft made its way through the river's currents. Talla's mother laid her hand on the top of her daughter's braids and muttered a word. The mind echo ceased.

"'Ware to port." Yorkshire George, a short, squat woman whose gray hair escaped the wrap covering her head and face, ducked down. "Ship yer oars, lads."

"What's amiss?" Nasty Face, so named because he was the youngest and handsomest of the lot, swung his oar over the side.

"Shut yer gob and get that lot hidden." Yorkshire George kept her voice low, but the spit in her words encouraged an urgency from her band. Towser, Nasty, and their fourth comrade, Toll the Miller, hastened to swing up their oars.

Towser kicked the soldier further into the hull, then spread a black tarp over Talla, her mother, and the man in uniform. The folds contained a crusty substance Talla didn't want to think about, and it reeked of fish and rot. A small hole in the canvas gave her just enough of a peek to see the smugglers stow their gear and produce a net which they proceeded to throw over the side of the boat.

"Ahoy there, vessel!"

The martial voice rang through the night, piercing the dark that even now began to yield to the first bits of false dawn. *Red sky in the morning sailors give warning…* Talla caught the snippet from the morass that was Nasty Face's panicked thoughts.

"Oy, wotcher goin' on about?" Yorkshire George demanded, uncowed by whatever or whoever had come upon them. "Yer scaring the fish. Honest folks gotta eat fer a living!"

There was a small silence. Finally, the voice came again. "Stand by for boarding."

Beneath the tarp, the man in uniform stirred. Talla felt a small dribble where she couldn't hold back her fear anymore.

To her dismay, Towser laughed out loud. "You're gonna board us?" He giggled again, a strange sound for an old man. "You put more'n two blokes on deck and we'll sink."

There was more silence. By now, the other vessel had drifted close enough for Talla to glimpse the massive wood-and-tar wall that dwarfed the smugglers' fishing boat. From where she sat, glimpsing her fate through a hole in an old tarp, the ship that had come upon them must have gone on forever.

Beside her, the bound man kicked again. Talla's heart leaped and she twitched, involuntarily.

Her mother pulled her even closer, placing Talla's hands on the beads around her neck. "Speak with me, daughter."

Talla nodded.

Her mother began the chant. It wasn't one Talla had learned, but luckily the syllables were short and repeated quickly enough that she could pick it up by the second or third repetition.

Under her hands, Talla's beads grew warm, the semi-precious stones responding to the chant. Her mother moved her hands along her own beads, the clear quartz spheres interspersed with onyx and ruby igniting with an internal glow.

They chanted, whispering at first, then growing in pitch as the power gathered around them.

"*Întunericul se ridică … întunericul se ridică …*"

Darkness rises. The words burned deep in Talla's heart, the flames smoldering until thick, black smoke arose around them.

The blackness spread, covering the woman and her daughter in its shroud, blanketing the muffled cries of the uniformed man who became a boy in its grip, creeping its desultory way along the boards and planks of the fishing boat until it gathered up the rest in its uncanny grasp.

Everything else—the smell of rotted fish, the looming Royal vessel, the man who had tried to take her life—faded from Talla's senses. In the dark, there was only the chanting of the flames that smoldered, grumbled, and then sparked.

That spark leapt and burst into a hundred more sparks, each point of light, a tiny, hungry flame. Each flame split and grew, split and grew, and massed together in a wall that swarmed up the side of the Royal ship. Where they touched, the wood of the ship grew black and thin. Wool pants and jackets disintegrated beneath the onslaught, the tender skin underneath melting from delicate bones.

The flames blanketed the ship, layering it in a mantle of fire that consumed every last morsel of canvas down to the wooden bones of the ship. In the furnace that danced to the beat of hellfire, nothing was spared, and nothing remained.

When Talla came back to herself, she sat, once again, huddled next to her mother. The tarp was gone. So was the large ship that interrupted their passage. She glanced in the bow behind her, but no sign of the bound man remained.

The smugglers sat in a tight group at the other end of the boat. It wasn't an overly large boat, but the distance between them seemed untraversable.

A soft bump at the bow signaled they had arrived at their destination. Without a word, Toll the Miller and Nasty Face jumped over the side, pulling the boat up and then stepping back. Talla's mother waited. Finally, Towser cursed and maneuvered himself over the side. He came around to the bow and offered his bare hand, which her mother took in her gloved one. After she was out of the boat, Towser extended his hands, swinging Talla out of the vessel, and set her gently down next to her mother. He tipped his hat and winked.

"Thank you, to you and your crew." Talla's mother spoke directly to Yorkshire George, who stayed seated in the stern, hand resting on the rudder. From under her cloak, the woman drew a purse and tossed it to the smuggler Lady. "It's all there."

Yorkshire George nodded. "All right, lads, we're casting off."

And with that, the crew pushed the vessel off the bank, splashing in the low tide that receded with every step until they were well into the river's embrace.

Talla watched as they drew their oars again, pulling with all their might amid the currents that led the way home.

"Talla." Her mother turned her back to the river. They had landed in a small cove. To the north, a stream trickled into the river. The rest of the cove was surrounded by almost impenetrable undergrowth, thorny branches and low shrubs. Along the stream, a small footpath gave them a way into the pine forest.

"Mama." Talla kept watching as the boat drew further and further away. "Why? Why do we have to leave? Why can't we fight?"

Her mother sighed and began walking along the footpath. Talla hastened to follow. Amid the dark pines, the silence broken by the calling of cautious birds and small, rustling things, her mother placed a hand on Talla's shoulder.

"When we fight, we call the darkness," she said. "And even though the flames burn bright, just the smallest piece of the dark stays with you, until one day there are no more flames."

"I don't understand," Talla said.

But her mother just kept walking. *You will.*

The Fifth Autumn After the Peace
A candle past midnight

The first crow waited for Talla as she closed the gate softly behind her. At this early hour, she wouldn't have seen it in the dark, except for the glint in its eye. The green flame of the wyrd-light flickered in its gaze, reflecting depths, as it perched on the gate next to the street lantern.

She didn't recognize this one, but then, new crows came and went, and it was dark in the wyrd hours. The fog had crept in over the stubbled fields during the night, and wisps of white mist playfully circled her as she headed down the lane.

The men had arrived just past midnight at the gate, asking for Talla and claiming sanctuary. The night watch woke her from a dream of burning, and she had bundled herself into her winter cloak, echoes of flames following her down the path.

The second crow waited for her at the Crossroad, perched on the gallows. No wyrd-light close enough to reach its eyes, but there remained a glint as it cocked its head and chuckled at her.

Once a simple intersection of two paths in a large clearing, the Crossroad was now a bustling center of the town. During the day, colorful stalls lined the paths, and deeper business dealings flourished behind the fluttering banners.

Now, though, the stalls were empty, their skeletal structures throwing harsh shadows under the full moon that spread its light across the square. Wyrd-lights flickered in corners, and the gallows that the crow hopped on from one end of the hanging beam to the next cast the harshest shadow of all.

Talla pulled her cloak closer around her, inhaling scents of rosemary and garlic, wood smoke from the hearth and the protection oils dabbed at her throat.

One for luck, two for a mate, three to snip the strands of fate…

Well, whoever woke her up four hours before she usually arose was going to need all the luck they could draw, and her wife was still curled up in bed, dreaming of roses. Sophia had briefly stirred when Talla, always the light sleeper, had gone to answer the door. But the images of bright pink flowers in a sun-filled garden had whispered at the back of Talla's mind shortly after, and Talla knew her wife was back, for a brief moment, in the carefully manicured gardens her family owned.

The town was arranged in rough circles around the Crossroad, with the last line in the wheel consisting of small cottages that opened onto the fields that buttressed the wall. Talla and Sophia lived in one of those cottages on the East side of the wheel, where the fields narrowed, and the stone wall glistened in the morning with dew on the shade side.

A large gate was set directly into the West side of the wheel. Ostensibly it was the only way in and out of the town, but Talla had never let a thing like walls and doors stand in the way of shortening her walk into the forest, where she spent much of her time gathering the supplies she needed. And for good reason. To enter the gate, especially on nights like this, required determining that no threat awaited outside, unbarring the doors, pulling the great, wooden beasts apart, and then ushering any travelers through the narrow barbican into the bailey, a flat open ground where the affairs of security and governance were typically conducted.

In fair weather, the courtyard would be bustling with council business or craftswomen conducting their business around the perimeter. Now, Talla knocked on the second, smaller gate set into the stone wall that surrounded the bailey. Through the iron trellis, she spotted a small watchfire burning and huddled figures standing before it, surrounded by women of the night watch, all of whom carried spears casually leaning in the direction of the figures.

At first, Talla thought the cough came from a member of the watch hurrying to let her in, but the short breath ended in another chuckle. She stepped back from the gate, heart suddenly pounding louder in her ears.

There, above the door on the stone lintel perched a third crow. The green wyrd-light torches danced in his eyes. He chuckled again, and Talla gripped her cloak closer, whispering words of protection against the night. Her mother's words came to her again, winding their way through her thoughts like shadows in the fog that chased her path.

Three to snip the strands of fate…

The Fifth Autumn After the Peace
Two candles past midnight

"Send them back." Talla glared across the bailey at the watchfire, eyes burning.

"We cannot." Glenna, tall and thin, cast a sideways glance at their council counterpart. They and Mayda made up two of the three council leaders. The third, Lundy Mae, was sick in bed and would only be called on if needed to break a tie between Glenna and Mayda.

They sat in the shadows of the blacksmith's cold forge, wrangling with the fate of three fugitives the night had coughed up onto their threshold.

"Then we must bury all trace that they were ever here," Talla offered. "The second wheel gardens are in need of soil refreshing."

Mayda snorted, but Glenna's face tightened, the shadows accentuating the sharp lines the years had etched into their narrow features.

"You were asked to take your mother's place on the council as the chief healer," Glenna said. "We have already heard their claim of sanctuary, a claim, they say, bolstered by the debt owed to them by Talla and Indigo Roundtree."

"My mother and I owe no person any debt," Talla said quietly. "And I did not see these three before tonight."

Mayda sighed. "No matter. We must meet these strangers with a voice of solidarity. Glenna and I have agreed that we shall allow them to pursue their claim of sanctuary—" She held up a hand as Talla opened her mouth to object. "No, as Glenna said, you are here on the council as our chief healer."

And the strongest of our Cunning folk.

The thought whispered around Mayda's head, ripe and expectant like low-hanging fruit. Talla felt an echo of her mother's hand slide across the crown of her head, and the thought vanished.

"We need to present a unified front as we debate their claim," Glenna continued.

Ever the consummate politician, Glenna remained stoic and impassive, as if they actually meant to consider and debate the claim in council. Yet, Talla did not need the gift of reading what others did not say to understand that she was included in this discussion as a courtesy—and a warning.

"I understand," Talla said. But she did not. She did not understand why the council had sent a runner in the night to wake her, and she did not understand why her dreams had been full of smoke she could not see through.

"Do you?" Mayda asked. "Good. Because these strangers asked for you by name."

The Fifth Autumn After the Peace
One candle before dawn

The sky lightened in the east as the watchfire guttered. The guard changed with quiet, precise movements. The new shift gathered up the bedraggled, dew-stained strangers and brought them to the council hall.

It was quieter than Talla expected. Most of the community had not heard the news, although that wouldn't last long. Rumors, gossip, and any sort of update that gave people the opportunity to talk about something other than the crops or the weather flew like wildfire across and through the wheel.

Two more auxiliary members of the council had arrived to join Mayda, Glenna, and Talla at the head table. Chief Agriculturist Xai had hurried from the fields; her mornings at the outer rim of the wheel started before the midnight candles had finished burning. Chief of Security Brytwen filled in the other seat; she sat alert, bright-eyed, and fully pressed in a clean, neat uniform. Talla reflected she must have an unending supply or a well-trained executive officer—she had never seen the chief in less than finely-tuned garb.

Chief Brytwen stood, grasping the ceremonial halberd she carried in the hall, and pounded its butt against the stone floor. The doors to the hall opened and two guards escorted three figures to the front of the table, where they hunched, their cloaks covering their faces.

Talla coughed, the faint odor of smoke lingering at the back of her throat. Or perhaps it was something more. She was older than she had once been, and a night without sleep weighed more heavily than it used to.

And then, all trace of exhaustion fled as the three figures pulled back their hoods, revealing two men and a woman, staring back at the council with burning eyes.

"Nasty Face!"

The man jerked his head up, a small smile creeping over his face. The harsh shadows from the morning sun emphasized the lines of his face, now ten years removed from that dark flight over the water, but it was him nonetheless.

"*Madama* Talla." Now, he grinned outright. "It's Orlan, now. You are looking well."

Glenna cleared their throat. Talla forced her face to stone, unwilling to reveal any other reaction to finding her past standing before her. This was the true reason why she'd been woken in the night. Glenna and Mayda must have discerned that the refugees had some connection to the sanctuary of the wheel and wanted to learn if she had foreknowledge of their arrival.

Talla sensed in their thoughts a certain satisfaction that she'd been caught unawares. She stilled her face even more, recognizing as she did so that she had played into their hands.

"Nasty Face." She nodded. "And where are your crew? These two are unfamiliar."

The smell of smoke returned, along with her mother's words.

Three to snip the strands of fate. Whose fate did this threaten?

Orlan's face darkened, a twisted grimace flattening his still-handsome features. "The old crew is dead."

Glenna and Mayda exchanged a look.

"I'm sorry to— When?" Talla asked.

"Two years into the peace," he snarled. "Once the Imperialists weren't too busy to overlook a little smuggling on the side. Yorkshire George and all the rest, plus any shipper independent enough to threaten the Empire's profits." He hawked and then, as the council members recoiled, reconsidered spitting on the stones at his feet.

Talla subsided, mulling over the strange sadness that whispered through her at the thought of the old man who'd smiled so kindly at her and hid her and her mother next to the dead body of soldier. With a start, she realized she heard no whispers from the three figures, no hint at all of what they thought or felt at the tale Nasty Face—Orlan—related.

"We were seized last Autumn, off the coast of Ringel Farr," Orlan continued, his companions strangely mute. "We've been running ever since."

Talla's fingers tingled at the ends, a curiously hot sensation. "And you ran here?"

Glenna frowned.

"We have no place left to go," Orlan said. "We came to claim sanctuary."

"And if we deny your claim?" Mayda asked mildly.

To Talla's surprise, the woman next to Orlan spoke up, her voice higher-pitched than Talla expected. "Then we will all swing from an Imperial gallows and let that be an end."

The Fifth Autumn After the Peace
One week past the Equinox
Mid-morning

"You're muttering to yourself again, love." Sophia packed rose petals into a large pot as gently as she could to avoid bruising the colorful flowers. "Last time you did that, it took weeks of scouring to remove the scorch marks from the lintel."

Talla forced herself to relax her fingers. She was poring over the spotty archives she'd borrowed from the council library as her wife prepared the rosewater she would barter later, sealed in small glass jars.

"It's just—this is exactly what I warned would happen," she groused. "We keep ourselves isolated from the world, we barely know what happens outside the wheel, and we are far too trusting of those who come knocking on the gate claiming sanctuary."

"Like us?" Sophia gently poured purified water over the petals.

Talla frowned again, the tiny script blurring on the parchment before her. "It was different with us. I know what happened to my mother and I. And I trust you."

"Do you trust me?" Sophia smiled. "Or do you love me?"

She lit a small fire under the pot, coaxing a dancing flame. She would simmer the water until all color had drained from the petals, then strain the concoction and pass it to Talla to be charged with its purpose. Then, she would pour it carefully into the row of small, glass jars that sat empty on the shelf, ready to be sold as a skin cleanser, an anti-itch serum, or for couples looking for a little extra glow.

"I do love you," said Talla. "*And* I trust you. But my trust ends at our cottage threshold, and we don't have enough word of the goings on outside the wheel to just be welcoming anyone who comes knocking on the gate."

Sophia sighed. She bent over the pot and wafted the air toward her with her right hand, then adjusted the flame lower. "Too warm."

"Did you know I dreamed of burning gardens the night you arrived?" Talla said abruptly.

251

"Yes." Sophia sat back down at the table and took Talla's hands, gently prying them out of their clenched position, resting their clasped grip over the parchment.

"For a solid week, I dreamed of burning roses," Talla mused. "The first night, the flames extinguished one bush. By the seventh night, I dreamed I was running through a labyrinth of close-set rose hedges, red and white and pink, and they were on fire. I ran as fast as I could, and when I woke, there were runs in my chemise and soot on my feet."

"Perhaps it was your dreams that showed me the way here." Sophia smiled, a dimple appearing in her left cheek.

Talla gripped Sophia's hand tighter. "That morning, you arrived at the gate."

Sophia smiled. "See? Your dreams brought me to you."

Talla shook her head. "I love you, my perfect rose, but that's not what I mean."

"You worry too much." Sophia withdrew her hands and stood, returning to the flame to gently stir the pot. "The council has this well in hand."

Talla closed the parchments. They were useless anyway. The most recent "news" contained therein was over a season old, related to the council by a refugee couple who had fled false accusations of witchcraft—and threats of forcible marriage to men. But they had arrived before the summer solstice, and no new folk had found their way to the wheel since.

The council itself was just as inadequate to her need for current information, although she would never say so out loud. Sophia had fled her noble family, but had settled comfortably into the gentle hierarchy of the wheel, with its lines of authority and expertise. For her, trusting in a pleasant system of rules and structure came as second nature.

Not for me.

Talla gazed at her wife—slender, pale, with long black hair that, even neatly braided, fell to her waist. A pink kerchief kept any loose tendrils from escaping, and her talented hands, callused and rough in areas, deftly stirred the pot. The smell of roses permeated the room.

The cloying scent tickled the back of Talla's throat, but when she coughed, a dark, scratchy taste of ash and soot burned her tongue.

The burning dreams came, always one week before another refugee joined the wheel. No matter how Talla tried to block them, no matter the protection oils and charms she charged, they still came creeping for her when night crossed the wall.

That was another reason why the council chiefs had called for her in the night. She was meant to reassure them that yes, these men and this woman were seen and foretold, and they should be welcome in the walls of the wheel. Instead, she'd told the council to bury them in the fields.

Was that warranted? She had not seen Nasty Face and his comrades in her dreams. Instead, in the week before her arrival, she had dreamed of a different burning altogether. The smell of smoke lingered after she woke, but all she remembered, each night, was the vision—the half-remembered dream—of ships burning and her mother standing before her, a dark silhouette against the flames.

You will…

"I'm sorry, love, what did you say?" Talla blinked her eyes.

Sophia stood at the now-extinguished flame, slowly lifting out rose petals with a strainer. She rolled her eyes. "I said, the council is calling for trials, and I volunteered to be a trial sister for Sceadu."

"Who?"

"The woman who arrived with the two strangers," Sophia said. "They were down the Crossroad earlier, in the market, under escort. We began to chat, and I found she has some talent with plants, so I invited her to be my trial sister."

Everyone who arrived at the wheel had to find their place; not everyone arrived knowing the extent of their potential talents. Each newcomer paired with a trial sister to find what profession within the wheel they were best suited to.

Some fled a life of drudgery while others, like Sophia, fled honor killings. She'd been caught in the rose garden in a compromising position with a person not of the rank nor gender her family would have preferred. Once at the wheel, she'd completed trials in the kitchen, in the fields, and in the armory, but it was only when she'd paired with Talla in the apothecary that she'd truly found her niche—and Talla the love of her life.

"Have they offered trials to the men, then?" Talla asked.

"I don't think so," Sophia answered. "I don't know if they've quite agreed what it means that two men arrived with Sceadu." She set the pot in front of Talla, who would take over, charging the liquid with the final energetic power it needed before bottling. "It would certainly be a change of pace, I think, men in the wheel?"

Talla barely kept herself from snarling in her beloved's face. She remembered a world with men—a world where they came to her mother, rich, poor, tall, short, married, unwed, all—grasping for charms and protection, for salves and potions. Sometimes, they would grasp for her mother. Or, as she got older, inquire after her. After all, cunning folk were known to make a bargain when it suited them.

And then, as the Empire's black iron grip inexorably closed around any who would not or could not live or breathe in that cold grasp, the burning times began. Those who could wield the flames slipped away, including Talla and her mother.

But so many more fell to the soldiers and their mundane fires.

Talla's mother never did explain how to make the flames burn without a flint, nor did she ever call fire again. No matter how much Talla begged, her mother would only admonish her against the use of the magic and warn her of the darkness.

"Well, if you're going to sit here all broody, I'm going to head out to the eastern fields," Sophia said. "There was a patch of mugwort I wanted to pull before it takes over. Plus, we're almost out of tea."

Talla nodded, not really listening. She needed to know what these warnings brought her.

She needed to talk to the strangers.

The Fifth Autumn After the Peace
One week past the Equinox
Early afternoon

Someone in one of the buildings facing the lane was baking a cherry pie. They must have been the last of the summer fruits. Either that, or someone had occasion to break into the overwinter stores. The tart sugar smells drifted across the way, and Talla swallowed against the sudden hunger.

She slipped into the council building with little fanfare, making her way through the wood-paneled hall, down the stone steps, into the former root cellar turned basement turned temporary confinement center. While the council may have opened the steps up to Sceadu joining the wheel, her two male counterparts would take more deliberation before earning the freedom to walk the wheel.

Access to the men was not controlled; the guard stepped to the side as Talla arrived, far enough away to pretend to privacy but close enough to ensure that her presence remained a threat.

As she approached the barred gate, Nasty Face—*Orlan*—and his companion turned away from a game of cards. They remained seated but gave her an up-and-down look that left Talla vaguely uneasy.

"I still see the little girl we hid under the tarp with the body of that soldier," Orlan said.

Talla heard the undercurrent to his opening gambit. The words didn't seep from his mind so much as the image of her mother and her as a little girl swirled in his aura. There was a slight greasy feel to the mind-picture, and she brushed it away.

"How did you find this place?" she asked. If he was determined to discomfit her, she would ask her questions and be gone.

"We knew where to start," Orlan said. His companion remained silent.

"Who showed you the trail?" Talla knew it couldn't have been them.

"Sceadu." Orlan's face closed in, his eyes narrowing and his gaze not moving from her face. "She was the one with the burning dreams."

He raised an eyebrow, staring at her, as if expecting her to respond immediately. If so, he was disappointed. Talla mulled that piece of information over in her mind. Sceadu, had she arrived on her own, would have raised no eyebrows, caused no concern for suspicion. Either she truly trusted these two men and cared for them enough to help them to safety, or she had been coerced to show them the way.

Orlan's companion spoke up, his voice scratchy and irritated. "After two weeks of wandering through the woods, she gets to roam free and we get stuck here while a bunch of women debate whether or not to let us out."

Orlan shot him a warning glance. Talla remained silent.

Orlan smiled at her. "There's more than women here in the wheel," Orlan said, more to her than his companion. "That council chief...Glenn?"

"Glenna," Talla responded, then kicked herself for the automatic response. She sighed. Glenna had arrived at the ripe age of eight autumns. Her mother had learned the story from the cunning woman who'd lived in the cottage before them and taken them on as trial sisters. Rarely, one like Glenna would arrive at the gate, but when they did, they were welcomed into the wheel. Talla suspected Orlan would not understand—or care—so she changed the subject. "Two weeks you were on the path?"

"Aye." Orlan and his companion exchanged looks. "I remembered the dock where we left you and your Ma, and Sceadu led us from there."

There were too many false notes in this song. The path to the wheel never took more than three days—the amount of time one could survive without water. The fact that Sceadu knew to come to the wheel, but that Orlan and his male companion somehow also knew of the sanctuary. Did Sceadu seek them out? Had Orlan offered to find the way for an unspoken price? There were too many questions without answers.

Talla opened her mouth to speak, but a voice came from behind, interrupting her before she had the chance.

"Talla, excellent, we just sent a runner to find you." Glenna and Mayda headed down the steps, followed by Chief Brytwen and two of the burlier members of the watch.

Talla found herself shunted to the side as Glenna gestured for Brytwen to unlock the cell door. She did so, and the two men inside stood up.

256

"Orlan, Danam."

So that was the other man's name.

"Yes?" Orlan smiled, a small grin that played around his lips.

"A quorum of the council has debated and voted."

Interesting that Talla had not been invited to that quorum. Perhaps the runner had gotten lost in the wheel.

"You will spend your nights here," Mayda continued. "But we will conduct a two-week pre-trial. You may continue to move about freely, under the escort of these members of the watch."

The two women assigned the duty outweighed each of the men by a good three stone, and the muscles and tendons in their forearms were defined in stark relief under their bracers. Still, Talla caught sight of the almost triumphant glance Orlan gave Danam. The slightest thought bubbled up from the two, a feeling of satisfaction. It quickly dissipated, but Talla wanted to see what would happen if either of the men challenged the watch. Their laughter wouldn't last long.

She waited as Orlan, Danam, and their escorts left the cell, traipsing up the stairs toward freedom. Brytwen followed them, then Glenna. Mayda stayed behind, waiting for Talla to say her piece.

"So now we open the wheel to men?" Talla asked. "Our own gate no longer separates us from the world so many of us ran from?"

The council voted to offer a wary opening of the wheel." Mayda's voice was studiously neutral. "They came seeking refuge. We must move with the times, and the wheel has always meant sanctuary."

Talla frowned, wanting to argue, but the council vote meant that anything she said would be left unheard. She waited until Mayda also left, and she was alone in the cool damp of the underground.

"It means the end of sanctuary."

The Fifth Autumn After the Peace
One week past the Equinox
Early evening

Beyond the wall of the wheel was the only place Talla could truly find quiet and peace. Within the wall, even at the edge of the fields, there was always someone about, the shadows of their thoughts swirling about, forcing Talla to tamp down her own walls against the unwanted intrusions.

As she'd grown, she'd found the hidden ways beyond the wall, and the secret paths through the deep, green forest that sheltered the wheel.

The evening was holding in the last of the late autumn heat as Talla reached her destination, a shady grove surrounded by beech and ash trees, still holding the full golden glory of their autumn dressing. A layer of soft grass mixed with wildflowers carpeted the grove, and in the center, a flat granite slab rose above the lawn.

Talla made her way to the slab as the setting sun cast long bronze and purple shadows through the trees. She placed her satchel next to the stone and pulled out the items she'd brought.

In the center of the slab, Talla set a charcoal disk. Withdrawing a glass bottle from a pocket of her skirt, she tapped out a generous amount of homemade incense. This one was a special blend of mugwort, bay laurel, lavender, and rose petals. From a special, wax-lined pouch, she drew a long match and a striker. Calling the flame, she carefully and quickly lit the charcoal disk until an even red glow shone all around the edges.

As the smoke from the charcoal and incense began to filter up through the air, Talla drew out the final item, wrapped in green silk shot through with black threads.

Reverently, she let loose the fabric, letting it drop to the grass below. The object, released from its bindings, glowed dully in the twilight.

Talla gently set her mother's skull over the burning incense and leaned forward to draw the smoke into her.

At first, the jumble of her thoughts drowned out the silence, a wave of chatter that threatened to bowl her over. Instead, Talla waited patiently for the incessant tide to run out and leave her with the peace and emptiness into which her mother's message would flow.

If her mother was aware enough to delve into the darkness with her, she would know soon enough.

The last whispers of her own thoughts faded, leaving a calm black emptiness. The smoke curled up in rivulets from the eyes of the skull. Talla breathed in again; the smoke burned at the back of her nostrils and throat with a pleasant tang.

It began with the tiniest flame in the dark void. Talla's eyes were open now. Gone was the grove. Gone were the late-autumn blooms and the shafts of evening sun. Instead, she stood in the black and watched as a second tiny flame joined the first.

Intunericul se ridică …

A third flame joined the others. Her mother's voice whispered, echoing loud, then soft, then loud again, as if wending its way through stone halls.

A wyrd-light fluttered to life in the dark, its green flame pulsing at the tip of a torch set into a brick wall. Three crows sat atop the wall, illuminated in flashing green and orange. One chuckled at her.

Talla gasped, caught in the throes of the vision. That was her wall, the gate to the cottage she shared with Sophia.

Darkness rises.

Now the smoke encircled Talla, choking her, smelling of burning wood and feces. The flames licked up and down the wooden cottage gate, and she put her shoulder to the door, pushing at it, clawing at it, pounding on the heavy threshold as the crows chuckled above her.

Finally, the door gave way, and Talla found herself standing in the middle of the burning rose garden, flames arising from each of the bushes in the labyrinth in weird colors of blues and purples and oranges and other colors not found in natural fire.

It was Sophia's family garden—but it wasn't, it was the rose garden behind the cottage—and then it became a garden in the shape of a wheel and in the center of the spokes stood her wife, tall, willowy, and her hair was black flame. As Talla reached for her love, Sophia threw her head back and screamed and the black fire grew, impossibly huge, and swallowed her whole.

259

"*No—*"

Talla jerked awake. The incense had burned out, and the granite was cold. The darkness in the grove was absolute; if not for the full moon filtering down through the branches, she would not have been able to see her hands in front of her.

She re-wrapped her mother's skull in its protective covering and shoved it in her satchel with the matches and the glass bottle with the remaining incense. With her right hand, she scattered the ashes from the burnt charcoal and herbs.

Unwilling to waste even a moment longer, she sought the signs only she could read—the trail that would lead her back to the wheel, where she hoped she would not be too late.

You will.

For the first time in her memory, her mother's words came not as a threat, nor as a warning, but as a promise to be fulfilled.

The Last Autumn After the Peace
One week past the Equinox
One candle before midnight

Talla ran, panting, through the night forest that opened its pathways before her, as if doing its best to speed her way back to the wheel.

She heard the screams almost before she saw the flames illuminating the underside of the thick, black smoke that sat over the wheel like an ugly toad licking its own feet.

Once inside the walls, lungs burning and heart pounding in her chest, she sprinted across the fields, heading for familiar bounds of the cottage she shared with Sophia.

Had she gotten turned around? Had her guides led her to the wrong path?

Her mind refused to believe the images her eyes fed it, even as she stood in front of the stone lintel, the embers on the ground burning through the soles of her leather shoes. The darkness of the night had been blown into shards of light by the flames that consumed her cottage—the roof, the door, blowing through the windows. The roar and crackle of the fire drowned out the screams that came from the other cottages around her.

Talla flung her arm before her face, burrowing into the fabric of her cloak, trying to force her way into the burning cottage. Each time, the heat and choking smoke drove her back.

"Sophia!" she screamed as loudly as she could, her voice cracking on the final syllable. "Sophia, where are you?"

The furnace inside the cottage continued, unabated. Talla whirled around, seeking help, but none was to be found. The flames had caught each cottage on this spoke of the wheel, and the fires burned brightly, creating the thick, black smoke that now concealed the sky.

Shortly, the flames would consume the path leading away from this section of the wheel, and Talla hesitated before resuming her flight. Sparing a thought for Sophia, she pictured her wife as she'd left her earlier that day—clean, cool, measuring rosewater for the apothecary. That was the picture she would hold until she found her wife safe and sound.

Sweating, Talla swiped at her forehead with the back of her hand, which came away blackened with soot. She stumbled past her neighborhood, retracing her steps of only that morning toward the Crossroad, intending to head to the council building, the bailey, wherever she could find any other residents of the wheel.

She broke through the last line of buildings and tripped. Hastily gathering her cloak from underfoot, Talla got back to her feet and looked down to see what had caused her to stumble.

The body was too small to be Sophia's. It was too small to be much past eleven summers. Talla recognized her—one of the refugees who'd arrived too young to be set in trial. Instead, the little girl attended the tiny schoolroom the teachers of the wheel set up.

Now, the girl lay sprawled and still, her empty gaze staring up at Talla, eyes wide and desolate, her face a bloody mask from the wound at her throat.

Talla swallowed and began walking across the Crossroad.

The little girl was not the only body. Trial sisters, merchants, refugees, fieldworkers—all peaceful, industrious inhabitants of the wheel—lay littered about the Crossroad. Most bodies showed signs of attack by blades, others still smoked, charred and shriveled husks of their former selves.

The smell of roasted meat hung in the air, and Talla tripped again. She fell to her knees and lost control of her stomach, vomiting into the freshly churned dirt. She heaved, over and over, the force of her convulsions loosening her bladder.

Closing her eyes, Talla contemplated collapsing into the dirt, crawling into a fetal ball, and pulling her cloak over her head, hiding like she had once hidden against her mother's side under a rotten tarp in the bottom of an ill-fated fishing boat.

Darkness rises...

Her mother's words pushed her to her feet. A swirl of light-colored smoke entwined around her as she stood, then vanished into the dark roiling smoke that sat low over the Crossroad.

The roar of the flames started to separate into distinct sounds as Talla pushed her way toward the western section of the wheel. Now, the steady rumble of the all-consuming fire resolved into the pops of dry wood exploding in the heat, screams of the residents of the wheel as they fled or cowered or pounded futilely on doors swelled shut. And now a new sound filtered through the cacophony—that of steel ringing on steel, sliding, striking—and the softer sound of blades burrowing into bone.

There, on the gallows, in the dancing light of the flames, three crows turned to face Talla, their eyes glinting green with a flickering wyrd-light.

She recognized the three on the gallows platform.

Sceadu stood, arm outraised, a pillar of wyrd-light erupting from her outstretched hand. The woman's face had aged, new lines deepening in her worn visage, as if the light sucked the life from her. The beacon did not flicker, and even Talla felt the call of the beam.

But whom had it called? Slowly, Talla realized that the shadowy figures clinging to one another in the smoke were not residents of the wheel seeking shelter from the fire.

Rather, in the shadows, she saw black uniforms with red crosses, swords with pommels that glowed blood red.

She froze, the memory of mail-gloved hands holding her down, choking her. *Burn... burn the witch...*

"No," Talla whispered.

On the gallows platform, Orlan and Danam flanked Sceadu, fighting the watch members who tried to fight their way to her, to cut her down, to extinguish the beacon.

Chief Brytwen thrust at Orlan, and he parried, then lunged in riposte, slicing open her cheek. Openly laughing, he attacked again.

This time, the Chief's foot slipped on the stair. Orlan leaped forward, the point of his blade tunneling through the air.

Talla watched in horror as Orlan kicked the Chief square in the chest. Brytwen slipped off the end of his sword, arms limp. Her body fell, blood spewing from the jagged wound.

She landed with a thud, her head almost severed, so that her body still faced the gallows, but her visage turned toward Talla. The light in her eyes faded, even though the flames reflected in their dull gaze.

"Welcome back, little mum." Orlan saluted from the deck of the gallows. On the other side of Sceadu, Danam sliced deeply into another member of the watch, who fell back. There was no one to take her place.

Talla stared at the burning vision of the past few weeks come to life before her, ripping away the sanctuary that had once grown green and soft for those in need of safety.

"Tell me true, Nasty Face," she shouted. "Did the soldiers kill your crew, or did you sell them for a price?"

Orlan laughed. "What a clever little witch."

"And what did you offer Sceadu to lead you here?" she shouted again. Her voice cracked and broke under the strain of the smoke and grief.

"A few more years." He smiled, triumphant, jubilant. "A few more years to hunt and burn all the witches."

Sceadu did not react, her face impassive as the beacon shone brightly.

"More are coming, more to burn this infestation of witches," Orlan continued.

Talla didn't bother correcting him. He had no more information that she wanted to hear. No matter that the magicworkers and cunning folk and, yes, witches in this sanctuary were few and far between. To the outside world, any private sanctuary for women beyond the rule of men would be an infestation of witches, good only for burning.

Under her arm, in the satchel, Talla felt her mother's skull begin to warm through the layers of her shift and dress and cloak. As if in a trance, she reached into the satchel, gently removing the cloth-wrapped bundle.

Talla let the green and black wrapping fall to the earth and raised her own hand aloft.

And now, she did not close her mind or heart to the words of others, or to the memory of her mother. Holding the smoke inside of her that she only hours ago burned in the grove, she called out for the words she knew it was time to release on the wheel.

"Întunericul se ridică...întunericul se ridică..."
Darkness rises.

The words repeated over and over again, gaining momentum, whirling in thick, white smoke in and out of her as she held the skull to the sky.

From all corners of the wheel, from those yet living, those releasing their grasp on the wheel, and those lying dead on the ground—all these voices joined hers in the chant.

"Întunericul se ridică...întunericul se ridică..."
Darkness rises.

Indeed, the crows had snipped the thread of fate—not only hers, but all those who called the wheel a refuge. But also those who sought to burn that refuge to the ground.

On the gallows, Orlan and Danam looked wildly around, at first not understanding what was happening.

Then the white smoke rose above the bodies. For the space of a breath, each smoke-body remained distinct. Chief Brytwen with her halberd. A young woman with her basket, who had been fleeing with her back to the gallows. An old woman who had stepped between the soldier and the fleeing girl.

With the quickness of a striking snake, the smoke unformed and rolled, combining into a wave of dense fog that swirled counterclockwise around the Crossroad, slowly at first, then faster and faster.

Orlan froze.

The smoke began reaching the invaders and inhabitants alike, and as it moved it *stripped* the flames from the buildings and the people and the bodies, extinguishing the fires in the space of a breath, and carrying them along to the next body.

But when it reached the soldiers, the killing began.

The smoke reached a man with a dark beard and bushy eyebrows who paused, sword poised over another member of the watch. The smoke enveloped him, swallowed him whole and spit him out the other side.

The screaming began, but Talla did not know how such a creature could still make a sound—stripped of skin and hair, all burned and boiled where the smoke had touched him.

And now the white smoke continued its path through the village. Wherever it touched, the flames in the wheel disappeared and the smoke joined the malaise. Where it alighted on the invaders, it left nothing but quivering, exposed muscle, dissolved flesh, and eyeless, hairless golems that stuttered, stumbled, and fell to the ground screaming until their very tongues and vocal cords decomposed into charred flesh.

Finally, the smoke congealed and swirled around the bottom of the gallows. It crept, stalking, like a cat with a favorite new toy.

Orlan screamed and batted at the fog with his sword. Danam swore and kicked, trying to shrink back against the encroaching smoke.

Inch by inch, the smoke consumed the figures on the platform. Sceadu, still in her trance, remained with her beacon aloft until the smoke rent her garments, skinned her body, and charred her to a fetal crisp.

Orlan wept as the smoke embraced him. His lower extremities melted, dissolving into charnel and viscera. As the mist crept up his body, he dropped his sword and pawed at his intestines, desperately trying to return them to his body, until his hands and arms and body separated into muscle, tendon, bone, and a slowly spreading pool of blood under a newly-whitened skull.

Danam screamed for his mother.

Sceadu made not a sound as the smoke embraced her like a wanton lover. Finally, as it reached the pinnacle of her body, the beacon winked out and silence fell over the Crossroad.

In the quiet, the only sounds that could be heard were sobs, soft and distant. Talla wondered briefly how far the destruction had spread. The white smoke had sucked all the flames and darkness into it, then released most of its mass.

All that remained stood before her. Slowly, as if whispering a poem into a lover's ear, it took a final, familiar form.

"Sophia?" Talla couldn't bite back the moment of hope, even as the pale figure shook its head sadly.

The smoke figure reached out and caressed Talla's cheek, then leaned forward and kissed her. The sensation on her lips was of a cool mist with a hint of charcoal, like the wisps escaping from last evening's embers.

My love…

In the darkness left after its passing, Talla knelt in the destruction and wept.

The First Autumn After the Burning Times
One week before the Equinox

The busy port bustled with men and women intent on their duties under the still-baking autumn noon sun. Customs agents, naval officers, trade representatives, merchants, and sailors hurried to and fro, desperate not to catch the eye of an Imperial agent or Royal peace officer. They merely wished to conduct business and move on to the next order of trade—returning to sea, or to their homes, safe from public eye or speculation.

In the midst of the controlled chaos, a slim, striking woman of slightly more than thirty autumns strolled down the gangway of the Imperial Trade Ship Princess Natya. At the end of the narrow plank, she stepped to the side and paused, taking in the sights before gingerly making her way down the crowded dock.

An Imperial customs agent caught sight of her and raised his arm to call to her to come and register at port. But a crow dove into his line of vision, trailing black feathers and smelling of smoke, and by the time he recovered from the distraction, the woman was nowhere to be seen.

Funny. She had looked familiar. Perhaps she had traveled through this port before.

He shrugged and moved on to his next in a long list of tasks due by the end of the day.

Talla strode away from the port and toward the depot where a wagon awaited to take her three days' journey into the interior. She had heard rumor of yet another refuge, a sanctuary right in the midst of the Empire's grasp yet free from interference. It was the sort of place only discoverable by those who possessed the sight of the cunning folk—or the desperation of those who fled the burning times.

In the satchel by her side, her mother's skull warmed briefly, then subsided.

Above her, wheeling black against the brilliantly blue autumn sky, three crows called to each other, chuckling against the humans below, clinging to their thin, desperate strands of fate.

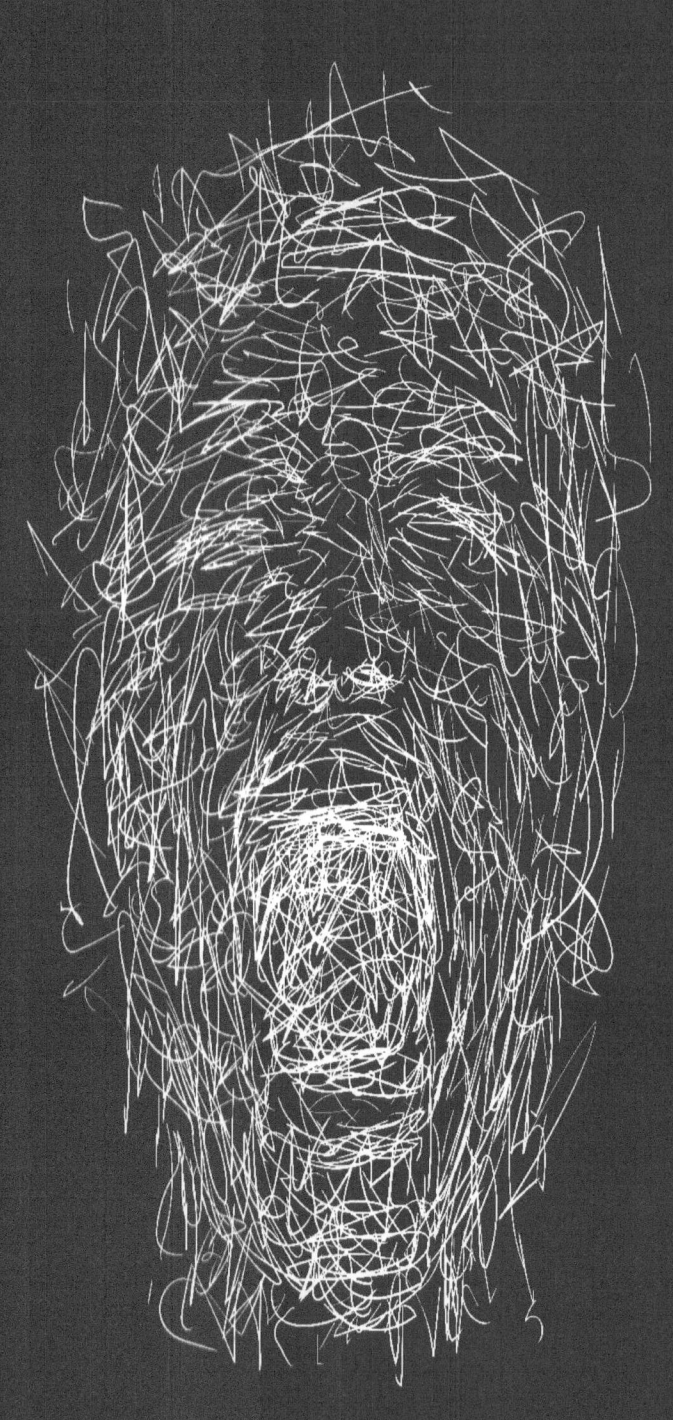

About the Authors

Nicole Givens-Kurtz

Nicole Givens Kurtz has been called "a genre polymath who does crime, horror, and Science Fiction and Fantasy (Book Riot)." She's the recipient of the Ladies of Horror Grant, the HWA's Diversity Grant, and a two-time Palmetto Scribe Award Winner (2021 and 2022) for her short stories and her novella. She's written for Pseudopod, Apex, Fiyah, White Wolf, The Realm, Baen, Subsume, and MV Media. Nicole has over 50 published short stories, including her story, "The Way Home," in Marvel®'s *Captain America: The Shield of Sam Wilson* anthology from Titan Books.

She has conducted workshops for Writer's Digest Online, Clarion West online, SAGA, and is the owner of Mocha Memoirs Press. Nicole is a professional level member of SFWA and HWA. You can find her at www.nicolegivenskurtz.net.

Michael G. Williams

Michael G. Williams writes queer-themed horror and science fiction celebrating the monstrous and the macabre. His books include the award-winning vampire series *The Withrow Chronicles* (Laine Cunningham Award); the thrilling urban fantasy time travel series *Servant Sovereign*; the sci-fi mystery *A Fall in Autumn* (Manly Wade Wellman Award); and a mess of short stories. Michael strives to present the humor and humanity at the heart of horror and sci-fi with stories of outcasts and loners finding their people and power. *Children of Solitude* is his thirteenth book.

Michael co-hosts *Arcane Carolinas* and *Data@Rest*, studied Performance Studies at UNC Chapel Hill and Appalachian Studies at Appalachian State University, and is a brother in St. Anthony Hall and Mu Beta Psi. He's a member of SFWA and HWA and serves as a Trustee of the NC Writers Network. He lives in North Carolina with his husband and a variety of animals.

JD Blackrose

J.D. Blackrose wrote The Summoner's Mark urban fantasy trilogy for Bell Bridge Books, consisting of *Demon Kissed*, *Fae Crossed*, and *Hell Bound*. She's published *The Soul Wars*, *The Devil's Been Busy*, and *Zombie Cosmetologist* novellas through Falstaff Books. She's published short stories such as "Don't Fool an Earth Witch," in *Mother's Revenge*, "The Book Burning," in *Curiosities*, and "Poisoned by Sugar," in *Witches, Warriors, and Wise Women*. Her short story, "The Ghost Train," was published by *Third Flatiron* in their Spring 2019 Anthology and Best of 2019 Anthology. "Welcome, Death," appeared in the *Jewish Book of Horror* in Fall, 2020 as did "The Space Ark," in the *HOZ Journal of Speculative Fiction*. Under the name Joelle M. Reizes, she co-wrote a children's Hannukah story entitled, "Courageous Candles." She blogs, reviews books, and does author interviews on www.slipperywords.com.

Jason Roach

Jason Roach is an American Writing Awards award-winning finalist in LGBT+ Fiction & Thriller Fiction for his book The House on Dead Man's Curve – inspired by his personal paranormal experiences. His new M/M Vampiric romance series, The Vampire Crusades, launched in August of 2024. He is also the owner and editor-in-chief of Gold Dust Publishing, a new indie publishing company for LGBTQIA+ and allied authors. He has previously been a paranormal/Sci-fi/writing guest panelist or presenter at GalaxyCon, Jordancon, ConCarolinas, Congregate 9 & 10, Ret-Con, and Multiverse. Originally from Statesville, NC, he now resides in Winston-Salem, NC.

When he is not working on the next big project or investigating the paranormal, he enjoys spending time with his family, their four cats – Lyma, Gandalf, Crooky, and Batman – and doggy Laylah. Concert-going, traveling, and a good paranormal investigation are the places he finds inspiration.

To learn more about Jason Roach, visit his website, www.authorjasonroach.com, and Gold Dust Publishing at www.golddustpublishing.com.

John Hartness

John G. Hartness is a teller of tales, a righter of wrong, defender of ladies' virtues, and some people call him Maurice, for he speaks of the pompatus of love. He is also the award-winning author of the urban fantasy series The Black Knight Chronicles, the Bubba the Monster Hunter comedic horror series, the Quincy Harker, Demon Hunter dark fantasy series, and many other projects. In 2016, John teamed up with several other publishing industry professionals to create Falstaff Books, a small press dedicated to publishing the best of genre fiction's "misfit toys." Falstaff Books has since published over 300 titles with authors ranging from first-timers to NY Times bestsellers, with no signs of slowing down any time soon. He is also the founder of the SAGA Genre Fiction Writers' Conference, where students hone their business and craft skills to write better books and make more money. In his copious free time John enjoys long walks on the beach, rescuing kittens from trees and playing Magic: the Gathering. John's pronouns are he/him.

Rachel Brune

Rachel A. Brune got her first publishing gig working for the US Army as a military journalist. Twenty years later, she writes, edits, and publishes speculative fiction, with an emphasis on the dark side of the literary spectrum. She brings a deep and abiding love of all the flavors of fear and foreboding to the Falstaff Dread line of horror fiction and the Crone Girls Press horror anthologies.

Also Available from Gold Dust Publishing

- The House on Dead Man's Curve
  By J. S. Roach

- Until Death: An Eric Kent Investigation – Case 1
  By Rey Nichols

- Reflections – Our charity book featuring over 40 authors contributing.

- The Purple Menace and the Tobacco Prince
  By Wade Beauchamp
- The Sword's Secret: Ancient Wonders – Book 1
  By Chris Cole
- The Vampire Crusades: The Acquisition – Book 1

  By J.S. Roach

- Mr. Tingles' Mysteries: The Curious Case of the Bodiless Head

  By Sean D. Roach

- Children of Solitude

  By Michael G. Williams

- Trial by Fire: An Eric Kent Investigation – Case 2
  By Rey Nichols

THRILLER · MYSTERY · GOLD DUST PUBLISHING · FANTASY · HORROR

www.ingramcontent.com/pod-product-compliance
Lightning Source LLC
Chambersburg PA
CBHW030633110726
47901CB00002B/426